Before

the

Magic

Coming of Age in 1970s Middle-America

Mark P Walsma, MD

Before the Magic
Coming of Age in 1970s Middle-America

MPW Publishing

Paperback ISBN: 978-1-7339764-0-4

Available through Amazon Kindle Direct Publishing
Amazon.com

Coming in 2020
the sequel
The Flight to Neverland

The following pages are dedicated
first and foremost to my best friend,
wife, mother of my children and
Love of my life,
Jane.

And to lost friends,
Luanne Bellar
&
Joe Williams.

Dear Diary,
My new town is very small. There are no stoplights. There is
no roller rink, bowling alley, indoor movie theater or mall. I
still can't believe there is no Catholic church and we have to
drive all the way to Kentucky for Mass. We've only been here a
few months, but so much has happened that I'm left to wonder
what the next weeks and months will bring. I'm happy to say
everyone I've met is really nice and I've already made lots of
new friends. My new best friend, Anne, lives just around the
corner and we talk almost every day. But she has a boyfriend,
so I don't know how long we'll remain close. My friends who
can drive, Gina and Patty, have taught me about cruising. We
go from The Village Market to Clifton's, to Jones's and then do
it all over again. Sometimes we drive a dozen or more laps in
one night. The best nights are the ones when we run into
Randy more than once. I wonder if he'll ever talk to me. Well, I
have to go to cheerleader practice now. I'll write more
tomorrow—there's always a new story to tell.

Table of Contents

Prologue

This is a true story. The vignettes stem from real people and events as seen through the eyes of a teenage girl in the mid-1970s. The middle-America setting is a fabulous backdrop for a coming-of-age story in one of the last pre-digital generations of our time. For presentation, there are many amalgamations of events and personalities, and I am compelled to address these in general before we begin this focused journey back in time.

First, most names have been changed to protect the innocent, the guilty, and those who didn't plan to be a character in a book.

Second, the characters, especially pivotal ones, represent composites of two or more people with similar but distinct histories and personalities. Let me emphasize, the reader would draw false conclusions if they would attempt to make a direct connection between any of the following characters with a "real life" person. So, if you believe you identify yourself in the storyline, don't take it personally if you feel I have misrepresented you.

Third, there are elements that draw upon my early medical training that reflect my confused and incomplete understanding of mental illness and chemical dependency, but impacted me deeply. I've integrated some of this confusion into the storyline.

Fourth, I have chronologically repositioned some events for the sake of presentation and, undoubtedly, some are temporally misplaced due to faults of memory thirty-plus years after the fact when no sources of confirmation are available.

Last, the first thirteen chapters of this book take place in what was a sparsely populated north-central Tennessee county in which I have never lived but provided an ideal backdrop and cast of characters for the issues of the day. The historical presentation of this county and its largest town (with a population of about 2,500 at the time of the story) comes from an "outsider" — me. My interpretation of the culture that existed in this particular county evolved from a combination of personal visits, an extensive review of the local newspaper from the mid-1970s, and hundreds of hours of informal interviews with dozens of current and former residents, including my beleaguered wife. Undoubtedly, some past and present locals will not agree (or at least openly admit that they agree) with some parts of the portrayal that follows.

The storyline follows no prefabricated book formula. It is a biographic presentation of the main character's mid-teen years. So, don't expect a standard paperback format. The heroine is

i

beautiful but has no superpowers, the hero isn't a wealthy thirty-something or unbelievably handsome, and the world is never at risk. There will be typical ups, downs, and mistakes in life that we all have made.

The seeds of this book were planted in late 2007 when I came across a sealed box while retrieving Christmas decorations from our basement to prepare for the holiday season. The box contained an assortment of personal mementos from our past, including my wife's pre-me teenage diary and 278 letters we wrote to each other during our college academic year of 1976–77. After decorating our Christmas tree that evening, we sat in our sunroom to relax and have a glass of wine. Picking up the stack of letters was like stepping into a portal to our past. Three bottles of wine later, dawn broke, and we watched the sunrise through our sunroom window. Then we took deep breaths and looked into each other's eyes with a new appreciation for the fabulous journey we've been sharing.

During the hangover of my happiness, I penciled a reconstruction of that year's events onto a makeshift calendar while I reread our letters page by page. As I scribbled summary comments into little boxes of time, the visual image of seeing all the events of that year juxtaposed so tightly together on a few sheets of paper came to life. The picture was simultaneously astounding and unbelievable.

A few days later, I added another page to the makeshift calendar to include the eight months between our introduction and our first letters and filled in known events as memory served. Eventually hitting a wall, I found that relatively simple research allowed me to fill in much of that year's calendar with enormous accuracy and completeness. The result was an incredible (at least to me) historical review of our early days together, and my jaw dropped more than once with awe and surprise; there were just so many significant events (for us, anyway) in such a short time.

Captivated by our history, I felt compelled to keep working backward in time through the days, weeks, months, and years before looking into my wife's eyes for the first time to learn more of her history. Her teen diary provided a good foundation but had spotty time gaps of various duration. From there, the process was slow and disorganized, but I continued to fill in the little boxes of time as random information became available. As a result, I came to appreciate my wife, her roots, and her story in a most unexpected way. It convinced me there was not only more to learn about her, but a bigger story with important life lessons. What I learned begs to be told.

The seeds sprouted while our youngest was in college, and we acquired more free time for ourselves. Maybe it shouldn't have been, but the treasure trove of play time was unexpected. We had been so busy with the business of life that becoming empty nesters caught us by surprise. I have to admit, it didn't take us long to adjust, and we soon took advantage of our newfound freedom.

Later that winter, in early 2008, while sitting on the beach consumed in rum and Diet Coke induced lateral-drift conversation, it hit like a bolt of lightning that although I knew most of my wife's pre-me life stories, the details were frequently fuzzy, and I had few mental images to go with them.

So began a ten-year journey of asking questions and listening to her to tell and retell her stories. I pushed for ever-increasing detail and she rewarded me with more profound revelations. Along the way, I integrated many of my own youthful parallel experiences into the fabric of the evolving storyline.

I splashed random notes on the individual vignettes onto a continuous broad mental canvas like a poorly organized collage. Evolution of the stories and the painting of mental images did not occur in a linear fashion but in discontinuous, and out-of-sequence spurts. Most of these spurts took place while sitting on the beach, hiking, biking, or floating in the pool; during pleasant lateral-drift time. Initially, the picture was fluid and ever-changing. Over time, however, I added fixed puzzle pieces, and the vignettes shifted into their proper chronology. As the collage became more defined and far less mutable, a coherent picture gradually emerged from the confusion and finally came to life in my mind.

It's a pursuit that will probably never really be finished, but for me, at least, it's an unbelievable image of my wife, part of her coming-of-age story and the ingredients she brought to the magic power that binds us together.

Writing didn't begin until January 2015, after a childhood friend called at midnight and asked me to meet him at White Castle. Without going into details, it was clear he was in deep psycho-emotional trouble. Attempting to focus him on positive thinking, I latched onto one of his long-time dreams: ". . . to write the Great American novel." I bet him a case of beer that I could write a novel before him. This was mostly a joke — he was the writer, while I was anything but. I'm sad to say that I will win by default. He died in July 2015.

The lessons of the story are not new. But they are timeless lessons that should be retold to every generation to help keep us from getting lost and may be more critical in today's struggling world than ever before.

───────── ◆ ─────────

I would ask the reader to keep in mind that this story takes place in the mid-1970s — before cable TV, the Internet, and cell phones. Our country was evolving new views on religion, sex, drugs, and politics that began in the 1960s. Most people considered long-distance phone calls a luxury, and actual letter writing was still a common form of communication. The decade started with Richard Nixon in the White House, most Americans were happy with their government, and the Watergate scandal had yet to unfold. The fall of Saigon and the start of our country's recovery from the Viet Nam war had to wait until April 1975. Flower power and peace symbols were common. Gasoline was under fifty cents per gallon and didn't increase much until the pseudo "gas crisis" near the end of the decade. Despite all of the sociopolitical tumult, most teens and young adults still believed in the American Dream.

The average kid owned his or her innocence longer back then, more in line with the Wonder Years television series. Undoubtedly, kids were kids and got into trouble as they always have, but in a more innocent way than they do today — something more in line with the movie Summer of 42. The average kid also grew up much as their parents did and, in my opinion, developed a better moral framework compared to today's youth. They understood they had to work and save for things they wanted and believed "being good" was important.

Kids who gave it any thought considered love and romance to be things for a lucky few. Kissing was considered a sacred act by most. It was a way of showing affection and part of building a relationship — not merely a prelude to having sex. Kids seemed to have more time to learn about love and respect its powers. Kids of today (especially girls) seem to have been misguided by Hollywood and television. All too frequently, they haphazardly give themselves away and destroy much, if not most, of the chance to experience true love.

I hope readers, especially teen to college-aged girls, and young parents will think about the lessons that follow and hold *them in their hearts. If just a few do, I will consider my efforts a success and believe the world will be a better place.*

To live only for some future goal is shallow. It's the sides of the mountain which sustain life, not the top.
Here's where things grow.
Robert Pirsig, *Zen and the Art of Motorcycle Maintenance: An Inquiry into Values*

Part I

The last rays of golden light slowly disappeared as the sun dipped below the watery horizon. Magic bands of brilliant red and orange hues stretched across the sky and melted into ever-darkening shades of blue as night slowly crept up from behind. Two pairs of sandy, middle-aged feet hung just over the edges of the beach loungers.

They looked at each other in the eye, gently touched glasses, and toasted the sky.

"We've been married for a long time. We made it through college, survived residency, and our kids are growing up fast; too fast. I probably know every important thing and most of the unimportant things there are to know about you. But the business of life — school, work, and raising kids — hasn't left much time to discuss the details. I'd like to hear more details."

"I'm not sure I know what you mean."

"Well, for instance, you've told me about your very first memory as a little girl. I can recite the story, but I have a very blurred mental image of it. Tell me the details. Draw me a picture with your words so I can see it in my head. Describe your movements so I can create a motion picture in my mind. I want to see you — to know you as a little girl."

"It's been a very long time. I'm not sure I remember that much. It's just a flash of a memory."

"Try. See what comes back as you tell the story."

"Well . . ."

Her words created colors and shapes that mixed to form flowing images. Rough at first, a more vivid scene gradually emerged from the muddled canvas. A little girl, not much over three years old with straight, shoulder-length, sandy-brown hair and bangs cut straight across her mid-forehead, wearing a knee-length, short-sleeve dress. It was white with light-blue

1

stripes, a white collar, and a matching light-blue cloth-covered belt. Her lightweight sweater was white with an embroidered rose on the left breast. White nylon socks topped by light-blue lace and folded over to the ankles disappeared inside black-and-white saddle shoes, neatly tied.

She sat with her mother on a train headed from St. Louis to Mexico, Missouri. Looking across the aisle, her tongue swept across her dry lips as she spied a drinking fountain. The bright-white porcelain bowl seemed to glow, and the shiny silver handle and faucet shot off beams of reflected light. Suddenly aware of her thirst, she politely asked her mother if she could get a drink. After receiving a nod of approval, she marched confidently to the fountain and grabbed the handle. Straining on her tiptoes, she couldn't get her mouth above the rim until her mother's fingers slipped around her waist to gently lift her toward her goal. Her eyes opened wide as the faucet came into view. When she turned the four-armed knob, the crystal-clear water rose and formed a smooth arch before splashing into the white bowl. Her lips intercepted the flowing stream. Swallowing what she could, she felt the excess water wet her cheeks and drip from her chin into the basin. Finally, she let go of the knob and a long, soft "Ahhhhh" vibrated from her throat as her mother gently lowered her to the floor. Stepping back to face her mother's gaze, she wiped her mouth with the back of her hand and said, "Thank you."

Life stories are all in the details.

Chapter One
There Is No Going Back
April 6–9, 1973

On April 6, 1973, NASA launched the Pioneer 11 space probe to begin a six-year mission to study the far reaches of our solar system before continuing on into endless interstellar space. The cold, lonely adventure would only become more so when the inevitable death of the probe's thermoelectric generators would end all contact with Earth.

The next morning, 14-year-old Mindy felt as if she was riding atop Pioneer 11 as she began her own adventure into uncharted territory. Although traveling at speeds far slower than a space probe, her family's car passed through Hartsville, Tennessee, in two blinks of an eye. Mindy's heart quickened with both excitement and fear as her father turned the car north onto State Highway 10 for the final fifteen miles toward their new home. Only a six-hour drive from her former home in St. Charles, Missouri, the trip had seemed an endless trek ever deeper into the unknown.

With seat belts all snugly tucked into the cracks of the bench seats, the entire Murphy family fit neatly into the broad body of a 1970 Bonneville sedan. Mindy's slim figure sat comfortably between her parents in the front seat while her three younger brothers, aged 8, 10, and 12, occupied the back.

Always chipper and chatty, Mindy's mother's lips rarely stopped moving. Mindy tried to be polite, but with thoughts elsewhere, she heard only some of her mother's words and nodded at what seemed to be the right times.

Glancing to her father, Mindy noted his hands fixed on the wheel at 2 and 10 o'clock with eyes glued to the road ahead and traveling below the speed limit. Reserved, logical, and business-like no matter the situation, Mindy didn't expect any words from him unless something needed to be said.

The gray early April sky stretching to the horizon was heavy and uninviting. The winding two-lane road disappeared around another hilly bend in the distance. Reminded of how little control she had over her immediate future, Mindy sighed softly. Her mother pulled out the road map, pointed to their location, and cried out, "Almost there!"

Pushing her gold wire-rim glasses up higher onto her nose, Mindy gazed ahead intently but saw no substantial change in the road or landscape. Bored by the unchanging scene, she pivoted to scan the back seat where her sleeping brothers sprawled like a directionless mass of boyhood; untucked shirttails, arms and legs intertwined, pretzel-like, heads all tilting in different directions. The boredom of the drive and a "Don't make me pull over" warning by their father had planted their directionless young brains in an uncaring netherworld; oblivious to where they had come from or where they were going.

Mindy's most significant source of joy in the back was the family dog. FiFi, a scrawny Chihuahua-Poodle mix, sat trembling in her youngest brother's lap. Referred to simply as Fi, the little mutt with Phyllis Diller fur reminded Mindy of the anxious but intuitive Fiver in *Watership Down*. Fi's intuition gave her an immediate sense of 'good' or 'bad' and, despite her small size, she'd growl and bark if someone of questionable value entered their home. Unfortunately, no one in the family learned to harness Fi's insight but focused more on the handful of tricks Mindy taught her as a young puppy; the demonstration of which would send everyone into hysterics.

Mindy sighed again. Just a few months ago, she'd been a happy, comfortable, scholastically challenged, and religiously balanced girl. For the first time in her life, Mindy had felt grounded, and in vague but exciting ways, the world beyond her sheltered home was inviting her into its future. She reached over the seat to scratch the top of Fi's head and soothe both the pup's anxiety and her own. Fi closed her eyes in appreciation, and Mindy's thoughts drifted.

Her friends! She would really miss them. Her family moved so often that it had been nearly impossible to forge lasting friendships. With their move to St. Charles, she hoped to keep her friends and maybe even find a true bosom friend like the fictional Anne Shirley. She wondered, "Will I have time to make new friends before summer? Will they even like me in Tennessee?"

Then there was her old school, Duchesne High. Wearing the same uniform every day took some getting used to, but it was easier than worrying about what to wear. Those uniforms, along with her literature and religion classes, had made her better. Teachers and classmates had encouraged her to think about life in novel ways. Impressed by the number of exceptionally bright students in those classes, she wondered how they ever came up with some of their insights? Being around those whiz-kids had made her work harder. They'd pushed her to grow up and seek her potential. As a result, her grades were never better.

The car rolled over a bump and startled Mindy out of her reverie for a moment. Her mother was gazing out the side door window, atypically quiet now. The boys still dozed. Mindy slowly drifted back into her thoughts.

She would miss the school dances. She loved to dance. Her best friend, Marla, liked to tease her and tell her how much the boys enjoyed watching her dance. "They like to watch the way you move — even some juniors and seniors," Marla had reported.

But Mindy had dismissed Marla's assessment, "I'm skinny. Why would they like to watch me? I'll bet Marla made it up."

She remembered her year-long crush on John Salvo. He had finally nervously smiled at her for the first time just a few weeks ago. And there was Glenn, a junior who was taller and undoubtedly stronger than John, who never seemed nervous around her. "Why did *he* ask *me* to prom?" Mindy had wondered. The thrill of being asked out by an older boy convinced Mindy to ask her parents, but she already knew she'd have to tell him, "Sorry, my parents won't let me date until I'm sixteen." That was more than a year away. "He would have been the perfect first date," she thought.

Scrawny little Fi was now fast asleep with her brothers. Mindy let out another soft sigh as she turned to face forward again. Images of her new reality approached at what seemed to be a snail's pace through the windshield. Another bend in the hilly road obscured her view and left her to wonder, "How did this happen?" Then she remembered.

"Your father has been transferred again," her mother had announced. With Mindy's gasp of angst, her mother continued, "Your father makes money to support the family, and the family will have to follow the work. I'm sorry, but it is a fact of life that affects us all. The good news is we probably won't have to be there for long. You can come back here to finish high school at Duchesne."

"We've only been here for a year and were only in Mississauga for a year and a half. How can you possibly know where we'll be next year or that we'll be able to come back here?" Mindy wanted to know. Her mother offered no reply.

Mindy's father gave a general overview of the move and what would be their new town at dinner that evening. "It's a small town in Tennessee with a population of around 2,000. There are no stoplights, there is no movie theater, no Catholic church, and no mall. It is a strong Baptist community. There will be few, if any, other Catholic families. I'll oversee the last phase of construction and opening of a new Carter Automotive plant."

Her brothers just shrugged and asked for more food, but Mindy shrieked, "What?! No movies! No mall! No Catholic church? How can that be? What do people do there?" Met with silence, Mindy protested, "So, does it have a bowling alley or even a skating rink?" she asked. Her father shook his head.

Trying to lessen the pain, her mother said, "Don't worry, we won't have to move until the end of the school year."

In her room after dinner, Mindy settled into her desk chair to study a road atlas. After scanning the two-page spread of Tennessee for several minutes, her finger stopped on a small circle labeled "Lafayette" at the crossing of State Highways 10 and 52. "Ah!" she cried out. Reaching to the back of her top desk drawer, she pulled her diary from under its notebook paper camouflage and placed it on her desk. She rubbed her fingers over the words "MY DIARY" etched in the cover, then studied the picture of a pair of worn saddle shoes below. "My saddle shoe diary," she thought. A moment later, she wrote:

Dear Diary,
I found our new town on the map of Tennessee. It took
a few minutes because it's so small. It's not even a dot!

A few days later, Mindy would gasp again when her mother announced, "There's been a change in plans. The plant construction will finish ahead of schedule, and they want to open early. So, we're going to move in early April."

"What?! Can't Dad just go?" Mindy cried.

Her mother tried to lessen the pain again by speaking soothingly. "Dad wants us all to go together. We move as a family. Really, it's better this way. The boys can get signed up for baseball, and you can be there for cheerleader tryouts. The only drawback is that we will have to live in a trailer for a few weeks because the current owner will still be in our new house."

"A trailer! We're going to live in a trailer? Will I still have my own bedroom?" Mindy shrieked.

"Compared to a house, it is small, and it will be very crowded with all six of us. But yes, you will have your own room. Most of our stuff will have to go into storage until we can move into the house. Everyone will get to take one suitcase of clothes," her mother explained.

Mindy went to her room in a huff.

Just before leaving Missouri, her father sat Mindy down for a rare father-daughter discussion. "You will be a big fish in a small pond. You will need to be a diplomat not only for the family but for the company. You must be respectful to all and never take advantage of your position. Another thing, the town is mostly

Baptist, and I hate to say this, but some Baptists don't think very highly of Catholics. I would suggest you not make a big deal of your religion and don't get too upset if you hear some odd or mean things about Catholics. Just ignore it."

For a happy-go-lucky, make-everyone-happy sort of girl, this lecture was some heavy-duty stuff. Mindy wasn't sure whether it should make her feel better or worse.

The loaded Bonneville climbed up what turned out to be the last hill of their journey as a sudden burst of wind shook the car. Mindy shivered, and her eyes widened as random snowflakes crossed their path. "I thought you said we were moving to the south. How can there be snow flurries?"

No one answered her question. The car slowed as it neared one of the few stop signs in town. Her brothers stirred, rubbing the sleep from their eyes and leaning forward with curiosity.

Just ahead on a quiet street, a man of indeterminate age wearing bib overalls and a worn, unzipped coat appeared to be waving his hand in the air and doing an odd dance. As they rolled to a stop, the image became clear. The lonesome creature was doing a little jig as he cracked a ten-foot bullwhip in the air. "*CRACK!*" sounded the whip, and the palpable vibrations sent goosebumps crawling across Mindy's skin. Her brothers leaned toward the left passenger window and sang, "Cooool" in unpracticed harmony. Mindy's jaw dropped, and her stomach sank.

Her father spoke his first words in the past 120 miles, "Here's the town square." The administrative and business heart of the town filled a short half-block square around City Hall. The small shops lining the perimeter displayed signs with local and unfamiliar names. "And there's the Spit and Whittle Club," he continued with a grin. The car crawled past the front entrance of City Hall as Mindy stared, wide-eyed, at two benches near the main entrance walkway occupied by three elderly men. Each wore a scruffy winter coat and held a small block of wood in one hand and a knife in the other with a dusting of wood shavings between their feet. One of the old men wore a scraggly, tobacco-stained beard and tracked the car's movement. Squinting with untrusting eyes, he spewed forth a thick stream of black tobacco chew onto the pavement, then smiled to reveal missing incisors bookended by brown stained canines. Mindy quickly turned away, pressing her back hard into her seat and wondering whether they were at the front door of the Twilight Zone.

With another quick left turn, they reached the north corner of the square and proceeded northwest on Scottsville Road. Just off the square sat several small businesses, a small strip mall, and a cattle-auction stockyard. Signs of human occupation then thinned considerably until they turned into a neighborhood dominated by single-story brick homes. Mindy found the more typical suburban residential appearance reassuring and thought, "At least our house will look normal." They pulled up in front of what would eventually be their new home on Ellington Drive. Mindy studied the scene: a ranch-style house set way back off the street, surrounded by a forest of tall oak trees and encircled by a long driveway with entrance/exits on both sides of the house.

"Well, there it is. Our new home" announced Mindy's mother. Mindy scanned the scene and smiled with pleasant surprise.

With everyone eager to get out of the car, they promptly retraced their path. In the few minutes they were away, almost all signs of life had deserted the square to create a ghost town atmosphere. The car exited at the south corner, and past several disheveled buildings. The cold, quiet surroundings quickly dissipated any feeling of warmth, and a sudden chill made Mindy shiver. She wondered, "What is this place? Why did they bring us here?" A moment later, the Bonneville pulled onto the gravel drive of their temporary home.

With most of their belongings headed to storage, Mindy lugged her one suitcase of belongings up the wood steps into the trailer. Stopping two steps inside, Mindy could almost touch the far wall. She scanned the narrow hall leading to what she assumed were the bedrooms, then turned to study the tightly packed kitchen, dining, and living area. The thought of having to share such a small space with three brothers left her queasy. Her mother pushed by and said, "Your bedroom is the first door on the left."

The only two pieces of furniture in Mindy's bedroom, a twin bed and a short chest of drawers, almost filled the floor space. Standing before the chest, Mindy quickly realized there was no room to open the drawers unless she kneeled on the bed. She shook her head and quickly unpacked.

The local stores closed early on Saturday, so Mindy's parents left her in charge while they made a trip to pick up basic food necessities. In their parent's absence, it didn't take long for her three brothers to become unruly and start fighting. Using threatening Can-Can kicks she had learned in jazz dance class, Mindy quickly broke up the skirmish and sent her little-boy siblings off to explore the trailer park.

A few hours later, Mindy set the table while her mother started dinner in the one-person kitchen. Without room to help, Mindy moved outside to sit on the steps of their temporary home with a jittery Fi in her lap. She felt alone and whispered, "Fi, I know we're not in Kansas, but we're sure not in Oz. I wonder how we'll fit in here?"

A short time later, a few neighbors wandered by to say, "Hey," "Wor y'all from?" and "Wey-come ta S-inn City." Visitors included a boy of about seven or eight wearing well-worn and too-small overalls who followed his father over to meet the new neighbors. As his father talked, the boy busied himself, pulling blood-filled ticks from his dog's neck and then crushing them with the heel of his shoe on a round concrete stone. Mindy sat speechless as she watched the bloody display unfold before her.

When the visitors left, Mindy scanned the surroundings. Most of the trailers seemed reasonably new, but several direly needed repairs. As far as she could tell, there were few other children in the park, and her parent's car was the only sedan in sight. Old pickup trucks and the occasional rusty tractor were the only other vehicles around. Overalls were standard attire for men and boys, and no neighbors crossed her path wearing a dress or tie. The collarless, free-roaming dogs were all scrawny, in much need of a bath, and looked as though they would enjoy eating little Fi for lunch. She scratched Fi's head and whispered, "I'll protect you."

After dinner, the kids were disappointed to find that the trailer's small black-and-white television could pick up only three stations. With little else to do, the kids were shuffled off to bed early after waiting their turn in line to use the bathroom. When Mindy finally curled up in bed, images of whips, tobacco spew, and ticks made it a restless night.

The entire family was up early the following morning and had time to practice navigation through the cramped quarters before getting ready for church. They drove 45 minutes to the nearest Catholic church, a Glenmary Home Missioners church in Scottsville, Kentucky, and were greeted warmly. In no hurry to get back to the trailer after Mass, Mindy's parents talked with other parishioners for what seemed an eternity before a leisurely family lunch at the Barren River Lodge.

With school registration the next morning, Mindy sat on her bed after dinner, considering her clothing options for the first day at her new school. She had learned the hard way that kids could be tough on students who showed up in unfamiliar or out-of-style fashions. Having worn one of two navy skirts and white button-down blouses to Duchesne every day, Mindy found her options limited and casual. She eventually settled on a white uniform shirt under a sleeveless lightweight sweater, flare-leg Levi's, and her favorite saddle shoes.

She lay in bed with open eyes for a long time, recalling the suburban life she'd left behind and wondering all the more what challenges and opportunities her new town would have to offer. Finally, closing her eyes, she prayed, "Dear Lord, thank you for all you have given my family and me. Thank you for taking care of us. Please, if you will, make tomorrow a good first day of school. Let me fit in and make lots of good friends. Amen." She had been in this situation before, and in her world, there was only one way to go, and that was forward.

Despite another restless night, Mindy was eager to begin her new life, so arose early to beat her brothers to the bathroom. After breakfast, they all hurried to the car. The first stop was Macon County High School (MCHS), where Mindy entered the school's front office with her mother. They quickly completed registration papers before her mother paused long enough to offer wishes for a good day, then was gone in a flash.

Mrs. Cutrell, the southern-accented school secretary, spoke in warm, inviting tones. "Mr. Blankenship, our Principal, will be with you shortly. Let me wey-come y'all ta Macon County High. We have four grades, ninth through twelfth, with a-most four hun-derd students total. I believe yer Class of '76 is one of the smaller ones but has over seventy students." She paused to check a file and then continued, "Yes, y'all will be student number seventy-four!"

"Seventy-four! Oh, my goodness! I thought my class of over two hundred at Duchesne was small," Mindy thought.

She didn't have to wait long for the principal to arrive and for Mrs. Cutrell to hand him a re-labeled manila file. "Wey-come ta Macon County High. I'm Principal Blankenship. Come inta my office." He closed the door and quickly slid into the chair behind his desk, where he silently reviewed Mindy's file.

The secretary's accent had been a minor challenge to manage, but Mindy was unprepared to decipher the monotone, ultra-southern, and soft-spoken principal sitting before her and had to focus hard on his words to interpret.

After a few minutes of silent transcript review, he continued, "Ya know, there's only six weeks left of school. I'll try 'n match yer classes the best I kin. I see y'all been takin' French One. We do French one 'n two ever' other smes-ter. We don't have French One now, so I'm gonna put y'all in French Two. Y'all will prob-ly know more 'n the teacher anyway. I see y'all has been takin' a religion class? We don't have religion here . . ." Mindy cringed and swallowed the joke she wanted to make. ". . . I'll just put y'all in Home Ec." He completed the class schedule and handed it across the desk. "The sec-er-tory 'ill get ya a lock-a, give ya a tour, 'n show ya yer classes."

Feeling numb, Mindy just nodded.

A moment later, back in the office foyer, Mrs. Cutrell smiled. "Y'all just come and see me if ever ya need anything." She turned to a young girl standing next to her. "And this is my dau-ta, Kim. She's in yer grade 'n helps out here in the office as part of her Office Assistant class." The girls exchanged hello's and then Kim led the way for a tour of the school. A single-story building with simple classroom numbering would not be challenging to navigate.

The students in each class greeted Mindy pleasantly, but she couldn't ignore the stark contrast to her previous school experience. She was used to seeing nuns in full habits, crosses on the walls, and students coming to immediate, silent, and full attention with the bell to start class. Here, the atmosphere was relaxed. It took at least a few minutes to quiet the room after class began, and only a handful of students remained attentive throughout the entire period. The teachers seemed more like friends than leaders.

Morning classes passed quickly. At lunch, Mindy declined the okra and grits but picked up a small carton of milk and took two pieces of cornbread for 35 cents. As she stepped out of line, classmate Carolyn Wix stepped up to introduce herself. "You have such a pretty smile, you must be nice. Come sit with me, and I'll introduce you to my friends." Mindy felt relief when she didn't have to sit alone.

"Where do ya live?" one girl asked.

Mindy paused. "We're in a trailer for a few weeks until we can move into our house. I think the trailer court is called Cin-City, like Cincinnati."

The girls at the table shared looks of surprise and giggled. "Well, we sure hope you can get out of there soon. That's not a place you want to be for very long," they sang in unison.

A little embarrassed, Mindy tried to change the subject. "My old school had at least one dance party each semester. Are there any school dances here before the end of the semester?"

There was a collective gasp. "You won't be going to any dances around here. We don't even have a prom. This is a Baptist town, girl. Things like dancing are considered a sin. No drinkin', no dancin', and no wild music."

Mindy blushed with more embarrassment and nervously asked, "Well, what kind of music do you guys like? Who are your favorite bands?"

The other girls traded blank stares and then agreed, "We don't get much choice in the matter. AM radio here is mostly country western." They named several country western artists and country rock bands, but Mindy was only vaguely familiar with a few of them and responded by taking an oversized bite of cornbread.

A lanky boy with thick brown curls stepped up to interrupt the girl conversation and asked, "Who's the new girl?"

After introducing Mindy, Carolyn grinned to say, "And this is Ricky Hicks. He's goofy, but everybody likes him."

Ricky stared star-struck and too tongue-tied to speak until Mindy smiled and said, "Hi. It's nice to meet you."

"I saw you walkin' down the hall. You're wearin' Levi's. Those are boys' pants," Ricky stuttered.

Mindy blushed again and tried to explain that she was wearing girls' cut Levi's. But Ricky was disbelieving and offered some advice, "Around here, you might do better in dress pants. Well, see ya," and then almost ran away.

The girls giggled, and all agreed, "Oh my, Ricky likes you already."

Mindy wanted to crawl into a hole, but felt more relief when Carolyn asked what seemed to be a more neutral question. "What did you do at your old school?"

Mindy had to ask, "What do you mean?"

"Here at Macon County High, girls can be in the band, play basketball, be a cheerleader or do nothin' but go to school. So, we want to know what you did at your old school?" Caroly explained.

Later, Mindy would come to learn there was far more truth in Carolyn's statement than she ever would have thought possible. Clubs and extracurricular activities were extremely limited, and part-time jobs for girls were virtually nonexistent. Because most parents rarely went out for the evening, even babysitting jobs were scarce. But Mindy didn't question this at the time. Instead, she explained, "I had planned to try out for cheerleading but broke my elbow while practicing just before tryouts. So, I was one of those girls who just went to school. But one reason we moved early was so I could try out for cheerleader here." An uncomfortable silence settled over the table. Mindy didn't understand the change and felt too out of place to ask.

To fill the void, Mindy peppered the group with questions about the school and town. To her disappointment, the group didn't have much to say and concluded with the general assessment that there wasn't much for kids, and especially for girls, to do in Lafayette.

Happy to have survived lunch, Mindy walked alone back to class. "They all seem like nice girls. I think I can fit in," she thought. Then she realized, "Other than asking what I did at Duchesne, they didn't ask a single question about the school, my house, my friends, hobbies, or even boys," but was uncertain what, if anything, it meant.

That afternoon, Mindy made a small study of the other students' clothing. They sported a wide range of attire that suggested significant differences in social status and wealth. This was in stark contrast to students at Duchesne. "In St Charles, we all lived in similar houses, shopped at pretty much the same stores and dressed pretty much alike."

At MCHS, the nicely dressed girls wore frilly feminine polyester dresses or pantsuits with wide bell-bottoms. Saddle shoes were common. Other than the Future Farmers of America boys in their corduroy jackets, polyester dress slacks, polyester dress shirts with wide collars and platform shoes dominated the boys' clothing. In general, styles seemed more than a year behind the times, and Mindy concluded, "My saddle shoes fit in, but I'll have to go shopping for clothes."

Mindy had become accustomed to aggressive, Socratic-style questioning and pointed dialogue at Duchesne, but these techniques appeared to be absent from her new school. Classes seemed easy, and the rest of the day passed quickly.

When the bell rang, and students filed out of the school, it suddenly occurred to her she didn't know which bus to get on. She hurried back to the office and explained her problem. "Where do ya live?" the receptionist inquired.

It hit like a ton of bricks. Mindy didn't know her address or even what direction she should go. She explained, "All I know is that it's a trailer court just outside of town."

"That don't help none. Which one?" the secretary asked.

"I think it's called Cin-City. Like Cincinnati," Mindy replied.

"Oh, my. Y'all mean Sin City," the secretary laughed.

"Yes, I think it is Cin-City," Mindy repeated.

"Git on bus number 22. It's right out yonder, girl. Just tell the driver where ya want ta git off. He'll know."

Mindy hurried outside, boarded the bus, and told the bus driver she'd like to get off at Cin-City.

He belted out a mighty laugh, nodded, and said, "Shore little lady."

Sitting in the first row, Mindy anxiously kept watch out the front window for a familiar sight. It didn't take long. The road ended, and the gravel drive of the trailer court began. Mindy jumped off the bus, but her quick pace soon slowed to a crawl. She felt her pockets as though she'd lost or forgotten something. Then it struck her, and she raised her hand to her forehead. For the first time in months, she was returning from school without a single minute of homework. She climbed into the trailer feeling disappointed; school suddenly felt like a loss. She plopped down at the small kitchen table with a Twinkie and a glass of milk where visions of blood-filled ticks and lack of personal space replaced thoughts about school.

After the snack, boredom set in and Mindy took a seat outside on the wood steps of the trailer with a novel but didn't open it. A short time later, the grade school bus returned her brothers and a few other younger kids. She listened to their chatter as they passed by and noted that she could understand them better than she could just two days earlier. Her baptism-by-fire immersion in the sound of Southern accent had quickly trained her ears to assimilate the new language, and somehow it felt like a minor victory.

That night, the sound of her brothers' heavy breathing passed nearly unobstructed through the thin wall and made sleep hard to find. Mindy wanted to feel sorry for herself, but frequent moves had forced her to become resilient and adaptable. She settled herself and prayed, "Thank you, God, for getting me through another first day of school. The girls all seem nice, but it sure is different, and I'll definitely need some new clothes. I think it will be okay. Besides, there is no going back, is there?" She paused and waited for a reply, but heard none. With a sigh, she concluded, "Amen."

Resigned to make the best of what fate had handed her, Mindy drifted off to sleep.

Chapter Two
It Doesn't Take Long
April 10–May 18, 1973

What is now north-central Tennessee was a sparsely populated region until land grants given in payment for Revolutionary War service prompted a modest influx of new residents. Macon County was incorporated in 1842 and Lafayette (pronounced Luh-fay-it by locals) was created by charter as the county seat in 1899. It is the largest city in the county with a population of about 2,500 and is approximately 50 miles east of Nashville. Rural Missionary Baptist doctrine has long been the foundation of the county's social and political landscape, while the economy is rooted in agriculture, predominantly burley tobacco. Geographically isolated, Lafayette and its economy grew slowly, but gas-powered vehicles and paved, two-lane roads eventually opened some doors of opportunity for growth beyond farming. Bolstered by U.S. government subsidies to grow hemp during the World Wars, the post-World War II years welcomed a small influx of light industry, but the effects were limited. Travel to and from Lafayette remained difficult on the winding, hilly, and narrow roads that fostered many limitations. Even radio waves and, later, television from larger cities required suitable weather conditions for good reception.

Small numbers of people passed through Lafayette on their way to the medicinal waters of nearby Red Boiling Springs, but the town itself hosted rare out-of-town visitors. Except infants born into this community, few new faces made their home in this county where farms are passed down through the generations, century farms are numerous, and a handful of surnames dominate the grave markers in the local cemeteries. It is generally believed that you only need to go back a few generations to identify relationships via blood or marriage between almost everyone in town, and "Everyone knows everyone and everyone's business" is a common saying. The corollary for meeting one's mate is, "If you don't meet your mate in high school, then try church. If that don't work, try a family reunion."

By the 1950s, cheap gasoline and the rapid evolution of farm machinery and operations placed unprecedented new pressures on the historical and religious foundations of Macon County. A substantial percentage of the workforce gradually shifted from farms into small factories or businesses in Lafayette. The flowering growth of local government and taxpayer-supported jobs compounded this efflux. Before long, the only secure jobs would be with the local government, school district, local banks, and the larger farms. As a result, the longstanding foundation of the community developed unstable cracks.

Relative isolation persisted into the mid-1970s as many side roads remained unpaved and many streams had no bridges. Tobacco continued to dominate as the primary cash crop, although some farms have seen their species of hemp "evolve" into hallucinogen-producing varieties and became an unofficial side business on more farms than any will openly admit. Ownership of large numbers of acres and livestock determine, in part, one's wealth and power within the county. Rural religious conservatism has promoted an isolationist mentality to protect the status quo, but honest, hard-working people coursing through life one day at a time form the core of the community.

Against this backdrop, Carter Automotive Products identified Lafayette as an excellent place to build a new production plant. The land was cheap, city council members were more than willing to cut tax deals, and a sizeable non-union workforce clamored for steady, well-paying jobs anyplace other than a farm. The Carter CFO, who was less concerned with economic factors and more concerned with specific prejudices, made the final decision on the location of the new plant. He wanted "a Protestant workforce and no blacks." Scoring 99% on both accounts, Macon County and Lafayette became a natural choice.

Charles Murphy, Mindy's father, was an energetic and focused manager who was working his way up the Carter administrative ladder. With an opportunity to escape an incompetent boss and climb another corporate rung, he volunteered to accept the challenging task of opening a new factory on relatively short notice. In Lafayette, this would be no ordinary factory. It would employ three hundred workers at start-up and up to one thousand when fully operational. The day he took the job, Charles became one of the most influential men in town; on par with the mayor, police chief, town physicians, and the veterinarian.

Despite her father's pre-move warning, Mindy had not foreseen the modest celebrity status her arrival in town induced. Although overstated, many perceived Mindy's father as "a big-shot corporate executive" and, by definition, "rich." This, along with being a relatively rare new face at school, made Mindy a frequent topic of conversation. Combined with her unassuming personality and stunning, girlish looks, she was an instant hit among her schoolmates, especially the boys. The exception to this was a small pool of teen female socialites who remained cool and aloof.

Although Mindy didn't fully understand the attention, she liked it. Her self-confidence grew rapidly, and she quickly integrated with her new classmates. Within days of her arrival, Mindy was rarely alone as boys and girls alike surrounded her between classes. There were even playful spats about whom she would sit next to at lunch.

At the end of her first week of classes, it surprised Mindy to learn that her plan to try out for cheerleader was common knowledge among the girls. When she questioned Carolyn about it at lunch, she learned MCHS had two cheer squads; one for football and one for basketball, with a limited number of positions for each class. "Trust me, the news of you trying out for cheerleader spread like wildfire. The girls from our class who were on the team this year are worried they'll lose their spot, and girls who were thinking about trying out for next year's team are in a tizzy," Carolyn explained.

Mindy had given no thought to which squad she would try out for, but there was no shortage of advice on the subject from fellow freshman Kathy (Kat) Shire. "Cheering for basketball is way better," she told Mindy. "You don't have to worry about the weather, and you get to cheer for a whole lot more games."

Because most of her clothing was still in storage, Mindy realized she would need to buy something to wear for tryouts no matter which team she tried out for. So, after school on Friday, she and her mother went to the Macon County Department Store on the square. Despite being the larger of the two clothing stores in town, it was small, with only seven or eight racks of clothes for girls and about half that for boys. Mindy looked through the limited options, but nothing captured her attention, so she asked her mother if they could go to a different store. Her mother shook her head. "I've already checked at the other store, and they don't carry anything for you, but we're not driving to a different town just to buy clothes." Mindy kept looking and eventually found something acceptable.

As they prepared to check out, Rose Belle and her daughter Anne entered the store. Being married to the local veterinarian placed Rose in the power and money club of the town by default. They had four children, with Anne being the youngest and assumed by many to be an unanticipated surprise. A petite fellow freshman at MCHS, Anne had been introduced to Mindy at school, but was one of those girls who had remained cold and standoffish to the newcomer.

Like Mindy, Anne was also shopping for something to wear to cheer tryouts. As the mothers chatted, Anne stood quietly with a distant stare that prevented much eye contact, but she couldn't avoid interaction when Mindy tried to engage her. Mindy soon disarmed her with her sweet personality and youthful kindness. Anne's eventual smile revealed two rows of dull silver braces. When they all left, Mindy and her mother headed for home while Anne and her mother drove to Nashville to continue shopping.

Over the next weeks and months, Mindy and her mother came to understand the limited shopping options in town. They also learned that driving to other cities, especially Nashville and Bowling Green, Kentucky, to shop for clothes was standard practice for most residents of Lafayette.

―――――――――――

The next afternoon, Mindy helped her mother put away groceries. As they worked, Mindy's father returned from Saturday morning meetings at the Carter plant and took a seat at the kitchen table. Her mother prepared his lunch and apparently forgot Mindy was within easy earshot as she weaved a short tale directed solely at her father.

"A pleasant woman about my age introduced herself to me at the grocery store this morning. She talked for several minutes about the town but ended on an odd note," Mindy's mother began. Summoning her thickest southern accent, she continued, "She said, 'Lafayette is jest a wuun-derful lil town. Ever-one is jest so friendly and hep-ful. Y'all gonna like it here, 'cept I 'spect y'all ain't gonna like the schoos much.'"

Switching back to her Missouri accent, she continued, "I asked, 'Why do you say that?' The woman paused, squeezed her lips together, and nodded her head before responding."

Shifting back to a thick Southern accent, Mindy's mother went on, "Well, I shouldn't ought-ta say nothin', but the schoos here ain't too good. The ed-u-cation yer kids 'il git probly ain't gonna be what yer used ta. I should know. I'm a tea-cha."

"I was surprised by the woman's honesty and wanted to hear more. I said, Oh, I'm sorry to hear you say that. What subject do you teach? The woman replied, 'In-glish.' I drove home wondering what in the world have we done," she concluded.

Mindy stood silently about ten feet away, wondering the exact same thing.

At lunch on Monday, Jill Dyer inquired about Mindy's plan for cheer tryouts. When Mindy shrugged, Jill explained, "Everybody considers football cheerleaders to be way better and way more important than basketball. They take two girls from each class for football. Kat and Anne were the freshman cheerleaders this year. So, if you go for football cheerleader and make it, one of them will get bumped. Hey, you're new, really cute and probably have a good chance. They're scared."

That same afternoon, Anne paused in the hallway to listen as Kat interrogated Mindy and repeated her earlier advice regarding tryouts. When Kat continued on to her next class, Anne pulled Mindy aside to warn, "Be careful what you say to Kat. She may use it against you. And take any of her advice with a grain of salt. She'll say anything to keep you from trying out for the football squad. She's afraid you will. If you do, she thinks you'll probably get her position."

Mindy had a flash of Anne's initial coolness, then recalled Jill's comment and wondered what Anne was really saying.

Hoping to avoid high school politics, this set of conversations seemed to settle the issue in Mindy's mind. She didn't want to make enemies, so chose what appeared to be the path of least resistance and mentioned her intention to try out for a basketball cheer position to a few girls that afternoon.

The next day, Kim approached Mindy to ask, "I hear you're planning to try out for the basketball cheer team. Is that right?"

Sensing some anxiety in Kim's voice, Mindy's thoughts backtracked and she hesitantly replied, "I'm not sure yet."

Kim frowned and looked away. Before Mindy could respond further, Kim rebounded with a forced smile to say nervously, "Well, good luck. But I believe you should think about being a football cheerleader. They're always more popular," then disappeared down the hallway.

Later, Mindy stopped Carolyn in the hallway to say, "This may sound like an odd question, but do you know if Kim is planning to try out for cheerleader?"

"She was a basketball cheerleader this year, so I guess she'll try out again for next year," Carolyn replied.

Mindy cringed, "Okay, thanks."

As the days passed, several upperclassmen stopped by Mindy's lunch table to introduce themselves. This included Bud Gentry, and the other girls at the table deemed it no minor event. One explained, "Bud is president of the junior class. He's quiet and very popular, but he's never shown even the slightest interest in any girl around here. Kat has had a crush on him for three years, but he won't even hardly talk to her."

So, it was another noteworthy event when Bud arrived at Mindy's lunch table for the second time. He cleared his throat loud enough to capture Mindy's attention. She turned to look up and gently pushed her glasses higher on her nose. Bud nervously combed his fingers through his hair, then wiped his palms on his pants and stuttered mildly. "Hi, Mindy. Would it be all right if I stopped by your house after school for a visit?"

With no reason to object, Mindy replied, "I think that would be okay, but we're not in our house yet. We're in the Cherry Hill Trailer Court for another few weeks." She silently patted herself on the back for learning the unposted but official name of her trailer court.

Bud anxiously replied, "I know — I mean, I know right where it's at. Well — great. See ya after school!" and bounced away with a little country jive in his step.

As soon as Bud disappeared out the cafeteria door, the other girls hummed a collective, "Ahhhh, he likes you!" and broke into a high-pitched gaggle about how lucky she was. Except for Kat, who sat staring at Mindy with cheeks aglow.

Embarrassed by the giggling, Mindy changed the subject by re-announcing her intention to try out for basketball cheerleader and was happy to receive much encouragement. She was less than thrilled after lunch, however, when she overheard someone at the far end of the table say with some disappointment, "Girls, we're in trouble. That new girl is going to have every decent boy at school after her."

After school, Mindy sat on the front steps of the trailer, finishing an oatmeal cream pie when a gold Dodge Charger pulled up. Bud emerged from the driver's seat with a little mechanical hitch in his step, like a teenage Geppetto. He was courteous and soft-spoken as they talked about the school, Lafayette, St. Louis, and farms. The conversation soon hit a wall and several seconds of uncomfortable silence ensued before Bud blurted out, "Would you go out with me this weekend?"

Mindy blushed. Bud seemed like a nice boy but had stirred not the slightest romantic interest in her. So, she was not unhappy to explain, "I can't date until I'm sixteen, and I don't turn fifteen until next week." Bud expressed his disappointment but asked if it would be okay if he came over to visit again. Mindy hesitated but responded with a silent nod of approval.

The mildly manic changes in Bud's demeanor whenever in Mindy's presence made it clear to everyone at school except Mindy that he was wallowing in a crush on her. When Bud began making daily stops at Mindy's lunch table, Jill couldn't resist stirring the lunch-table pot just for fun. "Ya know, Bud and Ricky both have crushes on you. Well, what we all want to know is, who ya gonna go for?"

Mindy sat quietly, but Kat jumped in to add, "Ricky is so smart and cute. He really is the one you should go for." The other girls at the table laughed hysterically.

That afternoon, Anne cornered Mindy to explain, "Because Bud is so popular, some girls are upset that he has a crush on you, especially Kat." She then took some pleasure in adding, "They're mad. They think it's mostly just because you're new in town. They think it's unfair, and it will be impossible to compete against you."

Mindy didn't believe Anne's report until the next day. Standing in the hallway outside the cafeteria, camouflaged by the crowd, she overheard part of a conversation that included "unfair" and "impossible to compete." When she heard her own name mentioned as the subject, she buried her head in her notebook and hurried away.

Over the subsequent week, Bud made three more visits to the trailer, and his confidence seemed to grow by the hour. But he was none too pleased when the presence of another would-be suitor, Ricky Hicks, complicated two of them. A fellow freshman, Ricky was too young for a driver's license but proudly arrived on his blue Stingray bicycle with a yellow banana seat, a weathered wood clothes pin (awaiting the return of an unworn playing card), and several small peace symbol decals that carried him from his home in town to the trailer park. Although the boys addressed each other politely, the unspoken competition was palpable and made for an uncomfortable trio. Hoping to outlast the other, each boy was unwilling to leave voluntarily and likely would have stayed until dark.

But Mindy was more concerned with fitting in at her new school and preparing for cheer tryouts than either of her suitors. She brought each of the visits to a premature end so she could practice cheers, cartwheels, and splits.

Bud returned the next day to anxiously inquire, "Would it be okay for you to ride with me to see my farm?" When Mindy hesitated, Bud asked to speak with her mother, to whom he presented a well-rehearsed speech that ended with a reassuring, "It's not a date or anything." It took a few seconds for Mindy's mother to suppress a chuckle before she gave her consent.

As Mindy slid into the passenger seat, she noticed that Bud's hands were trembling, but was uncertain what it meant. The drive into the countryside coursed through beautiful green rolling hills punctuated by broad swaths of recently plowed fields. The car suddenly slowed and turned onto an unmarked gravel road for a few hundred yards. After bouncing over the guttered path, they came to a stop next to a barn painted classic brick red. Standing before the barn, Mindy noted the quiet and closed her eyes. All she could hear was the occasional chirp of a bird and her own breathing. She took a deep breath to inhale the country air, but stopped short when the nose-burning scent of manure made her eyes water and nearly choke.

Bud laughed, then motioned toward the barn, and Mindy followed along. He explained the barn would be full of tobacco leaves for drying after harvest as he swung open the heavy doors. Random darting shadows across the dirt floor made Mindy gasp. Reading the uncertainty in her eyes, Bud shrugged. "Mice. Lots of mice in there."

Somewhat mouse phobic, Mindy shuddered and backed away. "I don't like mice. I don't like mice at all!"

They chatted for a bit about farming and tobacco as they walked toward a barbed-wire fence enclosing a broad, low hillside. Off in the distance, Mindy could see a herd of grazing cattle, and Bud proudly announced, "All these acres and the thirty head of cattle on that hill belong to me."

Trying to sound interested, Mindy inquired, "That's nice. How many cows are in a head?"

Laughing again, Bud replied, "Well, I don't know about cows in Missouri, but around here they only have one head each."

Embarrassed by her lack of farm savvy, Mindy blushed and wanted to escape. "I should probably be getting home," she said.

Bud seemed to panic and asked, "Want to drive?"

Surprised and excited by the prospect, Mindy nodded then admitted, "I've never driven a car before." Bud assured her that there was nothing she could hit but the barn. Mindy looked around and laughed. "I guess you're right about that."

As they walked toward the car, Mindy felt something move under her left foot. She glanced down to see a wriggling, four-foot black snake. She screamed, jumped backward, and danced with fear. "I don't like snakes either!" Apparently uninjured, the snake quickly disappeared into the tall grass along the fence.

Bud laughed for the third time, then stepped toward Mindy to deliver a hen-peck of a kiss. Mindy froze with wide-eyed surprise, then abruptly backed away.

Uncertain about what had just happened, thoughts swirled in her head. "Mice! A snake! A kiss almost all at once! Oh my!" Her thoughts raced more, "Does he think I like him just because I came to his farm? Kat will hate me if she finds out! No, she'll be heartbroken. I've got to get home!" She crossed her arms, hurried to the car, and almost dove into the passenger seat.

In hot pursuit, Bud squeaked, "Don't you want to drive?" With thoughts still racing and filled with concern for Kat, Mindy shook her head and stared straight ahead.

During the return, Bud tried unsuccessfully to engage Mindy in conversation. When the car pulled up at the trailer, she got out quickly. Bud hollered out the window, "Thanks for going to the farm. See ya at school."

Mindy waved over her shoulder without turning around and went inside, already planning to keep her trip to Bud's farm a secret from anyone at school.

Sitting on the front steps of the trailer, Mindy read a book while her mother prepared dinner and her brothers wrestled inside until the sound of shattering glass brought her to her feet. Inside, she found her brothers pointing fingers at each other over a broken lamp on the floor. Mindy's mother screamed and scurried the boys out of the trailer with an angry command. Mindy quietly grabbed the dustpan and began the clean-up while her mother fumed. "Don't you ever think about having four children! They will drive you crazy."

Mindy remained mum but thought, "Oh, don't you worry. I may never have kids at all. I don't want to get trapped like you. You're always stuck cooking and cleaning up their mess. I want to go to college. I want to have a better life than this." She looked around and realized the small confine of the trailer was taking its toll on all of them.

On her fifteenth birthday, Mindy's parents took the family to the Pioneer Kitchen to celebrate, but Mindy believed it was just an excuse to get out of the trailer for dinner. On the way home, they stopped at Clifton's for ice cream, and her mother presented

Mindy's birthday gifts: some money for clothes and the 1967-1970 Beatles greatest hits double album.

Shortly after returning from church the next day, Mindy's mother sat down and clutched her chest. When the sharp pain didn't pass quickly, her father became concerned and called Dr. Todd, who said he'd be right over. Moving cautiously to the couch while still holding her chest, Mindy's mother asked Mindy to sit with her. "I'm not sure what's happening, but if I die, I want you to take care of Dad and the boys for me."

Filled with fear that something might really be wrong, Mindy wrapped her arms around her mother's waist and held tight. Her mother kept talking, but Mindy's thoughts drifted. She recalled a homework project in her freshman religion class at Duchesne. Students had to fill out parallel surveys with their parents to promote family discussion and assess how much parents actually knew about their kid's school and social lives. One question for parents was, "Who is your son's or daughter's best friend?"

Her mother wrote, "Me. I've always been my daughter's best friend." But it wasn't strictly true. Her mom *was* her best friend for a time after each move, but not after Mindy had time to make new friends. Mindy suspected her mom would feel bad if she saw her answer, which was "Marla and Lisa," so tried unsuccessfully to hide her response. Mindy recalled how bad she'd felt and thought, "Poor Mom was so hurt when she saw my answer. But here we are in a new town, and she *is* my best friend again right now." Mindy squeezed her mother all the tighter.

Dr. Todd arrived a short time later, and Mindy's father shuffled the kids off to their bedrooms, where the wait in purgatory seemed endless. When her father finally knocked on their doors and told them to come out, Dr. Todd had worked his healing magic. Mindy's mother sat before them on the couch, looking happy and healthy.

Before falling asleep that night, the weight of her mother's words made it hard for Mindy to breathe. "I can't imagine what it would be like without my mother. Returning from school to do laundry, cook, wash dishes, clean, and help my brothers with their homework before doing my own." The image of being a fifteen-year-old head of household made her tremble. She went to bed with a deeper appreciation of her mother's role and very glad to have her around. "I hope we'll always be friends," she whispered, then drifted off to sleep.

Monday morning, Mindy walked into the main foyer at school to find a small cluster of female classmates surrounding tall and lean Loretta Weston. Hearing an overlapping chorus of congratulations and praise, Mindy peered through the crowd until she made eye contact with Loretta, who stepped forward to sing out, "I've been saaaved!"

With the image of a blazing house fire in her mind, Mindy said, "Um, that's good. What were you saved from?"

"Don't you know about salvation? Haven't you been saved?" Loretta questioned. "I was saved yesterday. I'm going to heaven and can't never go to . . ." She cupped her hands around her mouth to spell silently, "H-E-L-L."

"Well, I've been baptized. Isn't that the same as being saved?" Mindy replied.

A few of the girls shook their heads and stepped back from the young Catholic in their midst as if she had leprosy. A voice in the crowd announced, "No, it's not the same. You gotta be saved if ya want to get to heaven."

Embarrassed by her limited knowledge of local religious doctrine, Mindy tried to cover herself, "Oh, yeah. Well, I'm so happy for . . ." Interrupted by the morning warning bell, Mindy felt saved in her own way as the crowd quickly dispersed.

Sophomore Gina Autry must have read Mindy's uncertainty and gave a brief clarification as they walked to class. "Being saved means something different depending on what kind of Baptist you are. For some, it's like being baptized as a baby, but for most Missionary Baptists 'round here, it happens when yer older. It usually happens at church when they feel the hand of God reach down and touch 'em, and they know inside they've been saved. Sometimes it's an adult — usually a man who got caught cheatin' or drinkin' or lost his job. They git saved a lot. Most go up to tell the preacher, and he announces it to the whole congregation. Some preachers take ya to a creek ta baptize ya and wash yer soul of everything bad."

Mindy's eyes grew wide, and Gina continued, "Once ya been saved, yer suppos-ta be good. They know ya still won't be good all the time, but bein' saved makes it okay. For most, it means you've been saved forever, and ya don't ever have ta worry 'bout going ta hell even if ya do somethin' bad — especially if yer a Missionary Baptist."

The bell rang and left no opportunity for further dialogue. The combination of a southern accent, limited non-Catholic religious understanding, and a hefty dose of doubt left Mindy with much uncertainty on the subject of being "saved." But the concept bubbled in her thoughts and prompted her to seek clarification over the months ahead. Each attempt left her with a vision of an enormous loophole in the religious doctrine that she was learning dominated the social and political landscape of her new town. It sounded to Mindy as though being saved got one off the hook for sinning no matter how terrible you are, and that just didn't seem right.

Only vaguely aware of the slow avalanche of thoughts this unjust concept created over the next few years, Mindy questioned the meaning of her own baptism, the difference between Catholicism and other Christian religions, and the concept of sin in general. "I understand sin and the Ten Commandments, but outside of that, what is really a sin? Many around here believe dancing is a sin, but I love to dance! Who makes up these rules?" she wondered. She sensed these sorts of questions were only beginning.

———————— · ————————

Bud and Rick battled to monopolize Mindy's free time at school. This was no secret to Kat, who voiced her assumption that Mindy would eventually choose between them by repeating her advice. "Everybody just loves Ricky. He's so cute and smart. He really *is* the one you should go for."

Mindy wanted to ask, "If you think Rick is so great, why don't you go for him?" But she quietly explained instead, "Kat, they are both nice boys, but I'm not interested in either of them. You can have them both."

Relieved beyond measure, Kat asked, "Then would you talk to Bud for me? Tell him I like him and how nice I am?"

It took a few days, but Mindy did just as Kat requested and spoke first to Bud and later to Ricky on Kat's behalf. Both just smiled and walked away. To Mindy's relief, neither boy ever paid her another courting visit.

The following weekend brought welcomed respite from all the boy-girl talk at school, and Mindy enjoyed getting lost in the hype and pageantry of the Kentucky Derby. Home alone, she sat in front of the small black-and-white television to watch Secretariat race to victory with a yelp of joy.

After the race, the pageantry quickly evaporated. Alone in the quiet trailer, boredom settled in. Mindy stepped outside and took a seat on the front steps. Scanning the dreary surroundings triggered an audible sigh as thoughts of escaping the trailer and settling into their new house grew large.

The one respite from the dreariness of the trailer park was practicing hundreds of cartwheels, backbends, splits, and cheers to prepare for cheerleader tryouts. When the big day finally arrived, Mindy buttoned up a white Duchesne uniform blouse and slipped on her new culottes skirt. She smiled at her reflection in the mirror with an appreciation for the cute, flexible look of the outfit and tingled slightly, surprised by how it accented her young curves. She had difficulty concentrating during morning classes as the cheers she'd been practicing played over and over in her mind. Her excitement spiked when the bell rang, and the student body and teaching staff amassed in the gymnasium for the midday assembly.

All the cheer contestants reported to the cafeteria. En route, Mindy recalled the six years of dance and ballet she had taken in St. Charles. Although she had performed in dance recitals before packed auditoriums many times, she still had anxious thoughts. "This is different. I've never had to do a solo performance in front of my entire school before."

As Mindy arrived, she found the other girls tightly huddled and overheard the tail end of their conversation, ". . . when they heard Mindy was trying out for a basketball position, they dropped out and decided they'd just watch from the stands." Mindy looked at Kat and read angst in her eyes.

Mrs. Wilson interrupted the conclave and pulled the girls together to review the selection process. "Each of you will do one individual cheer, then one group cheer. The student body will cast their vote with applause. The Student Council will take those votes into consideration and then submit their recommendations to the administration, who will make the final selections. Teams will be announced overhead at the end of the day."

Mindy surveyed the other contestants, all of whom seemed confident. But Mindy was anxious and wished she felt as confident as they appeared. Her heart raced.

After what seemed an eternity, a brief announcement came over the loudspeaker and tryouts began. As the cheer contestants for football prepared to take the floor, Mindy felt a wave of relief and thought, "Finally, it's showtime!"

The first contestant strode confidently out the cafeteria door when her name was announced. Mindy listened carefully to the muffled sound floating from the gym, "Give me a **T** — give me an **I** — give me a **G** . . . What's it spell? **TIGERS!**" and visualize the very mechanical moves that went with the cheer in her head. Seconds after completing the cheer, the first contestant returned to the cafeteria, smiling as light applause echoed behind her. To Mindy's surprise, each subsequent contestant performed almost identical cheers, probably with similar mechanized moves, and she felt panic, "Did I misunderstand the instructions for the individual cheer?"

The grueling wait time continued as the basketball contestants prepared for their turn on the floor. Seniors, then juniors, and then finally it was time for the incoming sophomore contestants to take center stage. When Mrs. Wilson called Mindy's name, she felt a wave of exhilaration. She slipped off her glasses and entered the gym, bouncing with enthusiasm. Standing as tall as her 5'4" frame would hold her, Mindy faced the crowd with fists on her hips and a bright smile awaiting her introduction.

"Next up is Minnn-day Murrr-a-phay — for a sophomore position," boomed from the loudspeaker.

With a mental countdown, "3, 2, 1," Mindy nodded to the crowd and began:

> **Boogie down!**
> **Our team don't — MESS around.**
> **We got that SPIRIT now,**
> **We're going to SHOW YOU**
> **HOW — TO —**
> **Boogie down, boogie down, boogie down —**
> **(Followed by a cartwheel then the splits with arms raised in a V above her head)**
> **RIGHT NOW!**
> **(Points to the crowd and tips her head to the side)**

With inner-city jive and rubber band moves, Mindy belted out a cheer never before heard in this small middle-Tennessee town. Stunned silence gripped the gym. Most onlookers sat with dropped jaws and stares of disbelief until spontaneous combustion brought the crowd to life with hoops, hollers, whistles, and a rousing ovation.

Relieved beyond measure, Mindy jumped to her feet and joyfully bounced out of the gym to return across the hall to the cafeteria. Suddenly feeling more confident, Mindy relaxed as the freshman contestants completed their cheers. When Mindy retook the gym floor for the group cheer, groups of dancing boys stood to greet her, chanting, "Boogie down! More boogie down!" She smiled, synced on senior-to-be Patty Greggs, performed a flawless team cheer, and returned to the cafeteria, overflowing with confidence.

When Bud Gentry's voice crackled from the speaker to begin the end of the school day announcements, Mindy sat tall at her desk while Kat and Anne were already sharing smiles of success. As the only two sophomore-to-be contestants for the football positions, they won their spots by default, but that didn't dull their joy as their names sailed from the speaker.

Bud's static studded voice continued, "Now for the basketball cheerleaders. Let's just start with the new girl in town, Mindy Murrr-phay!" Overwhelmed by congratulatory praise, Mindy's cheeks flushed with pride.

Falling asleep in the trailer was easier that night. Mindy was happy that her schoolmates at MCHS were inviting her into their world with open arms, and thoughts of Duchesne were fading into her past.

The cramped quarters of the trailer continued to wear on the Murphy family's collective patience. For Mindy, the low point of living in the Sin City trailer park came when she couldn't escape the taunting from her brothers on Mother's Day after the embarrassing defeat of Margaret Court by Bobby Riggs in straight sets on national television.

But no one was happier later that week than Mindy when she climbed onto a different bus for the ride to her new home on Ellington. Her eyes lit up with joyful surprise when Anne slid into the seat next to her and pointed out the homes of several classmates along the way. Mindy was more surprised when Anne got off at the same bus stop, pointed down the street, and said, "I live right down there."

The movers had just finished unloading as Mindy walked up the new driveway and thought, "I'll be closer to many of my friends, I can invite people over to visit, and, thank goodness, I'll have a bigger bedroom where I can have a little privacy." She walked through every room in the house before stopping at the doorway of her new bedroom. She took in the spaciousness and smiled at the vision of two large closets, but wasn't sure of what to think of the bright-red shag carpet.

That night, she pulled her diary from the top desk drawer. It was like finding a long-lost friend, and she hugged it tightly to her chest. Gently laying it on her desk, she studied the image of the worn saddle shoes pictured on the cover, then stroked her fingertips across the etched letters of "My Diary" as she had so many times before.

Dear Diary,
I'm so happy to have you back. I'll bet it was boring for you in storage. I have so much to tell you . . .

She wrote one of her lengthiest diary entries ever with notes about the trailer park, various girls at school, Bud, being "saved," and cheer tryouts. She also included a somewhat detailed report on a particular boy who had caught her eye at school, but to whom she had not spoken a word, senior-to-be Randy Davidson.

With cheer competition behind them, Anne seemed less guarded. She sought Mindy out at school and called on the phone often just to talk. With the beautiful spring weather, they regularly shared the three-quarter-mile walk home. The trek provided private conversation time hard to find at school. As the days passed, Mindy believed they were becoming the closest of friends.

Being a lifelong resident of Lafayette, Anne provided a detailed teen insider's education on the town. She expressed an objective understanding of the county, its people, and its culture. Her perspective and insight seemed well beyond her age and impressed Mindy greatly.

But Anne detached herself from the small town-ness around her and often emphasized that she didn't count herself as "one of them." Mindy took to heart Anne's stern words of warning: "Be careful what you say and who you say it to. There are no secrets in this town. Your words will be twisted against you more often than you can imagine." Mindy was more surprised, however, to learn that despite Anne's lifelong presence in Lafayette, she felt isolated from her peers. By her own admission, Anne had no one she considered a bosom friend and told Mindy, "You are as much of a best friend as I've ever had." But Mindy sensed that Anne's distance from her peers was self-induced and wondered, "Who were her friends before me? Who did she hang around with?" She didn't know the answers, and the question gradually faded from her forethought.

The girls had walked home together several times before Anne revealed that she had a steady boyfriend. Matt Cummings lived fifteen miles away in Hartsville, attended Trousdale County High

School, and most assumed he came from a wealthy family because his father was part owner of a car dealership. Matt wasn't old enough to drive, so they depended on their parents to transport them between towns for weekend visits. The more Anne talked, the more she fixed Mindy's impression that it was an arranged relationship, with the parents acting as matchmakers. Still, Anne seemed genuinely happy, so Mindy didn't push for further explanation.

Cheer practice started immediately after tryouts. The group bonded quickly, and Mindy became especially good friends with Junior Gina Autry and Senior Patty Greggs. Both girls lived several miles out of town on family farms and had practical, straight-shooter personalities. As a bonus from Mindy's perspective, both could drive and had relatively free use of their family cars.

During the last week of school, Mindy cornered Patty for a private conversation and revealed a curiosity she'd been keeping to herself since her first week at MCHS. "How well do you know Randy Davidson?" she bashfully inquired.

Patty grinned. "Randy and I go way back. We've gone to school together since kindergarten and are good friends. Why do you ask?"

Mindy blushed and admitted, "He caught my eye right after we moved in, and I've just been curious. I haven't said a word to him, but I've caught him looking at me several times." She saw a flash of him in her mind — cute baby face, friendly smile, brown wavy hair, and from what she'd observed, very shy.

"Randy is really nice. Everybody likes him. His family owns a pretty big farm, and all the girls think he would be a good catch. But I wouldn't get your hopes up too high. He's been dating Rita Green," Patty explained.

Mindy's eyes opened wide. "Oh, okay. Thanks. I was just curious."

Mindy walked away with mixed emotions. She had heard plenty of girl talk about Rita, who many considered the queen diva of the incoming junior class. Mindy silently concluded, "I should probably forget about Randy. But I can tell there's something in his eye when he looks at me."

The academic year ended before Memorial Day. Final exams came and went uneventfully and didn't require much preparation. But Mindy was happy and content with how her move to Lafayette had unfolded. She had already settled into her new school community and felt more confident about herself. She had even developed a soft Southern accent of her own and used local slang with increasing frequency.

New friends, cheerleader status, popularity, and now relative mobility had all come Mindy's way in just a few weeks. Indeed, it hadn't taken long. Summer arrived, the doors to fun flew open, and Mindy was ready to play.

Chapter Three
Dandelion Wine
May 19–August 20, 1973

For Mindy, three long months of summer was the same as forever, with seemingly boundless time to lounge around or explore the world at one's own fancy. Other than setting the table for dinner, washing the dishes, and managing her own bedroom, Mindy had few fixed household responsibilities. Cheer practice twice a week on Tuesday and Thursday afternoons, cheerleader camp at Tennessee Tech, and a weeklong trip to Mississauga, Ontario, were the only scheduled events scattered over the summer calendar. As a respite from the constant noise and silliness of her younger brothers, Mindy spent much of her leisure time at Anne's. With no other siblings at home, the Belle house was always quiet. On a typical summer morning, Mindy put on a modest blue-and-yellow bikini covered by cut-off shorts and an old T-shirt. Quickly filling a bag with a clean towel and a bottle of Coppertone, she called Anne long enough to say, "I'm on my way," then walked or rode her bike directly to the Belle's. She never had to wait long after knocking on the door before Mrs. Belle greeted her with a cheerful smile. Anne would promptly bounce down the steps from her bedroom, and the two girls proceeded to the backyard.

Mrs. Belle enjoyed gardening and had planted both common and uncommon flowers that surrounded the small brick patio just outside the back door where a rich mixture of floral aromas filled the air. The girls carefully applied their tanning oil, adjusted the lounge chairs for the best sun exposure, turned on the hose, and strategically placed the brass spray nozzle between the loungers. With preparations complete, they assumed the horizontal position of young sun goddesses to soak up the warming ultraviolet radiation from the sky. With eyes closed facing the heavens, the dull red glow of sunlight burned through their eyelids. Initial minutes were usually quiet but gradually gave way to girl talk punctuated by intervals of reflective, peaceful silence.

The girl talk cycled through the usual topics: schoolmates, clothing styles, local gossip, music, and college. When it became too hot, one of them reached down for the hose, raised the nozzle toward the sky, and shot a fine mist into the air. They laughed when the cold micro-drops fell back onto their hot skin to trigger a refreshing chill that covered them with goosebumps. When the sun was just right, it treated them to a translucent rainbow. They reached out to the vaporous colors time and time again, hoping to be the first to touch the pot of gold at the end of a rainbow.

Anne frequently inquired about Mindy's former "life in the city" as if it had unfolded in another country. She expressed particular interest in boys, shopping, and "grown-up things to do." She ravenously consumed every descriptive word but never seemed quite satisfied. Sometimes feeling inadequate, Mindy wondered if Anne was looking for something that wasn't there. "Maybe she wants to hear something wilder? But we're just kids. How wild could it be?"

In turn, Mindy made a point of asking about Anne's past and her dreams of the future, but Anne routinely shifted the conversation to her boyfriend and what they had done the previous weekend. To avoid prying or getting too personal about Anne's romance, Mindy sat quietly as the conversation gave itself over to a monologue of Anne's everlasting love for Matt.

After the girls had been out long enough to cook their skin both front and back, Mrs. Belle would arrive with fresh-squeezed lemonade or over-sweetened iced tea, then take a seat to chat. Soon tiring of her mother's intrusion, Anne would deliver a cold piercing stare, prompting her mother to excuse herself with nervous politeness and disappear back into the house. Mindy always thought, "Wow. I don't think I'd get away with that with my mom," but learned to disregard it. The girls then shifted the lounge chairs and began another set of rotisserie turns in the baking sun before retiring to Anne's bedroom to play records and talk some more.

Although disbanded, the Beatles still reigned as the heart and soul of popular music and had released their two greatest-hits albums just a few months previously. One of these four LPs almost always found the turntable first. With no place to buy records in town, Macon County music lovers had to travel to the Kmart in Gallatin or RiverGate Mall in Nashville. Mindy occasionally stuffed some babysitting money into her pocket and tagged along with her mother to Kmart, where she slowly grew her own collection of albums including Jim Croce, Bread, and Elton John. Each new purchase relegated older records, such as those by Donny Osmond, Sonny and Cher, and Bobby Sherman to a dusty corner of her closet.

Mindy enjoyed listening to just about any kind of music, but quickly learned that country music dominated the local AM radio stations. Because most cars had only AM radios, FM radio was often only available at home but was frequently static filled. As a result, Mindy's exposure to popular music was quite limited.

When the opportunity to buy records arose, she typically purchased ones she was familiar with or had heard at Anne's house. Her first Tennessee album purchase was Elton John's *Madman Across the Water*.

Anne's copy of *'Madman'* got lots of turntable time. "Tiny Dancer" always captured Mindy's ear, and she would occasionally lift the needle at the last note to replay the song three or four times in a row.

As Mindy became lost in the melody, Anne often stood in front of her mirror to look herself in the eye and sing into a hairbrush. Mindy watched Anne's reflection in the mirror as she lip-synched every word and seemed to drift further away with each passing line. By the end of the song, Anne often appeared lost and, with the last note, took a seat on the floor against her bed to stare toward the ceiling. No matter how happy she'd been before the song, Anne was always sad and distant afterward, and Mindy wondered what had triggered the transformation. Several times, Anne seemed ready to express her thoughts but never cut loose, even after Mindy's prodding.

During lighter times, the conversation rolled nonstop as the girls flipped through Anne's teen magazines to critique the fashions and hairstyles. They often reviewed the small-type block ads in the back pages, several of which were for a "once in a lifetime opportunity" to purchase herbal bust enhancers. They often wondered whether the "money back guaranteed" product really worked. The $4.99 price of the gel pill bottles seemed reasonable, but the $9.99 for shipping and handling always dissuaded them from placing an order.

Sometimes they walked to Jones's Drive-in for soft-serve ice cream or Tooter's Cee Bee Foodtown, referred to by locals simply as CB's, for extra-large ice cream sandwiches. They rushed outside and sat on the store steps, where they tried to eat the cold treats before they melted. Anne liked to bare her teeth to show chocolate cookie mush packed in her braces, making Mindy turn away and cry out, "Oh, that's gross!" Girlish laughter would follow.

On one Friday afternoon in early June, Anne set a lighted mirror on her bedroom floor and took a prone position before it. She turned her head several times to make a careful study of her brow, then went to work with fine-tipped tweezers, plucking stray eyebrow hairs.

Mindy grimaced with phantom pain after each attack. Unable to tolerate the discomfort any longer, she had to ask, "Just what the heck are you doing?"

Anne scoffed with disbelief. "Why such a face? Don't you pluck your eyebrows?"

Mindy shook her head and winced again as another small hair fell victim to the crush and tear of the tweezers.

When the assault was over, Anne sat up and slid a tray of small bottles, compacts, and brushes in front of the mirror. Mindy watched in amazement as Anne deftly applied foundation, blush, eyeliner, and mascara with smoothness, precision, and practiced efficiency. Anne would occasionally look up at Mindy for silent approval.

Anne's transformation stunned Mindy, "Wow! I can't believe how different, how much *older*, you look." She thought for a second and recalled, "I've only used makeup twice. The first time I was about six and played dress-up in my mom's room. I put on one of her old dresses and high heels and then used her makeup. When she walked into the room, she just stared at me speechless. Then, all of a sudden, she started laughing and couldn't stop. But I don't remember feeling bad about it, though."

Looking to the ceiling to recall another incident, Mindy continued. "The second time was the beginning of ninth grade. Eye makeup was common at school, so I thought I'd try it and put on a little before dinner. My dad just made fun of me. First, he told me it looked like I'd been in a fight. Then he told me boys don't like girls who wear makeup, 'They like the natural look.' I ran upstairs feeling so embarrassed that I've never tried it since," she concluded.

As Anne finished her transformation with an eyelash curler and lipstick, Mindy had an unexpected spark of insight. "She's getting ready for a date!" and symbolically smacked herself in the forehead for her naïve awareness. She shook her head to clear it. "If this is what most girls go through for a date, I'm not sure dating is for me." Feeling awkward, Mindy stood to announce, "I guess I'll head home. I hope you have a nice time this weekend."

Anne jumped to her feet. "Wait! I have something for you." She pulled a small paperback from her bookshelf and handed it to Mindy. "Here, you might like to read this. I want you to have it. It's about a teenage girl and her problem with drugs. She died in the end, but nobody really knows what happened to her."

Mindy scanned the cover, *Go Ask Alice* by Anonymous. Always looking for new things to read, Mindy offered thanks and said, "I'll probably start reading it tonight."

While clearing the dinner table that evening, Mindy remembered her phantom pain that afternoon. She stopped to ask, "Mom, do you think I need to pluck my eyebrows?"

36

Her mother stifled a laugh and quickly composed herself, then studied her only daughter's eyebrows carefully. "No, I don't think you need to. Your eyebrows look perfect to me." Mindy smiled.

After kitchen chores, Mindy curled up on a chair in the family room with the gift paperback in hand and read. The horrific tale of a 15-year-old girl's drug addiction captured her entirely, and she finished it before going to bed. Over the subsequent week, she and Anne discussed the story at length. They agreed entirely on the conclusion: "Drugs are bad for everyone."

Biweekly cheer practices continued. The basketball squad had only six girls: Seniors Patty Greggs and Cathy Gates, juniors Gina Autry and Donna Powers, Mindy as the lone sophomore, and Beverly Dillon as the lone freshman. Each Tuesday and Thursday afternoon, the girls met at school to practice by themselves. They had no coach, no monitor, no supervision, and no outside push for excellence.

After tryouts, the first order of business had been to elect squad captains. As a general rule, the seniors became captains by default. But not this year. The relative originality of Mindy's "Boogie Down" cheer caught everyone's attention and prompted a pre-vote discussion of her dance and ballet experience. It was apparent that her background provided a perspective the other girls didn't have. So, it wasn't too surprising when the team voted for Mindy as co-captain along with Patty — but it didn't prevent a perturbed post-vote accusation by Cathy that Mindy had voted for herself.

Mindy considered the co-captaincy an honor and took the position seriously. She worked with Patty to plan practices to develop both individual and team skills. She paid attention to detail and interjected several new ideas. The other girls appreciated their captain's efforts, and the team bonded into a tight-knit unit.

Patty and Gina alternated providing Mindy rides to and from school with stops at Clifton's or Jones's after practice being routine. Their friendships grew, and Mindy enjoyed having upperclassmen as mentors.

With Anne unavailable on the weekends, Gina and Mindy became a standard duo, and Gina introduced Mindy to "cruising." The *American Graffiti* concept was simple: drive from one potential meeting spot to another with stops of varying duration depending on who else, mostly which boys, they might cross paths with at each location. Mindy stayed quietly on the lookout for Randy Davidson.

The cruising route from Ellington typically started with a short drive to The Village Market on Scottsville Road, continued through the town square to Clifton's Kwik Dip on Red Boiling Springs Road, then coursed back through the square to get to Jones's on Church Street before reversing the route back to The Village Market. The circuit covered approximately 2.5 miles, and a typical night of cruising included 10 to 15 laps covering 25 to 38 miles without ever leaving town. Traffic volume ebbed and flowed through the evening, but up to 20 other teen-toting cars might be out cruising at any given time. Except for a rotating handful of young adult males, cruisers were typically 16–19 years old. Boys usually came two to a car, although solo riders were not uncommon. Girls rarely cruised alone and usually rode in twos or fours. Narrow and repetitive as it was, cruising was a staple of teen entertainment throughout Mindy's time in Lafayette.

For Mindy, the best nights of cruising included crossing paths with Randy more than once. Although conversation remained elusive, Mindy caught Randy staring in her direction on several occasions. Once discovered, he would temporarily freeze as his cheeks filled with blood then quickly turn away. Mindy wasn't sure how to interpret this response, but Patty and Gina assured her it was a good sign.

About two weeks into the summer, Mindy and Gina sat on the hood of Gina's blue Mercury Marquis eating soft-serve cones at Jones's. The sun settled below the horizon, and the air cooled as the conversation drifted from one local topic to another until Gina lamented, "I wish you had known my brother. You would have liked him."

Gina's mention of her brother caught Mindy by surprise. Gina had a brother who had died a few months prior to Mindy's arrival in Lafayette, but this was the first time she'd brought him up in conversation. As Mindy weighed her response, Gina asked, "Would you like to see him?"

Filled with uncertainty, Mindy replied, "Ahhhh — okay."

"Well, get in," said Gina.

"Where are we going?" Mindy asked.

"To the cemetery. Where do ya think?" Gina replied flatly.

Hiding her confusion, Mindy gazed out the passenger window as they drove to the perimeter of town. The surrounding darkness became more intense as they continued further away from artificial light. Mindy shivered. She'd never seen a dead body before and wondered if she'd really see Gina's deceased brother. Visions of a quiet mausoleum housing a young corpse in a glass casket like Snow White danced in Mindy's mind. "How will he look? Will he be well preserved or mummified?"

A soft-blue streetlight marked the entrance of the cemetery. Turning onto the main drive, Mindy felt chilled as her own ghostly reflection in the passenger window floated by. She wanted to say, "Let's come back some other time," but didn't.

The car wove through dark turns to the back of the cemetery and then suddenly pulled off the road. With high beams illuminating a stone marker, Gina stared out the window then whispered, "Here he lies."

Mindy shivered again as she got out of the car and followed Gina toward the grave, imagining a glass cover over an in-ground tomb. As they approached, Mindy felt relieved but also more confused to see the gravesite covered over with grass. Gina slowly reached forward to an oval metal plate in the center of the marker and gently lifted the lid to reveal a photograph of her dear departed brother. "Cute, wasn't he?" Mindy nodded in agreement and let out a soft sigh of relief.

A week later, Mindy and Gina were joined by Loretta, who was well versed in all the small-town gossip and thrilled to be out boy hunting on the circuit. During a random conversation at Clifton's, Gina made a comment about a black-and-white pig she'd almost hit while driving. Mindy said, "Wait, pigs aren't black and white. They're pink!" as her city-girl ignorance glowed brightly.

Gina and Loretta shared puzzled expressions, then burst out in laughter. Gina retorted, "Pigs come in all sorts of colors, silly."

Convinced that they were trying to take advantage of her naiveté, Mindy searched her memory for images of pigs of any color other than pink.

"Don't believe us? Well, get in," said Gina. They drove to the nearby farm of John Cole, where Gina pulled up to a wood fence next to the barn. The high beam of the headlights revealed scurrying well-fed pigs of varying color patterns.

They returned to town and their appointed rounds with cold drinks, courtesy of Mindy.

Mindy loved to read and consumed books like snacks during the summer. So, it thrilled her to learn that her mother had joined a book club and would receive a set of new books each month. On a pleasant June morning, Mindy awakened early and finished breakfast before anyone else was up. Spotting the book that her mother had apparently just finished and left lying on the counter, Mindy scanned the cover as she returned to her room: *Once Is Not Enough* by Jacqueline Susann.

After changing into her bikini, Mindy returned to the kitchen where her mother noted the book in her hand and promptly stopped her. "Wait. That's probably not a book you should be reading. Do me a favor and find something else."

Mindy placed the book into her mother's patiently waiting hand and thought, "If it's that bad, why did you read it?"

With heightened curiosity, Mindy scanned the bookshelf for other recent book club arrivals. Her finger paused on *The Exorcist*. Lifting it from the shelf, she reviewed the back cover and then read a page from the middle of the book. She was only vaguely familiar with the storyline, but remembered hearing that it was terrifying. Learning that the main character was a young girl made it a natural choice.

She made the subsequent trip to the patio with her new book choice carefully concealed under a towel. As Mindy stepped out the back door, her mother inquired, "Did you find something better?"

"I think so," Mindy hollered back, then quickly closed the door. Immediately captured by the young girl's struggle with the Devil within and the torment to those around her, Mindy couldn't put the book down. She finished it the next evening and wasn't surprised she had trouble sleeping that night.

Later that summer, Mindy learned her mother was going to see *The Exorcist* with several other Lafayette mothers at a Nashville movie theater. The thought made her tremble, and she considered warning her mother not to go, but didn't. Her mother was still shaking when she returned and firmly pronounced, "I don't ever want you to see that movie!" Mindy didn't think that would be a problem.

——————— ———————

The first seven weeks of summer passed by with each week very much like the one before. Sun tanning, listening to records, taking walks, cheer practice, occasional picnic trips to a lake, B movie re-runs at the drive-in and cruising filled the days. But the first of two highly anticipated events of the summer, a trip to Canada, broke the routine.

In the summer of 1969, Mindy's father was transferred to Mississauga, Ontario, and the Murphy's lived there for 18 months. Vicki Lockton had been Mindy's best friend, and the two girls stayed in touch via letters and occasional long-distance phone calls. Both were excited for Mindy's week-long visit north of the border to visit her old junior high stomping grounds.

While Mindy was traveling to Canada, Anne was joining Matt's family on a trip to Florida. For Mindy, the concept of going on vacation with a boy was unthinkable. When questioned about it, Anne spoke with excitement and expounded about how serious they had become. The details made Mindy's head swim and left her feeling uncomfortable. Later, she would think, "We haven't even started our sophomore year yet. How *serious* can they possibly be?"

Just before Anne's departure, Mindy and Anne were enjoying a typical tanning day on the patio at Anne's when they were interrupted by the arrival of a senior MCHS male, recognizable but otherwise unfamiliar to Mindy. Standing at the corner of the house and out of view from the patio door, the visitor whispered, "Is Jimmy around?"

Anne glanced toward the patio door, jumped up off the lounger, and disappeared with the visitor around the corner of the house. Mindy could hear only unintelligible murmuring before Anne returned and went quietly inside. Mindy assumed she must have left the house through the front door when a moment later, she heard Anne's muffled voice again around the corner outside. Anne returned to the patio and without explanation resumed her sunbathing position. Mindy inquired about the visitor, but Anne just shrugged. When Mindy pushed harder, Anne ignored the question and changed the subject. At the end of the day, Mindy said goodbye with a somewhat heavy heart. She didn't understand why, but the incident left her feeling uneasy for weeks.

Mindy's flight to Toronto left a few days later. She was thrilled to be reunited with Vicki, and they filled their days with bike rides, floating in the pool, window shopping at the mall, a day trip on the GO Train to the Canadian Exhibition, and, of course, lots of girl talk. The trip seemed to be over in a flash, and before leaving for the airport, they took a flurry of pictures with Mindy, Vicki, and her family. When the shutter clicked, the biggest smile of them all belonged to Vicki's older brother, who had developed a crush on Mindy during her stay. Vicky's dad had commented several times about the brother's excellent behavior and improved attitude during Mindy's visit and playfully begged her to stay longer. At the airport, Mindy waved goodbye and yelled to Vicki, "See you next summer in Tennessee!" On the plane, she was excited to see Anne and share vacation stories.

The second highly anticipated event of the summer was cheerleading camp. But with Anne's late return from Florida, Mindy was disappointed she wouldn't get to see her until they arrived at the camp.

As the mini-MCHS caravan pulled into Tennessee Tech University in Cookeville, everyone in Mindy's car grew silent with amazement as they looked out onto waves of incoming camp participants before them. An army of girls from Tennessee, Kentucky and northern Georgia were arriving almost simultaneously. Many other squads came in large vans wearing matching outfits with matching bags in school colors. The Macon County High group arrived in farm-dust covered sedans and appeared a bit rag-tag in comparison, but that didn't dampen the electricity in the air as the mass of teen girls pushed toward the registration desks.

The MCHS football squad arrived just a few minutes later, and Mindy's eyes lit up. She waved and hollered Anne's name but got no response. After registration, Mindy forced her way through the crowd to Anne's side. "Hi, Anne! I'm so happy to see you. I can't wait to hear all about your trip," Mindy exclaimed.

Anne barely acknowledged Mindy's presence and reacted with irritation. "I can't talk now. Maybe later," she snapped, then marched off with her squad mates.

Crestfallen by Anne's cold-shoulder treatment, Mindy returned to her own group and walked silently with them to their assigned dorm. Gina apparently noticed something was wrong and inquired. When Mindy described Anne's reaction, Gina just laughed, "Welcome to cheer camp, girl. The football girls don't want to have much to do with us lowly basketball girls, and they sure don't want us to show them up. We'll be competing with them all week."

"That's bizarre," Mindy said. "We're all on the same team."

The dormitory tour took only a few minutes, and the two MCHS teams were assigned rooms at opposite ends of the hall. The rooms were plain: two beds, two desks with chairs, two small closet-dresser units, and no air conditioning or fans. Mindy roomed with Gina, and it took them no time to unpack.

An hour later, all the girls convened in the gymnasium for orientation. Mindy tried to approach Anne again, but she huddled with her gang and acted annoyed by Mindy's presence. Taken aback, Mindy returned to her small pack of basketball cheer mates feeling hurt. As everyone moved to seats in the stands, Mindy shook it off. "No matter. It's going to be a fun week," she thought.

The loud chatterbox noise in the stands quickly silenced when the camp director stepped to the microphone. After opening comments, the director introduced the camp counselors, and it surprised Mindy to learn there were several male college cheerleaders among them. She was more surprised by the buzzing sound from the crowd of teen girls as the male cheerleaders stepped forward with the announcement of their names. Afterward, the director outlined the daily schedule and made it clear, "It will be a week of work, not a week of play."

Counselors would closely monitor the teams, identify the best cheers of the day, and provide them with an opportunity to perform in front of the entire camp during head-to-head competition each evening. The team winning the "Spirit Award" would carry the red, white, and blue "Spirit Stick" to proudly display the next day. The "Most Improved" team would be announced at the end of the week. Mindy hoped her basketball squad could win one of the big awards.

The hard work made for long days by the time the evening competition was over. By the third evening of camp, most girls were already weary and chatted quietly in small groups anywhere they could find a cool spot.

When Mindy noted Anne wasn't seated with her cheer mates, she went first to her room to retrieve a gift for Anne from Canada, then quietly made her way down the hall. Uncertain how Anne would receive her, she hesitated before knocking lightly on her door. At first, there was no response, but Mindy could hear a rustling noise and noted moving shadows beneath the door. When she knocked again, the rustling and shadows stopped. Mindy whispered Anne's name, and the door slowly opened. Anne greeted Mindy nervously and invited her in.

Mindy promptly extended her gift-bearing hand, and Anne returned a broad, braces-adorned smile. Anne's smile faded when she opened the box to find a T-shirt emblazoned with the Molson Beer logo. Anne's expression reminded Mindy that a beer T-shirt was probably not a great idea for one from Macon County and prompted a red-cheeked apology.

After sharing a hug, the girls chatted, and the distance between them seemed to disappear as they traded reports of their trips. Anne described her thrills of swimming in the ocean, walking on the beach, playing putt-putt golf, and the wonders of Disney World. She seemed genuinely happy and excited about her future with Matt. But Mindy remained uncomfortable with the concept of a girl her own age to traveling with a boyfriend's family and talking so seriously about their future. She wasn't envious, but found her thoughts drifting to Randy and wondering what he had been doing over the summer.

With only a few minutes before curfew, Mindy considered confronting Anne about her cold shoulder but decided against it. "She seems to be okay now. I'll just wait and see how things go," Mindy thought.

When dorm curfew arrived, Mindy scurried back down the hall and slid under the sheet into bed. Gina was fast asleep within minutes, but the hot, stagnant dorm room air felt suffocating. Despite her fatigue, Mindy took a long time to fall asleep as wistful thoughts of her own dream date filled her head.

The morning alarm sounded unusually loud, startling the girls out of their slumbers. It was a new day and, despite lingering fatigue, Mindy encouraged everyone to put on their "spirit faces" for the counselors to see. Unfortunately, most of the girls were in flat-affect slow motion, and Mindy realized that showing genuine spirit was going to be a challenge. She attempted to rally the forces and reminded her squad mates of the "Spirit Award," but they didn't seem interested. She persisted and gave the basketball analogy of being six points down with only a few minutes left on the clock. "We can't quit! We can't give up," she urged.

At 7:10 AM, the day was already hot and humid, and Mindy's words of encouragement didn't go far. By 11 AM, the team was out of gas and the "Spirit Award" in obvious peril. Hoping to rescue her squad, Mindy jumped higher, did more cartwheels, and cheered louder than she ever had. Then, just before the lunch break, she felt lightheaded and nauseated. The 98-degree air felt like a dragon's breath. The sky spun, and her vision went dark.

The cold air blowing across her felt refreshing as Mindy came to. "Well, there you are. Drink this," came from a blurry, dark face dressed in white. Still weak, Mindy sat up slowly as cold packs fell from her forehead, neck, and shoulders. She blinked without seeing much as a cold cup was placed in her hand. Sipping slowly, Mindy felt a wave of embarrassment from the nurse's soft scolding. "Eat more breakfast and drink more juice ta-morrow mornin'. Y'all cain't go runnin' in the sun with nuttin' but nuttin' in your belly."

As the cerebral cobwebs cleared, Mindy remembered spending more time trying to energize her mates than eating that morning. She finished her drink, asked for more, and before long was feeling considerably better. The ultra-Southern-sounding nurse said she could leave the infirmary after proving she could walk without feeling woozy.

Patty and Gina arrived a short time later, wearing smiles of care and relief. They helped walk Mindy around the infirmary, then escorted her to the cafeteria where they made sure she ate and drank her fill. Re-hydrated and full, Mindy recovered her chipper personality, but it didn't wash away her embarrassment. Camp administrators shortened the remaining afternoon sessions because of the heat, and all the girls returned to the dorm early. Whether in bathing suits or in the buff, the girls enjoyed long, refreshing showers for the next few hours.

During dinner that evening, Kat made an unprecedented move and strode over to the basketball cheerleaders' table. Squeezing in next to Mindy, Kat held Mindy's forearm tightly and looked her earnestly in the eye. "Are you okay?" she asked. Without waiting for a response, she continued, "What was it like?"

"I really don't remember much, but I feel better now. Thanks for asking," Mindy replied.

"No, no. What was *he* like?" Kat persisted but received only a confused shrug in reply. "You know, the counselor that carried you. The guy with big arms and muscles everywhere?"

Gina and Patty came to Mindy's rescue and quickly filled her in. One of the male counselors, a real hunk by their description, had apparently seen her go down and was on the scene immediately to carry her off the field to the infirmary. He had apparently been the talk of the camp, but had gone unnoticed by Mindy.

As Kat drifted back to her table, she spoke wistfully, "He must have been watching you. He was there almost before you hit the ground. I wish it had been me. You get everything." Her eyes dropped to the floor as she drifted away.

Mindy watched her go and just shook her head while the other girls rolled their eyes in disbelief.

In the same sweep of the eye, Mindy noticed Anne seated at the far end of the football table. While the other girls talked and laughed, Anne remained silent and appeared distant.

The last days of the camp remained hot and humid, but the girls made it through the various rotations uneventfully. The basketball squad had shown significant improvement and bonded further as a team, but were out of the competition for any awards. Too many other schools had entire teams with dance and gymnastics experience. They integrated eye-catching flips and tosses into their routines while the girls of Macon County considered the splits and building pyramids as accomplishments.

In the presence of others, Anne resumed her unfriendly attitude, which left Mindy feeling hurt and confused. She tried unsuccessfully to make sense of Anne's behavior. "We are friends. Why would she treat me this way?" she wondered and felt uneasy whenever Anne was nearby for the rest of camp.

For Mindy, the highlight of the week was the grand performance by the counselors on the last night of camp. Dance numbers and short skits were colorful, imaginative, and demonstrated artistic skills beyond cheering. A dance sequence to the tune of "Mr. Bojangles" particularly captivated Mindy, and the combination of physical and emotional fatigue left her vulnerable. Absorbed by the music and visual imagery on the stage, the sad, lonely character isolated under the bright spotlight and surrounded by darkness brought tears to her eyes. When her teammates noticed, they shared looks of confusion and tried to understand what had overtaken her. "Mindy, why are you crying?" they wanted to know.

Mindy shrugged. "I don't know," she said, and a few others joined her with tears.

Two days after returning home from camp, Mindy answered the front door with some surprise to find Anne before her, acting friendly and cheerful. Mindy invited her in, and they retreated to Mindy's room. Anne acted as if there had been no distance between them. As they talked, the turntable spun the likes of "Leroy Brown," "Yellow Brick Road," and lots of Beatles tunes. Mindy considered confronting Anne about her coldness at camp, but believed she would deny it. They gradually settled into girl talk, and without missing a further beat, the two friends returned to sunning, walking, and riding bikes during the week.

The next day, Mindy accompanied Anne and her mother to Lebanon, where Anne shed her braces at the orthodontist's office, and they celebrated over lunch. During lunch, Anne became wide-eyed, distracted, and antsy. Mindy assumed she was excited to show off her pearly whites, but became concerned when Anne's hyper behavior escalated and Mrs. Belle anxiously suggested that they begin the drive home before lunch was over.

After returning to Lafayette, Mrs. Belle quickly disappeared into the house while the girls walked in the yard. Anne's excitement grew and morphed into mild mania as she talked endlessly about "making out with Matt without braces." Mindy tried unsuccessfully to interrupt Anne's racing thoughts and speech. Her gut told her something wasn't right, but didn't understand what was happening. Suddenly afraid, Mindy brought the afternoon to an end and walked home.

The hot days rolled on. Mixed carloads of girls made a few midweek trips to the Barren River to sit in the cooling flow of water and darken their tans. Cheer practice resumed, but cruising afterward waned considerably; it was just too darned hot.

Football practice began in mid-August. Because many boys had early morning farm chores, practice didn't start until late afternoon. The cheer squads didn't mind and made frequent visits to the football field under the guise of monitoring the team's progress. At the end of practice, several cheerleaders would take up position near the football field exit, where they stood nonchalantly to catch catcalls as the boys marched toward the locker room. Mindy watched the playful teasing from a distance, but felt uneasy when too many of the participants overplayed their roles.

Not long before the start of school, the cheer team gathered in the shade of the concession stand to watch as the football players received new game jerseys. Mindy couldn't ignore the thrill in Randy's eyes as he held up a jersey with the number 63 before him. She watched him carefully re-fold his prize and drape it over his forearm. As he turned toward the parking lot, his eyes suddenly shifted to meet hers for a brief but mesmerizing moment. His cheeks lit up, but he smiled and was much slower in turning away. When Mindy felt her own cheeks grow hot, she grabbed Gina's arm and pulled her toward the car.

On the third Monday of August, Mindy awoke and lay in bed staring at the ceiling with thoughts adrift. The bright morning sun quickly warmed her room, and she kicked off her covers to stretch her limbs like a cat waking from a long nap. As her arms fell limply back to bed, her heart sank with the realization that summer was almost over. The next day was Book Day, and the week would introduce the start of the school year with the preseason football jamboree. With the reality of the school year upon her, Mindy hopped out of bed, ate a quick breakfast, put on her tanning suit, and walked to Anne's house.

Mrs. Belle answered the door with a strained greeting and, atypically anxious, motioned toward Anne's closed bedroom door at the top of the stairs. Mindy bounced up the stairs and knocked lightly. She heard some rustling before the door cracked open just a few inches. From a darkened room, Anne peaked out and scanned behind Mindy with one eye to make sure the coast was clear. With a soft grunt, Anne pulled Mindy into the bedroom and locked the door behind them. An album was already spinning on the turntable, and Anne retreated to her usual position on the floor.   Already uncomfortable, Mindy joined her with some trepidation as Anne stared straight ahead into nothingness.

Without warning, Anne cocked her head and glared at Mindy with wild eyes. Frightened, Mindy asked with a trembling voice, "Is everything okay?"

Before the vibrations of Mindy's question faded, Anne blurted out, "We're gonna run away and get married!" She spun around onto her belly, pulled a blue hard-sided suitcase out from under her bed, and jumped up to toss it onto the bed.

"What!?" cried Mindy.

Anne's eyes darted about. "Matt's parents want to split us up. So, we're gonna run away and get married."

Unable to speak, Mindy watched in confused amazement as Anne dropped a hairbrush from her dresser, a small paperback from her headboard bookshelf, and a long satin and lace nightgown from a drawer into the suitcase and clicked it shut.

It all seemed surreal. Mindy wondered whether her eyes were fooling her.   Startled by another wide-eyed stare from Anne, Mindy grimaced when Anne, pointing to the suitcase, said, "I can't keep it here. My mom will find it and know I'm leaving. Can I keep it at your house?"

Massively confused and uncertain what to say, Mindy nodded. Anne motioned for Mindy to stay put as she tiptoed down the stairs and placed the suitcase outside the front door. Stealthily returning, she grabbed Mindy and pulled her down the stairs. As they passed through the front door, Anne shouted over her shoulder, "We're going to Mindy's."   Anne snatched up the suitcase with one hand, grabbed Mindy's arm with the other and they quickly disappeared around the corner.

Out of sight of the Belle house, Mindy came to her senses and resisted to slow their pace. "Anne, what's going on?" she demanded. Attempting to make eye contact, Mindy pushed, "*Anne* — What happened?"

Frantic, Anne replied, "Matt's parents think we're spending too much time together and want him to see other girls. But we're in love and won't let his parents interfere."

Mindy was full of doubt and questions. "Where will you go? Where will you live? What about money and food?" An image of the suitcase contents flashed in Mindy's mind, and the ever-present pragmatist added, "And what about socks, underwear, and definitely more clothes?" She received only Anne's blank stare into the sky in response.

They reached Mindy's bedroom unseen. Anne slid the suitcase under Mindy's bed. "I know you're a good friend. I know you won't tell anyone," Anne said.

Still confused, Mindy pressed her with more questions, but Anne responded with anxious talk of the upcoming school year and the start of the football season. She spoke of the big crowds and the "rush" of cheering before packed stands.

Mindy couldn't stand it any longer. "Wait. Just wait. If you are going to run away and get married, then how do you expect to go to school and cheer?"

Anne grew angry and clenched her fists. "Stop asking so many questions!" she snarled.

Mindy struggled to comprehend the strangeness of Anne's words and actions, but the unfocused wildness in her eyes was unnerving. It was apparent something was deeply wrong, and Mindy wondered what was happening. She wanted to help but didn't know where to start.

Without preface, Anne fell onto Mindy's bed and extended her arms in a cruciform loss. Her eyes stared blankly at the ceiling. Mindy watched in horror as Anne sighed and went limp in defeat. Her heart jumped into her throat as tears pooled in Anne's eyes and she plunged into despair.

With a few cautious steps toward the bed, Mindy whispered, "What can I do to help?" But Anne only rambled incoherently about school and cheerleading and Matt. Mindy tried several times to redirect the conversation toward happy thoughts and a happy future.

When Anne appeared to sink deeper, Mindy persisted with open-ended support until Anne's eyes regained some life. Anne gradually recovered and, at Mindy's behest, they walked to CB's for an extra-large ice cream sandwich.

They settled onto the steps outside as they had so many times before, and Anne eventually grimaced to show her white teeth speckled in dark chocolate. Mindy smiled. "Maybe that's not so gross after all," she said, then squeezed a mix of vanilla ice cream and chocolate cookie between her teeth. Both girls looked to the sky, laughing hysterically.

Anne's recovery seemed to hold as they returned, and they shared a warm hug at the turn to Anne's house. Continuing their separate ways, Mindy walked home full of doubt, confusion, sadness and questions — many questions.

That evening, Mindy pulled a worn and faded nightgown from a dresser drawer. She laid it on her bed and gently stroked it with her fingers. She thought, "I've been wearing most of the same nightgowns since sixth grade. They're old and worn, but I still like them." She then visualized Anne holding her royal purple nightgown before her. It was the most exquisite gown Mindy had ever seen: glistening, royal-purple satin, gathered sleeves, lace trim around the modest V-neckline, and a three-inch ruffle at the bottom. In Mindy's mind, it was fit for a queen. She envisioned herself wearing something similar someday. "But not yet," she thought.

Mindy's thoughts shifted, and she suddenly felt sad Anne seemed so lost.

The strangeness of the episode faded over the next few days, but Anne's suitcase under Mindy's bed wouldn't let it fade from memory. Mindy mentioned it to Anne when they next talked, but Anne just brushed it off as if it didn't exist.

Chapter Four
Farewell Summer
August 21, 1973–January 1, 1974

Tuesday morning seemed like a school day when the alarm went off early for the first time since cheer camp. Book Day, the last day of the summer break when students would pick up class schedules, check out books and meet teachers, was a slap-in-the-face reminder that the new school year was upon her. Mindy rolled out of bed and strolled into the kitchen. As she poured herself a bowl of cereal, her mother rounded the corner, fully dressed with hair and lipstick ready for the day. "I made an appointment for you this morning," she announced.

Uncertain what her mother was referring to, Mindy wrinkled her forehead to ask, "For what?"

Uncertainty turned to joy, and Mindy nearly choked on her Cornflakes when her mother replied, "Contacts. I know we said maybe when you're sixteen. But you're right, it will be hard doing cartwheels with glasses. So, Dad and I thought this might be a good time for you to give contacts a try."

Mindy was ecstatic that her pleas had finally been answered. After asking for contacts for two years, she had redoubled her efforts following cheer camp when she realized an elastic band for her glasses didn't coordinate well with her cheerleading uniform.

Lafayette had no optometrist, so as soon as Mindy dropped her Book Day books in her locker, she and her mother began the 45-minute trek to Lebanon, Tennessee. The initial stretch on State Route 10 was winding and well known for frequent car accidents. Considered "a corridor to booze" by many locals, some believed the accidents were God's response to sinners buying liquor in Trousdale County.

Within a few weeks, Mindy was a contact lens pro. Her self-confidence grew and, by the end of the first week of school, the effect of shedding her glasses was more than noticeable as boys began to swarm around her at school and while cruising.

Classes proved to be easy, and homework was minimal. Academic boredom prompted Mindy to recall many of the challenging thoughts precipitated by teachers and fellow students at Duchesne, especially in her favorite class, English Literature. She understood how the sometimes edgy and provocative class discussions forced her to think beyond her naiveté of youth. They encouraged academic competition and used it constructively. They pushed her to work harder and broaden her insight. "They made me *want* to be better," she thought.

But these elements were lacking in Mindy's MCHS experience, and as her popularity grew, academics faded in proportion. Quick reviews just before tests were enough to get above-average scores. Despite being academically passive, Mindy still earned a mix of A's and B's. No one pushed her. No one suggested, "You can do better." No one warned her there would eventually be a price to pay for her intellectual laziness.

The only comments she heard from teachers, parents, and relatives suggested they had minimal expectations of academic excellence for girls. Mindy heard repeatedly, "Being pretty and having a friendly personality is enough to take you wherever you want to go." In her mind, this translated to, "Being nice and cute is more important than good grades." But academic concerns were more than overpowered by her burgeoning self-confidence and growing social status. School became little more than a social platform as the academic atmosphere of Duchesne High became a historical anecdote. For a smart, pretty girl with everything going her way and no one to give her a push, academics became unimportant.

To add to the distraction, for the first time anyone remembered, the MCHS football team was off to a good start and delusions of a state championship soon dominated many conversations. Historically a football doormat, the 1973 MCHS football team grew larger each week as a source of community pride.

By the time the school year was only a few weeks old, Mindy had already settled into a comfortable pattern of balancing social life above academics. Lunchtime, especially, became highly interactive and full of questionable gossip.

Mindy's long golden hair, mesmerizing smile, and evolving teenage frame created a new focal point that most teen males found impossible to ignore. She was a vision that lured boys with dilated pupils in ever-increasing numbers for what the other girls called a "Mindy fix." But Mindy didn't mind. The low-current electricity generated by this attention was new, unexpected, and innocently exciting.

Over the subsequent days and weeks, rumors circulated to Mindy's ears that Rita Green was jealous of the attention she'd been receiving. Pleasantly developed, Rita reined as the unofficial queen belle of the junior class. In contrast to Mindy, Rita actively sought male attention and had no trouble finding it at the otherwise all-male lunch table that the other girls referred to euphemistically as "Rita Land."

Rumors of Rita's questionable behavior gradually grew and included promiscuity. Mindy was highly skeptical of such tales and always refused to comment, but the tales created a powerful thought: "I hope nobody *ever* talks about me this way."

The third week of September, Mindy shared a lunchroom table with her usual array of friends. Someone snickered and quietly pointed toward Rita Land, where the queen was in high spirits and commanding lots of panting male attention. She wore a tight, long-sleeved sweater that accentuated her full chest. The buttons were undone just low enough to reveal a sliver of cleavage and, to close observers, the white edge of her bra. She laughed and stood upright with a flip of her head to throw her long, brown hair over one shoulder and then the other to frame her round breasts. Spewing pheromones, she kept the circle of boys buzzing. The hormonal male harem came from all around to stare and drool. They all wanted more.

"Come on now, y'all. Pass me the salt. I meeean it! Quit teeeasin' me 'n jess pass the salt on o-va here," sang Rita with far more volume than necessary. More male heads turned in hopes of a cheap thrill.

As the antics in Rita Land continued, a voice from the end of Mindy's table snickered and then squeaked out, "Come on now, y'all 'n pass the salt on down o-va here." This started a chain reaction of copycatters, and the table roared with laughter. Mindy's laugh stopped abruptly when she looked up to see Randy's eyes fixed in her direction.

Many football players had staked an unofficial claim to a high-profile hallway crossroads adjacent to a dormant wall heater in the main foyer of the school. Loitering in this location, they capitalized on their celebrity status, socialized, and girl-watched. Virtually all these self-proclaimed kings wore Brut aftershave, the scent of which was pungent up to thirty feet away. The girls cheerfully dubbed this phenomenon the "Brut Cloud."

A near-permanent fixture in 'The Cloud,' Randy was in his usual position when Mindy passed by in mid-September. Mindy didn't fail to notice when his eyes widened and focused on her. Blushing brightly, he forced out a soft, "Hey."

Mindy returned a nervous "Hey," and felt her own cheeks turn hot as she continued by.

A similar scene occurred the next day and the day after that. Gradually, the greeting evolved into a much more formal "Hi," the blushes faded, and acknowledging smiles soon followed.

A few days later, Mindy was in her bedroom listening to records when the phone rang, so she didn't bother to answer. A moment later, giggles from her brothers outside her door preceded their sing-song announcement, "Minnn-dayyy — phone for you. It's a boi-oy."

"Randy!" she thought. Clearing her throat and settling her excitement, she calmly lifted the receiver and forced out a falsely unexcited, "Hello."

"Hi, Mindy, this is Mike McCarthy," rattled into Mindy's ear. Disappointed, she sat back slowly on the edge of her bed.

After brief pleasantries, Mike asked, "Would you like to go to dinner and a movie with me this weekend?"

Flattered and relieved, Mindy explained her parents' rule, "I won't be allowed to date until my birthday next April."

"Guess I'll just have to wait. Well, see ya at school," Mike replied with disappointment.

This scenario repeated itself a few days later with the voice of a different senior, Jim Harper, who nervously talked non-stop for twenty minutes before popping the date question. The outcome was unchanged.

Later that week, Mindy staked out territory in front of the family television right after dinner to watch what she hoped would be a rebound for women after the embarrassing defeat of Margaret Court by a much older adversary, Bobby Riggs. The media had championed the pomp and hype of the day by billing the upcoming match as "The Battle of the Sexes."

Billie Jean King entered the Astrodome Cleopatra style, carried by four muscular, bare-chested young men. Bobby Riggs, wearing a bright, yellow-gold "Sugar Daddy" jacket, followed in a rickshaw pulled by a team of young women he had dubbed his "Bosom Buddies." Soon after the match began, it became clear Riggs was in deep trouble. King ran the much older, unprepared, and out-of-shape Riggs all over the court.

When Mindy stood to cheer King's win of the first set, her brothers left the room in defeat. King swept three straight sets. As a result, Bobby Riggs became the embarrassing, older-male punch line of hundreds of jokes, and Women's Lib became more intrusive all over America.

The alarm went off at its usual time the next morning. With eyes barely open, Mindy walked directly to her stereo. She turned it on without looking at the knobs and it came to life with sharp static crackle. With deft fine tuning, she was happy to find a Nashville radio station coming in clearly because the local WEEN radio station played primarily country music and was too hard to listen to in the morning.

Jim Croce's "Leroy Brown" blared from the speakers as Mindy also came to life with a little dance shuffle to her dresser. Without commercial interruptions, the airwaves brought "Operator" and then "Time in a Bottle" as Mindy considered her clothing options for the day. A longer-than-usual pause of silence made Mindy freeze with uncertainty before the DJ's subdued voice announced, "In memory of Jim Croce, dead at the age of thirty. His chartered plane crashed following a concert last night."

Mindy sat on the end of her bed to absorb the shock. At length, she realized, "Things like hyped-up tennis matches are silly. They aren't important at all compared to death — especially untimely death." Her heart grew heavy as she wondered, "What things in life are really important?" The list she came up with seemed surprisingly short.

Teen parties were rare in Lafayette, so Mindy was thrilled when Cathy approached at the start of cheer practice. "Hey, my parents will be out-of-town Saturday night," Cathy said. "Let's have a slumber party at my house."

"That would be great!" Mindy replied. "We can all cruise together and then go to your place and make homemade pizza."

Cathy had another idea. "How about we pick up some wine before we go cruisin'?" she teased.

Everyone knew the cheerleader conduct codebook strictly prohibited smoking, drinking, and similar crimes. The thought of risking expulsion from the squad made Mindy shudder and reply cautiously, "Well, I don't know about the wine part."

"Aw, come on. It'll be fun," Cathy pushed, but Mindy remained hesitant.

The other girls overheard this exchange and chimed in to support Cathy. Mindy had never had more than a small sip of her mother's wine before, and the combination of curiosity and a hefty dose of peer pressure convinced her to agree.

Later that week, signs of an early fall had arrived. Nighttime temperatures were lower, rain was more frequent, and the leaves had already started to turn. Anne approached at the end of school and asked Mindy with some distress if she would walk home with her that afternoon.

Immediately concerned, Mindy replied, "Of course, but you look upset. What's the matter?"

"Matt called last night to break up. He wants to date girls at his own school," Anne explained with tear-filled eyes.

As soon as the sixth-period bell rang, the two girls scurried out the door shoulder to shoulder. Anne seemed to have regained her typically sturdy composure, so it didn't take much reassurance from Mindy to get her laughing again. By the time they parted toward their respective homes, Mindy felt all was well. With smiles, they made tentative plans to go shopping together on Saturday morning if they could get one of their mothers to drive.

Friday night came and went with another football victory. Mindy watched Anne closely from the stands and noted Anne was bouncy and more animated than usual, which she took as a healthy sign of recovery.

The next morning, they went shopping, and Anne's breakup was absent from their conversation. They returned early that afternoon to beautiful fall weather and decided to take a walk. They ended up almost a mile away at Sullivan's Pond, and stopped at the edge of the murky brown water. Anne sighed, pulled Matt's ring off her finger, rolled it for a moment in her palm, then tossed it with a girlish throwing motion into the middle of the pond and finished with an emphatic nod of her head.

Mindy applauded her strength and offered encouraging words of future love. As they began the trek home, Mindy felt an abrupt onset of cramps and said, "I'd better get home. I think I have a bad period coming on."

"I have something really good for cramps at home. Let's stop there," Anne replied.

After closing her bedroom door, Anne rummaged around in the back of a desk drawer and then handed Mindy two unmarked white tablets.

"What are they?" Mindy inquired.

Anne replied generically, "They're for cramps. I take 'em all the time."

Feeling better after the walk, Mindy wrapped the pills in a piece of paper and slid them into her pocket in case she might want them later. The girls took seats in their usual spots on the floor to listen to records and chat some more.

Before long, a sad tune spun on the turntable, and Mindy sensed Anne's falling spirits. She assumed Anne was thinking about Matt and tried to focus the conversation on happy thoughts. But she couldn't halt Anne's decline until Rita's "pass me the salt" story popped into her mind. Mindy added some hair tossing dramatics as she recounted the incident. Anne burst into laughter and requested an encore performance, so Mindy obliged but said, "I think that's enough," to decline a second request.

Anne laughed again, but her smile suddenly faded. She looked at Mindy earnestly to ask, "You know Rita is after Randy, don't you? You know they dated before you moved here?"

Mindy made no reply and Anne continued, "Judy told me Rita has been after him for months. It looked like they were going to be a steady couple until you moved to town. Judy is dating Craig Brooks, who just happens to be Randy's best friend, and she was hoping they could double date together. She told me Rita caught Randy staring at you the other day and was none too happy about it."

Mindy's thoughts swirled. She envisioned the look in Randy's eyes and couldn't believe she was misinterpreting their meaning. But the idea of competing with someone older and more physically developed was unnerving.

Shifting in her seat, Mindy looked out the window and noted the long shadows of late afternoon and excused herself. "Well, I guess I'd better be getting home to get ready for Cathy's slumber party," then leaned forward to whisper, "We might even have some wine."

Anne's eyes widened as she rose to her feet. She offered stern, almost angry, words of warning. "You're making a big mistake. You shouldn't go. If you get caught, they'll kick all of you off the team."

Mindy got up as well and, smiling with an appreciation for Anne's concern, assured her, "We'll be careful."

Anne persisted in her objection, "Don't go. Stay here with me."

When Mindy apologized and tried to explain her anticipation, Anne became angry with and released a guttural snarl. Unnerved, Mindy stepped back.

Anne reversed course and pleaded, "Please don't leave me alone tonight. Not on a Saturday night."

Mindy offered further reassurance but insisted she had to go. Anne's posture stiffened again. She slowly rolled her shoulders forward, glared through the slits of her eyes and snarled a second time. The almost demonic transformation scared Mindy and sent her in retreat to the bedroom door.

Anne's anger faded again but, confused and scared, Mindy shook her head and whispered, "I'm really sorry, but I *have* to go."

"Please stay. Please stay here *with me* tonight," Anne begged. Mindy didn't respond. Anne's tone changed again as she matter-of-factly continued, "My brother can get us some really good stuff." Mindy didn't understand, so Anne continued, "You know, pot. We can smoke some pot and get high."

Mindy couldn't believe her ears. During their many hundreds of hours together, they had talked about drugs only in relation to the book, *Go Ask Alice.*

"It's really good stuff," Anne repeated.

Mindy became angry. "*Now* who do you think is making bad decisions!"

Anne collapsed silently onto her bed, and Mindy left without another word.

It took almost an hour to clear her mind of Anne's unexpected outburst but, by the time Mindy had showered and dressed, her focus was on the evening ahead. Waiting in the living room, she kept a watchful eye on the driveway through the window. When Patty's headlights pulled into the drive, Mindy scooped up her overnight bag, hollered, "I'm going," and ran to the car.

Both girls were excited about the slumber party and drove to the Gates farm to rendezvous with the rest of the squad minus one. Donna Powers had backed out after hearing about plans for the wine. Along the way, Patty commented, "I don't know what Donna is all scared about. There's a six-pack hid in the back of just about every refrigerator in Macon County — including the Baptist ones."

All wound up, the five cheerleaders piled into Cathy's car and drove east on country roads unfamiliar to Mindy. "Where are we going?" she inquired.

"Got to stop by the bootlegger first," Cathy replied.

"A bootlegger? Are you kidding? I thought they were only in the movies!" Mindy exclaimed.

As a group, the girls filled her in. "Every dry county has bootleggers. Here, there are two main ones: The Lion at the bottom of the hill on Highway 10 and The King on highway 52 toward Red Boiling Springs. They both know the names of more teenagers in Macon County than most teachers do and are on a first name basis with the police." They all laughed.

Cathy added, "They know lots of adults too, especially those who don't want to be seen buying liquor in Hartsville."

The car rolled to a stop in front of a disheveled trailer partially obscured by trees. After a brief pause, Cathy honked twice, then pulled away. About a hundred yards down the road, she made a U-turn and came to a stop in front of the trailer.

They waited in dead silence, and Mindy's eyes widened when a scruffy-looking character in camouflage clothing emerged from the shadows of the woods behind the trailer. He scanned the scene suspiciously until he reached the car. He grabbed the upper door frame hard enough to rock the car and squinted to study each of its occupants. Mindy's breathing paused as his evil glare fixed on her.

A malevolent smile revealed the ruffian's poorly fitting dentures before he asked, "Well, what kin I git fer you ladies?" He smelled of sweat, booze, and gunpowder. Although only in his early forties, his weathered features made him look sixty.

With practiced confidence, Cathy replied, "One bottle of Boone's Farm Strawberry Hill." Their supplier nodded, disappeared into the trailer for a moment, and returned carrying a brown paper bag which he extended for Cathy to inspect. Cathy peeked in with a nod, then traded four one-dollar bills for the bag which she promptly slid under the front seat. She pulled away, spitting dust and pebbles from her rear tires.

"I can't believe it. I can't believe bootleggers really still exist!" Mindy exclaimed. The other girls just grinned.

The troupe headed back toward town and entered the cruise circuit. Mindy silently hoped to see Randy along the way, but felt disappointed when the streets and usual teen hotspots were quiet. During one stop, discomfort displaced Mindy's disappointment when her cramps flared and almost doubled her over. Hoping to keep the evening fun and pain-free, she pulled Anne's donated pills out of her pocket, swallowed them down with a cold drink, and took a seat away from the others for several minutes.

Later, they left the town lights behind as they drove toward the Gates farm. Cathy reached under the front seat and pulled out the bottle of Boone's Farm. She cracked off the cap, took a swig, then announced, "Here ya go girls. Drink up and be happy!"

Mindy watched the bottle get passed from girl to girl and tipped to the sky. When it reached Mindy, she didn't hesitate to do the same. Surprised by how much the cheap wine burned on the way down, she grimaced and shook her head. The other girls all laughed again.

They emptied the bottle quickly, and Mindy had to laugh when Patty jettisoned it out the window, and it spun into the darkness.

One bottle of cheap wine between five girls shouldn't have done much but at barely one hundred pounds, even the few ounces of wine along with the placebo effect of "being bad" left Mindy feeling giddy. Her cramps abated when her head started swimming and she felt all the giddier.

The other girls laughed harder at Mindy's mildly slurred speech and noted that she seemed "drunk or high." Mindy felt embarrassed and recalled the incident at Anne's that afternoon. In defense, she said, "It's not the alcohol. I think it may be the pills Anne gave me. She said they were good for cramps."

The others shared whispers, wondering what the pills might have been and seemed upset that Anne had shared them with Mindy. They gradually settled down and the rest of the evening was typical girlish fun. Not long after sunrise, the girls had a hearty farm breakfast, then said their goodbyes.

That afternoon, Mindy placed an album on the turntable and curled up on her bed to rest her eyes. It didn't take long for her thoughts to drift to Anne. It saddened her to think things might never be the same between them. She was afraid Anne felt betrayed and abandoned in a time of need, but she also remained frightened and angry by the mention of drugs. "How well do I really know her?" she wondered.

———————

Two days later, Mindy took her seat in English class and focused her thoughts on the day's reading assignment. Just before class began, Judy Green, who sat off Mindy's right flank, interrupted her concentration. In a loud deadpan voice, Judy barked, "Hey, Barb. I hear some people like ta do imitations."

Barb, seated behind Judy, responded much louder than necessary, "Yeah. I've heard the same thang." Mindy paid little attention to their conversation until Barb persisted. "Hey Manday, I hear ya do some really good imitations. Let's hear some."

Before Mindy could respond, Judy chirped sharply over her shoulder, "Yeah, I heard the same thang. Go on 'n do one. Do one fer us right now."

Confused, Mindy spun around in her seat to find Judy's angry eyes bearing down on her, and an image of Rita begging for salt flitted across her mind. Mindy flushed. Shaking her head, she said, "I'm sorry. I shouldn't have done that. It was just in fun, and I didn't mean anything by it."

Judy angrily commanded, "*No.* I wanna hear ya do it. I heard you do Rita really good."

Mindy declined and turned back to the front of the room as class began. The next fifty minutes seemed like five hundred. Mindy could feel fiery breath and burning stares from behind during every minute. When the bell finally rang, she scooped up her books and fled the room to escape further taunts.

Instead of walking home, Mindy took a seat near the front of the bus home that afternoon. Seeking safety in numbers, she didn't believe that Judy or Barb would have to gall to follow her onto the bus. Anne boarded the bus a moment later and slid into the seat next to Mindy, who was staring out the window.

Poking Mindy's arm to get her attention, Anne wore an innocent expression. "You'd better watch out," she warned. "Judy knows about you doin' Rita imitations and is really mad. Judy, Barb, and Pam say they're gonna beat you up before school tomorrow."

Mindy acted unconcerned and looked back out the window. "That's silly. It was just a joke," she flatly replied but her heart raced. Not only was she afraid they might actually come after her, but she was also furious that Anne had broken her confidence. She had done the Rita imitation for no one other than Anne, and sitting next to a Judas made her boil inside. The short bus ride was cold and silent.

Getting off the bus at their mutual stop, Mindy waited for the bus to pull away and then spun around toward Anne. "Why would you tell anyone that? I trusted you. You *knew* that was just between you and me."

Anne shrugged. "I thought it was funny. I didn't think it would bother anyone."

Unbelieving, Mindy glared at her. "*But you knew it would make them mad!*"

When Anne answered with an icy stare, Mindy turned away and marched home.

The alarm clicked on at its usual time the next morning, but Mindy was already wide awake. She lay in bed, breathing heavily. She thought, "Judy and Barb aren't big, but they are sturdy, broad-hipped country girls and Pam outweighs me by at least forty pounds. As a trio, they could undoubtedly do some damage. Oh, my goodness! How did I ever get into this mess? Anne. Anne got me into this!"

Mindy tried to convince herself that she had nothing to worry about, but feared otherwise. Catfights were a common occurrence at MCHS, especially over boys. The sound of "Fight, fight, fight!" followed by the flocking of bodies to the point of the altercation was all too common. Eight out of ten times, the two combatants were girls. The skirmishes were ferocious. Hair pulling, kicking, biting, and scratching was routine.

Mindy had never run to watch one of these battles, but couldn't help but overhear detailed post-event commentary from others. The reports made her shudder with fear and disgust. She had never imagined herself being involved in such a battle before, but now couldn't get the thought out of her head.

The morning minutes ticked by as Mindy lay in bed, stroking her fingers over her long golden hair and imagining what it would be like to have a chunk of it ripped from her scalp. She knew she couldn't avoid school, so she forced herself out of bed but purposely lollygagged while getting ready. With the start of school just minutes away, she sheepishly appeared in the kitchen to announce that she had missed the bus. Her mother grabbed the car keys, and in a flash, they were off.

The closer they got to school, the louder Mindy could hear her pulse pounding in her head. When they stopped in front of the main entrance, Mindy scanned the landscape before her. Only one other student was in sight as he raced to the door on foot, suggesting the imminent start of classes. Mindy took a deep breath and stepped out of the car.

With another deep breath, Mindy told herself, "Take the high road." Holding her chin high, she stepped through the main entrance with an air of pseudo-confidence. Standing together right in front of the main office were Judy, Barb, and Pam. Each sported a menacing scowl with a wide stance and held a mid-chest fist-in-palm.

Marching straight past them, Mindy turned to look Judy directly in the eye. Without showing the slightest bit of fear or concern, she said, "Good morning" and continued a confident march to her first class.

To Mindy's amazement, none of the girls involved ever mentioned the issue again. She had, however, learned a valuable lesson and would never make fun of anyone for any reason ever again but wondered, "Who can I really trust?"

———————————— · ————————————

Over the next few weeks, sadness and anger regarding Anne gradually faded into the background as football and boys, in general, became more interesting. The recipient of much playful flirting, Mindy bashfully returned the same, and an awareness that some boys would melt in her presence gradually grew. Sometimes, even simple eye contact would turn a boy into a puppet begging her to pull his strings. She soon understood the power of flirting but had strict, self-imposed limits and somehow knew to never take advantage of it.

Hallway crossings with Randy continued and became an expected part of each day. Mindy's smile was always slightly bigger when looking his way, while he stood taller when looking in hers. Mindy started pausing to say, "Hi. How are you today?" but actual conversation remained elusive.

By the end of October, Mindy learned through the lunch-table grapevine that Anne had a new boyfriend, senior Danny Meador, who was best known for his shady reputation. To Mindy's limited knowledge, only a few boys at school were quietly rumored to be involved with drinking and possibly drugs. Danny was one of them. Disheartened, Mindy tracked Anne down at school and matter-of-factly informed her she would return her suitcase that afternoon.

When Mindy arrived at the Belle's, she found Anne waiting outside, seated on the front porch step. Anne didn't get up and just stared blankly at the suitcase as Mindy placed it at her feet. Mindy said, "I guess you won't be needing this."

Gently laying her hand on top of the suitcase, Anne inquired, "What's in here?"

"Not much. I don't think you would have made it very far," Mindy replied.

Anne cautiously pulled the suitcase onto her lap and flipped the latches. Her eyebrows rose as she studied the contents. As Anne rubbed the lace collar of the nightgown between her fingers, Mindy could read her confusion. Anne then moved the gown to the side and cradled the book in her hands. Gazing at the cover, she showed no emotion as she stroked her fingers over the freckled face of the young girl pictured. After a moment, she asked without looking up, *For Girls Only*. Did you read it?"

Standing with arms crossed and feeling sad about the scene unfolding before her, Mindy shook her head, whispering, "No. I never opened the suitcase."

After a long pause, Anne looked up and waited to establish eye contact before extending her arm, book in hand. "Here, take this. I want you to have it. You might like to read it."

Anne seemed lost and genuinely apologetic, so Mindy reluctantly accepted the gift. She glanced at the young girl on the cover momentarily and was struck by the uncertainty of her distant stare. She looked back into Anne's eyes to ask, "Is everything okay?"

Anne didn't seem surprised by the question and flatly replied, "Yeah, sure."

The tone of Anne's response left Mindy doubtful. "Are things okay with Danny?"

Anne delivered another monotone response. "Yeah. Things are okay. We have fun."

Mindy suddenly felt afraid and didn't want to know or hear anymore. "Well, I guess I'd better get home. Lots of homework today," she lied.

Several seconds of awkward silence followed. Mindy turned and walked away but paused when she heard a sad and lonely, "Come back sometime."

Mindy looked back over her shoulder to force a smile. She nodded but said nothing. Resuming her trek home, Mindy felt a deep chill. Something was wrong, very, very wrong, and sadness filled her heart.

———————————

The regular season of football ended, and Mindy's anticipation for the start of the basketball season jumped to a new height. On the first Monday in November, she was more peppy than usual on her way to sixth-period cheer practice, but when she arrived, an unusual scene stopped her in her tracks. All the other football and basketball cheerleaders were in a tight huddle and speaking in skittish, low voices.

Mrs. Wilson stepped around the corner at about the same time, and a sudden hush fell over the entire group. Although she was the administrative sponsor of the cheerleaders, her physical presence at practice was unprecedented. She walked directly to the football cheer captains, pulled them in close, and whispered in their ears. The captains nodded and then quickly shuffled the other football cheerleaders into the cafeteria. Anne arrived just as the last girl entered the cafeteria, looking pale and frightened as she silently followed them in. Mrs. Wilson gave the basketball squad an expressionless glance, then looked to the floor and stepped into the cafeteria, closing the door behind her.

Mindy looked at Patty for an explanation. "They're having a meeting about maybe throwing Anne off the team. Somebody reported her for breaking the cheerleader code. I think they caught her smoking," Patty whispered.

After several minutes, Mary Sharp, the senior captain of the football squad, emerged and motioned for Mindy to join her down the hall.

Out of earshot of the others, Mary came straight to the point. "Tell me about the pills Anne gave you."

Mindy stiffened with surprise and whispered, "I was having bad cramps. She gave them to me for cramps. I don't know what they were called. Please don't use that against her. *Please, don't kick her off the team for that!*"

64

Mary nodded in understanding. "That's all I need to know," she said and started back toward the cafeteria.

Mindy caught her by the arm and repeated her plea. "*Please, don't use that against her.*" Mary nodded again and walked away without another word.

With a wave of fear, Mindy suddenly felt trapped. "How can I explain my giddiness that night? They might find out that nearly the entire basketball squad had been drinking. They might throw all of us off the team."

The other girls swarmed Mindy with curiosity, but she gathered her wits and remained mum. "It's nothing. Really, I don't think it's related to what's going on in there. Let's get to work."

A few moments later, the cafeteria door burst open, and Anne stormed through the doorway with tears streaming down her cheeks. As she disappeared down the hall, Mindy stood paralyzed, watching in horror-stricken disbelief.

Another moment later, Mrs. Wilson stepped through the doorway and walked away without further discussion. A subdued and distracted practice resumed. With neither squad showing much enthusiasm, the captains stopped practice early, and the girls drifted off in different directions.

Later, Mindy learned Mrs. Wilson had gagged the football cheerleaders with stern words of warning not to discuss Anne's expulsion. Following orders, they all remained extraordinarily tight-lipped. Other than "behavior unbecoming of a cheerleader," no other explanation ever emerged. Many implied or assumed that Anne was guilty of drug use, but to Mindy's knowledge, no one offered any proof.

Mindy considered calling Anne several times but, uncertain where to start and fearful of stoking a fire of revenge, she decided against it. She just wanted the whole thing to die down and fade away.

———————————

The football team ended the regular season 10−0 for the first time anyone could remember, and the community was flying high with dreams of a state championship. After a rousing pep rally, students boarded school buses for the neutral field first-round playoff game and a trip to MCHS football glory. As Mindy took a seat in the mid-rows with Gina and Patty, she spotted Anne sitting alone in the last row of the bus and felt ashamed for not inviting her to join them.

65

The buses unloaded at an upscale high school field near Nashville, where Mindy took a seat between Gina and Patty behind the Tiger's bench. With thirty minutes before kickoff, there was time to chat and let eyes wander. Mindy spotted Anne and Danny seated high in the stands at the far edge of the crowd behind them. When Danny stood and disappeared toward the concession stand, Mindy made her way up the stairs. Anne saw her coming and smiled.

Mindy offered an awkward, "Hey," then took a seat. Lightly touching Anne's forearm, she continued, "I'm so sorry. This must be really hard for you. Is there anything I can do to help?"

Anne took a deep breath. "Oh, it's all right. I really don't mind. It's good to have more free time anyway. Now I have a free hour at the end of every school day. I never have to take books home."

"Well, I see you're here with Danny. Is everything going okay with him?" Mindy cautiously inquired.

"Yeah, he's good to me. We have fun together," Anne replied. But her words were incongruent with her tone. She sounded lonely and sad.

They talked for several more minutes until Mindy spied Danny returning with concession goodies, so quickly excused herself. Settling back into her comfortable spot between Patty and Gina, Mindy was quiet and stared aimlessly at the field.

"You might not want to be seen with her too much," Patty whispered.

Mindy wanted to scream, "Don't so be harsh!" but bit her tongue. Weighed down by sadness for Anne, she sat silently wondering what she could do to help. Just before kickoff, Mindy looked upward in the stands. Anne and Danny were gone.

It didn't take long to dash the Tigers' championship dream. Hartsville jumped ahead early and crushed the Tigers 32-6. Disheartened Tiger fans emptied the stands quietly and made their way to the waiting buses. As they walked, Mindy realized she had been so absorbed by her thoughts she hadn't bothered to watch Randy play, and felt even worse.

Reaching the parking lot, she saw Anne standing off to the side. She asked Patty and Gina to save a few seats on the bus and approached Anne. "Would you like to sit with us on the bus?"

Wide-eyed and jittery, Anne looked around as if someone might be listening. "I'm going to ride home with Danny and his cousin." After an awkward pause, Anne continued, "We really do have a good time." With an unexpected burst of animation, she added, "Oh, my God. Compared to Matt, he's so much bigger. It's amazing when he's inside of me."

66

Mindy felt her cheeks turn cold and wondered, "*Who* is this girl I shared so much time with. Drugs — and now sex?" The avalanche of thoughts was hard to manage: "premarital sex is a sin," "drugs will kill you," "what about your reputation," "you're going to crash and burn."

Mindy implored Anne to think about what she was doing, but she was adamant that she was happy and being safe. A few seconds later, Danny stepped up behind Anne and stared, but said nothing. Numb and in need of an escape, Mindy nervously excused herself, "Well, I'd better get to the bus. See you later."

Stepping into the line for the bus, Mindy looked over her shoulder and watched as Anne and Danny walked away. Mindy could feel trouble in the making and sensed Anne was out of control. But Mindy didn't know whom to ask for help. "How can I tell my mother about this? She's good friends with Mrs. Belle. I don't want to be a snitch." With stomach churning, she kept her thoughts to herself during the subdued bus ride home.

Back in the MCHS parking lot, students with cars quickly disappeared while students waiting for rides dispersed more slowly as parents picked them up. Mindy rode home with Gina and shivered when they pulled out of the lot as the Belle car with Anne's father behind the wheel pulled in. "I wonder if her dad knows she went home with Danny?" she thought, but quickly dismissed it.

———————— · ————————

For the football cheerleaders, the season was over and the sixth hour of school morphed into a combination of study hall and social club. But the imminent start of the basketball season kept the basketball cheerleaders buzzing with energy. They didn't have the most athletic girls, but they took pride in their precision and worked hard to fine-tune their spirited performance. When the games started, they were ready to go.

The team's performance on the gym floor pleased Mindy, but the unexpected catcalls and teasing date offers drifting from the opposition stands surprised her. Although bothersome at first, Mindy soon learned to smile and either ignore them or return a soft verbal dart. Similarly, the rumor mill at MCHS suggested several boys had crushes on her and referred to her as "The Queen of the cheerleaders."

School continued smoothly until two weeks before the Christmas break, when a muffled rumor circulated around MCHS that Anne had been hospitalized in Nashville. Mindy's inquiries were unrevealing. No one knew what was wrong or how Anne was doing. Recalling their last conversation, Mindy's mind filled with fearful thoughts of pregnancy, abortion, and overdose. Deep in her heart, she hoped and prayed Anne would be all right.

As soon as Mindy walked through the door at home, she cornered her mother, "Do you know anything about Anne being in the hospital?"

Her mother offered a reserved response. "I really don't know much, but she's been in the hospital for about a week."

"What?! I can't believe you didn't tell me!" Mindy exclaimed tersely.

"Well, I just thought you had enough going on and didn't want you to worry," her mother calmly replied.

Sensing the inadequate explanation, Mindy stood firmly waiting for more, then inquired, "So, what's wrong with her?"

Her mother answered vaguely, "Well, I don't know the details, but it sounds like there is a mix of problems, but her parents hope things are under control now. I spoke with Mrs. Belle this morning, and she thinks Anne would be happy to have a visitor this weekend."

The evasive response was bothersome, but Mindy's inquest ended with her brother's arrival in the kitchen. She went to bed that evening with mixed emotions but resolved to pay Anne a visit and wish her well.

With Mindy's mother behind the wheel, the appearance of the hospital caught Mindy off guard. It didn't look like a hospital at all. It looked more like a resort and, although Mindy didn't want to ask, she started piecing the reality together.

The lobby was small and plush. The pleasant, sharply dressed receptionist took their names, punched four numbers on the telephone, and announced, "Visitors for Miss Belle." She smiled and motioned toward a large door, "An attendant will meet you momentarily."

With a light push, Mindy's mother suggested, "You go ahead. I'll wait for you here in the lobby. Visit as long as you like."

Mindy stepped back from the door when she heard the dull but decisive click of the lock. An attendant in a crisp uniform invited her in. As Mindy stepped into the antechamber, she looked to the far wall where a second heavy looking door with a small security wire-embedded window blocked the way. It was uncomfortably apparent that this was not a hospital for people with heart attacks, strokes and pneumonia.

The attendant stood back and made a visual head-to-toe scan, then inquired, "You have no purse or belongings with you?"

Mindy shook her head, and the attendant continued, "Do you have anything in your pockets or anything you plan to deliver with you, Miss?" Mindy shook her head again. "All right. Follow me," the attendant said politely before unlocking the inner door.

Mindy's skin crawled when she heard the door lock behind her with a mechanical thud. She stepped into a long broad hallway illuminated by a soft yellow, sunset-like lighting. In contrast, the far end appeared to open into a larger room that glowed with bright white light. She followed the attendant about halfway down the central corridor where he stopped and extended a hand toward an open door and announced, "A visitor for you, Miss Belle."

Mindy entered and found Anne sitting on a bed, wearing street clothes and surrounded by a thick cloud of cigarette smoke. Anne didn't get up but took a slow drag with a rebellious grin. After several seconds of uncomfortable quiet, Mindy said, "I heard you were in the hospital and thought you would like a visitor."

Leaning back against the wall, Anne replied flatly, "It's more like a prison than a hospital, but I'll be out soon."

"Maybe I shouldn't ask, but *why* are you here? *What's wrong*?" Mindy inquired.

Full of defiance, Anne clarified, "My parents don't like some of the things I do or sometimes the way I act. I just don't follow all of their rules. So, they thought I should be here for a little attitude adjustment. They put you on drugs, try to brainwash you and try to make you behave."

Unprepared for this conversation, Mindy felt off balance. Focusing on the cigarette in Anne's hand, she noted, "I didn't know you smoked."

Chuckling, Anne said, "*Everybody* in here smokes. The Macon County farmers should be happy."

Mindy tried to shift the conversation to school. "The football season didn't end the way we wanted, but I think it was a good year for the school and Lafayette."

Anne chuckled again. "It figures it would end the way it did. The whole school and the whole town just fell flat on their face. But I won't forget it. My parents don't want me with Danny — they hate him. My dad caught us when we got back to town after the last game. Whoo! He was mad and let me have it. But I still saw Danny at school, and on the weekends at my brother's house. Then my parents found out about some other stuff and caught me with Danny again and — well, here I am."

Astounded by Anne's lack of remorse, Mindy felt a little lightheaded and moved to a small chair in the corner. Perched on the front edge of the seat, she looked around and felt smothered by the surroundings.

After another long drag on her cigarette, Anne turned her head toward the window to shoot out a funnel of smoke and continued. "Danny and I went through a rough time, but we're okay now. He's not allowed to visit, but I can't wait to see him when I get out of here. I *can't wait* to get out of that crummy little town. It's run by a bunch of small people. It's going nowhere. There's never anything to do, there is never anything new."

Mindy sat taller to offer reassurance. "It's a *good place*. You have *good friends* and *people who care about you* there. *Not everybody has that.*"

Anne shrugged defiantly.

"Just where is it you want to go? Just what do you want to do that you can't do at home?" Mindy inquired.

"I want to go anywhere. *Any place but Lafayette*," she replied.

"Why don't you go cruising with us when you get home? Some nights, it's pretty fun," Mindy pushed.

Anne's eyes remained fixed on the window. Mindy followed her gaze to see what had captured her attention. She noticed the window was far smaller and situated much higher than usual. Its wire-embedded glass was coated thickly in cigarette tar, which made it virtually opaque. The only thing visible was the soft vertical shadows of exterior bars on the glass. There was no way to tell what else lay beyond.

The attendant leaned into the room. "Session in ten minutes, Miss Belle."

Anne nodded without otherwise acknowledging the attendant, then finally looked in Mindy's direction without making eye contact. "I gotta go. They won't let me have cigarettes if I don't go to group sessions. Thanks for coming," she explained.

Arising simultaneously, they each took a cautious step forward to share an uncertain hug. Mindy's fingers were shocked to find that Anne's slight frame seemed ominously thin and frail. Her bones were dreadfully easy to feel. Up close, the transformation from the young girl who Mindy had watched plucking stray eyebrows and putting on makeup just a few months earlier to looking wasted and worn was almost terrifying.

"You get better, girl. I'll be looking for you at school," said Mindy earnestly.

"You are a lucky girl. So smart and pretty. Don't mess it up," Anne replied.

Deeply touched by Anne's concern, Mindy honestly hoped her visit may have helped.

70

As the attendant unlocked the inner door to the antechamber, Mindy looked over her shoulder and watched Anne's silhouette disappear into the bright light of the day room at the end of the hall.

In the lobby, Mindy's mother asked, "How was Anne? Was she happy to have some company?"

"She's okay. I think she's doing okay," Mindy responded. But her words didn't match her thoughts. She didn't think Anne was okay at all and wondered what lay beyond the barred, opaque window of her future.

During the quiet ride home, Mindy reflected on her chilling visit to a world of which she had little knowledge or understanding and concluded, "It's not a world I ever want to live in." Then she considered the seemingly uncomplicated nature of her high school life. In some ways, basketball, cheerleading, and cruising seemed less important now, but it still felt reassuring to return to them. "There's just too much good stuff in life to spend it locked in a room and unable to see out the window. I have plenty of time for the more complicated stuff in life — whatever that is. But right now, all I want is to get home and wash the stench of cigarettes out of my hair and put on some clean clothes," she thought.

———————

The last week of school before the Christmas break was scholastically unchallenging and included two more evenings of basketball with two wins for the girls' team.

As expected, the boys' team was struggling and already seemed inconsequential to most observers. Feeling ever more confident on the court, Mindy took more notice of the random catcalls and date requests from the visiting stands. Wearing a big smile, she would occasionally point toward the voices, pause as if considering the offers to induce a wisp of silent anticipation, then gently shake her pigtailed head before dancing away. The boys in the stands would release a collective moan and melt back into their seats with laughter.

Christmas came and went uneventfully. Mindy got together variably with Patty, Gina, and neighbor Phyllis Brockett over the break to listen to records, shop, or go cruising. They were fun, happy, and well-balanced friends. They all expressed typical teenage dreams and anxieties, but didn't seem caught in a blinding maelstrom. Mindy found their teen paradigm to be pleasant and safe, but with at least one eye focused on the future.

"They don't know exactly where they are going, but they don't seem lost," Mindy thought.

The last Saturday in December was chilly, with gray skies and a light drizzle. About noon, Mindy sat in her room, mesmerized by an album spinning on the turntable as Jim Croce's "Time in a Bottle" filled the room. When the turntable clicked off, she made her way to the kitchen to pour herself a glass of cherry Kool-Aid. The phone rang, and she answered with a bland, "Hello."

"Hi — Mindy? This is Randy — Randy Davidson." Mindy almost spilled her drink as her heart fluttered in her chest. Although choppy at first, the conversation gradually smoothed. They talked about random subjects until interrupted by a party line caller at Randy's end of the line. Randy promptly announced, "Well, it was nice talking to you. See ya at school."

Afterward, Mindy danced her way back to her room, holding her Kool-Aid glass high in the air and singing, "It was Randy Davidson! It was Randy Davidson!" She set the glass on her nightstand, then jumped onto her bed. Rolling over to gaze out the window, she laughed with the realization that she couldn't remember much of their conversation. It didn't matter. It was a good day.

Mindy spent the remainder of the holiday break anxiously awaiting the start of the new semester and the chance to see Randy at school.

Chapter 5
Awakening
January 2–April 1, 1974

School resumed with Anne in attendance, but she was virtually invisible. Hallway sightings were rare, she didn't ride the bus home even on rainy days, and Mindy's phone calls went unanswered. Rumors suggested she was always with Danny.

Three weeks into the semester, Mindy sat in the hallway painting a poster for the next basketball game with the other cheerleaders when she spotted Anne seated alone in the cafeteria. Mindy put down her brush, walked into the cafeteria, and took a seat opposite Anne. They exchanged smiles and spoke for the first time since the hospital visit.

"We haven't had a chance to talk. How are you doing?" Mindy inquired.

"I'm okay," replied Anne, but her tone was unconvincing.

The strained conversation gradually warmed and Anne explained, "Danny and I broke up again after I got out of the hospital, but we're back together now. He can be really nice when he wants to."

"Well, let's you and I do something together before too long. Okay?" Mindy said. Anne nodded.

They talked a few more minutes before Mindy felt compelled to return to poster-painting. "Thanks for stopping by," Anne said.

"Call me any time," Mindy replied. Anne nodded again.

Returning to the hallway, Mindy could read question and scorn in her teammates' eyes. They seemed to silently ask, "What the heck are you doing?" but the entire group was silent for several minutes.

Mindy's thoughts made her heart race, "This is at least partly my fault. I can't just ignore her like you. I need to be a friend and help her if I can."

The basketball season rolled on and cheering remained the highlight of the early winter. The boys' team struggled to compete against moderate opponents, while the girls team became the winter talk of the town. With a few key upsets, they captured the conference tournament championship and triggered lots of conversation about a long run in the state playoffs. There was a welcomed resurgence of pride and excitement at school and around town.

At Mrs. Wilson's request, Mindy stopped by her counseling office before cheer practice the week following the conference championship. Mrs. Wilson began the conversation with excited talk about how well the girls' basketball team was doing and the possibility of going far in postseason play. Mindy acknowledged the obvious and politely asked why Mrs. Wilson wanted to see her. Mrs. Wilson paused and, despite being in her office with the door closed, looked nervously around as if to make certain no one else was listening. "Well, *some* have been wondering if it would be a good idea to put both cheer teams together for the rest of the season and have fourteen girls on the floor instead of six. What do you think of the idea?"

Sensing a trap, Mindy pondered the suggestion and its implications. It quickly occurred to her that if she was being consulted at all, she needed to be a decision maker but also felt she needed more time to consider it logically. When Mrs. Wilson started to speak again, Mindy interjected, "I can't give you an answer now. I think this needs to be a team decision. I'll let you know in the morning," then bounced out the door before Mrs. Wilson could object.

Mrs. Wilson's suggestion percolated in Mindy's mind, and she wondered why she had been singled out. By that afternoon, she concluded, "Mrs. Wilson thinks I am the key to making this suggestion fly. She thinks if I agree, the other girls will follow my lead and not openly object. But they will. I don't have or want that kind of power. I just want to cheer."

Mindy gathered her basketball cheer mates in the cafeteria before practice and gave a neutral presentation of Mrs. Wilson's suggestion. She waited for feedback, but the other girls all stood quietly until one of them broke the silence. "Well, Mindy, what do you think?"

They had become a tight-knit group, and Mindy knew it would upset most of them if forced to let the football cheerleaders "in on the glory." Disrupting their chemistry that had been months in the making just seemed the wrong thing to do, and Mindy softly admitted, "I don't think it's a good idea." Her words unleashed the storm that had been building in the other girls, and suddenly, five other voices were speaking in unison against the proposal.

The next morning, Mindy stopped by Mrs. Wilson's office to inform her of the team's decision. Mrs. Wilson was sadly disappointed but agreed to honor the team's wishes.

Mindy felt certain Mrs. Wilson was under political pressure and wished she'd taken a different approach. "Somewhere, somehow, there will be fallout from this," she thought.

Basketball excitement grew with first-place finishes by the Tigerettes in the District and Regional tournaments. For the first time anyone could remember, an MCHS basketball team had a real shot at making the Final Four. But consecutive losses in the Sectional tournament against more experienced teams quickly dashed any dreams of a state championship.

It had been a wonderfully successful season for the basketball team and fantastically fun for the cheerleaders, but it was suddenly over. Mindy felt unprepared for life without cheering until Spring's warmer weather induced a recovery with thoughts of spring flowers, her birthday and maybe even "car dates" all just around the corner.

Randy's phone calls gradually increased in frequency and soon settled into a pattern of just about every Monday and Thursday evening after dinner, with an occasional call late Sunday afternoon. By chance at first and later by design, Mindy calmly studied the phone sitting on her bed before her as it rang and would gently lift the handset from the cradle at the completion of the fourth ring.

The conversation was always polite but never ventured far from MCHS or Lafayette. There was limited discussion of current events, politics, sports, religion, and even music. Consequently, most of the conversations were short and superficial. Mindy's attempts to engage Randy in discussion of modestly abstract or complicated topics only resulted in accruing more knowledge of farming and country life than she ever expected. It succeeded, however, in giving her a better appreciation for the long days and hard work of farm life and how it cultivated not only crops but personal satisfaction and a future for the family. But she never imagined herself living that way.

Conversations tended to hit a wall whenever Mindy mentioned her dreams of college, a career, and world travel. Randy seemed to understand that his future was on a Macon County farm, and it was apparent he didn't plan to travel much beyond the borders of Tennessee.

What fueled Mindy's excitement was Randy's allusions to future "car dates." These included pizza in Gallatin, drive-in movies, cruising, and ice cream at Clifton's or Jones's. Each mention of dating triggered waves of goosebumps across Mindy's skin, but they would quickly fade with the melancholy sadness in Randy's voice at the end of each call.

With Mindy's sixteenth birthday just weeks away, the time arrived for driving lessons. Amusement park bumper cars were the sum total of her personal experience with driving, so Mindy's driver's education was essentially starting from scratch. She began preparations by memorizing every page of the driver's manual, then informed her father, "I'm ready for the road."

He announced, "If you're going to drive, you have to learn on a manual transmission first."

Mindy couldn't resist offering a sarcastic, "What's a manual transmission?" But the joke would be on her.

The first lesson turned out to be a short but wild ride. It was a smooth start out of the driveway and a right turn onto Ellington but, preoccupied with shifting gears, Mindy failed to look up or straighten the wheel and did an immediate U-turn into the chain-link fence along the street. Classmate Ricky Hire was an unplanned witness to the scene and dubbed Mindy a tongue-in-cheek "Mustang Mama," a nickname that stuck for the remainder of her days in Lafayette.

Subsequent lessons took place on weekends in the empty Carter parking where Mindy put many miles on the Mustang without ever driving on the street. Once she had parallel parking down cold, she hit the open road and had no further problems. She felt ready to take on the world.

————————— · —————————

The cafeteria discussion with Anne had narrowed their emotional distance but had not closed it. Anne remained distant at school, still didn't answer the phone, and didn't respond to messages. Subliminal anger over Anne's betrayal and the potential beating it had invoked lingered in Mindy's memory. Worse, Anne's allusions to drugs and sex made it clear to Mindy that they were on different paths, and Anne's path scared her. But Mindy couldn't escape her guilt related to Anne's expulsion from the cheer team and the subsequent problems it may have caused. She felt certain others had misinterpreted her report of Anne's pills as passing her drugs.

By nature, Mindy was forgiving and such thoughts and feelings were very uncomfortable. So, Mindy considered it fortuitous when her mother informed her the last week of February, "Mrs. Belle and I were at the Garden Club Meeting today, and we agreed to help with a March of Dimes charity. Everyone thought it would be a good thing to get our daughters involved in, so I signed you up to do a door-to-door collection with Anne."

A few days later, Mindy found Anne sitting alone in the quiet stands of the school gym. Anne looked lonely, and the image made Mindy's heart sink.

Full of uncertainty, Mindy took a seat whispering distance away, and they spoke earnestly and contritely. After a deep breath, Mindy confessed the story of the pills and the role they may have played in Anne's expulsion from the cheer team. Anne laughed and assured her, "There were other things. Trust me, I deserved my punishment."

Anne paused in thought and then laughed again. "You know, what you said about the pills explains something. I got a call last fall. It was from a girl, but I didn't know who it was. She just yelled at me for drugging her friend. She said, 'You could have really hurt her.' I didn't have any idea what she was talking about and wondered if maybe she'd called the wrong number. Before I could say anything, she hung up."

Mindy buried her head in her hands. "That was after the slumber party at Cathy's house. It was from Beverly. She told me she'd called you about the pills, but I didn't know she made it sound so bad. I told her she shouldn't have done that. She knew I was mad."

They continued to talk, and the walls of hurt, anger, and mistrust eroded. They agreed to do the March of Dimes collection together and to start their friendship anew. Mindy sensed Anne was genuinely happy to have salvaged their friendship and felt relieved. They smiled and shared a warm, caring hug. Mindy walked away at peace with Anne and looking forward to rebuilding their friendship.

Most sons and daughters of white-collar workers and small business owners in and around Lafayette were members of the high school extension of the local Rotary Club chapter known as the Interact Club. They didn't meet often, but Mindy enjoyed the social interaction it offered. As a bonus, delegates of the club got to attend a two-day conference with members of clubs from all over Tennessee, which provided a welcome break from the dreary late-winter weather and the monotony of school. The 1974 Tennessee convention was being held in a ritzy Chattanooga hotel and filled club members with anticipation.

Randy called the Thursday evening before Mindy's departure with far more energy in his voice than usual, and it didn't take Mindy long to understand why. He cleared his throat and took a deep breath. "I wanted to ask before you leave for the conference. I know you're not allowed to date until your sixteenth birthday, but do you think it would be okay with your parents if I take you to the All-Sports Banquet?"

Trying to hide her excitement, Mindy replied, "I would like that, but I'll have to check with my parents." She knew she would be hell to live with if they denied her.

"I'll miss seeing you at school tomorrow," Randy whispered.

Mindy tingled all over and danced alone in her room for several minutes after the call, then gathered her composure and quietly discussed the banquet with her mother in the kitchen. "I'll discuss it with your father," was the gist of her mother's response, but Mindy could read the answer in her eyes. She returned to her room with visions of fancy dresses and grand pageantry rolling through her mind.

———

Bolstered by her parent's approval to attend the All-Sports Banquet with Randy, Mindy confronted them after dinner later that week. "The All-Sports Banquet is less than a month away, and my birthday is less than six weeks away. What difference are a few weeks going to make? Why can't I start dating now?" Her parents shared eye contact and had no immediate counter, so hesitantly gave their consent.

The next day at school, Mindy wasted no time in making it clear to many, especially Randy, that she had received approval to go out on car dates. Fully expecting to hear from Randy that evening, she waited anxiously near her phone for a call that never came. When Randy called the next evening, he made no allusion to a pre-banquet date.

By Thursday, Mindy had given up hope when the phone rang at about 8:30 PM. "Randy never calls this late," she thought before answering on the fourth ring and was surprised to hear Bob Hackett's voice at the other end of the line. A senior and friend of Randy's, Mindy was more surprised when Bob got right to the point. "Would you like to go out tomorrow? Maybe grab a burger at Clifton's, then do a little cruisin' around town?"

It didn't sound very romantic, but it was a car date. Without the slightest hesitation, Mindy agreed, pending final approval from her parents. She hung up, feeling excited about her first date, but a little perturbed Randy hadn't offered first. When Mindy informed her mother, she furrowed her brow to ask, "What about Randy?"

Mindy hadn't considered any ramifications. She shrugged her shoulders and smugly replied, "He didn't ask," then promptly turned and marched back to her room.

Near the end of an otherwise typical hallway meeting the next day at school, Randy cleared his throat before nervously inquiring, "Would you like to go out Saturday night? Maybe get somethin' ta eat, then cruise a bit?"

Mindy replied with noticeable excitement, "That sounds like fun. I'd like that."

That afternoon, Mindy's mother was somewhat aghast with the news. "Just because we said you *could* go out doesn't mean you *have* to go out *every* night! My goodness, what have we unleashed upon the world?" That evening, Mindy laughed out loud as she wrote her mother's words in her diary.

By 7:00 PM on Friday evening, Mindy had been ready for over an hour. In fact, except for a few final strokes with her hairbrush, she had been ready since shortly after arriving home from school. Preparation hadn't taken long: wash face, brush teeth, and change into a white blouse and maroon polyester bell-bottoms with a striped white diamond design and matching blazer. The only pause was to review in her own mind that she hadn't worn this combination to school before. There was no plucking of eyebrows, no curling of eyelashes, and definitely no make-up.

The sight of Bob's car in the driveway sent Mindy to wait patiently in the foyer. When the doorbell rang, Mindy sprang to the door but opened it slowly to invite Bob in. "Good evening. It's a pleasure to see you. Won't you please come in?" As the words passed her lips, she had a flash of Eliza Doolittle reciting, "The rain in Spain falls mainly in the plain." She felt an urge to curtsy but didn't.

Bob stepped into the foyer, sauntering like a king and wearing a broad smile bookended by a pair of glowing cheeks. He wore a well-worn blue denim shirt with white piping that stretched tight across his chest, bulging slightly between the buttons. His flared Levi jeans looked newer and were complemented by a wide, silver-studded white belt and recently polished brown cowboy boots adorned his feet. Mindy had no difficulty reading his happiness to be in her company.

As Bob followed Mindy to the kitchen for an introduction to her parents, the heavy scent of Brut after-shave permeated the air. Mindy's father didn't have much to say as he mumbled, "Hi, Bob" through a mouthful of ice cream and walked away.

Mindy's mother was more talkative and greeted Bob pleasantly, but her trembling hands revealed her anxiety as she instructed, "This is Mindy's first date. We don't want her to be out late. She has a curfew."

In the car moments later, Mindy's fantasy image of her first date evolved from that of a proper Englishman into Joe Buck from *Midnight Cowboy.* Bob wasn't her ideal "Mystery Date" and wasn't, of course, Randy, but right then none of that mattered. She was just excited to be going on a date, *a car date*, for the first time.

In anticipation of eating at Clifton's, Mindy had skipped dinner with her family and was starving by the time they left Ellington. But it didn't take long to realize that there had been some miscommunication when Bob said he'd already eaten and planned to get only a shake at Clifton's. So, Mindy felt a little embarrassed, and Bob seemed surprised when she ordered a fried chicken meal. She offered to pay, but Bob scoffed at the thought. He did, however, do most of the talking between sips of his chocolate malt. When the waitress came by to clear the table, she complimented Mindy on her outfit, and they shared a brief conversation about clothes and styles.

They sat and talked more. Mindy gradually relaxed, and Bob did the same. But it was soon apparent they shared limited common ground, and the conversation hit several dead ends. After a long, uncomfortable silence, Bob nervously suggested they start cruising, and Mindy readily agreed.

Bob was courteous but, like Bud and Ricky, he simply didn't capture Mindy's imagination. The excitement of this first date lay not with him but with the "out there" beyond the confines of the car and in the mystery of what the next scene would bring.

Suddenly, Randy's face flashed in Mindy's mind, and she trembled ever so slightly. "What if we cross paths with Randy? What will I do? Why didn't I think of this before?" she wondered.

A half-dozen laps around town proved it to be a quiet night, and the excitement of "out there" quickly waned. When they pulled into the Village Market around 8:30 PM, the absence of other cars indicated the evening was over and Mindy suggested she should get home early on her first date.

Bob hesitantly agreed, "Well, I promised your mother I'd have you home early anyway."

It took only minutes to return to Ellington. As the car came to a stop, a wave of uncertainty prompted Mindy to preempt any driveway conversation. "Well, thanks. It was fun, but I'd better get inside," she said, then jumped out of the car. Bob followed hurriedly behind as Mindy moved toward the front door. Reaching the front porch, she stopped and turned to block Bob from following her to the door. Mindy shuddered to find intoxicated, innocent desire in his eyes.

Before now, Mindy hadn't given a moment's thought to the last minutes of her first car date. Now she worried he might try to kiss her goodnight. She gasped and jumped back when he leaned toward her to do just that. Retreating to the front door, she turned the doorknob to crack it open for safety, then said, "Thanks again," over her shoulder before escaping inside.

She stopped short when Bob said enthusiastically, "Let's go out again sometime."

Mindy looked down at her saddle-shoes and responded, "I'd better get in." Bob stood frozen as Mindy slowly closed the door and waited several seconds to let him make his way to the car before switching off the porch light.

Mindy didn't give Bob another thought. He would call each of the subsequent three weeks asking for another date, but Mindy did her best to gently extinguish his fire. "Sorry. I'm busy."

–––––––––––––– · ––––––––––––––

Mindy showered early the next day to give her long hair plenty of time to dry before Randy's arrival. The previous night's date with Bob had already disappeared into the deepest recesses of her mind as she prepared with great anticipation for her next venture into the dating world.

After slipping into one of many mother-made polyester pantsuit options along with her favorite saddle shoes, Mindy realized she was ready way too early. Too restless to sit in her room, she paced through the front of the house, peeking out the windows repeatedly. Just before 6 PM, she dashed to her bedroom for a few strokes of a brush through her hair. To her surprise, she found Randy in the foyer with her mother when she returned. She thought he looked sharp in a blue-and white-print polyester shirt with a wide collar, complemented by cuffed, navy-blue slacks and a wide white belt. Then it struck her; he seemed much taller than at school. She furrowed her brow and looked down at his feet to note a pair of brand-new patent leather platform shoes on his feet. A few seconds later, Randy's personal "Brut Cloud" overtook her and replayed clips of Joe Namath Brut commercials in her mind.

Recapturing her senses, Mindy motioned toward the kitchen where she introduced her new date to her father. With a mouth full of ice cream, he said "Hi" in acknowledgment, then walked away. Mindy's mother had recovered from the trauma of her daughter's first date the evening before and attempted to use her gift of gab to probe for insight into Randy's personality, but couldn't coax him past one or two-word responses. As the questioning continued, Mindy sensed Randy's growing unease, so interrupted the interrogation, and they left.

Randy skipped ahead to hold open the front door as Mindy exited and did the same for the front passenger door of his car. These simple acts made Mindy's skin tingle with pleasure.

Mutual nervous excitement spiked when Randy started the car, and both sat rigidly with eyes fixed forward as they drove. Groping for words, Mindy attempted to loosen the silent gridlock by asking where they were going for dinner. "I thought we talked about Clifton's," replied Randy.

"Oh, yeah. I knew that," said Mindy, and they both laughed.

The waitress at Clifton's gave Mindy a confused double-take as she took their orders. When the waitress paused, Mindy could read the question in her mind and cut it off with a subtle, wide-eyed shake of her head. The waitress nodded and walked away with raised eyebrows and a shake of her own head.

As the fast-food gradually disappeared, teen nervousness waned, and their conversation flowed more freely. They talked about school, classmates, the upcoming All-Sports Banquet, and graduation. Mindy inquired in some detail about Randy's plans for college. He explained he planned to take agricultural and practical business courses at Vol (Volunteer) State Community College for two years before working on the farm full time. He hoped to inherit at least part of his father's farm, but he knew additional acres would be necessary to make a living. Mindy froze for a moment. "Wow," she thought, "he's going to graduate next month. He's a lot closer to the real world and adult responsibility than I am." She felt happy to still be just a kid in school.

Silence ensued when they finished eating and continued until Randy suggested they hit the cruise circuit. He surprised Mindy by driving one full lap without stopping just to assess the overall scene. After a few more laps, Mindy realized the circuit would be unexciting for the second night in a row. With no alternate plan, Randy announced, "I should probably get you home early on your first date. I want your parents to trust me, and we'll have a lot more dates to do other stuff."

Mindy cringed with mild guilt but agreed, and before 8 PM they returned to Ellington. Stopping the car, sliding the transmission into park and turning off the ignition in one motion, Randy commanded, "Wait!" as he leaped from the car to open the passenger door. Strolling down the front walkway, each gave a nervous report of how much fun they had and how they were looking forward to the upcoming banquet.

Pausing on the front porch, Mindy thought, "He's a gentleman. He won't expect a kiss on the first date, and I wouldn't want to seem cheap by kissing on a first date." When Randy leaned forward, Mindy panicked, opened the door and stepped into the foyer. She looked over her shoulder to say, "Thanks again."

Standing frozen in the foyer, Mindy wondered if she was actually floating when her mother appeared to ask how the date had gone and if she had a good time. Answering with a dreamy nod in the affirmative, Mindy described what a gentleman Randy had been, and having doors opened for her became a foundation of her vision of romanticism. That simple act had made the evening unique all by itself and fueled her anticipation for the following weekend.

After recounting a detailed description of the evening in her diary, Mindy crawled into bed feeling happy and fell asleep with a smile.

———————— ı ————————

A protracted cold front kept the air chilly and dreary through the last week of March. Mindy sat with the rest of the student body in a midday assembly about nothing important when she saw the Administrative Secretary waving to get her attention and then motioning for her to come down from the stands. As they stepped into the hallway outside the gym, the secretary seemed distressed as she informed Mindy that her mother was waiting for her outside in the car. Mindy assumed that an eye or dentist appointment had slipped her mind. She stopped by her locker to get books and slipped on her wool cheerleading sweater, then skipped her way toward the main entrance.

Rain fell as Mindy slid into the front seat. As soon as she clicked her seat belt, her mother started the car but didn't put it into gear. The rain fell harder and her mother sighed. With sad eyes, she spoke gently. "I'm sorry, but I have some awful news. Anne is dead. She killed herself last night."

Mindy stared in disbelief but read reality in her mother's eyes. Overwhelmed by crushing sadness, she slumped limply forward. "No! No, no, no!"

Touching Mindy's arm lightly, her mother whispered, "I'm so sorry. I know you were good friends."

Mindy's mind and heart raced, hoping there had been a mistake. Tears started slowly, then flowed heavily down her cheeks as overwhelming guilt devoured her heart. "This is my fault. I should have seen something like this coming and got help. I should have been a better friend," she cried.

Rain fell harder. Mindy wondered, "Why? How could someone so young feel such despair that they would take their own life?" She could find no answers. Mixing youth and death didn't make sense.

Her mother offered no other details, and Mindy didn't ask. It was too late, details didn't matter. They pulled away from school for the short drive home, and a new river of tears began when they passed Anne's street. It would be thirty-two years before Mindy would travel down that street again.

Alone in her bedroom, Mindy lay on her bed with eyes swollen and red. Saturated tissues in her hand could absorb no more and the ring of tears grew ever larger on her pillow. A light knock came at the door, and her mother entered without waiting for a response. Taking a seat on the edge of the bed, she gently rubbed Mindy's back. "It's my fault!" cried Mindy as she buried her face in her hands.

"Why do you say that?" asked her mother.

"Because—" But the words wouldn't come out. Convinced that Anne's expulsion from cheer team was at the root of this tragedy, Mindy felt responsible for the start of her fall. What she now considered silly and exaggerated anger about Anne's betrayal and talk of drugs and sex, compounded her sense of guilt. Those concerns were real, but seemed so unimportant now. "I should have done more. I should have been a better friend." Mindy wept into her wet, tissue-filled hands.

Patting Mindy's back, her mother attempted to console. "It's not your fault. Anne had problems long before we moved here." Her mother didn't expound, and Mindy was too distraught to understand her meaning. It just didn't seem to matter.

After a kiss to Mindy's forehead, her mother said. "I am so sorry for your loss. Be patient. The pain will lessen with time but will never go away. Carrying happy memories of the days you shared. Those are the ones that will keep her living in your heart."

An hour later, there was another soft knock at the door. Mindy sat up to see Patty taking a seat on the bed. They shared a hug as they cried, then fell back on the bed, physically and emotionally exhausted.

"Why? Why did this happen?" Mindy cried. But Patty had no answers. As darkness filled the room, Mindy's mother returned with soup and sandwiches. After coaxing the girls to take a few bites, she left them alone, and they ate no more.

The phone rang. A moment later, Mindy's door cracked open again, and her mother whispered, "Its Randy. Would you like to take it now, or should I have him call back later?"

Mindy dabbed her eyes, blew her nose, and did the best she could to gather her composure before lifting the phone from its cradle to say a strained, "Hello."

"I'm sorry about Anne," Randy said. "How are you doing?"

"I'm okay, I guess," Mindy managed. "I'll just be glad when the day is over. It's just too hard to believe."

Randy did his best to offer comforting words and asked if she'd like him to come over.

Mindy didn't hesitate. "No. Patty is here. She's a big help, but thank you for the offer."

After a moment of painful silence, Randy said, "Well, call me if there's anything I can do to help." Mindy heard a pleading tone in his voice that gave her reason to pause, but overwhelmed by grief she didn't understand and couldn't muster the strength to say "thanks" or "goodbye," so quietly dropped the handset into the cradle.

Patty spent the night, and Mindy was glad to have her company. The temperature fell along with the sun, and the girls crawled fully clothed under the covers. In the cold, quiet darkness, Mindy's sorrow grew. She silently asked, "God, why did you let this happen?" but received no reply. Only the exhausted unconsciousness of sleep could relieve her heartache.

———————————————

Already awake as the last vestiges of the night gave way to dawn, Mindy lay quietly listening to Patty's heavy breathing. Questions without answers still dominated her thoughts, but the pale sky was a welcome reminder that a new day was forthcoming. Mindy took a deep breath and whispered to herself, "I've lived through tough days before. I'll do it again."

Chilled by her tear-soaked blouse, Mindy made her way to the shower. The warm water felt good but offered no baptismal cleansing, and tears flowed once more.

Eventually gathering her strength, she dried her eyes, dressed and took a seat alone at the kitchen table. Her eyes drifted to the back window and fixed on the trees standing like giants in the yard. The slightest hint of green was visible in the young buds at the tips of the branches. She wondered, "How old are those trees? Two times, five times, maybe even ten times older than Anne will ever be?"

Patty emerged from the dark hallway to deliver a morning hug and offer reassurance. "Would you like me to stay?"

Mindy sighed. "No. But thanks for being here last night."

It was a long day. Mindy received a few phone calls from concerned friends with each offering sorrowful condolences. They seemed to understand that Mindy and Anne had shared a special connection.

The hours ticked by and Mindy's mind spun looking for answers but found none. Anne had left no note. Her mother had found her lying in bed when she didn't get up for school. An overdose of one of her mother's discontinued heart medications had apparently induced death. No other information or explanation ever came to light.

That night, Mindy sat at her desk for a long time before opening the top drawer. She cleared some cluttered pens and paper to reach to a far corner where her diary lay face down. With fingers stuck on the etched letters on the cover, she scolded herself for being neglectful of it over the previous weeks, but writing something in it now seemed like the right thing to do. Tears welled in her eyes as she wrote:

Dear Diary,
Anne died yesterday. I feel like it is my fault. I am so
very sorry. There is so much to say, but I just can't
say it right now.

Preparing for bed, Mindy realized her habit of bedtime prayer had waned considerably in recent months, and triggered a resurgence of guilt. She got down on her knees and prayed longer than she ever had. But neither ears nor soul received any divine message of forgiveness or support. She understood she would have to work through any recovery on her own.

Friday afternoon, Mindy attended the funeral service with her mother. Harsh reality struck again as they stepped through the doorway from which the open casket was visible. Frightened and hoping to deny the presence of death, Mindy veered away, but her mother gently redirected her into the viewing line. The short procession moved quickly. Mindy's stomach churned, and her heart ached more with each step. In turn, they paused in front of the casket.

Anne lay with her small hands folded across a powder-blue dress Mindy had never seen her wear. She studied Anne's pale, lifeless face and felt the urge to scream, "Wait! Stop! She's not ready! They didn't fix her eyebrows or get her makeup right!"

With a soft gasp, tears flowed once more. Her mother gently tugged Mindy's arm, and they moved away.

The service was brief. There were no personal statements, no funny stories, no reminiscing. "What could anyone possibly say?" Mindy wondered.

The only spoken words came from the minister: a few Bible passages and prefabricated expressions of loss. They were words designed to lessen the pain and claim "she's in a better place." But for Mindy, all the holy declarations rang hollow. They were short sound bites composed of empty words that sounded good on the surface, but seemed devoid of substance. They changed nothing and relieved no pain. She thought, "Life after death is no consolation for one so young and so much life in the world ahead of her. What happened was a mistake." Then she realized that *never* and *forever* were two words that described the same very long period of time. At that moment, they both sounded cold, black, and lonely.

Patty rode with Mindy in the back seat during the procession to the cemetery with tears flowing uncontrollably. The interment service was also brief, and attendees disbanded with only whispered condolences to Anne's parents. There was no mention of happy times or good memories; no smiles or jokes about a life lived to its fullest. Only words of sorrow and loss.

After the service, Mindy spent a few quiet, contemplative hours alone at home. She wondered what Anne's future may have held but could only envision the window at the psychiatric facility; barred, meshed, and opaque.

"And what about *my* future?" Mindy wondered. She envisioned blue skies, personal fulfillment, and bountiful happiness and felt unfairly lucky. She pulled out her diary, studied the saddle shoe cover for a moment, then wrote:

Dear Diary,
I will be the most important decision maker in my
life. My choices will influence my future. I should
always try to make good decisions, but I know it
will be hard sometimes.

She only partially understood how difficult good decision-making could be with clouded vision or if misguided by misinformation and poor advice.

A soft knock on the bedroom door interrupted her musings. "Just a second," she hollered, then quickly closed her diary and stuffed it face down into its usual hiding place.

Her mother took a seat on the corner of the bed to inquire calmly, "Would you like to practice driving?"

Mindy was doubtful. "With you? Now? In the Bonneville?"

Her mother nodded, and before long, they were heading west on Westmoreland Road.

Mindy had never driven a full-size car and had never gone over 45mph, so the weight and power of the Bonneville shifted her focus from tragedy. The trip went smoothly until she approached a large, slow-moving tractor that obscured the road ahead. Uncertain how to proceed, frustration set in and she suggested they turn back. But her mother insisted they continue on. "As long as we live here, you will deal with these kinds of hazards. It's best to start learning now."

Mindy was hesitant. It was a risk she didn't feel prepared to take, but her mother encouraged her to pass.

After reviewing her approach, Mindy waited patiently for a relatively straight stretch of road. She checked ahead, then behind, then double-checked ahead before punching the accelerator with more force than necessary. The car lurched forward into the passing lane and pushed Mindy into the seat. With white knuckles gripping the wheel, she zoomed past the tractor and felt out of control. Her mother soothingly suggested she slow down. Mindy let up on the accelerator, took a breath, and forced the car back into the right lane. It took several miles for her vise grip on the wheel to relax, and blood flow returned to her knuckles. They turned around in Westmoreland, and the return drive was far more confident.

The weight of grief kept Mindy in bed much later than usual Saturday morning, and she felt too drained to answer the phone. When she finally emerged from her bedroom around noon, her mother informed her Randy had called twice. "He wanted to know if he could come over. I told him you were still in bed and to call back this afternoon."

When the phone rang again that afternoon, Mindy was hesitant to answer but gave in on the fifth ring. She wanted to be alone, but Randy pleaded with her, "I'd really like to see you today. How about we just drive around or maybe get some ice cream after dinner?" The longing in his voice and his need to offer support convinced Mindy to agree.

The greeting was subdued, and the drive began quietly, but Mindy appreciated Randy's caring tone. The heaviness in her heart lessened slightly as they drove two nonstop laps around the cruise circuit before Randy suggested they stop for ice cream. Although she wasn't hungry, Mindy nodded in agreement. When Randy pulled into a kid-packed parking lot at Jones's, Mindy recoiled. She didn't want to talk with others, so remained quietly seated in the car.

Randy must have sensed her unease and attempted to connect, but made the mistake of mentioning Anne. Without warning, what felt like a ton of pressure came out of nowhere and left Mindy gasping for breath. "I'm sitting here with a guy who treats me well," she thought, "but Anne will never have the chance to primp for another date."

A single tear left a glistening track down her cheek. Randy nervously apologized and reached over to wipe it away. Mindy forced a smile and suggested they keep driving.

During the next lap, they passed several cars carrying couples. Mindy noticed, as she had many times before, that the girls tended to sit snugly next to the driver, whose right arm draped across the girl's shoulders. The romantic vision had made Mindy tingle in the past but, steeped in sadness, she didn't want to see other people's happiness and asked, "Does anyone ever change the cruising route and go somewhere new?"

Randy considered the question and then flatly replied, "I don't think so." Mindy could hear the unspoken tagline, "Why would anyone do that?"

Sensing mounting tension in Mindy's demeanor, Randy seemed to surprise even himself as he drove right past Clifton's and continued east toward Red Boiling Springs. The unexpected path caught Mindy's attention and prompted her to sit tall in her seat. Seconds later, they were outside the city limit, and Randy turned to ask, "Well, is this better?" Mindy nodded with eyes focused ahead.

Randy captured her full attention a few seconds later when he suggested, "Scoot over here," with a wave of his hand.

Mindy flushed with uncertainty but did as requested and slid into the middle of the bench seat. A moment later, her eyes popped when she felt the hesitant weight of Randy's arm as it draped across her shoulders. Absorbing the sensation, Mindy sat silently. A quarter mile later, she sensed Randy's staring eyes, and her cheeks burned hot.

In those few seconds, the car drifted over the centerline. Looking forward, Mindy stiffened and pointed ahead to oncoming traffic in the distance. There was no real danger, but Randy gasped and jerked the wheel to swerve back into his lane. He gasped again when he glanced into the rearview mirror and said, "Oh, no — it's a cop."

Mindy shifted back into the passenger seat and looked over her shoulder to see flashing lights bearing down on them.

Randy pulled onto the shoulder, and the officer seemed to wait a long time before switching on a blinding searchlight. He approached the driver's door with a flashlight held high in one hand and an aluminum clipboard in the other. Randy nervously rolled down the window, and the officer peered in to study the occupants. "Son, you been drinkin'?" he inquired.

"No! No, sir. We're just out for a drive," Randy anxiously replied, growing pale.

"Well, it 'pears you be havin' trouble negotiatin' the centa-line," the officer pressured.

Shifting his flashlight directly into Mindy's eyes, the officer inquired, "And who might you be, young lady?" Ducking away from the sharp light, Mindy stated her name. The officer squinted with vague recognition. "You Cha-ly Murph's daughta? From the Cotta Plant?" Mindy nodded in affirmation.

The officer paused his interrogation for a moment and then turned back to Randy. "Well, son, I kin understand that it might be hard to watch the road with a pretty young thing next to ya. But y'all need ta be keepin' more eye on the road 'n less on yer pass-in-jah. Git along now 'n drive safe." He tipped his hat, returned to his car, and the flashing emergency lights promptly extinguished.

Relieved but shaken, Randy pulled back onto the road but took the first opportunity to make a U-turn and bring the adventure into alternative cruising territory to an abrupt end. By the time they reentered the Lafayette city limits, Randy's shakes had subsided, but Mindy had no difficulty convincing him to call it an early evening.

———————— · ————————

At church the next day, Mindy prayed harder than she ever had but still received no divine words of forgiveness or guidance.

The return to school on Monday was difficult, but it surprised Mindy to find an atmosphere that seemed oblivious to the tragedy. Nothing seemed to have changed. The same boys still joked in the hallway. The same clicks of girls stood in tight groups whispering about some boy. The same loners walked by themselves. No one spoke a single word to her or within earshot of her about Anne at school — that week or ever. There was no counseling, no debriefing and, incredibly, no gossiping. A new student or visitor would never have known that a terrible tragedy had recently occurred. "But this is Lafayette. Everybody has to know what happened. Don't they care?" Mindy wondered.

Walking home alone that afternoon, Mindy paused near Sullivan's Pond and remembered the fiery spirit Anne had shown with her girlish toss the last time they were there. She wondered how that flame had been smothered in just a few short months. Mindy remembered Anne's distant looks, strange behavior, and labile emotions. She recalled her mother's allusion to Anne's past problems and sensed that there was much more to Anne's story. It was a story that didn't seem to matter to anyone else, and she feared it would be lost. Mindy yelled at the pond, hoping Anne would hear her words, "But it does, it does matter! Things like this should never happen. Not ever!"

Continuing the trek, she and Anne had shared so many times before, Mindy paused at the turn for Anne's house. She took a deep breath, waved goodbye, then resumed her return home.

Mindy pulled the last ice cream sandwich from the freezer and took a seat on the steps just outside the patio door. She carefully removed the wrapper from the cold treat and took a bigger bite than usual. Staring into the yard, she thought, "Today and every day will be what I make of it. I want to make this a good day." She spread the mix of vanilla ice cream and chocolate pastry over her front teeth with her tongue and then bared them to the sky in Anne's honor, imagining that she could hear Anne's girlish laugh.

That night, Mindy sat at her desk and played the previous week's events through her mind. She knew her life would never be the same, then studied the cover of her diary with reverence. After several minutes, she opened it to the next blank page and wrote:

Dear Diary,
This day, this moment, this very second is important and,
even if not perfect, I should treat it with respect.

And what is good, Phaedrus,
And what is not good —
Need we ask anyone to tell us these things?
Robert Pirsig, *Zen and the Art of Motorcycle Maintenance:*
An Inquiry into Values

Part II

She studied the scenery as they approached the small middle-Tennessee town that had been home for two-and-a-half years, but struggled to capture visual recognition. When she mentioned it, he reminded her they were approaching from the west on Highway 52 instead of Highway 10 from the south. The Highway 52 Bypass project was just getting started when her family moved back to Missouri in 1975. She was traveling to her old town on a new road. "Things change the day you leave. You can never really go back," drifted through her mind. Her old town had other surprises: electric stoplights, a new motel, new restaurants, an indoor movie theater, and a Super Walmart.

They drove the old teen cruise circuit and made brief stops at various landmarks. Like cruising of the past, the tour didn't take long, even with questions and commentary on how many things had changed. Clifton's, closed and abandoned for over two decades, stood deserted with broken glass covering the parking lot as if to serve warning for old romantics to stay away. Jones's was almost unrecognizable with the old parking lot filled with junked cars, and The Village Market stood empty. It was hard to believe the lifeless shells that remained were once teen hotspots where rural life bubbled, and hormones raged. Once an energetic small business hub, the town square was sprinkled with only a few cars but no pedestrians in sight. It looked old and worn with several shops unoccupied, and windows boarded. The spit and whittle benches were gone; their former occupants buried years previous. The old high school was now a grade school and looked so much smaller than in her memories. As signs of 21st Century progress, a new high school had been built on the outskirts of town, and Sullivan's Pond is now maintained by the city with pretty aquamarine dye instead of its natural chocolate brown water. The house on Ellington looked the same, except the chain-link fence along the street had been removed, and the forest of trees surrounding it had been thinned.

She navigated as he drove with wide eyes, absorbing the details of his vision and her words. For him, hours and hours of conversation about his wife's roots had made everything about this town seem surreal. With each passing block and each turn, his contrived mental images were replaced by snapshots of real places. He attempted to repaint pictures in his mind to remove the wear and tear of time and see the town as it might have appeared in the 1970s. For her, vibrations of past events still seemed to hover invisibly in the air, and passing through them produced a barrage of memories, both good and bad.

Their musings on the potentially dangerous happenings, the culture that supported them and how she emerged from it thirty years previous prompted thoughtful contemplation and opened many doors of soul sharing discussion.

"I suspect your life and time here would have been much different had I lived here with you."

"Oh, don't I know that."

"I wish I had been here to be your friend when you needed one."

"That would have been nice, but it still worked out okay. Don't you think?"

"Yeah, it worked out fine, but it makes me tremble. No, it scares me to think it could have so easily gone another way. If you had made other decisions, it's likely you wouldn't have been the same person on the day we met. We might not have stuck the way we did. And that really scares me. Thankfully, you made good decisions at crucial times, and survived some challenges many other girls, probably the majority, wouldn't have. We're all at risk, in one way or another, whenever we walk out the door. It doesn't matter if it's a small town or a big city. What's different in your case is the significant cultural risk you faced. During a vulnerable point in your life, you faced cultural norms and expectations that lessened the value of young girls and encouraged them to give themselves away before they had a chance to see or experience life beyond the county line. Too many weren't encouraged to seek academic goals beyond high school or to explore the world. It was an incestuous culture designed for isolated survivalist mentality instead of encouraging personal and intellectual growth and, at least in the past, blinded many of its residents to the world beyond its local borders. More young girls than any care to admit got screwed by an older guy in a tobacco field, and their lives were changed forever — and not in a good way. The bottom line is the lost

94

opportunity and less fulfilling lives for far too many kids. Undoubtedly, it was teen girls who, as a group, paid the highest price. With that, I'll get off the soapbox."

"I was always going to go to college. Even if my parents had stayed here, I wouldn't have been back except for occasional visits. I knew there was more to the world and had to see it and experience it. I had to find you, even if you drive me nuts sometimes."

Chapter 6
Implosion
April 2–30, 1974

For Mindy, the dust of tragedy still hung heavily in the air and life resisted a return to normal. Lost in the sadness was the pre-sixteenth birthday All-Sports Banquet formal; the anticipation of which precipitated the return of uncertain smiles across Mindy's lips. But laughter was rare, and it would be many weeks before phone calls or conversations with friends regained their usual carefree teenage tone.

Although the All-Sports Banquet was the most modest of formal affairs, it was a major annual event for the student-athletes. The ceremony and buffet dinner took place in the school cafeteria, but paper tablecloths, dimmed lights, crepe paper streamers, and balloons added color to underscored the specialness of the occasion. The highlight of the evening was usually a guest speaker, typically an assistant coach, from a nearby college or junior college. It didn't matter that few, if any, of the students were familiar with them.

Much to her seamstress mother's silent disappointment, Mindy wore a long powder blue gown with a ruffled collar and empire waist purchased at J. C. Penney. But when Mindy walked out from her room, her mother had to admit, "Oh, my — you look pretty as a princess and graceful like a queen."

Randy arrived in his church suit, and Mindy thought he looked quite handsome. He presented a boxed white mum as big and heavy as a fist in hand and nervously handed it to Mindy's mother, admitting, "I'm not sure how to pin it on."

As pretty as it was, the mum was too big and way too bulky for the lightweight fabric of Mindy's dress. Despite several attempts, the dense corsage would sag and expose her bra strap. For all present, this, of course, would never do. So, Mindy erased everyone's anxiety, "I'll just carry it."

Mindy felt embarrassed when she forgot the mum on the seat of the car, and a bold underclassman openly chastised Randy for neglecting his date, "Man, you didn't even get her flowers! If she were my date, I would have got her a dozen roses!" Randy dropped his head in defeat.

The evening was otherwise pleasant. Mindy clapped loudest when Randy received his football letter, and he reciprocated when she received one for cheerleader. The closing speech and farewell prayer brought the evening to an end before 9 PM. Seniors said heavy goodbyes. For them, the glory days of high school sports were at an end. Although most students were dressed up and ready to party, the lack of options and the paucity of imagination brought the evening to an early end.

Randy drove slowly from school to Ellington, and Mindy waited patiently for him to open her door. He escorted her to the front porch where they exchanged pleasantries under the glow of the porch light until Randy hit an embarrassing verbal roadblock. Mute, he stared at Mindy with star-struck eyes until Mindy blushed as well and he nervously announced, "I wanted to give you somethin' — somethin' of mine." Suddenly too nervous to maintain eye contact, Mindy turned away with an uncertain breath, almost afraid of what was coming next. Randy continued, "I wanted to give you my letter sweater to wear at school." Mindy felt lighter, and her heart fluttered with romantic surprise as her mind filled with visions of other girls wearing a boy's letter sweater at school; they always seemed so happy and proud. But the bubble burst when Randy remorsefully concluded, "But my mom says I paid too much for it to give it away. I'd still really like for you to have it sometime." Mindy exhaled softly, feeling far more relief than disappointment.

The sorrow in Randy's eyes made Mindy's skin tingle all over. But when he leaned forward to deliver a kiss, she felt overwhelmed with the need to escape. She stepped to safety through the front door and said softly, "Thanks again. See you at school." The door clicked shut.

Shortened by a four-day Easter break, the next week of school passed quickly. Mindy wasn't sure why, but she kept phone calls with Randy that week short. They did, however, make plans for a car date with a new twist; an out-of-town double date with Randy's best friend, Craig Brooks, and his longtime girlfriend who, of all people, was Judy Green.

Since the threatened beating, Mindy and Judy had shared only the most superficial interaction at school. Judy had been polite but initiated no conversation or apology. Mindy never mentioned the threat to anyone and sensed that Judy appreciated this, but it didn't make them any closer. Mindy was uncertain how their chemistry would mix in the narrow confines of a car, but she planned to take the high road should any trouble arise.

The rendezvous with Craig and Judy at the Village Market belayed much of Mindy's anxiety. Judy greeted her as if they were long-lost friends while Craig and Randy had a brief discussion about who would drive. Apparently, the longevity of Craig's relationship with Judy made him the ranking male, and he ended up behind the wheel. So, Mindy and Randy loaded themselves into the back seat and seconds later the foursome began the forty-minute trek to Gallatin.

The pretty countryside was spring-time green and dotted with dogwood trees in full bloom. Judy was pleasant and talkative, but Mindy wondered if it would last. "Will she talk to me at school now? Will she even admit to Pam and Barb that she went on a double-date with me and had a good time? How will she expect *me* to treat *her* at school now?"

It surprised Mindy to learn that Judy and Craig had been dating for over two years and, although not officially engaged, they planned to marry not long after Judy's high school graduation. The concept of marriage at such a young age made Mindy tremble. "That's just too young!" she thought.

A moment later, Mindy looked up to find Randy's eyes fixed on her and burning with flames of passion. The heat forced her to turn away, but curiosity compelled her to peek back to find his fire had grown into a raging inferno. Despite the heat, Mindy's skin went cold when Randy's hand crept across the seat in her direction. Protective instincts jumped to the forefront, and she turned to point at something, anything, out the side window. A similar scenario repeated a few minutes later, and his third attempt to make contact nearly jettisoned Mindy into the front seat. "How much further?" she asked no one in particular.

"Not far. Maybe ten minutes," Craig replied.

The sun dipped below the horizon, and an old barn caught Mindy's eye. Tinted by twilight colors and shadows, it looked like an oil painting. Fixed on the vision, she wondered, "Why am I reacting this way? I like him. He's a nice guy, but I don't want to hold hands with him." Then she realized, "I just don't feel that kind of affection. Not yet, anyway. Holding hands would be a sign to him and to others we're a couple. I don't feel like a couple. Around here some people will start talking about us getting married. I'm not ready for that, and I don't want them talking like that."

When they pulled into the Pizza Inn parking lot, Mindy breathed a sigh of relief. She glanced at Randy, who looked like he had just stepped out of a cold shower. Entering, she felt a bit disappointed when they crossed paths with classmates who were just leaving, but the others didn't seem at all surprised. As they found a table, Mindy realized, "Silly me. I thought we were doing something special. I thought we were going somewhere people from Lafayette don't usually go. But they've all been here before and know this is a place people from Lafayette come to all the time for dinner."

When the waitress took orders, Mindy felt awkward when she was the only one to order a side salad. A few moments later, she quizzed the others about their plans for college and learned she was the only one with aspirations for higher education.

But Mindy wasn't shy about sharing her own plans. "I'm already looking forward to college. I hope to broaden my mind and meet people from all over the country and the world. I'm looking forward to college parties and drinking coffee during late night philosophic discussions. I hope to get a professional degree, become a career woman, maybe wear nice business suits, and work to help make the world a better place. I want to determine my own destiny as much as I can."

The others responded with silence and avoidance of eye contact. Mindy cringed as she imagined herself stepping off a soapbox. She didn't mean to make the others feel bad and was happy when relief arrived along with the pizza a short time later. The conversation shifted, and everyone seemed to recover quickly with smiles and laughter.

But Mindy's tension returned as they began the return drive and she sat plastered against the door. Back in Lafayette, the foursome said goodbyes at the Village Market where Mindy overheard Craig whisper to Randy, "We're going to take a little drive," with a wink and smile.

Randy let out an embarrassed chuckle and looked down at his shoes. It was almost 9 PM, and cruising activity would likely be slow, so Mindy suggested Randy take her home.

At Ellington, cars packed the street and driveway. Mindy explained her parents were hosting a party for Carter corporate executives and local elite, "I should go in and help my mom."

"Would you like me to come in and help too?" Randy offered.

Mindy stiffened. She had never vaguely considered this possibility. Beer, wine, and mixed drinks were undoubtedly being served, and Mindy wanted to avoid the possibility of Randy mentioning the alcohol at school. She quickly rejected his idea, "No. No — but thanks for the offer."

Feeling guilty, Mindy didn't wait for Randy to open the car door and hurried to the porch where she paused, and they chatted briefly. With mixed feelings, Mindy didn't move as Randy leaned forward. Without warning, the front door opened and two sharply dressed guests stepped out. They understood the scene and smiled. "Sorry to interrupt," said the gentleman.

Seizing the opportunity to escape, Mindy said goodbye and stepped into the foyer. She paused but didn't understand the unease in her gut. Her eyes fixed on the polished brass doorknob and noted her small and oddly distorted reflection. With a deep breath, she shook her head and turned toward the party. Seemingly out of nowhere, her mother stepped up and gave her a hug. "I'm glad you're here. I need some help."

Smiling and interactive with the relatively upscale guests, Mindy was an immediate hit as she delivered drinks and hors d'oeuvres. When her mother asked if she could borrow a few albums, Mindy was happy to drop the Beatles greatest hits album onto the turntable and was even more relieved she hadn't invited Randy in as guests danced.

Shortly after midnight, the visitors departed en masse. Mindy delivered dirty dishes and glasses to the kitchen, then quietly prepared for bed. She didn't want to discuss her evening out, so jumped into bed and immediately turned off the light. A moment later, there was a soft knock at her door. Before the door cracked open, she closed her eyes and pulled the covers close to her cheek. Her mother whispered, "Are you awake?" but Mindy returned only soft breathing. The light from the hallway gradually faded, and the door clicked shut.

The next day was the March of Dimes collection, but Mindy didn't want to go. Before Anne's death, she had thought, "The collection will be the first thing we've done together outside school since our talk in the gym. I hope it will be the first step in rebuilding our friendship." But feelings of guilt were still heavy and kept her keenly aware of Anne's absence.

Mindy's mother attempted to push her out the door, but Mindy resisted until her mother insisted, "You made a commitment and must see it through."

Lollygagging between houses, Mindy struggled to put Anne's death in perspective. She replayed her possible role in Anne's expulsion from the cheer team and chastised herself for not being more aggressive in confronting Anne about some of her choices. More than anything, Mindy punished herself for failing as a friend. "I should have said something. I should have sought help when I knew she was in trouble and making poor decisions. I should have been a better friend."

Then Mindy recalled Anne's vision of Lafayette, her skewed perception of what lay beyond the borders of Macon County, and mixed them with questionable decision-making. She realized, "Those poor decisions came with a price; a price that may have been hard to see at first, but should have been impossible to ignore if given a moment's thought. *She* made decisions that could only take her down a dangerous path."

Mindy gradually came to the understanding that the weight of self-imposed guilt was clouding her own vision. She took a deep breath and concluded, "I need to be more aware of *my own* decision making. I know sometimes it can be hard, but I must try to make good decisions. I need to make decisions about choosing a path, a direction, for my own life. I have to move forward each day on my own two feet and take care of myself. I hope others will help me, but I need to be able to do it on my own."

Her pace quickened, and Mindy completed her assigned March of Dimes rounds in good time and was happy with her collections. She returned home with a better understanding of life and responsibility.

At school, the absence of any discussion or even gossip about Anne still surprised her. She had to wonder if others didn't care about the tragedy in their midst or was the subject of suicide, especially teen suicide, taboo. Even attempts to find a sounding board among her closest friends were unsuccessful. No one was asking questions or offering any answers. She tried talking to Randy as well and divulged her feeling of personal responsibility in small disjointed pieces. But he could not piece together all the facts of the case or understand the degree of Mindy's guilt. Despite his caring ear, talking with Randy didn't help. So heartache persisted as their conversations drifted back to the mundane.

Despite having good friends and a supportive family, baring her soul was something Mindy couldn't do easily. To stifle her pain, she stopped discussing the tragedy with anyone and learned how to smile even when she hurt. Despite Mindy's outward socialness, she became a remarkably private person and rarely shared inner thoughts with anyone. The smoldering embers of the needless death of a young girl burned in her heart and dampened her spirit more than she would admit.

After dropping her books on her desk Monday afternoon, Mindy had an immediate sense that something was awry. Not a suspicious person by nature, she had to scan the room before realizing several things were slightly out of place. Her brothers never came into her room, and the only time her mother entered was to place a stack of clean clothes on her bed. Her bedroom was her realm, and nobody messed with it.

After closer inspection, Mindy's heart jumped when she noted that the top drawer of her desk was slightly ajar. She slowly pulled it open to find that several items were not as she had left them. Her heart jumped again when she found her diary face up and missing its usual notebook paper camouflage. Her jaw tightened when she realized her mother had been snooping in her room and had undoubtedly read her diary. Her mental wheels spun as she considered options for a return volley.

That evening, Mindy pulled Elton John's *Honky Chateau* album from her record rack. Placing the LP on the turntable, she carefully lowered the needle to the start of "I Think I'm Going to Kill Myself." Jumping to her desk, she read the lyrics on the album cover, then copied down the words as a plan came into focus. The stanzas dominated a blank sheet of paper without title or reference, and by themselves looked far more menacing than the reality of the mocking song. She placed the page face down, overlying her diary. Closing the drawer completely, she wondered, "Did anybody ever think that was a good song?"

When Mindy returned from school the next afternoon, her mother immediately cornered her in the kitchen and began a nervous interrogation, "How was your day?"

Expecting the trap, Mindy offered a monotone, "Oh, fine."

"Well, is everything okay?" was the anxious comeback.

"Yeah, I guess everything's fine," Mindy wistfully replied and overplayed her role as she stared aimlessly out the window.

Her mother pinched harder. "Is there anything you'd like to talk about? I thought you might have something you'd like to talk about."

Feigning innocence and ignorance, Mindy replied with irritation, "No. Why are you asking me these questions?"

Her mother hesitated before more nervously continuing, "Well, I don't want you to think I've been snooping, but I was putting some clothes away in your room, and I came across a letter and just thought I should ask you about it."

Still playing dumb, Mindy replied, "I don't have any idea what you're talking about. I haven't written any letters recently."

With disbelieving anxiety, her mother reached atop the refrigerator to produce the handwritten lyrics from Mindy's desk. Mindy shifted to the attack. "Where did you find that?"

"I was putting clothes in your room and just happened to see it on your desk," her mother lied.

Mindy knew exactly where she found it and stepped up the attack. "I can't believe it. You've been snooping in my room!" Caught red-handed, her mother looked exasperated and held the lyrics with a shaking hand. Suddenly feeling a wave of guilt, Mindy let her mother off the hook, "That's not a letter. Those are the words to an Elton John song. I wrote them down thinking I might use it in a paper I'm writing for school."

"So, you're not having bad thoughts?" her mother asked with a deep sigh of relief.

"Of course not. How stupid do you think I am?" A thought of Anne doused any lingering pay-back spirit. But she would never trust her mother in quite the same way.

Patty approached with some excitement on Holy Thursday. "I talked to Randy about maybe going on a double date this Saturday. He said if it's okay with you, it's okay with him." Mindy had no reason to object, so Patty continued, "I'll call you tonight with details."

Mindy couldn't deny her mild disappointment when Patty called that evening to say, "I talked to Larry, and he wants us to all go to the Pizza Inn in Gallatin." The thought of consecutive weekends at the same pizza joint didn't sound very exciting but, with no alternate suggestion, Mindy agreed.

Patty then spoke at some length about her romance with Larry and provided more personal detail than Mindy cared to hear. She finished with, "Since we met during the basketball season, we've been together almost every weekend. I think we'll get married sometime in the next few years."

Mindy hung up a short time later and sat on the end of her bed feeling a little confused and wondered if she had missed a between the lines message. "Getting married? We're teenagers," she said out loud to herself. Then Patty's words came together, and she had to wonder, "Have she and Larry had sex? Oh, my! Anne? Now maybe Patty? We're teenagers! Isn't it a sin?" Sadness settled in. "Patty has dreams. She wants to go to college. She's talked about traveling, about living in other places and seeing the world. She's going to lose her dreams. Why would she want to get married now?" Mindy saw no way to balance teen marriage with experiencing the world much beyond Macon County.

During Good Friday Confession, Mindy felt like she was only going through the motions. She prayed hard again for help and understanding about Anne, Randy, and Patty. Without a divine response, Mindy returned home to wait in what felt like Purgatory for a reply.

Randy arrived fifteen minutes early Saturday evening. He was all smiles and walked with an atypical hint of cockiness. As soon as they were in the car, he turned to explain with some excitement, "My parents and relatives really want to meet you. You can plan to come over for Sunday supper all summer long." Mindy felt a Ferris wheel drop in her gut.

They drove to the Village Market and waited in the car for Patty and Larry to arrive. After a moment of silence, Randy cocked his head and with puppy love eyes sung in soft, slow Donald Duck imitation, "Ah wuv woo."

Mindy didn't understand his jumbled words, but the look in his eye made her feel claustrophobic, and she jumped out of the car. "I need to stretch and get some fresh air." She drifted away from the car with arms crossed tightly and stared into the rolling hills in the distance.

The sound of footsteps approaching from behind induced Mindy to take a deep breath and hold it. "Everything okay?" Randy asked nervously. Mindy exhaled as her pent-up tension abated. She nodded with her eyes still focused on the distant hills and wished she were that far away.

Patty and Larry pulled into the lot seconds later and prevented any unleashing of thoughts. Mindy cringed when Randy quickly accepted Larry's offer to drive, and her uneasiness multiplied when she sensed the heat of Randy's creeping hand more than once. Reflexively, she would ask a question. Patty would turn around in her seat to answer, and Randy's hand would withdraw from Mindy's personal space.

At the Pizza Inn, Mindy found it hard to believe when they sat at the very same table they had shared the previous weekend with Judy and Craig. But she felt less surprised when the group ordered the same pizza, and she was the only one to order a side salad. Although Patty did most of the talking, the conversation over pizza was pleasant and unpressured. Mindy gradually relaxed and enjoyed the company.

But jitters returned as soon as they stepped back into the parking lot and prompted Mindy to make a pre-emptive move. "Patty, why don't you sit in the back with me so we can girl talk, and Randy can have more leg room up front?" The return trip was non-stop chatter in the back seat while the boys were virtually silent up front.

Back at the Village Market, the foursome said goodbyes and the short drive to Ellington was quiet. Mindy tried desperately to understand her feelings and put them into words. Randy must have sensed her distance and asked again as they pulled into the driveway, "Are you sure everything is okay?"

Relieved to be home and still feeling confused, Mindy hoped to avoid any confrontation and reassured Randy, "I'm fine. I'm just feeling a little crampy — probably from the pizza. Sorry." Randy seemed comfortable with her response.

The stroll to the front door was quiet and slow, but Mindy sensed both Randy's anticipation and her own emotional paralysis. Randy broke the silence to announce proudly, "There's something else I'd like to give you." Mindy froze in her tracks. Instead of being filled with warmth, she shivered with a chill. "I'd like to give you my class ring. I'd like you to *wear* my class ring. But my mom says I paid too much for it to give it away. At least, not yet anyway."

With an involuntary sigh of relief, Mindy thawed enough to step onto the porch. When she turned to say goodnight, Randy surprised her with a quick kiss on her cheek. Emotionally withdrawing and too numb to think clearly, Mindy forced a smile and disappeared into the house.

Seeds of romantic disenchantment had sprouted, and Mindy was beginning to understand that honest emotional commitment required a two-way street.

Easter Day passed without thoughts of Randy or personal guidance from God.

———————————

To Mindy's jaw-dropping surprise, she had learned several months earlier that fellow sophomore Brooke Cates was engaged to Randy's older brother Gary, and their wedding was later that summer. As soon as Brooke had learned of Randy's interest in Mindy, she took every opportunity to express her pleasure and suggested she talk with Randy about joining the Davidson family for Sunday supper. "I know they would love to have you over. Oh, just think, we may be relatives one day!" Brooke exclaimed.

A few days later, Brooke strode into the Home Economics classroom carrying her books and a shoebox. She anxiously gathered as many girls as possible around her desk, including Mindy, and giddily announced, "I have ta show y'all what I got Gary for his birthday."

She gently placed the box on her desk, carefully lifted the lid, and cautiously folded back the tissue paper to reveal a brand-new pair of shoes.

Several onlookers let out soft "Oooohs" and "Ahhhhs." Dumbfounded by both presentation and response, Mindy didn't make a sound and tried to figure out what she had missed. The morning bell rang, and the group dispersed in various directions. Mindy returned slowly to her desk and sat down heavily, feeling a little queasy. "I am just not ready for this kind of stuff," she thought.

Later that week, Mindy observed a change in the young man her friends now openly referred to as her boyfriend. He was more animated and expressed his excitement for the upcoming Junior-Senior Banquet. "I can't wait for the banquet. I'll get to see you all dressed up. You'll be the prettiest girl there."

Mindy paused later that day as she passed the dormant wall heater in The Cloud. Randy was so excited he could barely get his words out. Mindy calmed him down, then encouraged him to speak. "I can tell you have something to say. Just take a deep breath and spit it out."

Randy gathered his thoughts and then blurted, "My parents *really* want to meet you. I'm hoping we can stop by my house before the banquet on Friday."

Mindy felt a now familiar chill and looked away. She didn't want to meet his parents; she just wanted to go to the banquet and have fun. She looked back to reply earnestly, "I'd be too nervous. Let's just have fun at the banquet. Maybe I can meet them some other time." The bell rang and opened her escape hatch. "We can talk more later. See ya," she sang with some relief.

The next evening, Randy called and pleaded with Mindy to reconsider, "I'd really like to bring you by my house to meet my parents. You'll be all dressed up and pretty."

Mindy didn't back down. "I don't want to meet them all fancy. I'd rather meet them sometime when I'm just normal me."

Randy persisted, "Well, how about Sunday afternoon? You could join us for supper."

She had a flash of a handful of schoolmates who routinely ate Sunday supper with their boyfriend's family. This was a local custom that many considered a prelude to marriage. So Randy's invitation only pushed Mindy away. "I'm just not ready to meet your parents. Maybe some other time." The conversation came to an abrupt end.

After hanging up, Mindy sat quietly in her room and wondered, "Am I just being silly? Am I reading too much into this?" But the more she thought about it, the more uncomfortable meeting his parents became. "I'm just a kid. I just don't want to meet his parents. I don't want to meet *any* boy's parents. I want to have fun, but I don't want to be that *serious* or have anyone else think I'm *serious.*"

Then her thoughts shifted. "On the other hand, if he wants me to meet his parents so badly, maybe he *really* likes me. Maybe he likes me *a lot.*" She had never consciously considered the possibility that Randy might love her. "He's just a kid, too. He can't know anything more about love than I do. But what if he does really *love* me?" She couldn't finish her thought, but was surprised how the possibility of love warmed her heart.

The warmth persisted, and Mindy softened. She promised herself to suppress what she wanted to believe were unfounded fears of romance or local gossip. She wanted to open her heart.

Guilt over wearing a "store-bought" dress to the All-Sports Banquet prompted Mindy to ask her talented seamstress mother to make her a new dress for the Junior-Senior Banquet. In less than a week, her mother produced a perfectly fitting custom gown with a large blue floral print, a white lace collar and short puffed sleeves. Although still modest, the neckline was lower than any dress Mindy had ever worn, and every glance at herself in the mirror made her tingle.

On banquet night Mindy emerged from her room in her new gown with long strands of hair wrapped around her head like a crown and joined by a delicate blue bow with long trailing laces that mixed with the flowing waves of her hair. Even her father took notice. "My goodness, Mindy, you look like a princess," he boasted. Unaccustomed to such paternal compliments, Mindy blushed with embarrassment and pride.

The evening began as expected, except that Randy presented a wrist corsage to avoid any chance of a repeat flower disaster. But Mindy's pride changed to self-consciousness when Randy studied her gown, and his eyes stuck on her neckline.

They held the banquet in the cafeteria of the Imperial Reading shirt factory not far from the town square. The greetings and compliments they received as they entered made Mindy glow and Randy beam with happiness. When the photographer snapped their picture, no boy wore a bigger smile than Mindy's date who proclaimed, "If I can't get you to meet my parents in person, at least I'll be able to show them your picture." Mindy felt a wave of guilt for letting him down.

Mingling and chatting with the girls before the opening prayer reminded Mindy how much fun girl time could be. They all shared unimportant but funny stories and laughed almost continuously. There was no shortage of compliments on her dress, especially from Cathy, who described it as "elegant." Filled with pride, Mindy didn't hesitate to give her seamstress mother all the credit.

The senior class included several girls who were already married, so it didn't entirely surprise Mindy to note a handful of older males in attendance at the banquet. She was, however, surprised to learn there were at least a dozen other senior girls accompanied by young adult male boyfriends who appeared to be in their early to mid-twenties. At one point or another during the evening, Mindy was introduced to almost all of them, but committed none of their names to memory.

The after-dinner speeches reminded students of their Macon County roots, but Mindy found their lack of focus on the future somewhat unsettling. She studied the soon to be new graduates and realized that, for about half of them, the future was now as they went to work full time on family farms or in local small factories. Overall, their lives wouldn't change much. Mindy's thoughts drifted to dreams of her own future: college, new people, new places, and new experiences around the world.

With no music or entertainment, the evening passed quickly and ended with a closing prayer. Despite the lack in pageantry, Mindy left feeling good and thought Randy had been the perfect gentleman all evening.

On the front porch at Ellington, Mindy offered thanks for a pleasant evening. When she turned toward the door, Randy touched her arm and said, "Wait." Mindy stood motionless as Randy gazed upon her then leaned forward to deliver a soft kiss. She could sense the weight rolling off his shoulders as he sighed. Emboldened, he said, "I really wish you would consider coming for dinner on Sunday. I want my family to meet you. Brooke will be there with Gary, and I'd really like you to be there with me."

Lost in the moment, Mindy buckled and agreed, "If it means that much to you, okay, I'll go. I guess your parents won't bite."

"Woo-hoo!" Randy yelped and jumped with joy.

With a sweet smile, Mindy offered another soft, "Thanks again," then drifted slowly through the front door, quietly lost in thought of her first real kiss.

Inside, it didn't take long for romanticism to fade and uncertainty to return. By the time Mindy reached her bedroom, she was already regretting her response. "If I go, I'll be sending him a message that he might interpret as me saying I like him more than just a little. Brooke will tell others at school, and they will all think we're a serious couple. Others may make assumptions that aren't true, and there may be expectations I can't live up to. I'm not serious and don't want to be serious. I don't want to lead him on. I don't want people talking about us like we're going to get married. I just want to go out for fun once in a while and — Oh my God! — I don't want people wondering if we're having sex!"

Mindy crawled into bed as her thoughts crystalized. "He likes me. I think he really, honestly likes me. And I do like him. He's a nice boy; he couldn't be nicer to me. But I just don't feel about him the way I think he feels about me, and I can't force myself to like him more. I don't feel the excitement I used to. I was just an infatuated young girl, but I know he's not the boy for me. How in the world do I get out of this without hurting him?" She didn't have an answer.

Pre-arousal excitement awoke Mindy early Saturday morning, "I can get a driver's license today!" A short time later she took a seat behind the wheel of the Mustang and told her mother, "I'm going to do a lap around town and parallel park a few times to warm up before I take the test."

She parked in front of City Hall, and her mother said, "Good luck. I've got some shopping to do. Just come find me when you're done." Mindy nodded and walked through the doors less than one minute after the office opened.

Fifteen minutes later, Mindy bounced back out and saw her mother just leaving the pharmacy. Waving the pink temporary license over her head, she ran across the street to show off her prize. Her mother shook her head and asked with some disbelief, "You're done already?"

"I got one hundred percent on the written test, and then the deputy said he's seen me driving around town so didn't make me take the driving part. He just signed my papers," Mindy explained. Her mother just shook her head.

Mindy's sixteenth birthday coincided with the Miss Macon County High Beauty Pageant, and she spent most of that Saturday afternoon with classmates preparing the gym. As she worked, a few girls inquired why she hadn't signed up to be a pageant contestant. Mindy bit her tongue and shrugged, but recalled Mrs.

Wilson asking her to come into her office two weeks earlier to ask the same question. Mindy had explained, "I don't believe beauty pageants are in good taste and find them demeaning to women." Mrs. Wilson reminded Mindy that it was a fundraising event done for fun, then attempted to coax her, "I *really* think you have a good chance of winning."

Mindy knew better. She knew several girls who took the pageants seriously, and a few had expressed their belief that being crowned queen would open doors of opportunity for getting boys or even jobs in their future. But Mindy disagreed and thought, "It's just a bunch of young girls on display." She didn't want to be on display so refused to change her position but agreed to participate as part of the support staff.

After a brief trip back home for dinner and birthday cake, Mindy slipped on a pair of bright orange, made-by-mom slacks, and a classy mother-hand-me-down white silk blouse with puffed sleeves, topped off by a snug orange and white vest. Her mother dropped her back at school, where she assumed her duties at the concession table. Serving snacks and drinks in the hallway just outside the gym, Mindy was uncertain how to respond when several customers inquired, "Why in the world aren't you in the pageant?"

Mindy bit her tongue and quietly replied, "I'm just happy to be out here in the hall selling candy and doing my part for a good cause."

Randy arrived just as the semi-final round of the pageant concluded. He stopped by to say hi, then continued into the gym. Mindy closed down her concession table, then went to the gym where she took a seat next to Randy just as the final round began.

As the contestants circled the stage, an autonomous creepy sensation forced Mindy to clutch her arms to control her shakes. More than ever she felt confident she had made the right decision to avoid the stage and thought, "Even if done in good clean fun, strutting around and being voted on solely for looks and a smile just doesn't seem right." Otherwise, the pageant went smoothly, and they placed the 1974 MCHS Beauty Pageant crown on Cindy Porter's head.

During the drive to Ellington, Randy said with a boyish grin, "You should-a entered. You would-a won and been queen."

Mindy burst into a non-stop anti-pageant diatribe that continued all the way home. In the driveway, with the car illuminated only by a single light on the side of the house, Mindy continued her verbal assault on the teen beauty pageant concept. But with such pageants having a long history in Macon County,

Randy attempted to question the intensity of Mindy's women's lib perspective but didn't get very far.

Realizing that she had been ranting, Mindy apologized for her outburst and sat quietly to catch her breath. During the silence, Randy reached into his pocket to retrieve and present a small velvet-covered box, "Here. This is for you. Happy birthday."

Genuinely surprised, Mindy cautiously accepted the gift but hesitated to open it until Randy prodded. There was just enough pale-yellow light to reveal a heart-shaped pendant outlined with clear stones. With flushed cheeks, Mindy carefully removed the necklace from the box and held it before her. "It's beautiful. Thank you, but I don't think I can accept this. You shouldn't have bought me anything."

Randy shook his head. "Aw, it's not real. The diamonds aren't real. Someday I'll get you real ones."

Mindy studied the heart in her fingertips and considered handing it back. But Randy was beaming with pride, so she replied, "That doesn't matter. It's beautiful. Thank you."

At Randy's behest to put it on, Mindy tipped her head, and her long hair dropped off her shoulder and across her chest as she fixed the clasp. Sitting upright, she pulled her hair back and settled the pendant on her chest where it rested on her flawless skin.

"Someday I'll git you real ones," Randy repeated. He looked into Mindy's eyes and then took a deep breath to squawk out in a Donald Duck mimic, "Ah wuv woo."

Mindy didn't understand his words. "What?" she questioned.

Randy's cheeks glowed even in the darkness as he squawked again, "Ah wuv woo."

Mindy laughed. "*What?* I can't understand you. I don't speak duck talk."

Now wearing a crown of sweat, Randy geared up for one more try. "AH — WUV — WOO!"

Mindy's eyebrows rose in disbelief. "Oh! Now I get it," and fell back in her seat with a nervous laugh. Randy sat quietly, and Mindy wondered if he was waiting for her to echo his words. When Randy raised his eyebrows, Mindy felt overwhelmed with uncertainty and sputtered, "That's, ummm — nice. But I guess I'd better get inside," and quickly got out of the car.

In response, Randy jumped out as well and had to take several quick steps to cut Mindy off and slow her pace. Just before reaching the front porch, he grabbed her by the arm and pulled her to a stop to say, "My parents are really looking forward to meeting you tomorrow."

Everything was happening too fast, and Mindy needed it to stop. She gently placed her palm over the pendant and cleared her throat. "I really *do* appreciate the gift, and I *don't* want to hurt your feelings. But I'm not going to be able to make it tomorrow. My parents have made plans to meet friends for lunch at the lodge after church tomorrow, and I won't be back until late afternoon. I'm sorry."

The subsequent seconds of silence were awkward. Mindy gently took the pendant in her fingertips and looked Randy earnestly in the eye. "This was really sweet of you. Thank you so much. But, really, you didn't need to get me anything."

More awkward silence followed before Mindy said, "Thanks for the ride home," and stepped through the front door.

Mindy's mother almost choked when Mindy showed her the pendant. "Well, that's very nice." Mindy waited for more, but her mother only took a sip of wine and swallowed hard.

"My mother isn't any more ready for this stuff than I am," Mindy thought as she walked to her bedroom.

During the next few days of school, Mindy avoided Randy when possible, but when not, she rushed by, "I can't talk now. I've got some things I need to do — talk to you later!" She needed time to sort out what she was feeling but was sure it wasn't love.

Running late, Mindy missed breakfast Wednesday morning and arrived in the school cafeteria for lunch somewhat ravenous. She ordered double helpings of everything and slid into a seat next to Cathy at her usual table. The girl talk was already running in high gear, but Mindy noticed Patty, who sat directly opposite her, appeared detached and lost in thought as her eyes scanned the lunchroom.

Mindy whispered, "Patty, is everything alright?"

With eyes still adrift Patty matter-of-factly pronounced, "You can always tell which couples have had sex."

Mindy almost choked on her turnip greens and tried to follow Patty's eyes. "What? How can you possibly tell that?" she mumbled through the mouthful.

Patty wistfully continued, "Oh, you can just tell by the way they stand next to each other, the way they look at each other, and the way they hold hands." Releasing a mournful sigh, Patty pointed out several couples and declared 'they have' or 'they haven't' as she provided amateur detective observations to support her deductions.

113

Mindy's head spun with skepticism as she protested, "I don't think you can say that. Maybe they just like each other. Besides, sex before marriage is a sin."

"Not around here," Patty deadpanned.

Overhearing this exchange, Cathy interjected, "If you date any guy long enough, he's gonna want to get into your pants."

Angela Loomis agreed, "Guys really don't care about you. They just want what you have between your legs."

Several others chirped up in agreement before Cathy closed the conversation with the general summary, "Boys will be boys. All they really want is sex."

It seemed apparent the girls had discussed this topic more than once. As a group, the other girls seemed almost bored and considered the 'all they really want is sex' concept independent of love or even affection as not only acceptable but entirely natural. In fact, the general theme seemed so ingrained in their thinking, it didn't seem to bother them at all.

Mindy considered challenging them and wanted to ask, "But what about love? Where does love fit in?" But she bit her tongue when the conversation drifted another direction. Walking back to class, she felt sad and wondered, "Why do they accept such low expectations for boys and love?"

That afternoon, Patty cornered Mindy between classes to mention, "Cathy is too embarrassed to ask you herself, but could she borrow the dress you wore to the Junior-Senior Banquet? She needs a nice dress to take on the Senior Trip." Mindy was, of course, aware of the upcoming trip and having no plans to wear the dress any time soon was happy to help.

The warning bell rang and sent the girls in opposite directions with a parting agreement to talk more that evening. As Mindy hurried along, the lunchtime conversation popped back into her forethought. "Oh, my goodness! I wonder what Patty might think about Randy and me? Surely, she doesn't think — Oh, my God! I hope I'm *never* the subject of such lunchtime girl talk!"

When Patty called that evening, Mindy felt compelled to clarify her situation. "I hope you don't think Randy is like the guys you were talking about at lunch. He's been nothing but a gentleman. I hope you know that."

Patty laughed disbelievingly, "Yeah, right."

Mindy awakened at 2 AM with her heart racing, and it took a long time to calm down. As she finally drifted back to sleep, memories seemed to dance in the dark and drums pounded . . . *curious anticipation, embarrassed hallway smiles, hallway crossings, phone calls, corsages, and fancy dresses morphed into*

a gleaming heart pendant, duck talk, class rings, pressure to
meet parents, shiny leather shoes and missing her friends.

She thought she heard a door slam shut off in the distance. But now there was only darkness and quiet. Sleep took over, and Puppy Love was dead.

Brooke grabbed Mindy by the elbow before the first bell Monday morning. "We had a great time yesterday. We all really missed you, especially Randy. He seemed kind'a down all day. I know you'll be there when he gets back from the Senior Trip. His mom showed your picture from the banquet to everybody. She said you must be the prettiest girl ever in Macon County and just can't wait to meet you. I'm so excited, we may be relatives someday." Mindy was ever so happy to hear the bell ring.

Between classes, Mindy approached Randy cautiously in the Brut Cloud. "Sorry I couldn't make it yesterday. I hope everyone had a good time."

Randy was calm. "That's okay. My parents are going to have a graduation party for me after we get back from the Senior Trip. Just plan to make that. My mom will be happy, and so will I."

Pressing her books tight to her chest, Mindy looked him in the eye to explain, "I'm just not ready to meet your parents now. I'm happy to go out once in a while and have fun. Maybe I can meet them later." But she knew better and disappeared down the hall.

Transfer student Emily Harrison added to the weight of the day when she cornered Mindy to ask if she was planning to try out for the football or basketball cheer teams.

Mindy replied, "I haven't given it any thought."

"Well, I hope you try out for football. Being a transfer student, I don't think I can get enough votes for football, but I might be able to get a basketball position. Let me know as soon as you decide. Okay?" Emily pleaded.

Mindy thought about it all day. "If I try out for football, I'll probably be taking Anne's position. How could I ever do that?" The added weight made the walk home feel longer than usual.

That evening, Randy broke routine to call on a typically off night. The conversation began low-key but shifted when he asked Mindy to reconsider coming to his house for supper on Sunday.

Mindy felt something pop inside and said, "I'm just *not ready* for that," and felt the urge to add, "Let's just be friends," but couldn't bring herself to drop the guillotine. She had always known in the back of her mind that there would be an end, but had never considered what it would entail or that it might be painful. "He's been so nice. I don't want to hurt him," she thought.

"What would you like to do when I get back?" Randy tested.

"I don't think I'll be able to go out that weekend," replied Mindy.

"Well, when *can* you go out?" Randy urgently questioned.

"I'm going to be busy Friday and Saturday, and we won't be back until late after church on Sunday," Mindy lied.

The strength of Randy's voice failed as he asked, "You're not goin' to go out with me anymore, are ya?"

Mindy hesitated, then softly replied, "Probably not."

After an awkward pause, Randy sighed and said sadly, "Well, then I guess that's it."

A whispered, "Sorry," followed by more silence came from Mindy's end of the line. She didn't know what to say next or how to lessen the pain she sensed in his voice.

Randy was kind enough to end the torture for both of them. "Well, bye."

"Goodbye," whispered Mindy. Gently returning the phone to its cradle, she sighed with relief.

The very next day at school, Mrs. Wilson made another rare appearance during the sixth-hour and pulled all the cheerleaders into the cafeteria. "There are going to be some changes next year. The school administration has decided to have only one cheer team next year. The team will be made up of two girls from each class and will cheer at both football and basketball games. Good luck to all of you at tryouts."

Junior Debbie Lang spoke up, "I've cheered for football the past two years, then played on the basketball team. I won't be able to do both."

"Then you'll have to choose between them," replied Mrs. Wilson coldly. She turned and walked away without leaving an opportunity for additional questions.

Mindy wondered, "Is this is to hide the fact that Anne won't be here next year, or is this the fallout from not combining teams for basketball playoffs?"

Several of the girls traded looks of panic. It didn't take much math skill to deduce that fourteen positions shrinking to eight would create a significant increase in competition. Kat just stared at Mindy and trembled.

Chapter 7
Aftershock
May 1–June 29, 1974

Most of the senior class, including Randy, was still out of town for the senior trip and Mindy hadn't said a word to anyone, but news of their breakup was common knowledge at school. Mindy cringed with the thought of being interrogated by curious friends and gossipers, but only a few comments made it to her ears. To her surprise, each comment expressed a similar theme: "We knew it was just a matter of time. You guys weren't a good match. Shoot, everybody likes Randy, but nobody thinks he's good enough for you."

Mindy found this revelation disconcerting and had to ask, "Why didn't you tell me this before?"

The collective response was, "Hey, you're lucky. You weren't stuck at home every weekend. You got to go cruisin' with a boy and to Gallatin for pizza. I wish it would have been me. Heck, nobody thought you'd marry him." Their lack of romantic vision left Mindy feeling more unsettled.

A few days later, Mindy overheard parts of an animated conversation among some girls in the cafeteria. She was unaware she was the subject of their lamentations until she heard her name. "Mindy's back on the market. Now almost every boy at school will be after her. It's just not fair." Mindy hid her face in her books and quietly escaped unnoticed. Later that day, she heard, to her horror, rumors that the breakup had been the topic of a lengthy boys' locker room discussion, with bets being taken on whom she would date next. Her skin just crawled.

Mindy's mother approached the breakup with only superficial curiosity and repeated many of the same things from adult friends that Mindy had heard at school. Already perplexed by such talk, Mindy didn't want to discuss it any further with her mother, so flippantly replied, "Once I got him there was no challenge, and I got bored," and then walked away. Her mother would remember that response for a long time.

As the school year wound down, a wave of male schoolmates sought Mindy out between classes, and several started calling her regularly at home. She didn't mind the attention, but it didn't impress her, and she didn't let it distract her from preparing for cheer tryouts. In fact, she found the stretching, exercise, and practice to be a very welcome diversion from school gossip and boy-related politics.

Cheerleading tryouts was the focus of the mid-week assembly, and Mindy waited in the cafeteria with a large and very anxious pack of girls. Only Tammy Gregory, who everyone considered a shoo-in as the next Homecoming Queen, appeared relaxed. Several contestants had withdrawn just before tryouts, leaving only three junior-class contestants: Kat, Emily, and Mindy. When Mindy's turn came, she felt bad that she didn't introduce a new cheer as she had the year before. But her standard "Give me a T — Give me an I . . ." routine was flawless and earned her a place on the '74–'75 cheer team. Kat won the other junior position while Gina and Tammy claimed the senior ones.

The next days passed quietly until the tour bus carrying soon-to-be high school graduates returned to MCHS mid-day on Friday. Watching through a classroom window, Mindy smiled when Patty stepped off the bus and was already eager to hear about the trip. Her smile disappeared when an expressionless Randy appeared a few students later and hurried away from the crowd.

Mindy called Patty, who had never traveled beyond the Tennessee borders, right after school. Patty reported having a wonderful time and gave a detailed review of the trip. She didn't pause at the end to add, "Randy was okay at the beginning. Then he saw Cathy in *your* dress and asked her about it. I heard him say, 'Yeah, I know that dress.' He sounded sad and was pretty quiet the rest of the trip. He's probably glad to be home." Mindy expressed her pleasure to hear of Patty's good time, but made no comment about Randy.

Patty called back just an hour later. "Larry wants to know if you'd be willing to go on a double date with one of his friends and us. His name is Jack Robertson. He broke up with his girlfriend a while back and is a little depressed. Larry thinks a double date might cheer him up."

The concept of a blind date with someone recovering from a failed relationship sounded very unappealing, so Mindy declined. But Patty pushed and assured her, "He's a really nice guy who just needs to get out."

Mindy trusted Patty's judgment and rationalized, "I've never been on a blind date. What could it hurt? It will probably be a onetime thing, but it might be fun," so finally agreed to go.

Plans changed when Patty called Saturday afternoon to report that Larry was sick and wouldn't be able to go out that evening, but added, "Jack is still hoping to go out though." With an opportunity to establish some distance from the Randy era, Mindy agreed to talk with him by phone.

A short time later, Jack called to introduce himself. Mindy had a little difficulty deciphering his thick country accent, but they chatted for several minutes before Jack suggested, "I'll just head on ova if ya don't mind. Maybe we can git a bite at Clifton's or somethin'. Thars a farm not far that jess turnt ova a field that ain't been used fer a long time 'n is full of erra-heads. Maybe we kin git sum a-for dark." Searching for arrowheads sounded like fun, so Mindy agreed.

When Mindy opened the front door, it surprised her to find that Jack clearly fell short of Patsy's description; he was scraggly and unattractive by any measure. At first, he seemed pleasant enough, and they talked for a few minutes on the porch. It didn't take long to learn that he didn't have an ounce of wit, but there he was, expecting to go arrowhead hunting. From Mindy's perspective, there was no backing out, so she made a brief introduction to her parents, and they promptly left in Jack's car.

The sun sat low in the sky by the time they got to Clifton's. The conversation was awkward, and Mindy suggested they begin the search for arrowheads before the sun fell much further. They drove several miles into the countryside unfamiliar to Mindy, and the many bends in the road left her geographically lost. They pulled up along a recently plowed field where, to Mindy's pleasant surprise, she found herself to be either very skillful or very lucky in finding one arrowhead after another. Jack leaned up against the front fender of his car and watched her search.

As daylight waned, Mindy returned to the car where Jack put her treasures in the trunk. When he didn't start the engine right away, Mindy turned to question. In response, Jack aggressively reached his left arm across to the passenger window to trap Mindy in her seat. He moved in to deliver a kiss, but Mindy raised her arms in defense and screamed, "What are you doing? Stop it!"

Jack drew his head back without moving his arm. Smirking, he whined, "What? What's the matter, baby?"

Mindy could sense the Devil in him, and her mind raced. There was no farmhouse she could run to, darkness was coming soon, and she was geographically disoriented. Panic ensued.

With a deep breath, Mindy gathered her wits and then her adrenaline kicked in. With clenched fists, she glared with fire and growled, "You take me home. RIGHT NOW!"

Surprised by her tenacity, Jack withdrew, acting innocent. "What? What's wrong wit ch'all?"

When Mindy responded with only angry eyes, Jack shook his head with disgust and began the silent drive back toward town. Along the way, he would intermittently speed up then slow way down or take blind curves on the wrong side of the road to trigger new waves of fear. Mindy's own disgust for the nasty creature behind the wheel grew by the second. With each stretch of road, she planned a new escape scenario and kept her hand on the door handle, ready to jump out of the moving car if necessary.

At Ellington, Mindy was out of the car before it was at a complete stop and ran to the house. Just inside the door, she settled herself, then retreated to her bedroom without mentioning the scare to her parents. Anger and fear spun in her mind all evening, interrupted only by occasional thoughts of her lost arrowhead treasure.

The Murphy's returned from church in Scottsville without their usual stop at the Barren River Lodge for brunch the next day. Phyllis called a short time later and coaxed Mindy into cruising with her that afternoon. A year older than Mindy, Phyllis was short and full figured, with dark brown eyes and thick long brown hair to compliment her pleasant personality and cheerful disposition. Mindy always wondered why boys weren't pounding on her door.

Phyllis made the purpose of their outing clear before the first stop. She hoped to cross paths with her longstanding crush, Kevin Gerard. But still smoldering inside, Mindy didn't allow the conversation to stay focused on Kevin for long. She recounted her previous night's scare, and her anger grew with each word until Phyllis announced, "We'd better go to Jones's for ice cream and cool you down, girl!"

With mission Cool Down accomplished, Phyllis was glad when Mindy's sweet demeanor returned, and their trek about town resumed. Leaving the square on Red Boiling Springs Road, an entirely unexpected sight caught Mindy's eye. Approaching from the opposite direction was Jack's car with Jack behind the wheel and, of all people, Randy in the front passenger seat. Mindy sunk below the dash as they passed and went unnoticed, but she saw enough to tell the boys were sharing a hearty laugh. Out of sight, Mindy sat bolt upright in her seat with panicked surprise. "What in the world are they doing together? They don't even know each other! What do you think they're talking about?" she gasped.

Phyllis said sadly, "Probably about you, and it probably isn't good." That was precisely what Mindy was afraid of.

Mindy could come up with no plausible explanation for how those two particular boys ended up together less than twenty hours after the worst experience of her life. It made no sense, and she wondered what might follow.

The last week of school began the next day. Seniors would say goodbyes and prepare for graduation while everyone else was taking tests. Mindy had one other crucial, self-assigned task: to warn every girl she knew that Jack Robertson was a dangerous and disgusting pig. She didn't want any girl to face the fright and helplessness she felt with "the biggest dirtbag in middle-Tennessee."

Shortly after returning home, Mindy answered the phone with surprise when she heard Jack's voice. It was apparent her reports had yet to circulate to Red Boiling Springs, and it shocked her when Jack got right to the point. "I was wonderin' if I could have anoth-a chance?" he flatly inquired.

Anger and fear swelled within, and Mindy felt ready to burst. "Are you kidding me? I will *never* go out with you! I never want to see you again!" She slammed the phone onto the hook, then yelled at the handset, "You're a disgusting pig!"

"My goodness, what's that all about?" her mother inquired. With no way to escape, Mindy broke down and recounted the details of her frightful experience.

"Well, your father didn't like that boy. He didn't think you should be going out with him," her mother replied.

"Too frickin late," Mindy deadpanned in thought. She could only shake her head and walk away.

When Patty called that evening, Mindy's repeat tirade caught Patty off guard as she tried to downplay the incident. "Well, you know Jack had a girlfriend for a long time. He was probably used to getting whatever he wanted and probably didn't think he'd have to start all over with someone new, especially a city girl," she explained. When Mindy tried to interject, Patty ignored her and continued along lines of defense and diffusion, "You know, boys are just like that." Mindy almost exploded when Patty attempted to shift some of the blame to her. "I thought you knew about guys. I thought you could handle him. But you were just in over your head with someone like Jack. You probably could have handled him better," Patty matter-of-factly concluded.

Unable to control her anger, Mindy yelled, "Why are you defending him? He's a disgusting beast! I hope he never gets a chance to scare another girl. Your boyfriend needs to find a new friend!"

Rumors quickly passed well beyond the walls of the school, and Mindy's mother received several concerned phone calls from friends the next day. When Mindy returned from school, she was cornered and interrogated in more detail by her mother, who then asked, "Do we need to call the police?"

Mindy recoiled at this question without understanding. "No, it will die down and go away. I just want to warn other girls, then forget it ever happened." But the haunting memory of Jack's demonic eyes replayed in Mindy's mind for weeks.

The next evening, Jack called again and, without introduction, screamed, "Geez, what are you goin' 'round tellin' people 'bout me?"

Mindy responded in a flat and confident tone, "Nothing but the truth. Please don't call here anymore," and hung up with Jack's voice still screeching through the handset.

The kitchen phone rang again a few seconds later. As soon as Mindy heard Jack's voice, she interrupted, "I told you not . . ."

Before she could finish her sentence, her father pulled the phone from her hand to say, "This is Mindy's father. Don't call here again," and hung up.

Mindy watched as her father walked away without further comment or question and thought, "Oh, that's Mom's job, isn't it?" but Jack never called gain.

Over the next few days, Mindy came to better understand the power and efficiency of the small-town gossip machine. The rumor mill had churned her account of the near-assault and activated its metamorphosis into a tale far worse than the already evil reality. In some circles, it was even suggested that Jack tried to rape her. Consumed by anger and disgust, Mindy felt no guilt when she heard how big the story had grown, but it became a small-town lesson she would not soon forget.

The Jack Robertson incident played in Mindy's mind for weeks. Eventually, she came to an understanding, "I have no one to blame but myself. I should never have gone on a blind date without at least asking lots of questions first. I was asking for trouble. Stupid me."

The last days of school passed by without academic stress. No cumulative final exams, no term papers, and no late-night study. The biggest school event was the distribution of yearbooks, and almost everyone tried to inscribe a little piece of their soul into their classmate's hearts and memory.

Mindy hesitantly exchanged books with Brooke. When they finished writing, Brooke returned Mindy's book with some sadness, "I guess you won't be coming to Randy's house this

Sunday for supper. It's too bad. I was really hoping we might be relatives one day."

Those words were like fingernails on a chalkboard and made Mindy wince. But, just a few seconds later, her heart fluttered with uncertainty when she looked up to see Randy approaching with his eyes fixed on her. They hadn't spoken since the last phone call, and Mindy was uncertain how this first post-breakup conversation would unfold.

With cheeks aglow, Randy arrived to inquire politely, "Can I sign your yearbook?" Mindy quietly handed him her book.

He wrote in silence before gently closing the cover and handing it back. They exchanged a few pleasantries but quickly hit a wall. Randy swallowed hard and whispered, "Well, see ya 'round." Mindy just nodded and watched as Randy disappeared into the crowd down the hallway.

By the end of the week, Mindy's yearbook was crowded with notes and signatures of schoolmates; some were strategically placed, but most were scattered randomly. After finishing an after-school snack, she retreated to her bedroom and lay on her bed to review the entries in no particular order, but her eyes and mind focused longer on a few.

You are one of the reasons this year has been a very enjoyable one. I hope that whatever you do, you will be successful because you are a very deserving person. Stay the way you are, and you will never have any trouble making friends. Love always, Bud

It has really been fun going to school with you this year. You are a great girl. I hope you have everything you ever want and I hope maybe you and Randy will get back. I hope so. Brooke Davidson (Cates) P.S. Maybe some day we will be related.

It has really been fun, you are a great looking girl with a fantastic personality. I hope you never change. A friend forever. Randy

How do I begin to tell you what a friend you've been? All those times you talked to Bud for me and everything. Thank you so much for trying to help me with him. Oh, there's just so much I wanna say! I sure hope you figure out what you really want. (Boy wise I mean) I'm really glad you got cheerleader. I hope we have fun at camp this summer. Maybe we can hook

123

us a ride with somebody. HaHa (if we're lucky). Well, I don't know anything else to say except don't forget me, and we'll be even better friends next year! Your friend always, Love Kat

Similar entries went on and on. Mindy softly closed the cover and rolled over onto her back. She stared at the ceiling as the montage of recent events spun in her mind, and a sense of unease gradually crept into her cerebral meanderings.

She realized she had always viewed her life, and those that touched it with an accepting and unquestioning eye. But events of the past year were forcing her to look more insightfully at the world around her, at *life,* in a different way. Something was prodding her and demanding that she be more observant and more questioning of everything.

Mindy laughed at herself. "Wow, that's too much heavy thinking for the last day of school." With a shake of her head, she rolled back over to browse more yearbook entries. A moment later, she laughed again. "I need to ask more questions, and I definitely need to pay more attention to spelling and grammar all the time."

Friday evening, Mindy felt compelled to pay homage to the seniors who had made her first year in Lafayette so memorable and drove herself to the MCHS graduation ceremony.

In reviewing the graduation program, it was quickly apparent that the majority of new graduates weren't going far from home. The furthest steps away were to the University of Tennessee in Knoxville. Many would commute to Vol State Community College, and a handful would go to college in Cookeville or Murfreesboro. Half the class was staying behind, with most stepping directly from student to blue-collar worker in one day. She wondered how many would miss their best opportunity for exposure to the broader world.

The student and keynote speeches came from the heart, but Mindy found them lacking in scope and vision. She hoped the addresses at her own graduation would be more meaningful.

As names were announced, students marched across the stage to receive diplomas. Mindy's ears perked when one of the first graduates was announced with both a maiden and married name. She re-examined the program and did some quick counting. "Oh, my goodness! There are eleven girls in this class already married. That's almost ten percent! They've been in high school! How could this happen?" she wondered.

Mindy couldn't imagine herself as a teenage bride and being a teen mother seemed inconceivable. There were so many things she wanted to see and do before settling down, and she believed this should be true for most kids her age. She wondered how many of these girls would be happy or even still married ten or twenty years into the future.

When Randy crossed the stage, Mindy watched closely, and understood the adult realities of his world were upon him. She leaned back in her seat, very happy to be just where she was.

About four weeks into summer, Vicki arrived from Mississauga. Mindy and her mother picked her up at the airport in Nashville and left straight away for Gulf Shores, Alabama. The teen girls acquired pleasant tans to complement their modest bikinis and attracted small flocks of curious young gawkers hoping for a cheap thrill. Browsing through a tourist shop one evening, they came across $2 halter top-hot pant outfits on a clearance rack and snapped them up with plans to wear them as bikini cover-ups to and from the beach. In brightly colored halters and sunglasses the next day, they looked like a pair of budding movie stars.

Once back in Lafayette, Mindy introduced Vicki to small-town life with drives into the countryside and, of course, cruising. On the circuit, their tans, hip hugger jeans, mid-drift summer tops, and long shiny hair were an instant hit prompting packs of boys to track them like wolves.

Vicki was loosely aware of Mindy's months-long crush on Randy and its sudden collapse. So, a curious Vicki took the opportunity to talk with Randy when they crossed paths with him and his cruising buddy, Brian Witte. Mindy couldn't help but feel a twinge of jealousy when Vicki and Randy migrated away from the pack of teens to talk at length in relative privacy at the far end of the Village Market parking lot.

The sting of jealousy burned a second time when Randy called Ellington that evening and asked for Vicki. As they chatted, Vicki pushed Mindy out of the bedroom and closed the door. When the thirty-minute conversation was finally over, Mindy tried to be cool, but her own curiosity got the better of her. "So, what was that all about?" she wanted to know.

"He seems like a really nice guy and wishes you guys were still together. All he really wanted to know is if I thought you would go out with him again. I told him yes," Vicki replied.

Mindy winced. "You know I don't like him like that. Why in the world would you tell him I'd go out with him again?"

"He seems nice. You could just go out for fun. It doesn't mean you have to marry him or anything," Vicki explained.

"First of all, you haven't had any boy experience yourself, so I'm not sure you should be the one giving advice. Second, you don't understand. Around here, many people think steady dating in high school means you're getting married," Mindy argued.

Vicki apologized, "Oops. Sorry if I got you into any trouble."

At the airport. The girls said goodbye and discussed plans for another Canadian visit the following summer. Mindy returned home and sat on the edge of her bed, feeling washed out and torn until the ringing phone interrupted her thoughts. She calmly answered on the fifth ring but stiffened when she heard, "Hi Mindy, this is Randy."

They talked casually about Vicki and summer and cruising. Then, after a brief pause, Randy asked, "Hey, I was wondering if you might like to go out again sometime?"

A waterfall of thoughts rushed through Mindy's mind before "Maybe we could do that," slipped from her lips and she agreed to a dinner date the following Saturday.

Almost immediately after hanging up, Mindy had second thoughts. Randy *was* a very nice boy, but he *was not* somebody she could or wanted to be serious about. Her young girl infatuation had faded, and she was confident no fire of affection could ever be rekindled. Going out with him would just be taking advantage of his good nature and might give him the wrong impression. Most of all, she didn't want to hurt him again.

After a restless night, Mindy arose Saturday morning with her mind made up. She pulled out the local white pages, looked up Randy's number and dialed the phone only to hear a busy signal which reminded her the Davidson phone was on a party line. A dozen further attempts through the day had the same result.

As the date hour approached, Mindy stepped outside and met Randy in the driveway. He was all smiles, beaming with confidence and decked out in new, dark polyester pants, a new shirt, and shiny new platform shoes. But his smile disappeared when he saw Mindy was in a T-shirt and jeans and stood barefoot before him. She cut him off as he started to speak to explain, "I tried calling all day, but your line was busy. I can't go out. I have to go to church with my family."

"That's too bad. I was gonna take ya to the Pioneer Kitchen for a steak. Then I was hoping we could find a quiet place to talk." The bubbling excitement vibrating in Randy's words was easy to read, and Mindy cringed when she realized he didn't understand what was happening.

Just then, another car pulled into the drive, and Randy explained, "That's Brian. I worked on their farm today. He's bringing me my pay. I'll be right back." After a few steps, he paused and turned to confirm, "So, we're *not* going out tonight, right?"

With hands folded before her, Mindy nodded and whispered, "That's right."

Randy talked briefly with Brian and stuffed a stack of bills into his front pocket. Walking back, he looked Mindy's way and smiled. When she didn't return one, he stopped and stared emptily into the yard. His voice cracked, "You're never going to go out with me again, are you?"

Mindy gently shook her head. "No. I'm sorry. I really did try to call all day, but the line was busy."

Randy took a deep breath. He tried to speak, but his words wouldn't come out. With another deep breath, he summoned his strength and pronounced with a sweeping motion of his hand, "So, this is it. I'm not asking you out again."

"I really am sorry it happened this way," whispered Mindy.

After several seconds of frozen silence, Randy thawed. "Ah, it's alright. I'll just go get drunk instead."

Mindy felt a chill. "Oh, please, be careful."

"Why? What do you care?" Randy scoffed with a mixture of sadness and anger.

Trying unsuccessfully to make eye contact, "I would never want to see you hurt," Mindy replied.

He swatted the air and turned away. *"Yeah, right."*

Randy walked to his car and a last glance over his shoulder revealed the sorrow in his eyes. After he pulled away, Mindy stood alone, feeling sad and guilty for hurting him a second time. She sighed and thought, "He was born in Macon County and will probably die in Macon County. It's a good place for many, but I'm not ready to say I'll stay here forever." She sighed again.

That evening Mindy sat at her desk for a long time with a blank page of her diary before her. She realized she had learned a valuable lesson and wrote:

Dear Diary,
Feelings of affection are real and not to be trifled with.
I feel a little sad, but mostly guilty for hurting Randy
again. But I take comfort in knowing I did the right
thing, even if I did it poorly. I know what I felt isn't love.
I just hope I will be able to recognize true love if it ever
comes my way.

Chapter 8
Emergence
June 30–October 30, 1974

The next three weeks were quiet and routine. Mindy was happy to run errands for her parents just so she could get behind the wheel of the Mustang and spent lots of time cruising with Gina and Phyllis. Cheer practices were going well, and the warm, worry-free summer days floated by.

The only sting along the way was the embarrassment of getting caught breaking a parental rule. As a new driver, Mindy's parents prohibited her from leaving Lafayette. But one night, the girls convinced her to drive to Red Boiling Springs to assess the cruise circuit there. They found the streets in RBS were nearly empty and had immediately returned. The next morning, Mindy's mother handed her a piece of paper with pre- and post-trip odometer readings and demanded to know where she had gone. Mindy buried her face in her hands, admitted her crime, and accepted her punishment: washing and waxing both cars.

Mindy also dove a bit deeper into farm life when she spent a few nights with Gina. Farm duties began before dawn, and Mindy thoroughly enjoyed helping feed the animals, milk the cows and the heaping farm breakfast after chores. When the weekend ended, she had to laugh about her sore muscles from just a few days of farm work.

While out cruising with Phyllis, Mindy dabbled in the dual role of matchmaker and counselor whenever they crossed paths with Kevin. He always seemed happy to talk, but try as she might, Mindy couldn't shift Kevin's eyes toward Phyllis.

Not one to give up easily, Mindy was chatting with Phyllis in the driveway at Ellington when she spotted Kevin's car passing by. Mindy waved, and Kevin's car came to a screeching halt, then backed up and pulled into the drive. Kevin, along with his best friend, Wayne Schaefer, got out. The foursome chatted for a short time before Phyllis challenged Kevin to a drag race. Kevin looked at Phyllis's car and laughed, but accepted the challenge. Both vehicles drove down the street and came to a stop along a straight-away. With Mindy riding shotgun, Phyllis lost badly, and the boys enjoyed a good laugh, when they literally left the girls in the dust as they hit the unpaved road at the end of the street. The next morning, Mindy's mother informed her that a neighbor had witnessed the race and called to complain. Caught with no defense for a second time, Mindy felt embarrassed and wondered if it was possible to get away with anything in this gossiping town and its omnipresent eyes. She unhappily accepted her punishment to strip and wax the kitchen floor.

Cheer camp seemed to arrive sooner than expected. With only one team and the absence of intra-squad competition, the week away was relaxed and enjoyable. The team progressed nicely and melded into a solid unit. Mindy had the number 76, as in "class of," silk-screened on her T-shirt while most of the other girls all had a favorite boy's football jersey number printed on as usual. But this year, Mindy felt no surprise to find Lafayette as she had left it when they returned.

Phyllis called full of excitement the afternoon of Mindy's return. "I talked to Wayne while you were at camp. He says he'll get Kevin to go on a date with me if I can get you to go on a date with him."

Aware of Wayne's longstanding crush, Mindy frowned. "I don't think that's a good idea. I don't want to do anything to encourage him."

Phyllis begged and pleaded until Mindy broke down and agreed. Despite Mindy's complete ignorance about golf, she suggested they meet the boys at the country club for a round of golf and thus avoid a "date" label for the outing.

They met at the appointed time and immediately hit the links. The golf was terrible but generally fun for all, and afterward, everyone headed home happy. Phyllis thanked Mindy repeatedly for going along and hoped the casual outing would perk Kevin's interest. But Mindy didn't have the heart to tell her she didn't think that was going to happen. Despite Phyllis's attempts to flirt with Kevin, Mindy had sensed his eye uncomfortably focused in her direction much of the day.

———

The academic year began earlier than usual, and the summer seemed to have evaporated when Mindy awoke on August 5th with the realization that classes started in one week. So, she felt torn when later that day, Mrs. Wilson called to ask if she would like to represent the students of Macon County at a two-and-a-half-day drug and alcohol awareness conference in Knoxville. She explained that Mr. Gaines, Superintendent of the school district, would attend as the administrative representative, and would provide transportation.

Initially uncertain about giving up the last precious days of summer vacation, Mindy decided that getting out of town for a few days before school started and the opportunity to meet some interesting people would be nice. When she asked who else from school would attend, Mrs. Wilson explained there was only money in the budget for one student. Mindy didn't want to go alone, so asked if another student could go with her if she shared her room and they bought their own food. Mrs. Wilson didn't think Mr. Gaines would object. Mindy promptly called Gina, who was thrilled by the idea of spending a few quiet, lazy days watching TV in the hotel room while Mindy attended the conference.

The girls sat in the back seat and whispered while Mr. Gaines drove. After registration at the hotel, Mindy picked up her conference packet, then escaped to their room. Neither girl had ever been in such a fancy hotel, and the plush accommodations made them feel like queens. Curling up on her bed, Gina turned on the television while Mindy hurried back downstairs just as the conference was ready to begin.

The goal of the conference was to raise school administrator's awareness and understanding of teen drug and alcohol use through open and honest discussion with students in a non-threatening environment. After short presentations on various topics, students would complete brief surveys. Everyone would then split into small discussion groups with a mix of students and administrators. A moderator would ask students to share their survey responses with administrators and respond to any follow-up questions they might have. Hopefully, administrators would gain insight and become proactive in dealing with various teen issues in their own communities.

During the first group discussion, everyone introduced themselves and gave a brief description of their town, their school, and their perception of where they fit into the social structure of their school and community. As Mindy introduced herself, she noted the boy seated directly across from her kept his eyes sharply focused in her direction, so she listened carefully when it was his turn.

"My name is Connor Prewitt. I am currently a resident of Dahlonega, Georgia . . ." he began. He was confident, articulate, and startled Mindy with piercing eye contact. He outlined his father's military career and the various locations his family had lived. As a result, he had enjoyed the experience of life in different parts of the United States and Europe. What captured Mindy most was his apparent insight into other cultures, social structures, and political systems. These elements alone separated him from teen boys she knew in Lafayette and left her curious about this eighteen-year-old self-proclaimed man of the world.

The discussions finally got underway and the first set of questions related to the prevalence of drug use by students at their hometown schools. Initial responses estimated regular use of drugs or alcohol in 15 to 30 percent of classmates. Mindy was the dissenter. "Drug use in my community is rare. I can name only a few students who are *suspected* drug users, but I have never witnessed anyone with drugs. I'm only aware of a few instances of students drinking. If rumors are true, there is probably more drinking by boys at a nearby high school in Red Boiling Springs; which is even smaller than my small town. Still, it's unlikely that even those kids drink much. Macon County is a dry county. There is nowhere close to even buy beer except from bootleggers," she explained with a blush. She also pointed out that the population is mostly Missionary Baptists "who don't drink," and finally argued, "There is a large percentage of farm families in my county. Most of those kids have to be up early seven days a week and work long hours between school and chores. There isn't much time or opportunity for drinking and staying out late," she concluded.

Several students in the group reacted with disbelief and suggested that Mindy was naïve. They argued that many rural teenage boys drank and smoked pot regularly simply because there wasn't anything else to do. But Mindy staunchly defended her community, "Well, not in Macon County."

During subsequent discussions, Mindy noted that Connor skillfully managed tougher questions and smoothly deflected some questions to others by asking, "What do you think?" His self-confidence and people power made him stand out from the crowd.

After dinner, many attendees propped their hotel doors open to invite others in to socialize, and Mindy wasn't surprised when Connor arrived at her door. He invited himself in and quickly dominated the conversation in a group of eight. Before long, he referred to one of the more controversial conference topics of the day: teen sex. Most respondents had expressed their belief that premarital sex was not uncommon among teen couples at their schools, but Mindy had raised her voice in dissent and defense of Macon County for a second time.

The conversation swirled until Connor shifted forward to the edge of his seat and held up his hand up to command silence. Looking directly at Mindy, he pointedly inquired, "Well, what about you, Miss Virgin? Do you *really* think you'll wait till you're married to have sex?"

Seven sets of eyes focused intently on Mindy and the room became eerily quiet awaiting her response. After the blush in her cheeks faded, she sat tall and confidently replied, "I will wait until I am in love — and married."

Connor grinned and reached across the coffee table to stroke his index finger across a sliver of exposed bronze skin between Mindy's beltline and the lower edge of her tight ribbed blouse. "You won't make it wearing things like that." Mindy's cheeks glowed with embarrassment again as she pulled her shirt over her belt, and everyone burst out in laughter.

As the only one of legal age of eighteen in the room, Connor added to his glory when he excused himself and returned a few minutes later with a bottle of wine. It was only one bottle, but it made a big impression on the roomful of teens.

At the end of the night, Connor lingered as the group gradually dispersed, then pulled Mindy into the hall and out of Gina's earshot. "You are a delightful little girl. I'm so glad to have met you."

Somewhat offended by Connor's summary description, Mindy was more vocal and assertive during discussions the next morning. As a result, she acquired several male followers during breaks. Soon, three boys, in addition to Connor, were openly competing for her attention, and their verbal bantering became uncomfortable. When they all invited themselves to join her for lunch, Mindy apologized and tried to put them all off, "Sorry. I already have other plans."

Mindy grabbed Gina and thought they had escaped, only to find Connor and the other boys in hot pursuit. Unable to shake them, the group blended and walked to the nearby University of Tennessee campus. Along the way, Connor was rarely more than an arm's length from Mindy's side. After a brief tour of the college, they had pizza by the slice for lunch, then scurried back to the conference.

Students congregated in various locations again that evening, but Mindy talked almost exclusively with Connor. The wide range of interests of this mystery boy from another state both impressed and intrigued her. Before retiring, Connor asked for her address and phone number, showered her with compliments, promised to write her and concluded with, "I've never met anyone like you before."

When the conference ended after lunch the following day, Mindy wasn't sure what the administrators had learned but had to admit the other students had definitely changed her thinking. "There is probably far more drug and alcohol use and more teen sex in Macon County than I'm aware of." But she doubted the conference would have any lasting effect on the students or administrators and she didn't believe most adults at home could even talk openly and honestly about such things.

Back in Lafayette, cheer practice and school preparations quickly replaced lingering thoughts of the conference and the realities of day-to-day life dominated. The news of Richard Nixon's resignation from the presidency of the United States seemed inconsequential.

———————————— ‧ ————————————

It was hot when school began in mid-August. Mindy had matured considerably over the summer and arrived on the first day looking polished and beautiful. Much to her surprise, the first of five date requests came before lunch. She took the heightened male attention in stride but politely declined each offer. But her attitude changed shortly after dinner that evening. She answered the phone and to hear Tony Gann, a freshman and next-door neighbor, nervously introduce himself. He had difficulty finding his words until Mindy put him at ease and asked him how she could help. He lowered his voice to a whisper, "Paul Thomas, he asked me to talk to you for him."

The hair on Mindy's neck stood on end with an immediate flashback to a conversation the previous summer. Anne divulged a loosely kept secret that Paul Thomas, who had been dating Tammy Gregory steadily for almost two years, was having an affair with freshman Dawn Lawson. Mindy's first thought was, "This is Lafayette. Dawn and her mother have to know about Tammy and Paul. And they have to know Tammy will find out."

When Mindy suggested they inform Tammy themselves, Anne scoffed, "We could never do that! Tammy *has* been told before but she refused to believe it and made life difficult for the snitch at school." With no proof other than Anne's word, Mindy had reluctantly bit her tongue.

Tony continued, "Paul wants to know if you'll go out with him."

Mindy was beside herself with disgust. "Absolutely not! That's the most ridiculous thing I've ever heard. Everybody knows he's dating Tammy. I would never do such a thing to her, even if I liked him. *Which I don't!* You tell him I will never, ever, even think about going out with him. Not only is he a cheater, but he's also a coward. He doesn't even have the guts to talk to me himself!"

"He said you might say something like that, but he says it will be okay as long as you don't tell anybody until he breaks up with Tammy," Tony nervously replied.

Tony started to speak again, but Mindy cut him off to ask. "Would you meet with Tammy and me and tell her what Paul asked you to do?"

Tony's voice cracked, "Oh, I could never do that! Paul would kill me, and I'd probably get thrown off the football team. I'd never be able to go to school without getting beat up."

Mindy tried to convince him, "That's silly. I only want you to tell the truth."

Terrified, Tony replied, "No, no! I just couldn't do it!"

"Then goodbye!" Mindy said loudly and slammed the phone into its cradle.

Calming herself, Mindy sat in her bedroom wondering whether she should call Tammy. But with no physical proof of disloyalty and recalling Anne's advice a year earlier, she bit her tongue a second time. She considered asking Gina or Phyllis for their opinion but was afraid it would open gossip floodgates she didn't want to be part of.

Over the next few weeks, Mindy received two similar calls from the same freshman. She popped on the third one, "You tell him I think he's a low-class pig and I will never go out with him. You tell him if anyone calls me about this again, I *will* tell Tammy *and* every other girl at school what a cheater and loser he is." This seemed to put an end to the calls.

―――――――――― · ――――――――――

Kevin Gerard stopped by Ellington after school mid-week to show off his new car. After initial pleasantries, Kevin cleared his throat to ask, "Would you ever consider dating Wayne?"

Mindy gently shook her head. "Wayne is a nice guy, but I'm not interested in dating him, and I don't want to lead him on."

Kevin paused, then nervously inquired, "Well, if you won't go out with Wayne, would you consider going out with ― me?"

Mindy furrowed her brow. "You *know* Phyllis has a crush on you. I could never do such a thing to a friend, and *you* shouldn't be so silly to pass up such a good thing in Phyllis."

Ignoring Mindy's resolution, Kevin persisted, "Would you *ever* consider going out with me?"

She sighed and shook her head gently, "Never."

Kevin dropped his head, "Well, okay then. Guess I'll be going."

Mindy felt dirty and wanted to spit, but didn't know how.

―――――――――― · ――――――――――

A few days later, Mindy received a letter from Connor and continued to do so once a month for the rest of the academic year. His writing was well organized and usually included simple questions asking Mindy to reveal little things about herself. He also integrated quotes, poems, and song lyrics from various authors in a way that gave his letters a sophisticated appeal. Each ended with his dream of seeing her again. Although these things caught Mindy's attention, she was rarely timely about responding to Connor's letters. When she did, it was primarily because of her desire to maintain a mystery boy from far away fantasy. Written quickly, her return letters were generally factual updates and rarely asked questions in return. Later, they would evolve into a silent sounding board during less happy times.

Date offers continued to arrive regularly. Mike McCarthy, Virgil Goode, Jimmy Harper, John Cole, Dale Thompson, James Jones, Don Holland, Matt Wilmore, and MCHS graduate Harry Whitmire all inquired at least once via telephone within the first month of school. Except for Harry, they were all pleasant boys at school, but she considered none of them as date candidates.

The call from Harry struck Mindy as the oddest. With no previous introduction that she could remember, Mindy had no idea who he was. He mentioned he was a graduate of MCHS, knew of her through his friends, had watched her cheer at a basketball game and couldn't believe she hadn't at least heard of him. With not the slightest interest in another blind date, Mindy declined but later wondered if someone had failed to warn her that he might call.

Over the subsequent few weeks, Mindy received three similar calls. Each caller was a relatively distant MCHS graduate, each insisted that she had met them at the Junior-Senior Banquet, and each seemed surprised that she wasn't familiar with their name. Mindy politely declined and didn't bother to register their names in her memory bank for the second time. The bizarre fact that none of them had bothered to introduce themselves or talk with her in person before asking her out more than eclipsed the relative flattery of date offers from older boys. She had to wonder if these types of cold calls were a standard operating procedure for older boys in Macon County.

After making a few inquiries at school, it shocked Mindy to hear the general response, "They probably think you're cute and, because you're a city girl, think you might be loose."

"And really stupid," Mindy added bluntly.

Distraught by the possibility of an unwanted reputation, these calls left Mindy spooked, disgusted with boys in general, and hesitant to answer the phone. Her vision of courting and romance had taken a gigantic dive. "Where are all the *normal* guys?" she wondered.

Of the broad group of potential suitors, only Dale and Don succeeded in winning car dates. Dale, a fellow junior who was very nice, polite, and soft-spoken, came first. He quietly consulted some of Mindy's friends to ask if they thought she might consider going out with him. His youthful innocence sparked a matchmaking interest in classmates Kate Smith and Emily Harrison, who worked hard in his favor. Functioning as a tag-team, the girls approached Mindy on several occasions, only to have her decline. "I like Dale. He's a really nice guy, but I'm not interested in dating him," she explained.

A week later, they approached in tandem with a harder push, "Dale *is* really nice. You should at least give him a chance."

Bored with the Saturday night cruising ritual, Mindy succumbed to their pressure and said she would consider it.

Kate and Emily took no time in tracking Dale down at school to deliver the news. So, it was no surprise when Dale called that evening, and Mindy agreed to join him for dinner and a movie on the upcoming Saturday evening.

Dale was the consummate gentleman from the time he arrived at Ellington. They were soon off to a Steak and Ale restaurant near RiverGate Mall. Surprised by the prices, Mindy decided to order soup and salad. But Dale insisted money was not an issue, "I *want* you to order something special."

After dinner, they made their way to Mindy's first indoor movie since her move to Lafayette. *Earthquake* was one of a continuing string of 1970s disaster films that didn't live up to its hype, but it was an appreciated alternative to cruising.

During the return drive, Mindy knew Kate and Emily would inevitably inquire about the evening and pondered what she would tell them. Dale was one of the nicest and best-mannered boys at school, but Mindy wondered, "Why don't I feel better about this date or being with him?"

It didn't take long to answer her own question. As a date or companion, Dale didn't seem to come fueled with excitement and didn't generate any sense of wonder for her. She certainly didn't want to date anyone mean or bad, she'd already had enough of that for a lifetime with Jack Robertson. At the same time, a subtle teasing edge, a touch of mystery, or unpredictable wit would make any guy more interesting. But Dale lacked such attributes. He was more like the semi-fictional Fred Wright from the *Anne of Green Gables* series. Fred was "exceedingly good," but Anne had sensed no "could be wicked" in him. Mindy saw Dale as Fred's mirror image.

When Dale called a few days later about another date, Mindy informed him she was "busy." After checking several times with Emily and Kate, Dale accepted that fact that Mindy would be perpetually "busy."

Shy and reserved football team co-captain Don Holland was persistent enough to get Mindy to agree to attend a post-game party with him at Phil Phifer's house after the home opener.

Few things went well during the game, and the Tigers suffered a dreadful defeat. Although Mindy had been on the sideline cheering the entire game, she somehow missed the fact that Don had lost the ball more than once, leading to opposition scores. After the game, she waited near the concession area as the stadium lights were extinguished. Don was the last player out of the locker room. He approached slowly, eyes to the ground, and appeared to be holding something in his hands. As he approached, the image gradually sharpened. Between his hands was a football and what looked like an entire roll of white cloth tape encircling his hands and the ball. He explained, "Coach wants me to sleep with my hands taped to the ball so I'll learn to hold on to it better."

Don dutifully accepted his punishment and did not plan to rid himself of tape or the ball. Unable to drive, he dejectedly asked Mindy to get his keys from his pocket, the retrieval of which left her feeling very uncomfortable. As they walked to the car, she shuddered. "Oh, my goodness, what if he has to pee?" She opened the passenger door and helped him in so he wouldn't bump his head. It took Mindy a moment to figure out the three-on-the-column transmission before they could drive off in the party's direction.

Initially, Mindy felt terribly sorry for Don. He was a cute, hardworking boy who didn't deserve such a humiliating punishment. But her sorrow soon changed from dismay to anger. She couldn't believe that any boy would accept such a degrading penalty without a fight. Suddenly, her inner voice yelled, "Go to hell, coach. I quit!" as she envisioned herself ripping the tape off her hands then throwing tape and ball into the coach's face. Her guttural reaction surprised even her.

At the small gathering, Don still refused to remove the tape, making it impossible for Mindy to relax and have fun. Embarrassed and impotent, Dan apologized but finally asked her to drive them to Ellington. When they arrived, Mindy asked, "Would you like me to help get the tape off?" Don shook his head and refused any help.

"How in the world are you going to drive like that?" Mindy asked with some distress.

"I'll manage," Don pitifully replied.

It was evident that driving safely would be impossible, so Mindy protested, "I can't let you try to drive like that."

Don dropped his head. "I just can't let anyone see me take the tape off. I'll manage."

Mindy went inside and peaked out through a dark window to the drive. It looked as though Don was trying to get the tape off with his teeth. After watching the sad scene for a few minutes, Mindy decided to go back out and help him, but by the time she grabbed her sweater and a pair of scissors, Don and his car were gone. With fingers crossed, Mindy hoped he would get home safely.

Temporary relief came the following week. It was quiet on the boy front, and devoid of any annoying phone calls that required less than truthful excuses. Her concept of boys, dating, and romance continued to fall exceedingly short of her expectations.

The weeklong hiatus didn't seem long enough when Don approached at lunch. With less personality than Mindy could have imagined, he forced out his request, "I know things didn't go very well last week. I'd like to have another chance. Would you like to go out again this weekend?"

Mindy hesitated. Don was another polite and passively bright boy. But she knew "another chance" was a bad idea. She had, however, felt remarkably bad for him, and the little voice on her shoulder whispered, "You should help him rebuild his manhood." Against her better judgment, she agreed.

The following Friday brought with it MCHS Homecoming, which caused one unexpected but substantial paradigm shift in Mindy's vision of her future. A fair amount of hype and peripheral girl talk led up to the announcement of the Homecoming Queen, with most assuming that Tammy Gregory was the only logical choice from the senior class.

These same conversations sparked speculation regarding the next queen, and several classmates openly suggested Mindy already had a dominating lock on the 1975 Homecoming crown. Mindy took the compliments in stride and had little to say in blushing reply. Although she believed there were several other worthy candidates in their class, she silently enjoyed the fantasy and rationalized, "It's not like a beauty pageant. No strutting around on stage. No competition based on looks alone. Classmates, kids that actually know *me,* will make the decision."

Believing it would be a memorable way to begin her senior year, fantasy seeds sprouted and smothered remaining dreams of returning to St. Charles to complete high school. Without residual longing, she looked toward graduating from MCHS in the spring of 1976. For the first time, she consciously accepted the concept of being a Macon Countian for the foreseeable future.

Mindy watched from the sidelines as they placed the Homecoming crown on Tammy's head, but had to grimace when co-captain Paul Thomas delivered an obligatory kiss.

The subsequent game passed quickly in another lopsided loss. But Don's vise grip on the ball every time he touched it didn't go unnoticed by Mindy.

Don arrived at Ellington Saturday evening looking happier and more confident than Mindy had ever seen him. After eating at Clifton's, they made their way to the Macon County Drive-in, where Mindy's full stomach dropped when she saw the marquee: *Walking Tall* and *The Texas Chainsaw Massacre.* As the movie unfolded, the senseless violence kept Mindy's eyes turned away from the screen for much of the show but, much to her bewilderment, Don laughed during some of the bloodier scenes. Thrilled when the first movie ended, Mindy delivered an abrupt "No!" when Don asked if she wanted to stay for the second feature.

Minutes later, they were back at Ellington, where Mindy stepped onto the porch and turned with arms crossed to block Dan's path. "Thanks for taking me out," she stated flatly.

Trembling, Don asked, "How about next weekend?"

Mindy looked him in the eye. "I don't think so," she said before finishing the execution, "Let's just be friends." Don walked away like a man and never said another word to Mindy.

The following Monday, Mindy arrived at her usual lunchroom table to find energetic conversation already underway. She sat quietly and listened to a replay of the "all boys want is to get in your pants" theory. She found it demoralizing that so many girls openly accepted the "boys will be boys" philosophy and felt strongly that their expectations for males and love were unacceptably low. But her dating experiences had soured her own thoughts of romance, and the lunchroom brainwashing effect left her more accepting of their general conclusion: "Be ready to say no or be prepared to give in." Mindy felt empty as she returned to class. She realized that any acceptance of the concept as presented would require lowering her own standards considerably. Despite resistance, her own vision of love and romance took another significant dive.

The only other semi-eventful event during October was a party at Ellington. In Mindy's experience, parties in Lafayette were rare and always closed to a small number of carefully chosen invites. So, Mindy's mother surprised her when she suggested Mindy host an open party after the next home football game.

Fitting into all the social cliques at school but belonging to none, Mindy ignored unspoken local custom and invited a wide array of schoolmates to a post-football party the following Friday night.

The large turnout of students created an unusual but interactive mix of personalities and social classes. Mindy kept the music spinning on the turntable, but to her disappointment, no one ever thought of dancing.

There was a small band of alleged potheads whom Mindy had purposely not invited. Still, Brad Archibald and his sidekicks arrived late and made their way into the rec room from the side entrance. Within minutes, Mindy was made aware of their presence, and even Brad's own cousin anxiously warned, "They're probably here to case the house." But the party crashers escaped before Mindy could investigate, and a cautious inventory that night and again the next day didn't identify any missing items. Brad's presence, although brief, precipitated the departure of several attendees because "The party is getting too wild."

The next Monday at school, Mindy's history teacher, Mr. Tatum, pulled her aside to chastise her sternly for hosting a "drunken party." Someone had apparently informed him that Mindy's mother had been drinking beer. Engulfed by embarrassment, Mindy didn't deny that it may have happened but was angry that Mr. Tatum felt it was his business to comment at all.

At home, Mindy didn't hesitate to share Mr. Tatum's displeasure or to chastise her own mother for failing to anticipate such gossip and hide any alcohol in the house. Mindy's frustration with the negative feedback over an otherwise successful event convinced her to never host another high school party.

The death of puppy love, the previous summer's flatness, the disenchanting lunchroom talk about boys, and the disappointing dating experience through the early school year convinced Mindy that her fallen vision of romance was more than a simple matter of failed expectations. She believed "Mr. Right" would be unique but didn't know where he might exist and concluded, "Good thing I enjoy doing things with the girls."

Mindy also began to look at the limitations of the local scene differently and realized it provided little fuel for wonder, excitement, or personal growth. Other than beauty pageants, there were virtually no activities for girls outside of school; no sports, no dance, and no arts. There were a few school-sponsored clubs, but these were limited and poorly organized. Other than the annual state conference, even the Interact Club provided inconsistent social interaction. Mindy better understood Anne's perspective of the town's restrictions and felt frustrated by its sparse opportunity and lack of imagination. Worse, her own ideas almost always ran into roadblocks instead of finding openings.

On the boy front, date requests slowed but didn't stop. Mindy remained polite in her declinations and, "Sorry, I'm busy" became a conditioned response. She refocused her sights back to what she had always enjoyed most, her friends and girl time. Cheerleading, writing letters, shopping, reading novels, and dreaming about her escape to college happily absorbed the following weeks.

Babysitting in Mississauga and St. Charles had provided Mindy fairly regular weekend work and modest but renewable cash flow. But babysitting work in Lafayette had been minimal and inconsistent. When Mindy told her parents, she planned to look for part-time work, her father vetoed any of the low-level service jobs available for girls. When her savings account dwindled to almost nothing, she made a second pitch for work, but her father denied her again.

The employment clouds cleared when Citizen's Bank announced it was opening a new branch on Scottsville Road in November. At Mindy's request, her father spoke with Mr. Donnelly, President of Citizens Bank, and he was more than happy to engineer a part-time teller position for her. She began her training at the bank on the square and was thrilled with her schedule: Friday afternoons after school to closing and every Saturday from 8 AM till 3 PM. Once school was out, she would work full days on Friday and Saturday, with occasional weekly full-time stints to cover co-worker vacations. If there were ever conflicts with cheering, school, or travel, all she had to do was let the branch manager know, and they would excuse her from work.

The last Wednesday in October, Kat approached Mindy at school full of excitement. "I got a call last night from a guy who wants to meet you." Mindy's winced and wondered, "What are you trying to get me into now?"

Chapter 9
Saturday Night Fever
October 31–December 31, 1974

For Mindy, Halloween was a bigger priority than meeting any boy. She delighted in handing out treats to the little cowboys, goblins, and princesses that risked ringing the bell on Ellington. Most of the jokes they told weren't very funny, but the children were always delightful. Mindy laughed hysterically after listening to a Southern-accented little Cinderella and Snow White. It was like talking to an Asian with a Scottish accent; it just didn't fit any paradigm of auditory logic. Still, the adorable ones received twice as many treats as the rest, but no one walked away lamenting, "I got a rock."

Early the next morning, Mindy was already half awake before the alarm clock clicked on to mark the start of a new day. When it did, she pulled her pillow over her head to drown out the noise. Lying motionless, Mindy wanted to stay bundled in the warmth of her covers. But suddenly her eyes popped open, and she was wide awake. It was a game day and time to put on her cheer uniform. It was also a day with a twist, Kat planned to introduce Mindy to Damien Thorne after the game.

When Kat had mentioned "a guy who would like to meet you," Mindy was highly skeptical. A hefty dose of doubt regarding Kat's assessment and motive compounded her general lack of interest in boys. But Kat had been persistent in her sales pitch, "He's from Lafayette but in college now. He used to date Mary Sharp, but they broke up a few years ago. He's really good-looking and a really nice guy."

The reference to Mary was somewhat reassuring. Mindy respected Mary, a class of '74 MCHS graduate, and thought of her as a warm person with a good heart. As Kat talked, Mindy's mind drifted, "If Mary dated this guy, then he's probably okay. Plus, a college boy just has to be more interesting than a high school boy." Then she laughed. "At least this one is asking for an introduction. I guess I'll be at the game anyway."

Thoughtful drift was broken when Kat inquired, "Hey, did you hear anything I said?" and Mindy agreed.

The cheerleaders stayed on the field for a few post-game cheers and tried to ease the fan's pain after another disheartening home-field loss. The bleachers were all but empty when they finished the last cheer. Kat immediately grabbed Mindy by the arm and escorted her toward the stands. Mindy looked up to see a short, thinly mustached male sauntering down the otherwise deserted bleacher steps. He stopped at the fence separating the stands and field. From twenty yards away, the cockiness of his gait and body language ignited warning flares in Mindy's mind. The closer they got, it also became apparent that "really good looking" was an overstatement and Mindy wondered, "What *is* Kat trying to get me into?"

Less than impressed from a distance, Mindy's instincts were telling her to walk away, but it was already too late. After brief introductions, the threesome talked for a few minutes until Kat escaped to catch her ride home while Mindy was polite and stayed to chat a little longer.

As they talked over the fence, it surprised Mindy to find that Damien seemed reasonably articulate and polite. It was evident he was older, but his helmet hair and mustache made it hard to tell just how old he was. At the end of the conversation, he asked if he could call her sometime the following week. Mindy didn't care one way or the other, but had no reason to object.

Predictably, Damien called a few days later and invited Mindy to grab a burger with him after the next football game. Almost always hungry after games, the prospect of a post-game burger and fries sounded good, so Mindy consented.

The following week, the field lights had just gone dark, and Mindy was waiting near the concession stand when she spotted Damien waving from the shadows of the parking lot. She said goodbyes to her friends and made her way through the stadium gate. Damien seemed to be in a hurry. With minimal salutation, he pointed to his car, and they quickly pulled away.

When Damien announced they were going to Jones's, Mindy furrowed her brow because Clifton's was the more popular post-game meeting place. There was little opportunity for conversation during the sixty-second drive, but surprise grabbed Mindy a second time when Damien objected when she started to get out of the car at Jones's, "Let's just wait for car service."

The arrival of food helped to smooth the otherwise choppy conversation. By the time Mindy finished the last of her fries, she had confirmed her initial impression that Damien was reasonably articulate, but it was apparent he wasn't a recent MCHS graduate. She had to ask, "So, what year *did* you graduate?"

Damien frowned, shifted in his seat several times and answered evasively, "Oh, a few years ago." Before Mindy could clarify, he changed the subject.

This response invited uncertainty, and Mindy suggested she should get home. Damien stiffened and spoke with some urgency. "Would you like to go with me, my cousin Larry, and his girlfriend, Holly, to hear a band and go dancing in Nashville next weekend? You probably know Holly, she graduated last year."

It was like offering candy to a baby. Nashville, live music, and dancing were not things that had been even vague possibilities on any previous outing. So, Mindy accepted the offer; not for the boy, but for what promised to be a refreshing change of pace and the excitement of being "out there."

Conversations with other girls at school with older boyfriends percolated in Mindy's mind and raised questions that prompted a minor investigation into her new suitor's history with only limited success. The only concrete information was a repeat of what she'd already heard. Although several friends knew of Damien in general, nobody Mindy trusted could offer any insight into his history or personality. Kat was the only one who had positive things to say, "You're so lucky. He's such a great guy and was so popular in high school."

Mindy wondered how Kat could know these things when no one else did. In fact, not one friend seemed to know anything about him other than he was from Lafayette. Mindy had her doubts, and her own first impression had been lukewarm at best, but Kat's persistent sales pitch made her wonder whether she was missing something.

Further inquiries remained unrevealing. Mindy wondered why he wasn't dating someone his own age, but rationalized her doubts away. "He's older and acts more confident, but he doesn't seem any more mature than typical high school boys, and the presence of others should keep it safe." Mindy convinced herself that the trip to Nashville wouldn't be another Jack Robertson outing.

For a mid-teen with grand visions of the world, the thought of Nashville, music, and dancing seemed like the doorway to Oz, and her desire to experience "out there" overpowered her concerns.

Products of small towns themselves, Mindy's parents were sympathetic and well aware of Lafayette's entertainment limitations. So, they didn't question her when she informed them of the trip to Nashville. Mindy then mentioned in passing that Damien was an MCHS graduate but didn't elaborate further and her parents didn't ask.

Damien arrived fifteen minutes late and cowered on the front porch as Fi snarled and guarded the doorway in her miniature defensive posture. Mindy picked her up to soothe her, but Fi became unmanageable as Damien crossed the threshold. Mindy ignored the little dog's warning and handed the furry alarm off to her brothers. Damien cautiously followed Mindy to the kitchen for introductions which, already running late, were brief.

They met Holly and Larry at the square minutes later and began the nearly hour-long trek from Lafayette to Nashville. The initial conversation along the winding two-lane road was strained but loosened considerably thanks to Larry's laughter producing wit and observation. The talk about college and politics was something new, and being out with "older people" gave Mindy a sense of maturity.

As they approached Nashville, Mindy's eye caught sight of a highway sign that read: To St. Louis next right. The sign instantly revived visions of returning to St. Charles to finish high school, and she spoke with excitement about the possibility. She cut herself short when she realized that her innocent ramblings about her former home were irritating Damien, but made a silent mental note of his reaction.

At the nightclub, they waited in the ID line, where Larry's eyes fixed on Mindy's feet before he whispered something into Damien's ear. Damien glanced down at Mindy's feet, then condescendingly inquired, "Are those your only shoes?"

Unaware that they were going to an age-restricted bar, Mindy hadn't thought twice about slipping on her favorite shoes. She sarcastically thought, "What? Do you think I have another pair in my purse, or do you think this is the only pair I own?" But she bit her tongue and explained that her saddle shoes were very comfortable and she wore them everywhere. But the boys worried they would be a clear sign Mindy was underage and might prompt the bouncer to card her. As it was with most bars, it didn't matter; cute girls were allowed to enter unquestioned.

Inside the nightclub, as the boys referred to it, cigarette smoke already hung heavily in the air, and the group moved to a booth near the back. The poorly cushioned seats were covered in worn imitation red velvet, and the dim lights helped to hide dirt and stains. A waitress came by to take drink orders just a moment later. She looked to Holly first who, without hesitation, ordered a Tom Collins. The waitress turned to Mindy, who paused while trying to decide between a soda or ice tea. Reading her indecision, Larry jumped in. "She'll have a Singapore Sling, and two Budweiser drafts for the gentlemen." Mindy had not the slightest clue what went into a Singapore Sling, but didn't want to risk embarrassment by asking.

The drinks arrived, and Mindy enjoyed feeling "grown up" as she cautiously sipped the sugary alcohol concoction. Subsequent sips were far less uncertain, and the unfamiliar taste made the drink disappear quickly. When the band started a short time later, Mindy was ready to dance. Happy to cut loose, her arms stretched to the sky, her long, silky hair flew through the air, and her hips caught the rhythmic beat of the music. Mindy was a dance floor sensation, and it was immediately apparent that Damien was out of his dance league. His Popsicle-stick limbs moved mechanically, and his sense of rhythm was nonexistent. It didn't matter to Mindy. In the middle of the floor, she had a dozen dance partners riding the rock-and-roll waves.

Early evenings had never remotely threatened Mindy's 10:30 PM curfew before, but tonight it brought the dancing to an end when the troupe began the drive back to Lafayette at 9:30 PM. Despite the early conclusion, this nightlife already had Mindy hooked. Dancing and live music in such a small venue offered a type of fun she had never experienced before. She didn't really care who she went with, but she wanted to go to Nashville again.

After dropping Larry and Holly at the square, Mindy took the opportunity to ask again about Damien's age. Much to Mindy's surprise, she learned he would graduate from college at semester and would turn twenty-two in the spring. "Oh, my goodness, he's *five* years older than me. He *is* old! If I'd known that at the football game and told my parents, I'm pretty sure they would have said '*No way!*'"

She recalled his elusive responses to her previous inquiry about both his age and year in college, and realized, "He *knew* he was too old for me but wanted to hide the fact until he considered it safe."

———————— • ————————

"Nashville" as a destination, was a misnomer. With a merger in the early 1960s, Nashville and Davidson County became one, but the downtown area existed south of the Cumberland River while the area north of the river remained mostly suburban and gradually transitioned into farmland. The boys lumped the north of the river suburbia along with small towns just outside the city limits into one collective term for descriptive convenience.

The boys' use of the term "nightclub" was also a significant stretch. Most of these "clubs" were free-standing motel restaurants by day and bars by night. After serving pancakes and eggs for breakfast followed by burgers and fries at lunch, they became nightclubs when they turned on dim-colored lights for ambiance and hosted live music on the weekends with 12-x-12-foot acrylic dance floors illuminated by flashing colored lights from below. For a sixteen-year-old, these realities were unimportant; it was new, it was different, and it seemed only as playfully dangerous as a roller coaster ride.

Not one of Mindy's friends or acquaintances from Lafayette had ever mentioned "nightclub" destinations, and she quickly realized that between drinking and dancing, there was little wonder why. From the very first trip, Mindy believed she should never discuss these locations with her schoolmates, not even her best friends. Experience had taught her that the rumor mill was powerful and potentially dangerous. With dancing, she risked reprisal from her Baptist friends, but drinking could precipitate her expulsion from the cheer team. Larry confirmed these fears in no uncertain terms, "Don't tell anyone where we've gone. We don't want Holly's dad to find out." But Mindy read through the screen and suspected the boys were more concerned about themselves than Holly.

It was apparent that Mindy would need to keep Nashville nightlife at a safe distance from her happy-go-lucky world as a high school cheerleader as much as small-town life might allow. A dual existence would be necessary. That suited Mindy just fine, but she was uncertain why.

But Mindy's hope for near-total secrecy lasted one day. Somehow, Kat was aware of the date, minus the nightclub details, and spread the news Monday morning at school. At lunch, several girls gathered around Mindy to interrogate. Mindy downplayed the evening but couldn't ignore the other girls' accolades. "You're so lucky to be going out with a college guy. He'll get a good job and be able to take you to nice places." In their eyes, dating an older guy clearly elevated one's social status.

The next day, the lunch table was unusually quiet until one girl laughed and announced, "Ha! The boys must have all heard the news about Mindy dating a college guy. None of 'em are showing up for their Mindy fix."

Another voice belted out, "Of course not, silly. Teenage boys can't compete with an older guy with a car."

Mindy sat wide-eyed and uncertain what to think.

The "older guy" concept percolated in Mindy's mind that night. "Maybe there are some advantages right now, but they are time-limited — they will fade away in just a few years. Don't they see that? I'm going to college and can't imagine not marrying a college educated guy someday."

The football season already seemed like ancient history when the basketball season began. Most observers already believed the boys' team would struggle to compete, but viewed the girls' team as a ray of hope. With the core of the team returning, many held tight to high expectations for the Tigerettes. They had done well the previous year, and a real run at a state title seemed within reach.

The opening game of the season was against county rival, Red Boiling Springs. At halftime, the MCHS cheerleaders made their way to the RBS side of the court to offer a 'hello and thank-you' cheer for the opposing fans. After the cheer, a nameless boy with a generic country face wearing a John Deere ball cap stood and cupped his hands around his mouth to holler, "Hey, you! Girl with the pigtails. What's your name?"

Mindy playfully turned her head to send her pigtails flying. Looking in the general direction of the voice, she replied with a faux Southern accent, "Minn-day."

"Can you come cruising in RBS this weekend?" the boy hollered back.

Mindy laughed and hollered, "Sure" before marching away with her cheer mates. The pool of teen boys around the instigator let out a yelp of joy and then erupted with good-natured laughter. By the time Mindy returned to the visitor's side of the court, the incident was already lost in her past.

Damien called from his apartment in Murfreesboro the next evening. Before Mindy finished saying hello, he sharply interrupted, "What are you planning to do this weekend?"

Mindy innocently replied, "Oh, I don't know yet, but I'll probably get together with the girls. Maybe go cruising."

Damien responded coldly, "Well, that's not what I hear. I hear you have plans for this weekend."

"What are you talking about?" Mindy asked.

"I hear you're going over to RBS," he barked.

Intimidated by his sharp tone, Mindy replied, "No, I don't have any plans to go there. Why would I go over there?"

Damien continued, "Well, that's just not what I hear."

Now angry, Mindy fired back, "Well, what *did* you hear?"

"Well, that's just not what I hear," Damien repeated.

"What *are* you talking about?" Mindy demanded.

Damien finally explained that Kat had called him with a report of the RBS flirtation with the anonymous boy the night before, and he felt it necessary to call and confront. Mindy put her fist on her forehead and shook her head in disbelief. She laughed, "That kind of stuff happens all the time. None of us pay any attention to it." What she thought but didn't say was, *"It's none of your business, anyway!"*

Mindy's response seemed to smooth Damien's ruffled feathers, and he bluntly informed, "I'll be home over Thanksgiving weekend and want you to come over to watch me play in the Turkey Bowl."

Unfamiliar with the event, Mindy had to inquire. Damien explained that the Turkey Bowl was an alumni flag-football game at the high school on Thanksgiving Day. Mindy hedged, "We have out-of-town family coming to visit, and I'm not sure if I'll have time."

Damien pushed. "Really, you need to be there."

Mindy remained non-committal. "I'll try to stop by if we're not too busy."

Relatives from Missouri and Alabama arrived Wednesday afternoon, and the mini-family reunion of adult siblings and their families began. Old stories, laughter, food, beer, and wine-fueled a three-day party, and Mindy took pride in providing much-needed assistance to her hostess mother. The family fun continued on Thanksgiving as the turkey roasted and appetites grew. As Mindy worked aside her mother, the adult relatives commented on how much she had matured and warned, "The boys will be busting down your doors."

Once the feast was served, it didn't take long for the food to disappear and Mindy cleared the table as the adults settled in to reminisce, drink more than a little wine and laugh about days gone by. This is when Mindy kept her ears particularly sharp and knew she would hear old family stories unlikely to be recounted at any other time. They were often reminders that her parents, aunts, and uncles had enjoyed their own PG-rated wild and crazy days.

Preoccupied with family fun, the afternoon hours faded into history. The Turkey Bowl game didn't cross Mindy's mind until the sounds of NFL football on the television reminded her of it. She considered driving over to the school to watch the last minutes, but the drizzly, uninviting day convinced her to stay warm inside and enjoy the company.

That evening, Mindy received another angry phone call. "Where were you today?" Damien asked sharply.

"I told you I didn't know if I could make it. My mom needed my help here," she explained.

Aghast, Damien retorted, "Well, you know, Holly was there for Larry. How do you think it made me look?"

Mindy couldn't believe his possessive attitude and thought, "We've been on one date. I don't owe you anything" but felt too intimidated to say so. Instead, she brought the conversation to an abrupt end, "I have to go help my mom. Bye."

Dropping the handset into the cradle, she said out loud to herself, "I'll go to Red Boiling if I want to, and I won't go to a lousy huff-and-puff football game if I don't want to," and nodded sharply.

Docility, but no apology, came with Damien's phone call the next day. "Would you like to go to another nightclub in Nashville along with Holly and Larry Saturday evening?" he inquired. Visions of doing "grown-up" things vaporized any residual angst, and Mindy agreed.

Saturday evening, Mindy left her favorite saddle shoes in the closet and the boys introduced her to a Tom Collins before she wore them both out on the dance floor. But the fun came to an early end once again, and on the way home, Mindy made a mental note to discuss a later curfew with her parents.

Work, basketball, the annual Christmas Parade, and church occupied most of the following weekend. The highlight for Mindy was throwing candy from atop the MCHS Cheerleader float to the outstretched hands of children along the parade route.

Saturday evening, Mindy returned to the local cruise scene with Phyllis and Gina, where she was happy to be talking with the girls but cautiously avoided any discussion of Damien. After the first few laps, the route seemed remarkably small, and Mindy sensed no anticipation for "out there." She returned home happy to have spent an evening with her friends, but distracted by the desire to see more of the world. The growing allure of Nashville made Lafayette seem even smaller, and Anne's voice rang in her head.

With the college semester nearly over and his apartment lease expiring, Damien called the next week to invite Mindy to Murfreesboro to tour the MTSU campus. Mindy discussed the excursion with her mother and purposely revealed Damien's age. Surprised, her mother seemed uncertain how to respond, but Mindy's interpretation was, "She thinks if she didn't object before, she can't object now." When Damien called back to confirm, Mindy simply stated, "My mom said okay."

With the winter solstice approaching, daylight was already beginning to wane as Mindy hurried home to freshen up after work at the bank. A short time later, Damien stood on the front porch. With a foreboding sky as a backdrop, he looked taller than usual and appeared anxious to get started. So, Mind didn't dwell on his height change, and they began the ninety-minute trek to Murfreesboro. With fanciful visions of campus life dancing in her head, Mindy's end of the conversation focused on the upcoming tour and the nature of dorm life.

When Mindy mentioned her vision of late-night political and philosophic discussions, Damien frowned and flatly informed her, "That doesn't happen much at MTSU."

The cloudy December sky still held enough twilight for a walk through the small campus which ended at the bookstore. Mindy perused the book aisles, where she flipped through the psychology and philosophy texts, hoping to absorb some essential and meaningful secrets of life. Her search ended when Damien pushed her away from the books and said, "It's time to go."

When they stepped outside, Damien smugly produced a bouquet of dried flowers from behind his back. "I got you some flowers. Dried ones are better than fresh because they last longer."

After offering thanks, Mindy added a tongue-in-cheek, "And thanks for the explanation of their longevity," but Damien missed her playful sarcasm.

With darkness upon them, Damien became impatient. He suggested they stop to see his apartment and drove the few blocks far more aggressively than necessary. He jumped out of the car and scanned the area as if someone might be watching, then hurried Mindy to the apartment door.

The tour of the two-bedroom apartment with a one-person kitchen and tiny living room didn't take long. Damien reached into the refrigerator to grab two bottles of Coke. Handing one to Mindy, he pointed toward the sofa. Mindy sat at one end, and Damien coiled into the other squarely facing her. Still hoping to learn more about college life, Mindy launched into a laundry list of questions that had accumulated in her mind during the tour.

Damien answered with short, blunt responses and soon became agitated. Sensing his irritation, Mindy halted her interrogation and was greeted by several uncomfortable seconds of silence. She took an uncertain sip of Coke, and Damien seized the opportunity to interject, "Are you a virgin?"

Mindy choked on her drink. Taking a moment to recover and assuming she had misunderstood the question, she shook her head, "What did you ask?"

"Well, you don't have to answer — *if* you don't want to," he replied, then smiled as if he knew the answer.

"I don't think I heard you correctly. What did you ask?" Mindy innocently inquired.

Damien flatly repeated, "Are you a virgin?"

Mindy failed to comprehend the straightforward nature of the question and frowned to question, "You mean, like Mary?"

Damien reacted as if he'd been punched in the nose and shook his head with befuddlement. *"Mary?* Who's Mary?"

"You know, Mary — Virgin Mary, the mother of Jesus?" Mindy calmly replied.

"Virgin Mary? What's *she* got to do with it?" he hissed.

Looking squarely into Damien's empty eyes, Mindy nonchalantly explained, "Well, I go to church every week, but I don't think I'm as good as Mary," then took another extra-long drink of Coke.

"I meeean — *have you ever had sex?"* Damien quipped.

Mindy nearly shot Coke fizz through her nose and choked out, "Well, *of course not.* Why would you ask that? Do you think I'm *not* a virgin?"

Lowering his head in defeat, Damien shrugged his narrow shoulders. "Don't you remember last summer when I passed you going into CB's?" Trying to understand the direction of the discussion, Mindy returned only a blank expression. So, Damien squealed, *"Don't you remember?* I was walking into CB's, and you were walking out. You *smiled* at me."

"I have no memory of that — of ever seeing you before Kat introduced you. But what in the world does *that* have to do with anything?" Mindy asked, more confused than ever.

Sitting tall, Damien earnestly replied, "Well, most girls who smile *like that* have had sex."

Mindy just blinked in stunned disbelief, and then a shook her head several times to clear it. This was one of the dumbest things she had ever heard. She couldn't see any logic in his assumption. "That's just silly. Just because any girl smiles doesn't mean she's had sex. Why in the world would you *ever* think that?"

The conversation abruptly died, and suddenly uncomfortable, Mindy stood to announce, "Let's go. I'm hungry."

Damien stood as well and looked around the apartment, reeling in defeat. Suddenly filled with frustration, he blurted, "Let's go get some pizza. You can bring your Coke with you."

The pizza disappeared quickly, with sparse conversation from either side of the table. Minutes after the last bite, Mindy was happy to begin the drive home. Her mind spun with questions, but she arrived back in Lafayette no worse for her mental gyrations.

———————— · ————————

The MCHS basketball teams hosted Whitehouse on December 20th. The Tigers fell while the Tigerettes improved to 7–0 in a 50–36 blowout. The games marked the end of the first semester of school and the start of Christmas break. Mindy would miss the fun and excitement of game days, but by the time she was preparing for bed, basketball was unimportant. She was looking forward to another trip to Nashville for music and dancing. But she had to pause when she thought, "The boys will probably buy me more drinks. It may be grown-up stuff, but I know it's wrong, and so do they." She reminded herself that her Saturday nightlife would have to remain carefully hidden from her friends and schoolmates lest she follow Anne's cheerleading fate.

Confiding in her mother had waned considerably, but Mindy reviewed the first trips to Nashville, including her assessment of mixed drinks. Her mother expressed no concern but had mentioned the drinks to Mindy's father. While Mindy was waiting for Damien to arrive, her father stepped into the kitchen to offer a rare bit of advice, "Don't drink any of those fruity drinks. They just make you thirsty and want to drink more. Order a whiskey on the rocks and just sip on one drink all evening."

Her mother overheard this advice and cleared her voice to ask, "How old did you say Damien is?" Mindy's interpretation was that her mother hoped her father would hear the age difference in context with drinking and intercede. To the contrary, he let the question slide by and noted, "At least she'll get to go out to nice places instead of Clifton's and the drive-in."

The third trip to Nashville was very much like the first two. Mindy tore up the acrylic while Damien proved to be a perpetual dance floor failure. It was not uncommon for other males to slide into dance motion with Mindy, who would playfully share a few dance minutes with anyone who displayed decent moves. A frustrated Damien never attempted to stop them.

To escape embarrassment, Damien would ask Larry to step in for him occasionally. Larry would coolly reach into his back pocket for a comb, slowly stroke its teeth through the strands of his thinning hair, grow a big smile, and happily oblige his cousin's request. This was just fine with Mindy; he was a better dresser and a far better dancer. Lost in the shuffle was Holly.

Curfew approached and departure time arrived. Having spent most of the evening on the dance floor, Mindy was the only one in the group sufficiently sober as she slid into the front passenger seat ready to turn up the eight-track tunes. Larry and Holly flopped into the back, curled up for the drive home, and fell asleep in minutes. About ten miles into the return, Damien begged, "I've had a really long day. Would you mind driving?" Still running on a dance-adrenaline high, Mindy happily agreed. The car pulled onto the shoulder, and Mindy flew around the front of the car like a Chinese fire drill. Damien quietly collapsed into the front passenger seat and was also asleep within minutes. Mindy cruised down the road toward Lafayette, lost in the music and quietly singing along to a Linda Ronstadt eight-track tape playing at low volume.

As the car came to a stop on the square, the three sleeping occupants awakened. Startled to see Mindy in the driver's seat, Larry looked around with some confusion. After piecing the scene together, he squawked out an exasperated, "Oh, man, I can't believe you let her drive!" Damien shrunk low into his seat with embarrassment.

Damien re-assumed command of the car and drove Mindy to Ellington, where he pulled up deep into the driveway, beyond the reach of the carport light. When the passenger door clicked open, Damien barked, "Wait." When Mindy looked his direction, he softened his tone, "Ya know, I like you."

But his words sounded empty, and Mindy thought he was just trying to be nice. She nodded in appreciation but offered no other response. When he added, "I *really* like you," she felt confused. His tone made him sound like a salesman rather than an admirer. Then she realized she had *never* sensed affection *from* him and knew she had never expressed any *for* him. Going out with him was simply a ticket to a night on the town.

Damien reached under the seat to pull out a satin-covered black box and extended it toward her. Quite surprised, Mindy stared at it blankly and felt embarrassed because she hadn't even considered buying him a Christmas gift. "Thank you," she said, "but you really shouldn't have bought me anything."

"Open it," Damien pushed. "Go ahead, open it."

Mindy opened the box to find a cross-shaped necklace. She strained to examine it in the pale light, but could tell only that it felt large and heavy. "Thanks, but I really wish you hadn't bought me anything. I'm sorry, but I don't have anything for you."

Wobbling his head with a mix of pride and intoxication, Damien said proudly, "It's a Catholic-Baptist cross."

"There's no such thing," Mindy concretely retorted as she slipped the heavy chain over her neck. Glancing at Damien, it surprised her to find that he had shifted in his seat and was leaning toward her. Uncomfortable but unafraid, Mindy pushed the car door open.

Damien followed closely as she made her way to the house. When they stopped at the side door, Damien said, "I hope you like the necklace." Still feeling embarrassed, Mindy didn't move as Damien delivered a quick, cold, mustache-inhibited kiss.

Now more embarrassed, Mindy could only reply, "Thanks again. Goodnight," and escaped indoors.

Standing at the bathroom sink, Mindy closed her eyes to recall the pleasure of dancing under the flashing lights and smiled. Opening her eyes, her sightline shifted to the pendant sitting heavily on her chest. She thought of the other inexpensive but elegant cross necklaces she owned. This one was quite large in comparison and looked out of proportion to her petite frame. She leaned toward the mirror to study it closer. It had a flat pewter finish and twisted arms. A few lines of finely carved scrolling offered the only hint of polish. Compared to Randy's heart pendant, it was massively heavy.

Mindy wasn't sure what to think or feel about the necklace. Peering into the reflection of her own eyes in the mirror, she tried to appreciate the thought behind the gift but couldn't help wondering if it had been offered as a sign of God's grace or for some other reason. She knew it wasn't affection.

Christmas came and went uneventfully. Mindy received a few albums from "Santa" along with some money for clothes. Aside from work, the days were lazy and spent happily with girlfriends who were unaware of her more recent dates. Mindy's desire to maintain the dichotomy between Nashville and school friends intensified, so she never volunteered any information. A split social identity felt safer than a blended one.

The next weekend, the same foursome, Larry, Holly, Damien, and Mindy, drove to Gallatin for pizza. Sitting at the same Pizza Inn table she had shared twice with Randy, Mindy recalled the excitement that had tickled her heart just six months earlier. She felt none of that anticipation or wonder now, but didn't stop to consider the implications. She had a vague understanding that she was generationally separated from Damien and rationalized that the absence of excitement was part of the trade-off.

The conversation over pizza touched on a variety of current topics and added to Mindy's sense of being out with grown-ups. Their views were different, but she was more than capable of holding her own during the group's minor debates, and this seemed to irritate Damien. Mindy sensed he thought she should be more submissive, but that only encouraged her to battle all the harder.

The boys tried to avoid the hottest topic of the day: the second anniversary of the *Roe vs. Wade* decision. But there was no escape for them once trapped in the car during the return drive. Mindy inquired, "How do you guys feel about abortion?" They both cowered, but Mindy wouldn't let them off the hook. "Catholics are taught that life begins at conception, so abortion is considered murder. The unborn baby is stripped of the opportunity to live a life full of potential and opportunity. I want to hear what you guys think?" she pushed.

The boys exchanged pained expressions before Damien whispered, "Baptists don't think it's a sin."

"So, you're telling me you believe drinking and dancing is a sin, even though you do it every chance you get, but ripping a defenseless baby out of a mother's uterus isn't?" The two young adult males nodded without comment.

"That's just ridiculous. I can't believe you guys!" yelled Mindy. The remainder of the drive was quiet.

The evening out ended early with Damien's routine of pulling up to park in the dark corner of the Ellington driveway. Verbally trapping Mindy in the car with a monologue, he talked at length about his high school football career and boasted about his football glory. Considering his short stature, Mindy found most of his discourse implausible and was soon bored by his bluster. When she opened the door, Damien panicked and leaned across the center console to deliver a kiss but stopped short when bright headlights pulled into the driveway behind them.

Mindy said, "That must be my parents. They went out to dinner with the Donnelly's."

Damien slumped into the shadow of the driver's seat. Mindy said goodbye, got out of the car, and waited for her parents by the side door. Her father didn't pause as he walked past her into the house, but her mother waited by the side door with Mindy until the Donnelly's, and Damien, pulled away. Sounding anxious, her mother asked, "How was your evening?"

"Oh, fine. We just went out for pizza," replied Mindy.

Her mother started to speak again, but seemed flustered and diverted to, "Well, let's get inside."

The reason for her mother's mild agitation became apparent the next morning while Mindy was helping prepare breakfast before church. Her mother nervously inquired, "So, how was your evening out?"

"I told you last night. It was fine. We just went out for pizza," Mindy said.

Her mother hesitated, then continued with some distress, "Mr. Donnelly says Damien is just trying to get into your pants. He told Dad he was a fool to let you go out with him."

Embarrassed and surprised by her mother's directness, Mindy gasped. "What?! Mom, it's not like that. He hasn't tried anything. He's kissed me once, that's it."

With her own little gasp, her mother questioned, "Where did he kiss you?"

Mindy cringed at the question and silently wondered, "Why in the world are you asking that?" and then grimaced when she remembered images of many schoolmates sporting hickeys at school. Some tried to hide them, but most did not. Blushing, Mindy replied, "On the lips. Where do you think? But I didn't kiss back."

"No, no. *Where* were you when he kissed you?" Mindy's mother persisted.

Wondering why it mattered, she said, "At the side door." She paused to consider her mother's initial question and continued, "But he did ask me if I was a virgin."

Her mother froze momentarily and then anxiously asked, "You are — *aren't you?*"

Now more angry than embarrassed, Mindy yelled, "MOM!"

Flustered by the crash and burn of this mother-daughter conversation, her mother stuttered, "Well, well — you just — you just tell him — it's none of his business!" then returned to breakfast preparations with a shake of her head.

Waiting for a more substantive response, Mindy watched her mother's eyes dart in every direction, trying to understand her own unease and looking for words as though she knew she should say or ask something more. Uncertain how to proceed, she said nothing at all.

That evening, Mindy struggled to understand the source of her mother's unease. Generally trusting and accepting of everyone, Mindy saw only the good in people and never worried that someone might intend harm. She concluded she was safe with Damien. "He has too much to lose. He wants to come back to

Lafayette and get a white-collar job. He's too afraid he'll ruin his reputation and nobody will hire him," she reasoned. Mindy certainly wasn't infatuated with Damien, but didn't dislike him either. Because she sensed no threat, she didn't consider declining his subsequent date requests.

Larry hosted a New Year's Eve gathering at his mother's duplex. The partiers listened to records, played cards, and the boys drank beer when Larry's mother wasn't watching. Having grown up in a family that played a variety of card games regularly, Mindy had developed good card sense. The others, especially Damien, apparently lacked this quality and were disbelieving when Mindy won almost every individual game they played. When they shifted to Spades, Mindy found herself frustrated with Damien's general lack of card sense and had to explain to him more than once why it was a bad idea to overtake her winning tricks.

Mindy's parents had granted permission for her to stay out until midnight, and she watched the central time zone replay of the Times Square ball drop on the portable television to introduce 1975 with some excitement. When Damien approached at midnight with the apparent intent of planting a New Year's Eve kiss, Mindy reacted immediately to block any public display. Damien looked around to see if the others had noticed, then glared at Mindy with disbelief. While the others sang "Happy New Year!" Damien pounded his thigh with his fist and walked away. But he seemed to recover by the time everyone was leaving a few minutes later.

During the return drive, Damien repeated, "I really like you," then added, "You're really pretty." Mindy blushed at the unexpected compliment, but the sensation didn't last long when Damien continued, "I hope we can get closer."

Pulling into the driveway, Damien stopped abruptly and slammed the transmission into park. Without preface, he grabbed Mindy by the arm and tried to pull her toward him. His aggressiveness triggered a flash of Jack Robertson, and she stiffened with fear, stifling his kiss before it began. She pulled away and launched a defensive volley, "I told my mom you asked me if I was a virgin. She said it's none of your business."

Damien reacted as if someone had kicked him in the groin and slumped over to bang his forehead against the steering wheel. He then slowly turned his head as it lay against the wheel and whimpered, "Do you tell your mother everything?"

"Pretty much," replied Mindy. The passenger door clicked open, and the evening was over.

Chapter 10
Subjugating Lucifer
January 1–May 14, 1975

The New Year began with the convictions of John Mitchell, H. R. Haldeman, and John Ehrlichman in the Watergate cover-up scandal, but many Americans had lost interest. Busy with the day-to-day realities of making a living and keeping up with inflation, Watergate became little more than a political soap opera for the average American. One thing was clear, the disconnection between the U.S. government and its citizens was underway and picking up steam.

New Year's Day passed quietly at home, and the second semester rolled to a start the following day. Classes would remain unchallenging, and despite performing below her academic potential, Mindy still received good grades — but not as good as they should have been. It didn't matter, no authority figure seemed to care. Not one person in Mindy's small world encouraged academic excellence from her. Those closest to her didn't hide their belief that her good looks and pleasant personality would carry more weight than academic performance in her long-term success.

The first Saturday in January, Mindy hurried home from her job at the bank and was soon off to Donna Power's house with a wedding shower gift in hand. A senior, Donna had befriended Mindy as a basketball cheerleader the previous season. But the combination of increased competition, her mother's disapproval of "skimpy" uniforms and her twenty-two-year-old fiancé, who didn't want her busy cheering on weekends, dissuaded her from even trying out her senior year. Instead, she was getting married.

Mindy enjoyed the modest bridal shower until, after opening gifts, Donna shifted to the front edge of her seat. "Everyone, can I have your attention. I have an announcement to make. The wedding has been pushed back one week. I hope the change doesn't cause you any trouble." The crowd responded with concerned expressions and waited for an explanation. Donna blushed and leaned forward as the guests followed her lead into a tight huddle. "I moved it back so I wouldn't be on my period," she whispered.

A harmonious hum vibrated from the guests as they sat back in their seats with nods of understanding. Mindy covered her mouth and thought, "That's just too damn much unnecessary information!" then slapped herself for using a silent cuss word.

Driving home, Mindy reflected on the responsibilities and demands of any new bride. The thought of balancing school with cleaning, cooking, laundry, and other wifely duties seemed overwhelming. "And what about college? I thought she was planning to go to college? How's she going to do that?" Mindy wondered.

The second week of the new semester, a school-wide vote took place for various categories of "the best of" in the student population. The winners would have their names and photographs prominently placed in the front pages of the school yearbook. Most students considered it a relative honor and took the voting seriously. There were no campaigns or open nominations, so students had to be liked and respected to win in any category. School administrators would tally and review the votes, with winners announced the following week. Mindy made a point of voting for classmates whom she felt needed a boost, and she quietly tried to get others to do so as well.

Feeling achy and tired despite a good night's sleep, Mindy put on her cheer uniform Friday morning with less excitement than usual. She felt worse as the day progressed and had a difficult time getting through her shift at the bank. When she returned home flushed and fatigued, her mother placed a hand on her forehead, then pronounced, "You have a fever. You're not going to any basketball game tonight, my Madame Queen."

Mindy notified Gina, then curled up in bed, where her mother promptly delivered a double-shot of honey and whiskey.

Damien had never come to watch a basketball game, so Mindy never considered informing him of her illness. But when he arrived at MCHS between games and couldn't find her, he talked with Kat. Immediately suspicious, he drove to Ellington, where his heavier-than-necessary knock at the front door brought Mindy's mother scurrying to ward off a second knock. Damien stood rigidly as she informed him that Mindy was ill and sleeping. His agitation revealed his doubt as he peered past her mother's protective stance and ask, "Can I see her just for a minute?"

Mindy's mother shook her head, "I'll tell her you stopped by," then closed the door.

A visit to see Dr. Froedge the following morning confirmed Mindy's mother's suspicions. The doctor started Mindy on antibiotics for strep throat, and she spent most of the weekend curled up in bed.

During her convalescence, Mindy had time to flip through several teen magazines. One of the fashion styles being pushed was a 1950s retro look with pant legs rolled to the mid-calf to reveal high argyle socks. Aware that she might have to endure some teasing, Mindy decided to give the style a try at school. She put her hair in pigtails, copied one of the magazine models as best she could, and then went to school looking as though she had just stepped out of a Dobie Gillis short story. To her mild surprise, the style was a hit with the girls, and by lunchtime, a small army of throwback females was running around the school sporting high-riding ponytails, with pant legs and shirt sleeves rolled high, and socks stretched to the calf.

That afternoon, a secretary interrupted cheer practice to inform Mindy that Mr. Blankenship would like to see her right away. Mindy became worried that someone had identified her as the culprit behind the flashback style, so she paused outside the office to roll her sleeves and pant legs down but left her pigtails untouched.

Mr. Blakenship, who no longer sounded almost unintelligibly southern to Mindy's ears, said, "Take a seat, young lady." Mindy promptly complied, and her fears grew as Mr. Blankenship silently sorted through a short stack of papers before him. She jumped when he finally broke the silence. "Well, we have a problem and I'm not quite sure what to do," he said. From the tone of his voice, Mindy was now sure she was in trouble, and her heart raced faster. "You've been voted Miss Junior, Miss Personality, and Friendliest," he announced. Mindy sat frozen with surprise but relieved and uncertain what to say. "Well, I think it would only be fair to the other students if y'all only got one award. Which title would you like to have?" he asked.

She didn't take long to decide, "How about Miss Personality?"

"It's all yours. I believe you've made a good choice. Now, y'all understand, this conversation is just between you and me?" was Mr. Blankenship's monotone reply. Mindy nodded in understanding and bounced out of the office.

Hosting dinner for corporate visitors or local leaders was an unending task for Mindy's mother, and the upcoming weekend included a payback dinner for the Donnelly's. So, Mindy's mother took the opportunity to suggest that Mindy invite Damien to join them. Mindy suspected her mother wanted to give Mr. Donnelly a chance to interrogate Damien and avoid the task herself.

Arriving fifteen minutes late, Damien remained quiet throughout dinner except for short, nervous responses to Mr. Donnelly's questions. Damien gradually revealed he had recently graduated from college, had no job prospects, and planned to work his father's farm until an appealing white-collar job in Macon County presented itself.

By the time dessert was served, Mindy believed the other adults perceived Damien as a typically unpolished and harmless country boy and assumed she was in full control. Before leaving, Mr. Donnelly softened and suggested Damien stop by the bank for an interview.

Damien interviewed the next day and started training as a bank teller immediately. With gasoline selling at thirty-four cents per gallon and dinner for two rarely exceeding $15, including drinks and tip, making a little over $200 a week sounded like a fortune. More importantly, Damien would be one of the few college graduates working at the bank, thus leaving his door of opportunity to climb the short managerial ladder wide open.

To celebrate, Damien arrived the following Saturday, full of cockiness, to take Mindy to Nashville. But this late-January trip sported only three passengers. For reasons never made clear to Mindy, Holly had ended her relationship with Larry over the holidays, but it was no surprise to Mindy. Larry was still in college in Murfreesboro, and Holly was at the University of Tennessee in Knoxville. The one hundred eighty miles of separation for most of the academic year sounded like an insurmountable obstacle.

Larry sat depressed and dejected in the back seat but, by the time they arrived at the bar, Mindy had helped to rebuild his manhood with playful banter. Feeling more optimistic about life, Larry marched straight to the counter and ordered a double-shot Sloe Gin Fizz in payment. As Mindy finished the blood-colored drink, the band struck up "China Grove" by Larry's favorite band, The Doobie Brothers. When Mindy offered to join him on the dance floor, Larry didn't hesitate to jump to his feet.

The unlikely pair heated up the acrylic for four consecutive songs until, after a short pause, the lead singer announced, "Here's a slow one for all you lovers out there."

Larry's eyes opened wide, and he took a step toward Mindy with arms extended, but stopped short after a glance in Damien's direction. He laughed, "I guess we'd better not. I'm outta breath, anyway. Ya know, *all* his friends want to date you too."

A moment after they returned to their table, another couple walked up. The male visitor gave Larry a slap on the back and said, "You're a lucky man. Your girlfriend can really dance."

Larry leaned back in his seat, proudly folding his hands behind his head and smiling from ear to ear. "Thanks. I think so, too." Damien shrank in defeat, and Mindy just laughed.

As Larry slept in the back seat during the return trip, the thought crossed Mindy's mind that the two boys in the car always went to Nashville as a pair. After a moment's thought, she realized why. Damien was afraid. Damien was vulnerable outside his small Lafayette pond, and even his platform shoes wouldn't help if forced into defending his date's honor. Larry, on the other hand, could hold his own in the bar crowd and would gladly jump in to protect a girl at any time. "Larry is Damien's security blanket," Mindy concluded.

January quietly drifted into the past along with the Nera White basketball tournament at Vol State, where the Tigerettes won the championship in front of large Friday and Saturday night crowds.

Illness, school, and cheerleading had significantly limited Mindy's exposure to Damien for most of the month and allowed the uncertainties surrounding him to drift out of her forethought. But Kat's persistent inquiries only reinforced Mindy's resolve to keep anything associated with Damien separate from school as much as small-town life would allow. Damien continued to call during the week, but conversations were limited to factual exchanges and current events while history, politics, and religion became lost topics. Having such incongruent frames of reference of life meant that even Damien's generation of friends were virtually excluded from their discussions. The walls impeding communication were tall and left little room for growth. But that didn't prevent Damien from whining about lost weekend time.

The second Saturday in February, Mindy and Damien met Larry and his new girl on the square to drive to Murfreesboro to take in a college basketball game at MTSU. The sharp, bright colors and the sounds of the pep band filled the college arena to mesmerize Mindy and fan her college fantasy flames. During the game, she spent more time watching the cheerleaders than the action on the court and noted that her MCHS cheer squad had comparable athletic abilities. This sharpened her interest in attending a small college where she thought she might be able to make the cheer team.

The electricity in the stands quickly faded as the Blue Raiders struggled through a mismatched game and a lopsided score. Nonetheless, Mindy wondered more than ever about what her own college experience would bring. During the return trip, Mindy's words wove the fabric of her personal college dreams and plans to experience the world beyond Macon County. But Damien scowled and fidgeted as Mindy spoke. Soon, Damien's growing agitation counterbalanced Mindy's excitement, and the last miles of the drive were quiet.

Back at Ellington, Damien tried to entice Mindy to stay in the car, but the longer-than-usual trip made her want to stretch her legs. She went inside soon after receiving an awkwardly forced goodbye kiss that left her wondering, "Does he think I owe him a kiss after every date?"

Valentine's Day arrived the following Friday. At MCHS it was the common practice for boys to have flowers delivered to their girlfriends at school as an acceptable display of affection. Mindy was quietly embarrassed to receive flowers from three different schoolmates. Carrying three dozen roses between classes, she sought out each gift giving boy to offer a smile and say, "You really shouldn't have bought me anything, but thank you." Each suitor melted where they stood, and Mindy continued to class, leaving three pairs of rosy cheeks behind. At home, Mindy found another dozen roses from Damien awaiting her.

Bobbie Hauskins, the owner of the gift shop where most flowers in town were ordered, had called Mindy's mother earlier in the day. Her mother laughed heartily as she recounted Bobbie's tale of taking orders and saying, "Didn't you just call a little while ago?" only to realize that four different boys were ordering flower deliveries for the same girl. As long as she'd been running the shop, she had never experienced such a coincidence before.

That evening, the basketball bus returned from away games at Whitehouse, and Mindy planned to ride with Gina to Jones's for a snack before heading home. As the bus pulled into the school parking lot, she felt a wave of disappointment when she spotted Damien's car parked in the shadows. As Mindy stepped off the bus, Damien rolled down his window to flag her down. Hoping to avoid mixing school and Damien, she quietly informed Gina of the apparent change in plans and then waited until the crowd thinned before walking toward his car and his dark silhouette waiting inside. Mindy cautiously slid into the passenger seat and felt uneasy about this intrusion into her school world. "I didn't expect you to be here," she said somewhat nervously.

"Well, I wanted to make sure you got your flowers," he replied.

Absorbed by cheering and basketball, she had forgotten about the flowers. A vision of the roses transformed her disappointment into guilt that grew when she realized getting Damien anything, even a card, hadn't crossed her mind. Trying to recover, Mindy said apologetically, "Oh, yes. They are beautiful. Thanks so much, but you really didn't need to get me anything."

"What did they say about the flowers at school?" Damien pompously inquired.

It was clear he expected to hear accolades, so Mindy hesitated, then explained the shop had delivered his flowers to Ellington. This triggered a short tirade that made it clear he was more concerned about his loss of absentee glory than offering a sign of affection.

His outburst left Mindy shaken, and she trembled with uncertainty. Damien noticed and worked hard to recover his composure. By the time he pulled into the shadowed corner of the Ellington driveway, he was all smiles. When Mindy opened the door, Damien squawked, "Wait, I have something for you." He reached into his pocket and, bobbing his head wildly, handed her a small, cube-shaped box.

Caught entirely off guard, Mindy was uncertain what to think. Instead of feeling pleasant surprise, she feared what the little black box might hold and was hesitant to look. After repeated prodding, Mindy finally pried it open. She squinted in the shadows to see a ring with a flat silver finish with three molded offset hearts across the band. The center heart held a small, transparent stone. Mindy felt a sudden chill when Damien asked, "Do you know what this means?"

She shuddered as the possibilities flashed in her mind. "Oh, no — what *does* this mean? What does *he* think this means?" she wondered. She shuddered again and took a deep breath to respond, "No. What *does* this mean?"

With great pride and condescending arrogance, Damien replied, "Well, silly. It means you don't have to worry about getting a date on Saturday night."

His tone made Mindy flinch. There was no trace of romance or affection in his words. There were only false assumptions. But his response happily washed away the fear of a promise ring or a cheap engagement ring out of her mind.

"Well, put it on," he pushed.

Mindy slid the oversized ring onto her right hand and then received an obligatory kiss but offered none in return. She got out of the car without further reply. Damien walked with her to the side door where she said, "Thanks again for the flowers, but you *really* shouldn't have bought me anything," and took a half step toward the door.

Damien interceded to touch Mindy's weak spot, "How about we go to Nashville tomorrow night?" Unable to reel in the thoughts swirling in her mind, the image of dancing and music shifted her focus, and she unthinkingly agreed.

In her room, Mindy studied the ring on her finger and felt suffocated by the pressure it generated. The uncertainty in her gut forced her to consider the implications of wearing any boy's ring. In accepting it, she felt for the first time she was being forced to make a commitment; a kind of promise she had never considered before. She understood that wearing any boy's ring would be a sign she was taken — *owned* by someone else.

She already knew the obvious in her heart, "I'm not committed to Damien, and I shouldn't limit my options just for show." She pulled the ring off her finger and laid it on her nightstand. Her heart felt lighter, but she didn't understand why. Then she remembered the promise of a perpetual Saturday night date and the many date requests she'd declined. She laughed. "Worried? Does he really think no one else will ask me out?"

She shivered and pulled her bed covers close to her chin. "I want to go out now and then just for fun. I don't want to limit myself, and I don't want to feel guilty about talking with other boys. I will feel certain obligations if I wear any boy's ring," she thought. Then it struck her, "*Obligated* — that's it!" She understood the source of her unease, "Accepting a ring should be a sign of affection, a pinnacle of romance for any girl. I should wear it because I *like* him; because I want others to know I like him. I should want to wear it because I want to and because it makes me feel proud. But I feel none of that. I feel only the weight of obligation."

Staring at the ceiling, the limitations of the town came crashing through. Getting out of town occasionally, even if just for a change of scenery, seemed important. Mindy had always enjoyed "girl time" immensely, but understood that going out on a date with a boy opened up different options and opportunities for adventure. She closed her eyes to visualize other 'just-for-fun' date options at school, but could think of none that were likely to offer live music and dancing occasionally. "If I want to do those kinds of things, I'll probably have to do it with Damien," she thought. Then another wave of insight struck her. "Trapped! I'm trapped. If I want to go to Nashville to dance, I'm pretty much trapped into going with Damien."

Fatigue settled in, and thoughts became less focused. Before falling asleep, Mindy concluded, "I'll wear the ring for now, but I will hand it back before accepting a date with someone else." This was as committed as she'd ever been.

———————————— · ————————————

Larry and another new date were waiting at the town square Saturday evening. Mindy slid into the back seat with the somewhat nervous young lady and quickly put her at ease. En route to the RiverGate Mall area for dinner, Damien pulled into a small market in Hartsville and returned with an eight-pack of Miller Ponies. The girls declined, but the boys promptly chugged a little bottle and pulled out another. Mindy sat quietly and thought, "Miller Ponies? Aren't those for women?" Her doubts grew larger when Damien tried to order a bottle of Boone's Farm Strawberry Hill at the restaurant.

After dinner, they were off to the Rodeway Inn bar, where Mindy had a wonderful time on the dance floor, lost in her own world of silky rhythmic moves. The next few hours passed quickly, the extended curfew was upon them, and Mindy hurried the group to the car.

During the return drive, Mindy rode shotgun and mentioned having to be up early for Mass the next day. This opened one of the few discussions she had with anyone from Lafayette about religion. From the back seat, Larry asked, "Why do you Catholics worship idols? Moses had his brothers and cousins slaughter thousands of people 'cuz they worshiped idols."

Aghast, Mindy replied, "Well, Moses did have lots of people killed, but Catholics *don't* worship idols. What do you mean by that?"

"Well, like Mary. Don't you guys pray to a statue of Mary? She's not a god. Why would you pray to her?" Larry replied, and Damien nodded in agreement.

Taken aback but feeling a responsibility to educate them, Mindy explained, "The idea is to take the time to give thanks for what we have, confess our sins, reflect on how we are living our lives, and thank God for his support. The statue is a focal point. You don't worship *it;* the statue is simply a place, *a reminder*, for meditation and prayer."

The boys didn't seem to understand, so Mindy simplified it for them. "Just because you kneel down next to your bed to pray doesn't mean you're praying to your bed. You kneel next to your bed to show reverence and penitence. It's a standard place where you to take time to reflect, pay tribute, give thanks, and ask for forgiveness at the end of the day. You don't give thanks or pay tribute to your bed."

Shaking his head, Damien held firm, "Sitting in front of a statue to pray still sounds like worshiping an idol to me."

Sensing their beliefs were ignorantly intolerant, Mindy went on the attack, "Many Baptists, including the two of you, believe drinking and dancing is a sin, right? But you guys do it every chance you get. So why aren't you guys going to hell?"

They sang out in unison, "Because we've been *saved!*"

Mindy pushed back. "So, if you go out and kill somebody — say you kill ten people in premeditated cold blood — you still go to heaven if you've been saved?"

"Absolutely. Being saved is forever," Damien barked.

"Well, that's just one of the most ridiculous things I've ever heard. That is not right. If Catholicism is a cult, then you guys are a bunch of hypocrites."

With no immediate response, Damien and Larry sat quietly as they shoved future discussions of religion into a closet and locked the door.

After dropping Larry and his date at the square, Damien and Mindy had to hurry to Ellington to make the new 11 PM curfew. Parking as usual in the shadows, Damien quickly turned in his seat to face Mindy and keep her in the car. He spoke like a salesman, "We've gotten a lot closer these last few weeks. I think it's time to talk about moving to the next step."

Not for one second had Mindy considered their friendly relationship as "close," she cocked her head with uncertainty and wondered, "Closer? What does that mean?"

Damien stopped her thoughts and continued with a business-like tone, "I think it's time we consider having sex."

Utterly unprepared for this quantum leap in expectations, an avalanche of thoughts and emotions poured through Mindy's mind. Damien had kissed her a few times, but she had never returned one. They had never shared any mutual affection. She had never sensed any romance in his gifts. They had never held hands, shared a hug, or uttered the word *love* to each other. They had never discussed thoughts of devotion or a future together. His talk of sex entirely outside the bounds of love, marriage, or even affection, overwhelmed her reason.

Reading Mindy's obvious distress, Damien pressed, "I'm not saying right now — but soon."

Mindy felt the blood drain from her cheeks, and she suddenly felt chilled. The seconds of silence that followed rapidly raised the pressure within until she burst out, "Oh, my God! That is *never* going to happen! I'm not ready for that! I'm *not* going to have sex before I'm married! I believe sex outside of marriage is a sin, and my religion doesn't let sinners off the hook as easily as yours!"

Damien threw up his hands in false innocence, "Hey, I understand. I don't want you to do anything before you feel ready. I can wait."

Parked in the driveway, Mindy never felt in imminent danger or without escape, so his words were falsely reassuring. She took off the ring and handed it back to him, "It's too big." He thoughtlessly dropped it into his shirt pocket as Mindy walked unescorted to the side door.

Preparing for bed, Mindy felt an odd ache in her gut. She tried to calm herself and remembered the matter-of-fact, almost nonchalant, attitude of the girls at her lunch table. She had never once considered herself as the focus of such talk, but now recalled their emotionless conclusion: "That's just the way guys are. They don't really care about you. All they want is sex." She wondered if she should accept the excuse of a genetically hard-wired sex drive over expectations of love and a higher quality of being, as many of them had. As her tension eased, she told herself, "Don't ever let yourself fall victim to girl-table brainwashing."

The age difference between Mindy and her pursuer couldn't have been more significant. She was looking through the eyes of a young teen, not a manipulative young adult. She didn't understand that the trips beyond the borders of Macon County, gifts and flowers had accumulated substantial debt, but suddenly could sense the debt collector pounding at her door. Damien was demanding payback, and it scared her.

The dull ache in Mindy's gut kept phone conversations with Damien short and cold the following week. Damien sensed her distance and attempted to recover, "How about I take you to a nice place to eat in Gallatin next Saturday?" Mindy's responded with silent hesitation, so Damien pleaded, "I didn't mean it. I'm sorry I ever brought it up." He sounded sincere, so she softened and eventually agreed, but hung up still feeling uneasy.

The school week went well, and by the time Saturday arrived, Mindy's unease had largely abated. She made a point to dress more formally in anticipation of going to a "nice place," only to feel a sting when Damien pulled into the Gallatin Shoney's. Conversation during the drive was tense and remained so through dinner, causing Mindy's unease to return.

In the driveway at Ellington, Damien rambled on about nothing important, and Mindy had the distinct impression he was purposely trying to limit her opportunity to speak. Without warning, he leaned across the center console to deliver an emotionless kiss that missed the mark and failed to narrow the emotional chasm between them. The passenger door clicked open, and the night was over.

Preparing for bed, Mindy wondered if she was being silly and overreacting. Influenced by girl-table talk, bad movies, and cheap romance novels, she had gradually developed a sense of "payback" along the lines of "when a boy takes you out, you owe him kisses in return." Her experience with Damien only reinforced this notion; he clearly seemed to expect payback.

Mindy felt alone. She didn't believe she could confide in her friends for fear of the rumor mill and doubted her mother would understand. No one she trusted seemed likely to offer meaningful advice. So, Mindy learned to accept a "business of dating" philosophy and believed the business required balanced books. An empty kiss at the end of a date balanced her books psychologically, but she gradually understood they came with emotional walls that effectively drowned out any chance of genuine affection. Romance was absent from her equation, but Damien either didn't notice or didn't care.

The girls' basketball team became a rallying point for many Macon Countians who hoped a long run in the playoffs would make Lafayette bigger on the middle-Tennessee map. Mindy was happy to be on the Tigerette bandwagon, but Damien grumbled, "Basketball is taking up too much weekend time. I can't wait till the season is over."

The Tigerettes won their conference but had to bounce back from a shaky start to win the District tournament. The following weekend, they pulled off consecutive wins against favored opponents and needed only one more win to reach the final four.

Mindy hoped as much as anyone that the team would play the following weekend. If not, she would attend a three-day Interact Club conference in Gatlinburg. When Damien learned of this, he practically oozed venom and complained, "Basketball and school are getting in my way."

"Remember, I'm still in high school and time with my friends, cheerleading, and my family are important to me. I can't ignore or forget them," Mindy explained.

The confident Tigerettes took on perennial power Ooltewah in the mid-week sub-State game on the MTSU court. Static electricity made the air pop, and Mindy took every opportunity to scan the nearly packed stands to drink in the excitement of the moment and brand the images into her memory.

The Tigerettes played their hearts out from the opening tip-off, but fame and glory would not belong to the players, MCHS, or Lafayette this year. They lost to the eventual state champions, and their dream season was suddenly over. The defense had faltered, and some players wondered if they lost, in part, because their star player had been "dealing with terrible morning sickness and just wasn't herself on the court."

Basketball and cheerleading seasons were suddenly over, but for Mindy, the conference in Gatlinburg would absorb the Ides of March weekend. Damien made his first but brief weekday appearance at Ellington on Thursday evening to return the resized ring. Fi growled in Mindy's arms as Damien stood on the porch and commanded, "I want you to wear it to the Interact Conference as a reminder of me. I want you to think of me while you're gone so you'll be excited to see me when you get back." Fi snapped at the intruder and his dominant tone. With uncertain thoughts, Mindy stroked the top of the little mutt's head and silently nodded her own in agreement.

That evening, Mindy examined the ring sitting in her palm. The jeweler had cut out a small section from the side of the band and welded the two ends back together. The misshapen hoop was hard to push onto her finger, and it never felt right.

Shortly after boarding the bus, Mindy felt a sharp pain in her gut and was more than happy when it faded. She glanced at the ring on her finger, fulfilled her promise with a distorted flash of Damien in her mind, then rotated it heart side down to push him out of her mind for the weekend.

The days of socializing with people her own age were refreshing, and Mindy considered handing back Damien's ring. Her first thought was, "I'd like to do more things with people my own age." But she stumbled on her second thought, "Who would I go out with and what new things would we do?" She had no definite answers, and the ring remained on her finger.

Damien called mid-week, trying to sound cool, "Easter is getting close and I want to take you out for seafood." Mindy appreciated his apparent recognition of Catholic Lenten tradition, and the thought of seafood was exciting. She had tasted shrimp, crab, and lobster on only special occasions and remembered how her mouth watered with each bite. So late Saturday afternoon, she slipped into a fancy pantsuit in anticipation of going to an elegant seafood restaurant.

Full of fanciful visions, Mindy thought Damien was joking when he pulled into a Long John Silver's and flatly questioned, "Okay, where are we really going?"

Damien bobbed his head and proudly replied, "Right here. All of their seafood is on sale. You can get whatever you want." Mindy tried to look happy as she ate fried popcorn shrimp out of a plastic basket, dipped them in the cocktail sauce from a gallon pump jug, and got three free self-refills on her cold drink. Suppressed feelings left her mildly sarcastic in thought, but she still appreciated the gesture.

The real treat of the weekend came the next night. Damien had purchased tickets to see one of his fantasy girlfriends, Olivia Newton-John, in concert. The show opened with a set by a little-known artist who was just making his name in Nashville, Billy Joel. With the crowd well primed, Olivia walked out onto the stage to rousing applause, bowed, and started singing. The bright lights, pageantry, and fabulous acoustics of the Ryman Auditorium were intoxicating. Mindy's eyes and ears never wandered from the stage as she sat mesmerized by the view and the music. Fifty minutes later, the music stopped. Olivia bowed, waved to the cheering crowd and walked off the stage. Mindy left the concert euphoric, looking forward to the rest of her life and dreaming of the adventures it would bring.

About ten miles from Lafayette, Damien asked, "Did you like the concert?" He, of course, already knew the answer.

Mindy sighed with pleasure, "Oh, it was fabulous. Thank you so much for taking me." Her eyes sparkled as a gleaming smile grew across her beautiful face. Damien clearly felt proud of himself as he grinned and wobbled his head.

But Mindy's exhilaration evaporated when she read the look in his eye and he pompously inquired, "So, have you given any thought to us moving forward?" as if he knew the answer.

"I told you. I'm not ready for that. It's not going to happen," Mindy coldly replied.

"You know I love you? I think you are more ready than you know," he persisted.

Mindy quietly digested Damen's words and then replied, "Don't tell me what I think or know. I believe sex before marriage is a sin, and no amount of being saved will change that."

He repeated, "Don't you know I love you? I just want us to be closer." Mindy crossed her arms tightly across her chest and remained silent for the rest of the drive.

The passenger door clicked open before the car was at a full stop in the Ellington driveway. Full of urgency, Damien whined,

"Don't you know I love you? I just want us to be closer. Having sex is part of getting closer. Just think about it."

"Thanks for the concert," Mindy deadpanned then marched to the side door, angry that Damien had ruined the evening.

Mindy went to bed feeling unsettled but had difficulty putting the sensation in her gut into words. She had heard over and over from other girls how much they wanted to be "loved and desired." These were supposed to be good things. But she didn't feel that way; she didn't feel that way at all. She felt dirty. "He doesn't love me. He just wants what's between my legs. He must know I don't love him. That's why he doesn't ask. He knows what I'll say if he does. But he doesn't care about love. He doesn't care about *me*."

Damien's words trickled through Mindy's mind as she lay in the darkness of her room. She began to ask questions and doubt infiltrated her thoughts. "Is it possible he really loves me? I sure don't see it or feel it. He's okay most of the time, but I don't love him now. Is it possible I might love him later? Will I really ever love anyone? Is pre-marital sex really a sin, or am I just being a prude? What will people say if I stop dating him now? What will *he* tell people about me? Will he tell them I was a tease, and that I led him on? Will he lie and tell stories about me? Will I be happy just cruising with the girls? If not, then what?"

Mindy took a deep breath. "I know the answers to these questions aren't complicated, so why do they weigh me down? I'm not old enough to know all the answers. Do I even really know what is right all the time?" She trembled. The Devil was tempting her, and God had abandoned her to her own sixteen-year-old decision-making.

In her heart, Mindy knew she would never love him and wouldn't blindly walk away from her faith. She knew she should tell Damien to go away forever and retreat to safety. But she also felt the pinch of teen restlessness that made the kaleidoscope of opportunities and enticing impressions of what lay beyond Macon County curiously appealing, while the routine of the local cruise circuit was very much less so. Anne's comments about this same small town danced in Mindy's memory and built a better understanding of what she was saying.

Mindy's stomach churned and ached. Trying to rationalize the "boys will be boys" concept was ineffective and interpreting her thoughts was difficult. The pressure was building. Sleep didn't arrive until well after midnight and was restless when it finally took over.

The ache was still present when Mindy awoke, but gradually dissipated at school. Her classmates seemed young, innocent, and honest. They unknowingly made her feel better and helped unload the weight from her shoulders. She came to appreciate even more the safe world in which most of them lived.

Good Friday arrived and, along with it, a late-afternoon excursion to Scottsville for church. Mindy's father surprised everyone by driving over the speed limit to get them to the church in time for confession, and Mindy soon sat face to face with Father Dominic. There were no confession booths or option for anonymity here. With fewer than sixty parishioners in his flock, Father Dominic knew everyone's voice. It didn't matter, Mindy liked and trusted the Father. He was personal friends with her parents and even conducted Mass in their living room on Ellington occasionally.

With feet crossed at the ankles and hands tensely folded in her lap, Mindy avoided eye contact as she tried to unload her guilt. She began by admitting she was mean to her brothers at times. Father Dominic quickly absolved her, "Mindy Murphy, you don't have a truly mean bone in your body. I worry less about you than anyone else here today."

With trepidation, Mindy forced out a barely audible, "I am doing things and having thoughts about things I shouldn't."

Images of nightclubs and drinking passed through her mind, but they never made it into words. "And sometimes others want me to do things I know I shouldn't." Damien's pressure made her squirm, but she offered no detail.

Mindy desperately hoped Father Dominic would hear her calling for help. She wanted to scream, "Please, somebody ask the right questions." She was feeling pressure from the world before she was ready, and her self-imposed gag prevented her from asking for help and guidance.

"You are a good person with a kind heart and good common sense. I know some things can seem difficult when you are young, but trust your faith and let your conscience guide you through difficult decisions." He completely missed the anxiety in Mindy's voice and the pain it reflected. He asked no questions, and her gag remained in place.

Later, Mindy rationalized that Father Dominic was too close to the situation to see it clearly, and she returned to Lafayette, feeling no better. But the time away from Damien offered some respite from the ache in her gut.

The next morning, Mindy was up early and dressed for work at the bank. Confession hadn't unloaded any weight, but she felt stronger anyway. Already absorbed in her work and happily distracted from disturbing thoughts, her heart sank when she looked up to see Damien slinking through the front door of the bank and had a flash of Uriah Heep in her mind. He crept to her counter to entice her humbly, "Your birthday is coming up in a few weeks. How about I take you shopping at RiverGate Mall to get you something for your seventeenth birthday?"

Damien ignored the fact that Mindy didn't immediately respond before her pleasant middle-aged co-worker Brownie chimed in, "Oh, that sounds so exciting and so romantic. Mindy, I'm sure we can get you out a little early that day." Feeling pushed onto her heels, Mindy agreed to the shopping trip but didn't wave as Damien seemed to slither back out the door.

Rosa Carter was a classmate of Mindy's who did homeschooling most of her sophomore year to accommodate pregnancy and nursing her infant. Keeping up with her studies from home, she returned to MCHS at the start of her junior year but was one of a few classmates Mindy had never had a conversation with. Their introduction occurred by chance at the beginning of the second semester when Rosa signed up for a minor role in the school play, and Mindy signed up to be a stagehand, prompt and understudy for a few minor characters.

Too busy with school, cheering, and work for even a modest role in the play, Mindy felt a wave of panic when Mrs. Wilson stopped her in the hall just four weeks before opening night to say, "Rosa is missing practices and doesn't know her lines. You'd better be prepared to play her role come April."

Mindy immediately went in search of Rosa to encourage her attendance at practices and worked with her one on one. No one wanted Rosa to be ready more than Mindy.

The final dress rehearsal took place on April 1st. While focused on the script, Mindy was the recipient of April Fool's madness when Ricky Hicks appeared out of nowhere to plant a kiss on her cheek before running away. With a clipboard on her hip and pointing a menacing finger, Mindy belted out, "That will never happen again!" Ricky blushed and smiled as he disappeared around the corner.

Emily witnessed the off-stage scene and stood in frozen disbelief. She thawed enough to cry out, "I can't believe he just kissed you. I wish he'd kiss me." Mindy laughed under her breath with the thought of how goofy teenage boys could be.

Rosa responded well. She played her role, small as it was, flawlessly in both performances, and Mindy offered Rosa much praise for her excellent work. Rosa smiled and returned a tear-filled hug of gratitude.

The following Friday, Mindy stood at a cutting table in Home Economics with several classmates lost in idle teen chatter. Mindy looked across the table and made eye contact with Emily, who immediately grew a playful grin. "Hey, girls. Tell me, what's the best kiss you've ever had? Not necessarily a boy you like now, but overall. Just the best kiss you've ever had?"

Mindy knew where Emily was headed and returned a tight-lipped shake of her head.

The other girls at the table couldn't resist the temptation and jumped in with their stories. Mindy glanced around and could see Kat was anxiously waiting her turn. Considering Kat's ongoing crush on Bud, Mindy recalled the shock wave she felt after his unexpected kiss at his farm. She cringed at the thought of hurting Kat's feelings and crossed her fingers some distraction would deflect the question before it reached her.

But the question marched inexorably around the table and presented itself to Mindy, who looked to Emily for help. Emily smiled, and Mindy suspected she was expecting to hear Ricky Hicks's name. But Mindy's mind stuck on Bud, and could come up with no alternatives. Emily wouldn't let Mindy off the hook, "Well, go on, Mindy. Spit it out. What's your best kiss? Or maybe we should we ask, who have you been kissing lately?"

The longer Mindy delayed, the more the entire group's stare burned until "Bud Gentry" sprang from her lips. The other girls froze with expressions of utter disbelief. Mindy blushed and looked across to Kat, "I'm so sorry. You know I don't like him like that. He just surprised me one day, not long after we moved in. It sent a shock wave through me, and I guess that's the best kiss I've ever had." Kat trembled with cheeks aglow.

That evening, Mindy laughed as she described the episode in her diary:

> . . . *my thoughts were stuck. Neither Randy nor*
> *Damien even crossed my mind. Ha!*

Damien ignored the unwritten Saturday "date night" convention and arranged a Friday trip to Nashville for music, dancing, and probably more than a few drinks.

Looking forward to hitting the dance floor, Mindy rushed home from work, ate a few quick bites of dinner, and changed into a plaid pantsuit. Damien arrived at Ellington just a few minutes later, wearing a brown, pinstriped leisure suit. When Larry saw them, he stomped his foot with disgust for their lack of fashion coordination. "Man, you guys just don't look right at all!"

The evening proceeded as usual, except that Damien bought Mindy a drink before Larry could offer. Not to be shown up, Larry delivered a second drink before Mindy worked her way to the dance floor. The drink rotation continued, and the boys never left Mindy empty-handed when away from the dance floor.

With only a few bites of dinner, the alcohol didn't take long to circulate from Mindy's gut to her head. Suddenly lightheaded, she sat down as beads of sweat grew across her forehead, and waves of nausea weakened her knees. She could see the pallor of her trembling hands even in the dusky light and felt nauseated. She took a deep breath and pulled together her thoughts, "I have to work tomorrow morning. I need to get home."

Damien was resistant, but Mindy demanded they leave immediately. She stumbled toward the car, and Larry barked, "Man, you can't take her home like this. She needs something to wake her up. She needs some coffee!"

Damien dejectedly drove a few blocks and pulled into a Dunkin' Donuts. After one bite of a warm glazed donut and a sip of acid-tasting coffee, Mindy's nausea intensified, and she knew vomiting was inevitable. Shuffling quickly to the bathroom, Mindy dropped to her knees just in time to heave into the commode. Several times she thought the heaving was over and attempted to arise, only to fall back to her knees and vomit again.

Time seemed to pass slowly, and Mindy wondered why no one from her group checked on her until a noise from behind prompted her to turn. Standing over her was a short, round caricature of a woman with bleach-blonde bouffant hair, painted-on black eyebrows, long false eyelashes, with enough blue-green mascara to paint a picture and wearing a shiny, black-vinyl skirt and go-go style boots. With fists on her hips, she said, "Oh, honey, you are much too young to be doing this."

The woman helped Mindy to her feet and over to the sink where she rinsed her mouth and washed her face. The paper towels felt like sandpaper, but Mindy thanked the Good Samaritan for her kind assistance then wondered if the others had abandoned her. She was almost surprised to find them still in the booth, staring into their cups. She moaned, "I just want to go home," then walked out the door to the car.

During the trip back, she tried to sleep but couldn't. The drive was long enough to allow her mind to clear, and she wondered,

"What happened? I don't think I had that much to drink. What did they give me? Did they order double shots?" Her gut churned, and she wondered just what else was happening inside. Offering no words of comfort, Damien remained in his seat as Mindy got out of the car and walked to the house without looking back.

The next morning introduced Mindy to the sensation of hungover embarrassment. Despite persistent, gnawing upper abdominal discomfort, she went to work less than her usual chipper self. Around 10 AM, Damien cautiously stepped into the branch bank to confirm plans for the evening. Mindy announced a self-imposed grounding, "I can't go out tonight. I still feel too bad."

Frustrated, Damien tried unsuccessfully to get Mindy to change her mind. She quickly doused Damien's suggestion that he come by Ellington after dinner; she knew his presence would only make her feel worse. Damien was less than understanding, "Well, just what am I supposed to do tonight?" he wanted to know. Mindy shrugged, and Damien walked away angrily.

Mindy spent much of that evening and the next day reflecting on her relationship with Damien. She concluded, "Usually he seems nice, but he is too self-centered, and I don't trust him." She reminded herself, "Nobody I know or trust knows him at all. He has grown up in this same small town as my friends, but he's literally from a different generation."

Considering this further, their age difference became ever more obvious; he *looked old* while she was still clearly a mid-teen. The paradox was that she had never perceived him as being more mature, despite his age and college exposure. "He's just like most teenage boys around here. He's not much different from Ricky Hicks. Maybe I need to cut him some slack and overlook his shortcomings, just like any boy my age," she thought.

In the final analysis, Mindy's sixteen-year-old mind saw few alternatives for fun and entertainment in town. Damien offered transport into a post-high school world that no boys her age could. With hammer and chisel, she chipped away at this thought and convinced herself to separate the pathway to fun from the path of the heart. She understood she didn't feel any particular fondness for him and didn't respect him any more than someone her own age. Still, he offered an opportunity for fun and experience outside Macon County. So, Mindy decided to accept Damien's shortcomings while taking advantage of his age but without emotional commitment and without loss of her virginity. This logic kept his ring on her finger, but she knew she would never love him.

Mindy tried to reconnect with Gina and Phyllis with phone calls and daytime visits when not working. She quickly learned that her own busyness had blinded her to their news. Both girls were now sporting boyfriends and described relationships that tickled the realm of genuine romance. Although their weekday time would be minimally affected, by late spring, time with them on the weekends would largely evaporate. Mindy didn't foresee the impact this would have on her decision making in the weeks to come.

———————————————

Just home from church on an atypically warm early April Sunday, Mindy changed into a T-shirt and hip-hugger jeans and was putting her hair up in pigtails when the phone rang. Answering on the obligatory fourth ring, it surprised her to hear Damien's voice, and it surprised her more when he announced his plan to stop by for a visit. Fifteen minutes later, the doorbell rang, and Mindy answered the door looking youthfully casual and stunning. Fi stood in a staunch defensive posture between her bare feet, snarling at Damien.

Stepping back in fear of the miniature mutt with a sixth sense, Damien motioned for Mindy to come outside. "Let's go get some ice cream," he said as he backed further away from little Fi.

"Okay, but I need to get my shoes," she replied.

"No, no! That's perfect. We'll just sit in the car," he replied while holding both palms to ward off Fi's incessant chant.

Mindy hollered to her mother in the kitchen, "I'll be back in a few minutes." Under the assumption that they were going to Jones's, Mindy frowned when Damien turned west and headed out of town. "Where are we going?" she demanded to know.

"My parents really want to meet you," he replied.

"Oh, no. Not like this! I don't even have shoes!" she objected.

"I told my parents I was going to kidnap you. They'll understand," he said.

Thoughts tumbled and Mindy was very unhappy with what was unfolding, "You tricked me! Take me home." But Damien just grinned and refused to reverse course. Mindy didn't want to meet his or any boy's parents. If not for her residual embarrassment, she would have considered more drastic measures, and a glance at her bare feet reminded her it would be a tough walk home. Against all the voices of common sense screaming at her, she conceded, then removed her hair ties and combed her fingers through her hair.

Damien's parents were awaiting their arrival and stood frozen in the small front yard. From a distance, they looked worn and hard; as if they had just escaped an iron-framed copy of *American Gothic*. But one look at Mindy quickly softened Damien's father, who smiled and was instantly pleasant and cheerful. His mother, however, studied Mindy's petite, feminine lines and long, impractical hair through squinted eyes, then turned to glare silently at Damien. Mindy shuddered with the sensation she could read his mother's telepathic message: "Just what in hell are you doing with such a young girl?"

Mindy apologized for her appearance and explained her lack of shoes. As they chatted, Damien's mother gradually softened as well, but Mindy still felt she could read her thoughts: "This city girl is not destined for any life on a farm."

The invitation to come inside for cake and ice cream made Mindy shudder again. Her dislike of what it meant to dine with a boy's parents on a Sunday afternoon made her very uncomfortable. Mindy apologized and insisted that she needed to get home for Sunday dinner with her own family. During the return drive, Mindy felt angry about Damien's deception but realized that nothing harmful had happened. By the time she walked into Ellington, her anger had dissipated. Anger was not something she ever held onto for very long.

Judy had remained distant at school, so Mindy didn't question it when she entered History class to find Judy with her head buried in her folded arms on the desk. But Mindy became concerned when the bell rang, and Judy didn't move. As the class progressed, Judy didn't raise her head even once. Mindy became more doubtful when the teacher seemed to ignore the scene and made no display of it. When the ending bell rang, Judy finally stirred slowly but appeared pale and sluggish. Mindy helped her to her feet and quietly inquired if she was all right. Judy nodded, "I'm just really tired."

The same scenario replayed the next day. Mindy quietly observed and wondered why other students seemed to ignore Judy, but it baffled her that why Mr. Tatum still took no notice. On Wednesday, Judy's seat was empty, and Mindy suspected Judy was ill. "I'll bet she has mono," she thought.

The next week of school ended with work and the All-Sports Banquet. Mindy had never considered inviting Damien and looked forward to an evening with friends. But he was familiar with the annual event and pushed his way into Mindy's teen world by inviting himself. Mindy felt she had little recourse, so begrudgingly accepted his intrusion.

Damien wore a vintage plaid suit, and Mindy was happy to wear more of her mother's seamstress handiwork; a modest, full length, off-white sleeveless dress with a small flower-bouquet print. Mindy quickly mixed with her friends, and Damien took a seat by himself

As some of Mindy's friends commented on her cute dress, Kat stepped up to question her about the heart pendant hanging around her neck. Mindy shuddered with the realization that she had unthinkingly put on Randy's birthday gift and that he might be at the banquet escorting his new girlfriend, Pam Driver. Mindy didn't want Randy to see her in attendance with Damien or wearing his previous year's gift.

They held the banquet, as usual, in the school cafeteria, which was decorated with a few paper chains and balloons. Mindy cringed when she and Damien took seats at a table with the other cheerleaders. The collection of youthful faces made Damien stand out, and the uninformed might have mistaken him for a teacher-chaperone.

Following the invocation, students and guests made their way through the buffet lines to fill their plates. A short time later, the keynote speaker gave an uninspiring speech followed by WEEN radio personality Bill Speck to present varsity letters and individual awards. Festivities wrapped up with a closing prayer before 9 PM, leaving the students all dressed up and no place to go but home.

In the shadowed corner of the Ellington driveway, Damien showered Mindy with compliments. But she could sense animalistic hunger in his voice and reacted coldly. When he persisted with needless accolades, Mindy became uncomfortable and afraid he might broach the subject of her virginity again. She withdrew from the conversation, and the passenger door clicked open. Damien panicked, "Wait! We've been together for a long time, and it's time to find out if we're really right for each other. I don't think we'll know until we've had sex."

Mindy felt as if she'd been stabbed in the chest by an icy shard and screeched, "I said no! Stop asking me!"

Damien chased her to the door and whined, "You know I love you? It's only right for you to share yourself with me."

Mindy cut him off, "Stop it. I'm going inside."

Damien grabbed her arm. "I'm sorry. Don't be mad. It's a good thing that I want you. I'll wait till you're ready," he lied.

"I'll never be ready for you," Mindy growled as she pulled away.

Mindy avoided conversation with her mother and crawled into bed with burning pain in her stomach. Damien's words percolated in her thoughts through the night to create broken and restless sleep. She awoke early the next morning feeling cold, anxious, and empty. "He hasn't actually done anything," she tried to reassure herself. They were just words — but they scared her.

After balancing her window at the end of work at the bank, Mindy stopped at home for a quick bite of lunch but was soon off to school to help with preparations for the Miss Macon County High Beauty Pageant that evening. Mrs. Wilson had tried unsuccessfully for the second year in a row to convince Mindy to be a contestant and even went as far as asking her mother to pressure her to reconsider. Mindy held her ground, "I don't care if it is a fundraising activity. Someone is making money by having young girls parade around on stage, and that's just not right. But I'll do my part to help."

With pageant preparations complete, Mindy returned home to shower, then slipped into the same pretty blue dress she had worn to the previous year's All-Sports Banquet with Randy. With a wide-eyed double-take at the mirror, she noted that the dress still fit her but was noticeably fuller in the chest. "Wow. When did that happen?" she wondered.

Mindy worked as a "Runner," delivering and retrieving ballots to and from the judges. As the last rounds approached, a middle-aged, heavyset judge stopped her. Mindy felt uncomfortable as he scanned her from head to toe and seemed to linger on her chest. "Well, young lady, just why in the world, are you not on stage with the other contestants?" he inquired. Mindy held back no punches in delivering her opinion on beauty contests, but that didn't stop the judge from voicing his disappointment.

After the final cuts and all votes were counted, Rita Green wore the queen's crown. Following the coronation, the same heavyset judge asked Mindy whether she thought they had made a good choice. Surprised that the judge would even ask such a question, Mindy struck back, "She's obviously a cute girl, but no, you didn't. There were other girls up there with warmer hearts, but you would never know that, would you?"

Driving home, Mindy thought, "That judge was just a dirty old man," but she felt ashamed of her outburst and wished she had answered him with more political correctness. She wondered if her internalized ills and the pain it was causing in her own life prompted her harsh response. "Those words just aren't me or who I want to be. I don't even really know Rita," she thought.

With further reflection, Mindy realized she knew Rita only as the rumor mill had painted her at school. That picture was not pretty and undoubtedly tinted by far more rumor than fact. She concluded it was likely many girls were jealous, and that Rita was probably just a normal girl who had fallen victim to the rumor mill simply because she was more developed and drew more attention than most girls. Mindy shuddered again to think of herself as a similar victim and the potential consequences of such in a small town.

Still hoping for divine guidance, Mindy prayed hard the next day at church but received no reply. During the drive home, the weight of the previous few days became intolerable, and she decided it was time to consult her mother. Mindy took a seat at the kitchen table and folded her hands tensely. Her mother was rushing to prepare lunch and too busy to read the anxiety in her daughter's eyes. So Mindy opened the conversation, "After the Banquet Friday night, Damien asked me if I would have sex with him. Not right then, but sometime."

Her mother almost dropped a knife and froze with disbelief. Thawing, she glanced around to make sure no younger-brother ears were listening to ask, "Well, what did you tell him?"

"What in the world do you think I told him?" Mindy returned with some irritation. Her mute mother offered only a blank stare. "I said no, of course. I told him I wasn't ready and would wait till I was married."

Her mother blinked as Mindy waited for more, then stumbled through her response. "I'm glad to hear that. It's the right thing to do. I hope you know you can always talk to me about such things," she tried to assure — but didn't sound very convincing.

That was it. Mindy sat quietly at the kitchen table for several minutes, waiting for her mother to explode. She wanted to hear her mother scream, "You tell him you're not allowed to ever see him again! You tell him if he shows up here, we'll call the police!"

But the conversation was clearly over from her mother's perspective. With weak limbs, Mindy pushed herself up from the table and plodded to her room. Her veiled attempt to ask for help during Good Friday confession and the more direct approach with her mother had failed. She believed the risk of lighting a rumor mill fire was too high if she discussed it with friends, so she kept further thoughts to herself.

Mindy recovered her spirits enough to join schoolmates on a March of Dimes charity walk that afternoon. It was a cherished time that she did not want diluted or distorted by Damien's presence. With her hair in flying pigtails, she enjoyed a pleasant afternoon with friends.

The following Friday brought with it the Junior-Senior Banquet which was, as usual, held in the cafeteria of the Imperial Reading shirt factory. Mindy looked stunning in a royal purple, sleeveless, empire-waist gown. Damien invited himself again and suggested that they have a photo taken, but Mindy declined.

Like the previous year, older, post-high school boyfriends escorted several other girls as well. The pack of out-of-place young adult males banded together and shared a table with their teen dates. The group included Julie Crist with Ed Cartwright and Barb Gentry with Harry Whitmire.

Julie, a fellow junior at MCHS, began dating Ed in 8th grade while Ed was a senior. Ed now worked for the highway department and was on the road five days a week, but would spend every waking minute with her on the weekends.

Barb had recently started dating Harry. She had somehow learned that Harry had asked Mindy out the previous fall and took the first opportunity to ask Mindy why she had declined. Mindy explained, "I had no idea who he was when he called. I'd never talked to him before or even been introduced. But he talked like I should know who he was anyway — it was just too weird."

Barb shook her head in disbelief, "These older guys don't come along very often. Sometimes ya just gotta grab 'em when ya kin."

Mindy felt a wave of nausea and so very sorry for Barb.

The small-time banquet and speeches passed quickly. With no music or dancing, festivities ended before 9 PM. After the closing prayer, the older boys jumped out of their seats toward the exit.

A short caravan carrying young adult males and their teen dates pulled away from the shirt factory and drove several minutes out of town. The cars pulled off the main road and up a small incline into a gravel parking lot that had two picnic tables illuminated by a single dull yellow streetlight. Larry, who did not attend the banquet, had arrived before the caravan to throw old blankets over the tables and set a cooler of beer on one of them. The girls huddled beneath the light pole to talk while the boys each grabbed a beer, popped the tabs in unison, and tipped their cans to the sky in an old-fashioned chugging contest.

A short time later, Damien made his way over to Mindy to offer her a beer. Mindy scrunched her nose, "No, thanks. Are you *trying* to get me kicked off the cheerleading team?" Damien scoffed and returned to the boys.

The evening air cooled considerably, and Mindy had just pulled her shawl up over her shoulders when Damien returned. He tapped Mindy on the shoulder and motioned toward the far picnic table. Mindy reluctantly disengaged from the girl pack and followed his lead. Damien asked, "Would you like to sit down?" Mindy nodded in agreement, but felt uncertain when he picked up an extra blanket and moved toward the road. Walking away from the group and light, he stopped at the edge of darkness, then spread the blanket on the sloping grass-covered hillside that overlooked the winding road below. Damien sat first and patted the blanket. Mindy took a hesitant seat a full arm's length away, wishing she had gone home to change into jeans. The streetlight and pale moon glow provided just enough light to make out Damien's shadowed features, but his eyes looked pitch black.

When Damien suddenly leaned over to deliver a kiss, Mindy quickly withdrew. Embarrassed, she glanced over her shoulder, happy to see that no one had noticed, then stiffened and chastised, "Don't do that when people are around."

Unfazed, Damien whispered compliments, noting how elegant she looked and how jealous all his friends were. Mindy sat silently. When she didn't reply, his tone shifted, and he spoke intensely. "Look at you. You are all grown up now and ready to be a woman. Tomorrow you'll be seventeen and old enough to do what you really want to do. Having sex will make us closer."

Worried others might overhear him, Mindy glanced over her shoulder again. Then she turned back and glared into his empty black eyes to whisper, "Shhh. I told you, I'm not going to do that until I'm married."

"Don't you want to be close? I can get a motel out of town. You need someone that knows how to be gentle the first time," Damien pressured.

Mindy's stomach churned, and acid burned her throat. Hoping to avoid making a scene in front of her friends, Mindy felt trapped. She shook her head and said through clenched teeth, "No. It's not right, and it's a sin."

"I don't want you to do anything before you are ready, but I still think you are far more ready than you know. Don't you know I love you?" Damien whispered.

Mindy looked to the sky and sighed to proclaim, "You just ruined another nice evening."

"Just think about it," he pleaded.

An approaching car hit the curve at the base of the gravel drive and briefly flooded them with high beam lights. Damien covered his face, and Mindy turned away. By the time the car lights moved past and returned them to darkness, Mindy was on her feet and headed back to the crowd. "I don't need to," she said over her shoulder. What she wanted to say was, "It won't happen because I don't love you and never will." Then she wondered, "Why is that so hard to say out loud? It shouldn't be."

Mindy studied the girl group as she returned. She had heard their "boys will be boys" philosophy but had rescued herself from accepting it. With another long sigh of relief, she felt a sudden paradigm shift within, and the pressure felt lighter. "He's just going to keep asking, and I'm just going to keep saying no. I guess boys *will* be boys, but it will be on *my* terms." Rejoining the small band of girls, Mindy no longer felt angry, upset, or even embarrassed by his request and planned to let such future requests roll off her shoulders. Full of confidence, she believed in herself and her moral values.

The loosely defined post-banquet party soon dissolved. During the return to Ellington, Damien tried to recover but didn't apologize. "Tomorrow will be different, I promise. I'll pick you up after work and take you shopping at RiverGate Mall, and you can get whatever you want for your birthday. Then we'll stop by my parent's house for birthday cake." The lure of shopping out of town outweighed the downside of cake with his parents but, most importantly, the plan sounded safe. So, Mindy agreed and accepted a cold, budget-balancing kiss before going inside. Her trust and naiveté were a dangerous combination.

As the evening replayed in her mind, and Mindy concluded that having to say "No" over and over was a necessary trade-off for getting a taste of being "grown up." It was a trade-off that she felt comfortable making and consciously decided against discussing it further with her mother or friends.

Mindy awoke genuinely excited for the day, and her anticipation grew through the morning. She hurried home from the bank and stood before her closet, considering her clothing options. Her eye settled on a yellow silk blouse with delicate blue flowers. It had a broad, overlapping breast lapel with hidden buttons, and its gently puffed shoulders and sleeves gave it a touch of elegance. While brushing her hair, she felt proud of the attractive reflection in the mirror.

During the fifty-minute drive, Damien was all smiles and acted uncharacteristically lighthearted. As they entered RiverGate Mall, he asked Mindy if she had a favorite store. Slightly embarrassed, she replied, "No. You know my mother makes most of my clothes, and most of what she doesn't make I buy at K-Mart in Gallatin."

"Well, let's go to County Seat. That's where I buy most of my clothes," Damien boastfully announced.

A chipper young sales girl met them at the door and guided them toward new pantsuit arrivals. She quickly pulled a bright yellow blazer with matching flare leg slacks from the rack. Mindy nodded her approval, and the clerk added, "And here is the perfect blouse to go with it."

The style and color caught Mindy's attention. She studied the selection carefully, then turned to find the clerk focused on Damien. To escape, Mindy said, "I'll just go try them on."

The attractive young clerk followed her into the dressing room, where Mindy felt a wave of self-consciousness when she noticed the changing stalls had no doors. She took a deep breath, overcame her modest personality, and plunged into a nearby stall. After slipping on the outfit, Mindy glanced into the mirror and smiled with approval. Turning to view the back, she saw to her dismay the dark floral print pattern of her underwear faintly visible through the fabric of the pants. Aghast, Mindy quickly slipped on the blazer and was thankful it covered most of her derrière. She took another deep breath and just hoped no one else would notice.

Stepping out of the stall, Mindy came face to face with the waiting sales clerk. Scanning the clerk's pretty face and intuitive eyes, Mindy's immediate impression was that she was smart and insightful. But the clerk's expression became doubtful as she asked, "Is that guy out there your boyfriend?"

Mindy gasped. No one had ever used the term "boyfriend" in reference to Damien before. Mindy didn't want to explain, so took the path of least resistance and silently nodded her head. The clerk frowned, and Mindy could envision a flashing neon sign floating above her head that read: "Are you crazy?"

Mindy wanted to run out of the dressing room. As it was, she moved toward the sales floor, where she realized, "Ugh, I'm going to be putting on a fashion show; strolling in front of him just like a pageant." Suddenly she felt cheap and queasy. The thought of him looking at her with elevator eyes made her gut ache.

She emerged from the dressing room to find Damien anxiously waiting. His eyes lit up as he scanned her curves.

The clerk asked, "Would you like to try on anything else?"

In desperate need of a quick escape, Mindy replied, "No. I like this combination. I'll take it."

With shopping over so quickly, Damien struggled with what to do next, but Mindy helped him out and suggested they wander through a record store. Curiosity took over, and Mindy didn't resist when, for the very first time, she sensed an attempt at romance as Damien took her hand and pointed toward the far end of the mall.

Entering the record store, Damien instructed, "Pick out any album you want." They went their separate ways down the aisles, thumbing through the stacks. Twenty minutes later, Mindy returned to the front of the store with an Elton John album. Damien snarled, shook his head, and suggested an alternative as he held up a Linda Ronstadt album. It was like being doused with ice water. The transient romance of the day promptly washed away, and they left the record store seconds later without a purchase.

With a sudden shift in demeanor, Damien became anxious and suggested an early dinner, which passed quickly and with little conversation. The atmosphere lightened during the return drive, and Mindy lowered her guard. The more comfortable she became, the more distracted Damien acted.

Just a short distance from his home, Damien slowed and made an unannounced turn onto a muddy farm service road then said, "I want to show you something." He continued down the dirt road for about one hundred yards then pulled into a small clearing facing the setting sun. With only a field of tobacco before them, Mindy surveyed the view, wondering what could be so interesting. Damien made it clear as he boasted, "This field and tobacco will be all mine one day."

Mindy's eyes continued to scan the scene and wished she could appreciate it more. Damien seized his opportunity, "Do you really like your birthday gift?"

With an innocent smile, Mindy replied, "Oh, yes. I'll wear it the next time we go to Nashville." Damien turned sideways in his seat and leaned across the center console to deliver a kiss. As he sat back, Mindy looked down at her hands folded loosely in her lap and wondered, "Why don't I ever feel the urge to kiss back?"

He leaned across the center console again and raised her chin with his left hand. Mindy closed her eyes in anticipation of another kiss. The light pressure of his hand on her chin disappeared, only to reemerge heavily just inside the wide lapel of her blouse. His probing fingertips, inhibited by the hidden buttons, landed just over the edge of her bra. He pushed down firmly but quickly withdrew. It lasted only seconds, but felt like someone had driven a hot poker through her gut. Damien leaned back in his seat, sighed heavily, and grew a victorious smile.

Mindy rotated her shoulders to prevent a second attack and stared wide-eyed out the passenger window. Caught so off guard, she was confused about what had just happened. A rush of uncertain thoughts swirled in her mind, and wildly mixed emotions ran through her veins. "Is this my fault? Did I somehow invite this? Do I owe this to him for a nice day? Payback? Is this included in the business of dating? What will happen next?"

Her frozen surprise gradually thawed, and her mind cleared as the answers came to her one by one. "No. He's going to demand more and more. I didn't have a chance to say no to this." Anger settled in. "He took this from me. He had no right! This is wrong!"

She took a deep breath to compose herself, then glared at him to say, "Take me home. Now!"

Impotent panic replaced Damien's victorious smile. He tried to disarm the bomb sitting in his car by reminding her that his parents were expecting them for cake and ice cream. The low sun cast long shadows all around and triggered flashes of Jack Robertson. Fear replaced anger, and Mindy just wanted to take the fastest route to the safety of other people.

Damien reached for the key in the ignition and then sat back without turning it. "Look, you are seventeen now and really are all grown up," he said. "We've grown so much closer. I really think it's time we take our relationship to the next . . ."

"Stop! I said NO! Let's go — *right now!*" Mindy popped.

Filled with bitter defeat, Damien dropped the transmission into drive and stepped hard on the accelerator. The rear wheels spun on the rain-soaked turf, but the car didn't move. Slamming the transmission into reverse and punching the gas pedal brought the same result. After multiple futile attempts to rock the wheels backward and forward out of the soft, muddy trap, Damien screamed, "God damn it!" He tried rocking the car a few more times but only sank the tires deeper in the mud. Breathing hard with embarrassment and frustration, Damien banged his head on the steering wheel and whimpered, "We'll have to walk."

With flat-soled shoes, Mindy strolled atop the soft surface like an elf, but Damien struggled with every step against the mud's suction grip on his four-inch platform shoe heels. It took a long time, and by the time they traversed the quarter mile to the house, Damien was exhausted.

Damien's father must have seen them approaching in the waning twilight and met them outside to ask, "Where's the car?"

Damien sheepishly explained his car's situation. He seemed to shrink into his shoes as his father chastised him for being such an idiot and concluded, "I'll pull it out with the tractor in the morning."

They moved inside, where the conversation over cake and ice cream was tense. Mindy was pleasant with his parents but ate quickly and spoke only when spoken to. Immediately after swallowing the last bite, she apologized to his parents but insisted she had to get home. Damien grabbed the keys to his father's truck and began the drive to Ellington as darkness won the battle for the sky.

Damien alternated between apology and defeat, but Mindy heard none of it and got out of the truck without a thank you or goodbye. When her mother inquired about the shopping trip, Mindy wanted desperately to confess the whole truth but couldn't force out the words. Her mother missed her hesitation and continued with her duties to finish another long day of running the house.

Mindy went to bed feeling Damien had wrongfully taken something from her, but she was angrier at herself for allowing it to happen. She seriously considered telling Damien not to call again, but illogical uncertainty grew as the tobacco field incident interjected a new twist to the concerns in her teenaged mind. Although she believed the truth shouldn't be able to hurt her, Mindy now feared more than ever what misinformation Damien might feed to the rumor mill. She didn't want people talking about her in the distorted way they gossiped about Rita.

From Mindy's perspective, the tobacco field incident had pushed her across a one-way bridge. She wanted to confide in her mother and ask for guidance, but was afraid her mother wouldn't believe her or might even blame her for what had happened? She went to bed feeling weak and more alone than ever. Damien had cracked her shield of confidence. Feeling trapped again, she wondered if she could continue to say no if his pressure persisted. The burning sensation in her gut interrupted her sleep many times that night.

Monday morning, Mindy awoke well before the alarm clock with her heart racing, gown soaked with sweat, and stomach aching. She felt slightly better after forcing down some breakfast and left for school, only to endure intermittent flares of pain and sweats throughout the day. After school, her mother noted a subtle pallor on her usually rosy-cheeked daughter, which prompted a few questions. After Mindy described the discomfort and the progression of her symptoms, her mother called Dr. Froedge's office and scheduled an appointment for the next day.

Concerned Mindy might have developed an ulcer, Dr. Froedge started her on appropriate medication and scheduled her for an outpatient upper GI. With a radiologist in town only once a week, the study would have to wait until the following week. In the meantime, he cautioned her against ingesting potential stomach irritants, including aspirin and caffeine, but failed to mention the avoidance of alcohol or cigarettes.

The next day, Mindy noticed that Judy's seat in History class remained empty. Thinking she must really be ill to miss so much school, Mindy quietly asked Barb if she knew what was wrong. Barb whispered in reply, "Don't you know? She's pregnant. Her morning sickness is so bad that she can hardly eat." Mindy's heart grew heavy with sadness and uncertainty. Judy's seat remained unoccupied for the rest of the semester.

Returning home from school, Mindy hoped a Twinkie and a glass of milk might soothe her aching stomach. As the first cold swallow eased the fire in her gut, mental images of her pregnant classmate mixed with the anxiety of the past weekend and burned in her mind. She moved to the patio door and scanned the backyard, and the peaceful scene of early spring gradually soothed her thoughts. The fantasy of a private garden allowed her to relax and take a deep, cleansing breath until the ringing phone interrupted the calm. In no hurry to answer, she lifted the receiver after the fifth ring. A boyish voice whispered, "Hi, is this Mindy?"

Her heart dropped when the voice continued, "Paul Thomas asked me to call. He'd like to know if you'd go out with him this weekend?" The soothing effect of her after-school snack was instantly reversed and re-ignited the fire in her stomach.

Forcing herself to remain calm, Mindy chose not to kill the innocent messenger. "Everyone knows he's dating Tammy and *no*; I won't ever go out with him," she said evenly.

"He said you'd say something like that. But he said to tell you he plans to break up with Tammy soon," the youthful voice chirped.

"You tell him he's a cheat and a liar. You tell him if anyone ever calls me like this again, I'll tell everyone in town what low life scum he is. Goodbye!" Mindy bellowed, then hung up.

Mindy turned around to find her mother scowling. "My goodness. What was that all about?" she wanted to know. Mindy didn't want to discuss it, but saw no way to avoid it. She delivered a brief historical review of Paul and his indirect phone calls. Her heart sunk even further when her mother's only question was, "Are you doing something at school to encourage him?" as if it were her fault.

Marching to her room, Mindy carried the weight of anger and confusion. The ache in her gut spiked and doubled her over in silent, gnawing pain. After several minutes, the red-hot skewer in her belly cooled but killed her appetite, and her dinner went mostly untouched.

Paul broke up with Tammy later that week. In response, Tammy abandoned her typically sharp attire, perfect hair, and make-up to arrive at school looking as if she'd just rolled out of bed for what little remained of the semester. At the lunch table, Tammy's friends reported that depression was dissolving all of her happy high school memories. The break-up also triggered a tidal wave of gossip, with many girls expressing sadness and disbelief over the fall of "the perfect couple." Mindy felt guilty that she and others aware of Paul's history of cheating said nothing in response.

Feeling poorly, Mindy nixed plans for going out and spent a quiet weekend at home, but Damien didn't hide his frustration.

Feeling better on Sunday, Mindy enjoyed a few solitary hours sitting on the back porch under a beautiful blue sky. She flipped through pages of a book but read with little comprehension. She just wanted to enjoy the peace and quiet.

The sound of the patio door sliding open interrupted Mindy's solitude. Her mother stepped outside and pulled up a chair and said, "Oh, my, what a beautiful day it is," as she sat. Mindy acknowledged her but could read something more substantial in her mother's eyes. After an uneasy moment of silence, her mother continued, "Well, your father is unhappy at work right now. You can't tell anyone, but he's sending out some feelers to see what else might be available," then quickly changed the subject.

Mindy's heart sank as she thought, "She means we'll probably be moving — *again*."

Mindy spent the following Tuesday morning at Macon County General Hospital. The barium for the UGI was grainy, but Mindy choked it down before the technician fired pulses of radiation through her body. Dr. Froedge called late that afternoon with the results: a three-centimeter gastric ulcer. The good doctor instructed Mindy to stay on the ulcer medication for at least six weeks.

Curling up on the couch that evening, Mindy watched the evening news in stunned silence as they played and replayed evacuation scenes from the fall of Saigon. The Viet Nam war was a conflict that few Americans understood, but Mindy wondered along with them, "How did we lose this war? We are the United States of America. We only win wars. How did we lose this one?"

───────────── · ─────────────

By the following week, the ulcer medication was helping, and Mindy felt considerably better in time for cheer tryouts. The school administration had decided to expand the team so that more girls could participate. When tryouts began, boys who remembered Mindy's first tryout yelled out, "Boogie down! Boogie down!" as she took the floor, but she disappointed them with a playful shake of her pigtails. Although not physically at 100 percent, her standard tryout routine was flawless. When it was over, Mindy and Kat made the team again along with fellow senior-to-be, Loretta Weston.

Emily Harrison was selected as an alternate for the second year in a row and didn't hide her hope that some circumstance would arise to make her an active member of the team. Her chance would come sooner than anyone imagined.

The Murphy family left early on the first Friday in May for Mindy's cousin Lynn's wedding in Tuscaloosa, Alabama. Mindy enjoyed seeing her extended family, dressing up for the wedding and toasted the new bride and groom with a glass of water. She consciously suppressed any thought of Damien and welcomed the miles between them. But the return to Lafayette rekindled fears of what Damien might feed to the rumor mill and triggered a flare of abdominal pain that was almost overwhelming. She wanted to run, but there was nowhere to go.

Mindy's mother notified Dr. Froedge, who immediately arranged for a hospital stay, additional testing and an evaluation by a gastroenterologist in Nashville.

When Mindy informed Damien of her plans to spend the weekend at home, he became angry and openly doubtful of her illness. When Mindy questioned his lack of concern, he didn't seem to understand. He did, however, say he would visit her in the hospital Monday evening after work.

Mother's Day began with church, followed by brunch at the Barren River Lodge. Mindy's mother encouraged her to "eat up" because she and her mother were leaving for the hospital upon their return to Lafayette. From what they knew of the tests she would undergo, it was doubtful food would be plentiful after admission. Mindy took her mother's advice and happily ate her fill at the all-you-can-eat buffet.

As soon as they returned home, Mindy packed an overnight bag and reviewed the hospital checklist. Her eye stuck on "Remove all jewelry and leave all valuables at home." She pulled the misshapen hoop off her finger and dropped it into a box with her other costume jewelry.

In the hospital, they took blood samples shortly after admission and delivered only a tray of clear liquids for dinner. The bowel-prep for a barium enema began an hour later. The many cathartic induced trips to the bathroom and the nagging ache of the IV in her arm limited Mindy's sleep that night. An upper endoscopy the following morning confirmed the ulcer, and biopsies were taken. That afternoon, she endured the humiliation of a barium enema and felt angry about what was happening to her. Despite her anger, Mindy had never been hungrier. The hospital food was less than appealing to look at but felt so good when it hit her stomach late that afternoon.

Although feeling weak and tired, Mindy took a few minutes to clean up in anticipation of Damien's visit that evening. She pulled on a full-length robe, then took a seat in the recliner to talk with her mother while she waited.

The scheduled arrival time came and went with no visitors. Still hungry, Mindy asked her mother to get her ice cream sandwich from the cafeteria. A moment after her mother left, the phone rang. Mindy was silent as Damien unapologetically explained, "Mr. Donnelly asked me to go fishing with him after work, and I couldn't pass up the opportunity to get in good with the boss."

Mindy questioned disbelievingly, "Fishing? On a Monday? After work?"

Caught in a lie, Damien replied, "Don't you know I love you?"

His empty words sent cascading thoughts, images, and memories tumbling in Mindy's mind. When the subconscious haze cleared, her vision of his escalating pressure came into conscious focus, and she finally fully understood the source of her pain and illness.

He had used the word "love" with increasing frequency in the past six weeks, and always in reference to sex. She now understood his use of it as a means to an end. "I said I love you, so that means I should get a free pass to have sex with you."

Mindy had always considered the word *love* to be the biggest and most powerful word in the English language. It was a word to express pure affection and total commitment. It was the sacred pinnacle of all emotions. But there was a complete absence of love in his words.

Mindy's heart turned cold and hardened. True Love's pathway to her soul was closed by an avalanche of disappointment. She wouldn't be able to hear, say, or believe in the word *love* in a positive or caring way for a long time. His manipulative use of the word had poisoned her, and she felt an enormous loss.

She snapped, "I'm in here because of you! This is *your* fault!"

Damien whimpered, "Why is it my fault?"

"This *is* your fault, and you *know* why," Mindy said more calmly, then hung up.

More unpleasant testing the following morning completed the hospital evaluation. Mindy's mother checked her out, and they returned to Lafayette immediately after lunch. Fatigued but not too weak, Mindy ate and drank anything she could find.

When Damien called late that afternoon, Mindy refused to come to the phone. He told her mother would stop by after work the next day.

Mindy went to school the next morning but felt physically exhausted by the time she returned home. She found energy to devour a few Twinkies and washed them down with cold milk, then slowly made her way outside to the back patio. She took a seat and enjoyed the relaxing late-afternoon sun. The warm rays thawed some of the coldness within as her strength gradually returned, and she released a long sigh of satisfaction.

Damien arrived and Mindy's mother directed him to the patio. When Mindy heard the patio door slide open, she didn't budge and maintained her gaze into the yard.

Damien tiptoed to position himself a safe distance in front of her to ask, "Are you feeling better"?

Mindy turned toward him with cold, uninviting eyes. "I'm feeling much better today," she said with surprising strength, but no emotion.

Damien whispered, "That's good. I was thinking . . ."

Mindy could see the manipulative devil in Damien's eyes and cut him off. "I need to be away from you. You aren't good for me."

Her words cut deep and stabbed at his devil within. Damien stumbled backward as the blood drained from his face. "No, no. I don't want that. I'm sorry. It's really not my fault."

Mindy's cold response was not long in coming. "You are not worth my time. I have allowed you to make me ill and cause me pain. I won't allow it anymore."

"But everybody expects us to be together. Give me another chance. Let me take you to Nashville," he pleaded.

Mindy laughed to herself thinking, "Nashville — his only real attribute is a ticket to Nashville." She pitied his lack of substance and softened. With unemotional eyes, she pronounced, "I don't think you deserve another chance. I don't think you'll change."

Beaten into submission, Damien stumbled again and almost fell. "Please!" he begged.

The pathetic vision before her softened Mindy some more. "I won't agree to anything right now, but if I ever go out with you again, there will be new rules. There will be no pressure. There will be no talk about sex. There will be no touching. There will be no expectation of kisses or payback. If you break any of these rules, I will walk away."

Damien nodded his head in acceptance of her guidelines. Mindy sat silently with hands calmly folded in her lap. Damien wilted more with the silence and finally whispered, without a single ounce of manhood, "I understand. I think we can get past this."

Mindy gave no reply. She didn't believe him and knew whatever relationship they had was over. She had never felt any significant affection for him, and now even the smallest innocent sliver of respect she may have had for him was gone.

"I'll call you," he said, and quietly walked away.

Mindy remained seated as Damien disappeared around the corner of the house. When the sound of his car faded, Mindy went inside. Her mother glanced up, and Mindy could tell she wanted to say something but was too busy preparing dinner. Mindy continued to her room and closed the door.

Chapter 11
Metamorphosis
May 15–June 5, 1975

Aware of Mindy's hospitalization, her teachers went easy on her the last few days of school. Her math teacher even allowed her to skip the final exam and offered, "Just come by my house any time in the next few weeks to take it."

The lost days resulted in fewer yearbook signings, but most echoed similar sentiments as the year before. The boys uniformly made a note of how much they liked her, how cute she was, and how they hoped to see her over the summer. Several even asked for a date, yearbook-style. Gina and Phyllis, both of whom were graduating, wrote long notes expressing appreciation for her friendship and for being supportive as they prepared to step into new roles and responsibilities.

As she flipped through the warm notes of high school friendship that afternoon, Mindy's thoughts drifted back to events that already seemed like ancient history but had occurred only a year ago: breaking up with Randy, the Jack Robertson incident and entering the summer without Anne. She chuckled with the thought, "This school year hasn't ended very well either. I wonder what next spring will bring?" If a prophet had read her future, she wouldn't have believed it.

With her brothers all fast asleep, the house was calm, and Mindy sat at her desk to finish schoolwork she'd missed while in the hospital. After closing her books, she walked to the kitchen where she sat quietly dipping Oreo cookies into cold milk and enjoying the sensation of them disintegrating on her tongue. The soft, sweet cookies soothed her stomach and filled her with pleasant satisfaction. She smiled for what felt like the first time in weeks.

Mindy's mother made rounds to double-check doors and windows before retiring to bed. She paused in the kitchen, nervously folding and refolding a dish towel. Then she cleared her throat to say, "There's nothing definite, but Dad has been talking with a headhunter. He will probably interview for a new job this summer. If he makes the changes at the plant that the corporate office wants, Dad thinks the workers will vote to unionize. If that happens, he thinks the company will close the plant, and he doesn't want to be here for that. It's still a secret, so don't talk about it with anybody."

Mindy didn't hear much past "new job." Thoughts of packing, loss of friends, loss of cheerleading, and yet another new school filled her mind. Her cookie-induced satisfaction faded, and she went to bed feeling cheated.

Lying in the dark, emotions churning, she knew there was nothing she could do about it. She took a deep breath. The school year would be over in another two days, and she resolved not to let the threat of a move ruin her summer.

Mindy hadn't discussed her breakup with Damien with her mother, so she felt obligated to take the phone when he called a few days later. He tried his old tactic of dangling a trip to Nashville like a carrot, but only succeeded in making Mindy mad by suggesting a nightclub just days after her discharge from the hospital. But Mindy's anger rapidly dissipated when Damien hit another sweet spot, "I bought tickets to see Linda Ronstadt at the Opry on Monday."

"I didn't say I'd go out with you again," Mindy replied.

"Oh, come on. I'm trying to make it up to you," Damien whined.

"No. You're trying to make me owe you something. I'll think about it, but I'm not making any decisions now," Mindy tersely replied.

On the last day of school, Mindy returned home and lay across her bed to review the day's yearbook entries. Her classmates were good and honest people. She would miss seeing them at school, but hoped to share lots of time with them over the summer. In contrast, thoughts of Damien represented a double-edged sword. He was a threat to her wellbeing as well as the most practical ticket out of town.

Her thoughts drifted to being "unobligated," and it occurred to her that returning Damien's ring was the right, if not the only, thing to do. Then she could move forward in her own way. Public dissolution of any association with Damien was no longer a question of *if* — only *when*.

Mindy attended the MCHS graduation ceremony on Friday evening and sat alone. She shared her friend's exhilaration as they completed their rite of passage into a new chapter of their lives. But melancholy sadness seeped in with the realization of how much distance had grown between herself and them during the past months. "I've traded away so much time with them in search of the world beyond Lafayette, but I only succeeded in gathering more worry, pain, suffering, and embarrassment than I would have ever predicted. Worse, Gina and Phyllis are dating every weekend. It's likely our distance will continue to grow," she thought.

The dichotomy of Mindy's world blocked her from confiding with those she trusted most and bonds with her friends and mother had weakened considerably. Emotionally isolated, Mindy wondered what the word *best* in the concept of *best friends* really meant. She realized she really had no best friend and drove home after the ceremony with a heavy heart. It felt even heavier when she concluded, "I've never really had a *best* friend."

Mid-Saturday morning, Damien arrived at the bank and approached Mindy's window wearing a crown of sweat. Mindy raised an eyebrow but said nothing. "What have you decided about the concert?" he nervously inquired.

"I've given it a lot of thought. As long as you follow my rules, I will consider going places with you occasionally, but I am making no promises. Linda Ronstadt is one of my favorites, and I would enjoy seeing her in concert. So, I'll agree to go," said Mindy matter-of-factly.

Damien nodded. "That's good. I'll pick you up at six on Monday." He hesitated before continuing, "Would you like to go out and get something to eat tonight?"

"No. I have other plans," Mindy said bluntly. Damien stood mute, and Mindy raised her other eyebrow as if to say, "Are you done now?" He turned and limped out of the bank, clutching his wounded manhood.

By chance, Gina's boyfriend was out of town for the day, so Mindy grabbed the opportunity to mend their neglected bond as they listened to records at Ellington. When the sky darkened, they drove to the Macon County Drive-in, where they had fun watching a B movie, then finished the evening with ice cream at Jones's.

Damien called Sunday evening to report, "I'm sick and won't be able to go to the concert tomorrow. But my mom will meet you at the square with the tickets and my sister Rhonda if you want."

He didn't sound sick, so Mindy had doubts about his claim of illness and wondered if this was his way of punishing her. But she was not at all upset by the change in plans. She would have preferred to take a friend but thought, "Rhonda will be just fine."

Late Monday afternoon, Mindy put on her yellow birthday pantsuit and carefully reviewed a map and directions with her father before leaving to pick up Rhonda at the square. She exchanged brief pleasantries with Damien's mother as Rhonda nervously took a seat in the Mustang. Neither of them mentioned anything regarding Damien's illness.

The unlikely car mates had met briefly only once before, but they had shared no conversation. Mindy's attempts to engage Rhonda as they drove met with limited success, and Mindy wondered if Rhonda, a fifth grader, was just very shy or had other personality concerns.

The show opened with a forty-minute performance by a newcomer on the American music scene, Al Stewart. Popular in Great Britain for almost a decade, Stewart's British folk music was virtually unknown in the United States. The audience showed their approval with a standing ovation.

For Mindy, the big show began when Linda Ronstadt strode out on stage and sang for nearly an hour without otherwise engaging the audience with talk or commentary. Her voice was fabulous and made Mindy's spine tingle with each high note. Ronstadt never ventured beyond the bounds of a six-foot circle around the microphone and was unaware of a "streaker" who traversed the stage right behind her wearing nothing but a pair of PF Flyers. Poor little Rhonda just sat wide-eyed and frozen while Mindy laughed and wondered whether the culprit's shoes would really make him "run faster and jump higher" in his escape.

When "You're No Good" began, Mindy sang along with extra gusto and pointed her finger at an imaginary image of Damien floating in the air. Mindy laughed again when little Rhonda's expression oozed uncertainty and surprise at Mindy's vocal outburst.

After the last song, Ronstadt bowed to the audience, smiled, and walked off the stage without a word or wave. Mindy had a wonderful time singing along with most of the songs and departed the Opry with exhilaration.

Despite ongoing efforts by Mindy to connect, Rhonda had remained nearly nonverbal and flat affected most of the evening. So, it surprised Mindy when she reacted with animated happiness as they pulled onto the square in Lafayette to find her mother waiting. Rhonda hopped out of the Mustang and into her mother's truck without a word or wave. Mindy waited patiently as they pulled away and just shrugged.

Loretta called the next morning to ask, "Hey, why weren't you at the softball game last night?" Mindy summarized the concert and Damien's illness. Loretta replied, "Well, he must have made a quick recovery. It was the opening night of the softball league last night, and Damien played in both games. I wasn't the only one that missed you because I heard several people ask him where you were at." Mindy silently shook her head and promptly changed the subject.

The next morning, Mindy's mother presented a quiet update. "Your father has been considering a few job options but doesn't think he'll take any of these. So, he's still looking."

To Mindy, this statement was the equivalent of, "A move is definitely on the horizon," and put a new spin on her thoughts about Damien. "I'll probably be gone soon. There is no need to leave behind bad feelings or rumors. I should avoid confrontation if at all possible," she decided.

―――――――――――・――――――――

Tuesday-Thursday cheer practices resumed the next day. Afterward, Mindy and a few of the other girls would grab dinner at Clifton's or Jones's and then drive to the ball field to watch "the boys" play. Someone would usually remind them, "They aren't boys anymore. They're grown men who just act like little boys. They all think they're stars."

Having watched her father play in the same league with his Carter Automotive team, Mindy knew the reminder was accurate. The boys tried to live out their sports fantasies to win pseudo glory in their small, slow-pitch pond. Defensive play was shoddy and the games were typically high scoring. For Mindy, that didn't matter; it was just good to be out with the girls in a relaxed, unpressured atmosphere.

Mindy kept post-game interaction with Damien to a minimum. She did, however, take the opportunity to make him squirm, "So, I hear you recovered from your illness and were able to play in a double-header instead of going to the concert."

Caught in his lie, Damien mumbled an unintelligible reply.

"If you didn't want to go to the concert, all you had to do was tell me the truth and say so," Mindy said, then turned and walked away.

The dissolution of any "obligation" was already set in Mindy's mind, but the details of delivery of that fact were not. She felt strongly that it needed to be done quietly to minimize rumor mill gossip. Most of Mindy's closest friends seemed to understand that she was less than enamored with Damien, but they were unaware of any discord. Many others, however, assumed by local cultural default, that they had a future as a couple. So, Mindy was undecided about what to say should they inquire and tried to avoid conversation about boys or dates in general. The few times that Damien's name came up, it was not uncommon to hear the same old and inaccurate accolades. Mindy knew better, and she felt uncomfortable with many of the girls' blanket expectations.

This indirect peer pressure was unwanted and left her feeling guilty for not setting them straight.

The next weekend, Mindy enjoyed Friday evening with the girls and took part in the inaugural "Hillbilly Day" at Key Park after work on Saturday. The small-scale event included amateur folk bands playing bluegrass music, booths for homemade crafts and foods, and a few circus-type arcades sponsored by the local banks. Mindy went to work that morning with pigtails adorned with big red bows, wearing a red-and-white checkered shirt and overalls held snug by a rope belt around her waist. Afterward, she arrived at the park to volunteer in the Carter Automotive tent selling hotdogs and brats. Sales skyrocketed as teen boys stood in line just to see Mindy dressed like Elly May Clampett from *The Beverly Hillbillies*.

Mike McCarthy was Mindy's best customer, returning three times before asking in a whisper if she'd go out with him sometime. His innocent devotion made her smile, but she gently shook her head and softly whispered in return, "This one's on the house." He appreciated the offer but dejectedly laid a dollar on the table. Mike apparently walked away with the understanding he would never date the girl he openly referred to as "the town's one true princess," and he disappeared into her past.

Hillbilly Day ended, and Mindy went home to clean up before a dinner date with Damien. A record spun on the turntable while she dressed, and thoughts turned in her head as she became lost in self-debate on how best to become "unobligated" with political correctness and minimal confrontation. Mindy strongly considered doing it during dinner but decided against it when she remembered Randy was taking her to the Pioneer Kitchen when she handed him a "let's just be friends" bomb. "That would be too creepy," she thought.

The Pioneer Kitchen had a reputation for top-notch BBQ pork steaks and a pretty decent charbroiled steak. Damien was on his best behavior as they took a table by the dormant fireplace. But Mindy found her mind wandering back to Randy and wondering how the year might have gone differently had she accompanied him to this same restaurant the previous June.

The possibility of a move, fear of the rumor mill, the safety of her new rules, and Damien's submissive demeanor kept her distracted for much of dinner. Her thoughts mixed and impeded her logical resolve to deliver the final blow in the upcoming hours or days. Naively trusting, she concluded, "It would be okay if things stay like this and I can avoid confrontation." Damien had avoided, at least temporarily, final banishment.

One other small thought dangled like a carrot on a stick before Mindy. "If somebody interesting asks me out, I'll pick Damien's ring out of my jewelry box and hand it back." In her mind, she relegated Damien to the role of a backup plan for getting out of town occasionally.

The next week was similar, with visits to the ball field after cheer practice. Interaction with Damien remained limited, although Mindy accepted a ride home one evening. When he pulled into the shadowed corner of the driveway, Mindy shot to alert status. She reminded herself not to lower her guard and didn't linger to talk for more than a few minutes.

It was already hot and humid when Damien's softball team planned a Memorial Day weekend picnic outing to Dale Hollow Lake. Lounging on rafts with the girls sounded like fun to Mindy, so she bounced out of the house when Damien arrived Monday morning. She carried a small bag containing a swimsuit and a change of clothes. When she noted he was wearing a heavy T-shirt and jeans, she inquired, "Did you bring shorts or a swimsuit? It's going to be awful hot."

Damien dropped his head. "No. I don't have any shorts, and I don't know how to swim."

Julie and Ed arrived a few minutes later, and the foursome left for the lake with boys in the front and Mindy comfortably chatting with Julie in the back. For Mindy, the trip was filled with simple pleasures: girl time, horseshoes, eating sandwiches on the boat dock and dangling her feet in the water. Her internal alarm sounded only once when Damien tried to entice her into sitting on a blanket with him. Mindy declined. She did not want to be seen isolated with him or play into his desire to send false messages to his teammates.

The only disturbing aspect of the day was the way many other girls expressed their impression that she and Damien were a committed long-term couple. While Mindy was detaching herself from him by the day, her peers were pushing them together through cultural expectation. Mindy recoiled from the peer pressure but didn't bother to correct them.

Revivals are the financial, if not spiritual, heart and soul of many small churches and Damien's church was no exception.

When Damien called to say his parents were pushing him to take Mindy to a revival service, Mindy had to pause and wondered what message that would send. But she rationalized and laughed, "Maybe they just want to introduce the Cult Catholic in their midst to their Missionary Baptist ways." Always curious to see and experience new things, she agreed.

It was a mid-week, after-dinner service, and the drive into the country seemed to take a long time. Mindy was beginning to wonder where they were really going when Damien pulled onto a gravel drive that disappeared into a thick grove of trees. The car came to rest in front of a one-room building designed for a tiny congregation. The relative isolation felt eerie, so Mindy was surprised but not unhappy to see Larry waiting by his car, then wondered why he was there.

When Larry stepped up with a broad grin, Damien grabbed him by the arm and pulled him close to deliver firm instructions, "Make sure to keep her *between* us. Don't let anyone get close to her." The tone of his voice conjured up visions of snakes and pagan animal sacrifice in Mindy's mind, and she trembled.

Within minutes of the preacher's first words, Mindy found herself surrounded by unintelligible chanting and slowly gyrating bodies. The dim lights and dark windows added to the strange scene and covered Mindy with goosebumps. Feeling uncertain and out of place, having a relative buffer standing on either side was oddly reassuring.

As the show continued, Mindy's anxiety gradually abated, and her curiosity took over. She studied the unfamiliar sights and sounds, and eventually, the crowd seemed harmless. Damien remained passive and silently moved his lips in prayer. Larry, on the other hand, chanted loud enough for Mindy to overhear several admissions of sin and repeated requests to forgive him for drinking and dancing.

About halfway through the service, several people presented themselves to the preacher to announce, "Praise the Lord. I've been saved!"

The preacher would place his palm on their forehead, look to the ceiling, and ask God to confirm their salvation with far more drama than necessary. Then the preacher would pause before proclaiming, "I can hear God's voice, and he's extending his divine power through me to give you everlasting victory over the Devil!"

One of the newly saved parishioners added some drama of her own as she slumped to the floor. Apparently, overcome with the power of the Holy Spirit, she had to be carried back to her seat. Fully absorbed in observation, Mindy wondered why no one seemed too concerned as they nonchalantly seated her in a chair. But the scene caused the creep factor to jump higher.

Mindy's trio left immediately after the service, saying nothing to the boys' friends or family. When they reached the cars, Larry said, "Hey, how 'bout we hit a nightclub this weekend?"

"Sounds good to me," replied Damien.

Mindy shook her head in disgust. "You guys *are* a pair of hypocrites. You stand in there confessing your sins, and you're not even out of the parking lot before planning your next escapade of debauchery. And you think the Catholic Church is a cult. Just what the . . ."

Damien interrupted her and hurried her into the car. Others had overheard part of Mindy's comment and glared at them. Damien sighed with relief when they hit the paved road and drove away much faster than they had arrived.

"You should come to a Catholic Mass," Mindy suggested.

Damien didn't even pause to consider the invitation. He just looked away and mumbled, "I don't think I can do that."

As they approached Ellington, Mindy announced, "I got a call from a guy I met at the Drug and Alcohol Convention last summer. His name is Connor Prewitt, and he'll be in Nashville to tour Vanderbilt University on Thursday. He plans to stop in Lafayette for a visit on Friday. I'm going to show him around town, and we'll swing by the bank so you can meet him. Maybe we can all do something together Friday evening."

Damien snarled, "No! I don't want to meet him."

Surprised by Damien's anger, Mindy whispered, "He's a nice guy. I just thought you might like to get to know him."

Damien responded with venom. "No! I don't want to meet him or get to know him. Why would I want to do that?"

Unprepared for and intimidated by Damien's bitterness, Mindy sat in silence for the remainder of the drive. Damien gradually calmed and softened his words, but didn't apologize for his outburst.

Avoiding any further discussion of Connor, Damien suggested vague plans to play cards at Larry's mother's apartment Friday evening. Still shaky, Mindy didn't mention that Connor was planning to spend the night in town and went inside still baffled by Damien's reaction.

Preparing for bed, Mindy realized that her post-revival rant had removed the possibility of Nashville from the weekend schedule. With a wave of disappointment, it reminded her that the opportunity to dance and get beyond the invisible walls of Macon County occasionally was important to her.

A flash mental image of Connor rekindled Mindy's girlish fantasies about a worldly mystery boy from a faraway land and was happy to think of the unfamiliar face in town as a welcome diversion for the day. Then she realized, "Damien got mad because he's afraid of being compared to other boys. He knows he won't look good. *He's* the one who's really intimidated!"

Mindy described Damien's response to Connor's visit and her predicament that evening to her mother. "Damien's planning to pick me up after dinner to play cards, but he doesn't know Connor will still be here. What should I do?" she pleaded. Her mother was unsympathetic, offered no solutions, and left Mindy to deal with the dilemma on her own.

Mindy took the morning off work in anticipation of Connor's arrival Friday morning. When she opened the door, Connor stood with arms spread expecting a hug. But his arms fell with disappointment when Mindy stepped back to invite him in. After introducing Connor to her mother, Mindy took him for a tour of the town. She drove the cruising route and made the usual stops while providing descriptive summaries along the way. Relaxed and maybe a little cocky sporting a new boy, Mindy cheerfully made introductions to any friends and acquaintances they met along the way.

As they chatted between stops, Mindy realized Connor knew much more about her than she knew about him. So, she asked her own set of probing questions and quickly learned that Connor was more interesting in her fantasies than in reality. "But that's okay. He's a nice guy and will be a welcome change for the day," she thought.

The conversation's tone shifted when Connor mentioned his girlfriend. He had written in letters, "things are going really well," but had given no specifics. When Mindy asked more about her, he reiterated they were "very close" and deeply "committed" to each other. This description tickled Mindy's repressed visions of romance and made her feel warm inside. Connor's non-local status also provided an opportunity to use him as a neutral sounding board. Hesitant at first, Mindy gradually revealed details of Damien's pressure, and how it had made her physically ill, along with the pain and embarrassment of her hospitalization.

Connor was quick to cast his vote to exile Damien. Mindy explained that she had considered doing so several times and outlined her concerns about the potential fallout. "All he has to do is say I was a tease or suggest that I did things that never happened. That stuff flies through the rumor mill, and people believe it. I've seen what it's done to reputations of other girls, and I'm scared it will happen to me." Connor had no answers for such small-town politics — real or imagined.

As they passed through the square, Mindy decided it was time to reveal her predicament. "I was going to stop by the bank and introduce you to Damien, but he got mad about you being in town at all. I didn't know what to say. He's picking me up after dinner tonight, and I don't think you are invited." Connor's pale expression revealed only fear.

Dishonesty was not part of Mindy's nature, but faced with a dilemma, a minor deception suddenly seemed necessary and maybe even exciting. She proposed a general plan, "After dinner, you stay out of sight until Damien picks me up around seven. Then you can hang out with my brothers, and I'll make something up and get back home early — no later than eight." Connor nodded in uncertain agreement.

After ice cream at Jones's, Connor recovered his poise and recycled the conversation about his girlfriend, then mentioned the concerns she had about being left behind when he went to college. "I told her not to worry, and we came to an agreement. We decided it will be alright to see other people while I'm gone, but we'll only see each other when I'm at home."

Mindy took his words at face value but found the concept of a "committed" couple dating other people very disconcerting. "Just how in the world can that possibly work?" she wondered.

Migrating to Clifton's, Mindy introduced Connor to several more schoolmates before returning to Ellington. Connor left to get checked in just down the street at the Ellington Motel while Mindy got ready to face the rush of Carter employees swarming the bank to cash payroll checks.

Connor returned to Ellington just a few moments after Mindy's return from work. During dinner, Connor capitalized on a military connection with Mindy's father and their conversation dominated the dinner hour. Seeing anyone trying to schmooze her father was rare, but watching someone young pull it off was new and wholly unexpected. Mindy found Connor's smoothness almost too hard to believe.

After dinner, Mindy and Connor moved to the family room to converse in private. The minutes passed quickly, and Damien's arrival at Ellington was imminent. Connor nervously arose and whispered, "I should probably get me and my car out of sight."

Mindy agreed. "Come back in about twenty minutes. My brothers can entertain you until I get back."

A short time later, Mindy answered the front door with Fi snarling between her feet. She grabbed her side and acted uncomfortable. "Oh, hi," she said, acting surprised by Damien's arrival. "What time do you think we'll be done playing cards?" she added.

Damien frowned suspiciously. "I'll have you home by curfew. Why?"

"Um, well — I'm not feeling very well and may need to come home early," said Mindy without making eye contact.

Damien scowled. "What's wrong now?" he questioned without apparent concern for her wellbeing.

"Oh, I'm just having bad stomach cramps," she replied. Aware of Damien's modest germaphobia, she added, "And I feel like I'm coming down with something." She turned her head and feigned a weak cough.

With impeccable timing, her father stepped into the doorway with menacing abruptness. He looked down coldly at Damien on the porch and sternly announced, "Mindy hasn't been feeling well. I want her to be home early."

Mindy felt lightheaded. This unsolicited act of support both shocked her from surprise and impressed her with how convincing her father could be as an accomplice in a lie. Either way, her pallor was more pronounced than it would have been otherwise.

Despite the warm air, Mindy slowly slipped on a light sweater as if she were achy and then mechanically stepped outside. Lagging behind, she could hear Damien grumbling unintelligibly all the way to the car. As soon as they pulled through the driveway, Damien glared at her to ask, "So, *what* were you doing today?"

"Nothing much. Connor came into town this morning, and I showed him around," she replied.

"I know. I *know* you showed him *all* around town. People *saw* you riding around with another guy, and *I* had to hear about it all afternoon. Just how do you think it makes *me* look when people see you riding around with some other guy?" he barked.

Damien's attitude and the efficiency of the gossip machine instantly angered Mindy. She wondered how long it had taken the gossipers to run into the bank, approach Damien at his teller window and report her non-indiscretion. She fired back, "I *told* you he was coming into town and even offered to introduce him to you at the bank. But noooo, you didn't want to. I wasn't hiding anything, and I didn't do anything wrong. You have no right to be mad!"

Damien retreated but repeated softly, "Well, it just doesn't make *me* look very good when people see you with another guy."

Mindy stared ahead through the windshield with cheeks burning and said, "I don't owe you anything."

Forty minutes after their arrival at Larry's mother's apartment, Mindy reported she was feeling worse and wanted to go home. Damien, with smoldering anger, begrudgingly returned her to Ellington. Mindy embraced her role and disarmed him. "I'm sorry for being no fun. I think I've got a stomach virus that's giving me stomach cramps. I don't want you to catch anything. I'll probably feel better tomorrow." She walked to the house and wondered why she didn't feel guiltier about her deception.

Mindy paused at the door as Damien pulled away to scan the driveway and street, but there was no sign of Connor's car. Inside, the house was quiet, and Mindy didn't hear any voices. She started checking room to room until she found her two youngest brothers in the family room giggling with innocent guilt. Mindy smiled and asked, "Where's Connor?"

Her brothers giggled some more and pointed through the hallway to the closed bathroom door. As Mindy turned, the bathroom door cracked open but revealed no light. The door continued to open a few inches at a time until Connor cautiously emerged from his dark hiding place with a juvenile smirk.

"What in the world are you doing? And where's your car?" Mindy wanted to know.

"I didn't want to get caught if he came inside, so I hid in the shower. I parked my car down the street so he wouldn't think you had company," Connor replied.

Mindy's first thought was, "That was smart" until her intuition kicked in and she realized he had done it entirely out of fear and self-preservation. She laughed and shook her head. Connor definitely wasn't the chiseled, dynamic young man she had envisioned in her fantasies. Mindy wondered, "*Are* there any real men in the world?"

The teens left the younger brothers behind and moved to the rec room where they chatted until curfew arrived. Mindy escorted Connor to the door where he nervously said, "I don't want to sound silly, but what does your boyfriend look like and how big is he?"

Mindy laughed. "You don't have anything to worry about. Don't get lost on the way to your car — wherever it is."

Preparing for bed, Mindy wished Damien *would* discover her deception. "I hope he finds out I left him to see another boy. Now that I think about it, it would probably be better for *him* to tell everyone we've split up. Ha! — as if we were ever together. But him announcing it might minimize the gossip."

Up early and dressed attractively for work, Mindy answered the knock at the door to find Connor ready for his drive back to Georgia. When he stepped into the foyer with a heavy scent of Brut aftershave, Mindy thought, *"You have got to be kidding me!"*

They wandered into the kitchen to say goodbye to Mindy's mother and then proceeded through the rec room toward the side exit. They paused, and Connor expressed his hope to see Mindy again over the summer. They chatted for several minutes until Mindy needed to leave for work. Connor jumped ahead to hold open the door. As Mindy stepped through, she looked up to offer an acknowledging "thank you" but stopped when Connor grabbed her arm. Without warning, he delivered a light kiss meant for her lips but only partially hit its mark.

Surprised beyond imagination, Mindy felt the heat rise in her cheeks as she stepped away with her heart pounding. Several seconds of awkward silence followed as they walked the short distance to Connor's car. She finally looked up with a strained smile and said, "Have a safe trip home."

Also sporting flushed cheeks, Connor said nervously, "Well, have a fun rest of the summer, but not too much fun."

Mindy forced another smile that quickly faded and waved aimlessly while Connor pulled away. When he was out of sight, she paused, trying to understand why she felt so uneasy and not at all unhappy he was gone. She replayed the unexpected kiss in her mind and felt a wave of warm tingling all over. It was a sensation she had not felt since Randy's first kiss on her front porch, but there wasn't time to dwell on it as she rushed off to work at the bank.

Wearing invisible chains of Catholic guilt, Mindy moved slowly at work and was more polite than she might have been when Damien called later that morning. His older sister, Jenny, had acquired several free tickets to a rescheduled Eagles concert in Nashville the following week. Mindy accepted his invitation after confirming it was a group outing.

Still feeling guilty, Mindy replayed her false illness deception in her mind after church the next day. She didn't consider herself Damien's girlfriend, but was aware that he thought otherwise. Still, she rationalized, "You can't call it cheating cheat if you're not committed to someone."

But her heart sank when she thought of Connor's girlfriend. "She *is* an innocent victim of our deception. Her boyfriend kissed me and stirred my emotions, and I know it stirred something in him. What would his girlfriend think? How would *she* feel about what happened? Can Connor possibly say he didn't cheat? No. I felt flushed and embarrassed — but I didn't slap him hard across the face. I liked it. So, *how can I say I didn't cheat?* How can I absolve myself? It was wrong. Everything about it is deceitful and wrong — dreadfully wrong."

Mindy lounged on the patio under a clear sky and bronzing sunshine until late afternoon. After showering, she wound her internal springs by playing an Eagles album without listening to the words. While brushing her hair, her eyes locked on her jewelry box. She hesitantly lifted the lid and looked inside. Lying atop the disorganized costume jewelry was Damien's ring. She picked it up and studied the misshapen band. It wouldn't fit right, but obligation took hold, and with more effort than should have been necessary, she forced it onto her finger. The album continued to spin and allowed magical images of the band under bright stage lights to displace the sense of obligation from her mind.

Full of summer radiance and concert anticipation, Mindy felt wired. After a stop at the square to pick up Larry and his date, they drove to Jenny's apartment, where they met several other concertgoers and picked up tickets. A short time later, the caravan crossed the Cumberland River into downtown Nashville. The cityscape before them spiked Mindy's youthful curiosity and excitement.

After dinner, the group proceeded to Municipal Auditorium, where they dispersed to scattered seats. Making their way through the main halls, Mindy noted the crowd was considerably different from those at the Newton-John and Ronstadt concerts. They were younger, wilder, and predominantly male. Inside the auditorium, the atmosphere was charged, and the crowd roared when the lights darkened and the Michael Stanley Band took the stage for an opening set. The intense stage lights popped on, and the rippling bass vibrations gave Mindy goosebumps.

The short set turned out to be unmemorable, and it seemed an eternity waiting for the Eagles to take the stage. The crowd grew impatient and clapped in unison, demanding that the show begin. Mindy clapped as well until a strange aroma caught her attention. Looking down the row to her right, she furrowed her brow when she saw what she assumed to be a joint being shared as it passed, zigzag, from one set of lips and hands to the next and heading her way. Before she could process what was happening, a ruddy set of fingers extended the smoldering stump just inches from her nose. Mindy calmly put up her hand to decline the offer but watched with curiosity as the twisted loser's hallucinogen was passed to the next desiring hand and slowly disappeared into the crowd.

When the Eagles finally took the stage, the energized crowd became even more hyper. Mindy had never listened to the lyrics carefully before, so was surprised that many concertgoers sang along. She tried to join in on the chorus lines but didn't bother to decipher any of the song's meanings. She scanned the scene around her and realized that she didn't need any drugs to enjoy the show. The strangeness of the experience brought with it sights, sounds, images, and now aromas that were far more potent stimulants for her imagination.

The Eagles played most of their popular songs of the day but, to Mindy's disappointment, omitted "Desperado" from the setlist that night. She enjoyed the overall big-concert experience tremendously, but none of the music or any part of the performance created any lasting memories.

During the return trip, Mindy's thoughts randomly drifted a dozen different directions but dwelled the longest on college, travel, other cultures, and the concert. Damien spoke, but Mindy's distracted thoughts only allowed some of what he said to register, and he became agitated with her inattention.

Until now, it had been an enjoyable evening, but Mindy wondered whether she could continue to balance his age advantage with his many shortcomings.

The make-up concert was short, and the group returned to Lafayette much earlier than expected. After dropping Larry and his date at the square, Damien drove slowly to Ellington. The night air was clean, crisp, and comfortable. Still riding the wave of concert euphoria, Mindy was in no particular hurry to go inside. She was honestly thankful for the evening and felt the need to say so. So, she sat quietly, willing to balance the books with the most valuable thing she could offer; her time.

Without preface, Damien came out of his seat to grasp Mindy by the back of her neck and pulled her toward him. Guard down, Mindy didn't resist but was glad that the kiss missed her lips. Then she froze when she felt Damien's hand slide around from behind her neck to settle at the base of her throat. Paralyzed by curiosity, she sat rigidly still. In the next instant, he drove his hand inside the collar of her blouse, then pushed down hard onto her chest. It felt like an out-of-body experience, and she wondered, "Is this really happening?" Still frozen, she remained motionless as he tried to work his fingertips deeper. It lasted only seconds but long enough to fill her cheeks fill with blood. Thwarted by the restrictions of the collar and the awkward positions of their bodies, he strained to reach lower. Suddenly, Mindy needed to breathe. With a gasp, she pushed him away.

Waves of anger, guilt, and shame came crashing over her head. The suffocating weight pushed her beneath the surface, and she felt like she was drowning. Gathering her strength, she fought and kicked her way to the emotional surface. Breaching, she took a deep breath, and her mind cleared. She knew she should save private moments of passion for someone else. Her mind screamed, "Not him! Not *ever* him — but for someone I love. For someone who truly loves me."

He leaned toward her again, and she pushed his torso hard back into his seat. Mindy straightened her blouse, then mechanically turned toward him. Her eyes glared into the blackness of his as she growled, "You'll never change."

The passenger door flew open, only to be slammed shut with unnecessary force and loudly enough to alert Mindy's parents of her return.

Mindy ran to the side door, and Damien yelled, "Wait!"

"No. Just go!" she fired back and stepped through the door.

The house was dark and quiet. Her mother had apparently expected a later return and had gone to bed. Mindy moved quickly and quietly to the bathroom. She didn't want her mother to get up and ask how the night had gone. She didn't want to talk to anyone. She felt dirty and violated.

Hoping a shower would offer a baptismal cleansing, Mindy stood under the flowing water for a long time. By the time she retreated to her bedroom, she was angrier with herself than with Damien. Mindy eyed the dull ring on her finger. She had taken it off before going to the hospital and now recalled the hesitancy she felt when she forced it back on that afternoon. Angry for making such a stupid mistake, she twisted his ring of obligation off her finger, dropped it into her jewelry box, and swore she would never wear it again.

Another reluctantly accepted gift, Damien's college graduation photo, stared at her from its cardboard frame on her dresser. Mindy scooped it up, folded the stand, and closed the cover hard, vowing never to look at it again. She stuffed it into the bottom drawer of her desk along under a mixed collection of old pictures and mementos of days past.

Damien called the next day. He spoke as if nothing had happened and wanted to confirm plans to meet at the ballpark that evening.

"I won't be there. I don't want to see you," Mindy flatly replied.
"Why? What's wrong now?" he stupidly inquired.
Mindy returned only silence.
"Wait. Let's talk about this," Damien begged.
"There is nothing to talk about," Mindy replied and hung up.

Chapter 12
The Valkyrie Rises
June 6–July 9, 1975

Mindy awoke the next morning feeling better and stronger than she had for a very long time. She had no preconceived notion of what the day would bring, but was ready for whatever it might offer and hoped to "move forward" in her own way. She would find it easier said than done.

When Mindy made no announcement at breakfast regarding plans for the evening, her mother inquired. Mindy flatly informed her, "I don't have any definite plans, but I'm going to call Gina and Phyllis. I won't be doing anything with Damien. I told him I didn't want to see him anymore."

More curious than concerned, her mother cornered her in private after breakfast, looking for more information. Mindy didn't want to discuss it, so bluntly stated, "He kept pressuring me to have sex, and I got tired of it." She didn't have to provide any other details, that little three letter word struck her mother mute.

Mindy studied her mother's face. It was clear she was unprepared to discuss such topics with her little girl. "She wonders if something has already happened but is afraid to ask. She doesn't want to know," Mindy thought.

When Mindy started to walk away, her mother recaptured her voice and found an alternate route. "It's probably just as well. It looks like we may be moving. But there's still nothing definite, and you still can't say anything to anyone."

This was not the response Mindy needed or wanted to hear, and it took all of her willpower to contain her frustration. She wanted her mother to scream, "We should never have let you got out with that bastard. He doesn't deserve you. I don't want you to see him again — ever!"

But mother and daughter only exchanged blank stares for a moment. Mindy could tell her mother was gearing up and waited anxiously, hoping to hear her explode. To the contrary, the subsequent motherly advice left Mindy dumbfounded. "Well, if you do go out with him again, be careful not to get him excited. Boys are just like that. It doesn't take much sometimes. Don't sit for a long time in the car, especially after a date. Don't kiss in the car, get out of the car quickly and walk to the door. Don't let him kiss you too many times in a row, even at the door. If you kiss, just make it quick. Don't do any *prolonged* kissing. Be careful how you sit or stand next to him, don't seem inviting or affectionate. Those things will just get him excited." She leaned forward to whisper, "And *for God's sake*, don't let him touch your breasts! That will really make him crazy."

Mindy's heart fell to her shoes. This was not the lecture she expected. Her shoulders slumped, and head dropped in defeat. Emotionally reeling, she walked away to her bedroom shaking her head and thought, "These mother-daughter talks don't seem to help much."

———————————

Business at the bank was slow, so Mindy called Gina but was disappointed to hear she would spend most of the weekend with her beau. Her disappointment grew when she received a similar response from Phyllis.

Determined to enjoy the summer despite its unknowns, Mindy brushed her concerns off her shoulders and stepped into the next morning happy and lighthearted. The morning air was clean and light and invited her to come outside and breathe it in. Grabbing a towel, she bounced out the back door to the peaceful solitude of the patio and dove into a book.

The next two weeks were similar and delightfully relaxing. While tanning, Mindy experimented with Sun-In on her hair. To her surprise, her long golden strands lightened considerably in just a few days, and she stared wide-eyed at the reflection of a beaming bronze-skinned blonde in her mirror.

She also began a daily exercise regimen, and it didn't take long to gain size and strength. Her arms became fuller, and her stomach more sculpted. In the weeks ahead, she would scan her reflection in the mirror again and be pleased with the result. She was petite, toned, and pleasantly shapely.

It was a struggle, but Mindy corralled Gina for an evening of cruising and Phyllis for a rerun at the drive-in the following weekend. The girl time was delightful, but the luster of the drive-in and cruising had faded considerably. Boredom infiltrated at least part of most days and gradually became more intrusive. Outside a book, there just wasn't much to stir her imagination in town.

Cheer practice followed by snacks at Clifton's or Jones's continued as usual. But to avoid seeing Damien, Mindy would say goodbye to her mates and drive home while the others migrated to the ballpark to watch "the boys" play softball.

It soon became apparent this approach was a poor solution. It required Mindy to punish herself by boxing herself out of social interaction and away from her friends. She also knew that the smallness of the town would preclude avoidance of Damien forever. So, the next week she joined the rest of her friends for a trip to the ballpark.

Mindy hadn't mentioned her split with Damien to her friends, but, despite their limited knowledge, she thought it odd that none of them inquired. She was more surprised to find that none of Damien's friends at the ballpark seemed to be aware of it either. Then she realized, "Damien hasn't told anyone."

In the stands, Mindy heard several similar reports. "Oh, we're glad you're here. Damien has just been a mess in the field and at the plate with you being sick and not here to watch him. The other guys have been teasing him about keeping you locked up somewhere. They *all* like you."

Their comments made Mindy cringe, but she otherwise enjoyed the evening talking with the girls. She paid little attention to the action on the field until the last innings of the second game when Julie commented, "We really thought Damien would play better tonight with you here, but he hasn't had a hit all night." Mindy left the field and drove home before the final out.

It had been almost a month since the Eagle's concert, and Damien had been remarkably scant in Mindy's thoughts. So, it surprised her to answer the phone and hear his voice. He sounded weak and defeated as he pleaded with her to meet with him. The girls' reports at the ballpark, the pathetic tone of his voice, and Mindy's relative boredom combined to soften her stance. With significant reservation, she agreed.

At the appointed time, Mindy drove to Key Park, where she found Damien sitting atop a picnic table next to the parking lot. Uncertain she was doing the right thing, she sat in the car for a moment studying him through the windshield. He looked small and worn. She laughed at the concept of dating older guys as advantageous and couldn't balance those time-limited advantages against either Damien's shallowness or the absence of affection.

The word *advantage* stuck in Mindy's mind. She was still angry Damien had tried to take advantage of her youth and naiveté but realized that she had done a similar thing. She had been just as unfair by taking advantage of his age, freedom, and money without personal commitment.

Eventually making her way toward the picnic table, Mindy looked him in the eye without emotion and said nothing. She waited patiently to force Damien to break the silence. "Are you really going to break up with me for good?" he inquired.

"I already did break up with you for good," she bluntly replied.

Damien plunged into a sea of apology and begged for another chance.

"I don't think you deserve another chance. I already gave you a second chance. I don't think you'll be any different. I think it would only be a matter of time before you'll try to pressure me again — *and you would fail again,*" Mindy frankly responded.

Damien's expression revealed his defeat. He sounded feeble as he promised not to make the same mistakes if given one more chance. "Will you be at the softball game tonight?" he feebly inquired.

"No, I won't," said Mindy.

"What about this weekend?" he continued.

"I have to get back home, and I won't agree to anything right now. I need to decide what's best for me." Mindy walked away.

During the short drive back to Ellington, questions rolled through Mindy's mind. "Should I even consider going out with him again? I know he will eventually try to pressure me again, but what are my alternatives? Will I sit home bored? What will he tell people? It doesn't really matter, we'll probably be moving, anyway."

Mindy drove home after cheer practice and Jones's while the other girls went to the ballpark. She placed a Jim Croce album on the turntable, then stretched out on her bed. Her thoughts drifted and mixed before they coalesced and shot with clarity into her forethought. "There are some basic things I need to consider in my decision making about this summer. First, Gina and Phyllis have boyfriends and won't be free much on the weekends. It will be lonely without them. Second, there just aren't many ingredients for the imagination here, I will want to get out of town once in a while. Third, we're probably moving soon so it would be silly to be confrontational or stir stuff up that will get twisted in the rumor mill. Plus, it sure wouldn't be fair to date other boys and not tell them we're moving. My parents need both cars here. I won't be able to take one out of town for the day very often. As much as I hate to admit it, going out of town with Damien now and then might be the only reasonable alternative. I don't trust him, but I *can* control him."

This confounding set of issues made it difficult to chart a logical short-term course. Mindy had faith, family, and friends but didn't believe they would guide her with wisdom. Supported only by the unstable pillars of her seventeen-year-old logic, she was left to her own decision-making. She was bound to make mistakes, and Damien's door of opportunity cracked open.

The end result of Mindy's mental gyrations was a time-limited plan to go out with Damien occasionally as long as he followed her rules. Any relative reconciliation with him would be superficial and strictly on her terms. She didn't trust him; she would never trust him again. She knew she would have to be in *and* stay in control. He would be safe and submissive, or she would leave him cold in the tobacco fields of Macon County.

If they moved, she would happily let him fade away. If her parents delayed their move, she would make their dissolution public knowledge before the start of school, and would be thankfully "unobligated."

Before putting her mind to rest for the evening, Mindy had one more thought that fine-tuned her plans. "My chance of being voted Homecoming Queen will probably be better if nobody thinks I have an older boyfriend. If we don't move soon, I'll announce the break-up to everyone right before I leave for Canada. Most of the gossip will have died down before I return, and I can start the school year fresh and ready to go."

The Valkyrie had risen.

Mindy drove herself to the softball field with some trepidation after cheer practice. She chatted with the girls and paid little attention to the games. As she made her way back to the car, Damien approached and begged, "Please give me another chance. I won't make the same mistakes."

Mindy asked, "Why would you even want to go out with me again? Nothing is going to change."

"Because all of my friends think we're together. They all think I'm the luckiest guy in the county," Damien explained.

It suddenly became clear. Damien was more concerned about his appearance and his social status than her heart. Mindy pitied him for his shallowness and realized that even empty, budget balancing kisses stoked his predatory flame — they made him want more. She finally understood that her ability to say no infused her with power over him.

Mindy continued, "We may be able to work out an arrangement. I enjoy getting out of town occasionally and I will consider going with you but would prefer to have others join us. Let me be clear, *I don't ever want a physical relationship with you.*"

"Never?" Damien whimpered.

"Never," Mindy concretely replied.

223

"Well, how do you think that makes me feel," Damien stupidly questioned.

"I don't *care* how it makes you feel. If you want me to go out with you for appearances, then that's the way it will always be," Mindy responded.

Damien nodded and said he would agree to whatever ground rules she set, then inquired, "Would you consider going to Nashville this weekend?"

"I haven't agreed to go out with you at all," Mindy reminded him.

"Please — people around here, my friends and everyone else, they expect it," he pleaded.

"If I do, I wouldn't want to go to Nashville now. You need to have a track record of safety first. I'll think about it. Call me later this week." She gave him no choice but to agree.

When Damien called a few days later, Mindy had made up her mind, and agreed to accompany him on a dinner outing with Julie and Ed.

The summer solstice sun still sat high in the sky early Saturday evening when they met Julie and Ed on the square with plans to go to Gallatin for pizza. Ed drove with Damien riding shotgun. Not far out of town and without explanation, Ed turned onto a dirt road that made a sweeping curve down into a shallow valley. Mindy shot a questioning glance toward Julie, but she didn't seem surprised. So, Mindy leaned forward from the back seat to question, "Where are we going?"

"Gonna do some quick giggin'," Ed replied. This twist to the evening hadn't been mentioned before, and Mindy looked at Julie, wondering why she didn't seem interested or concerned.

The car came to a stop next to a narrow path through the tall grass that led to a small pond about forty yards further down the hill. Near horizontal sunlight set the haze in the air aglow as small flying insects became sharp points of light dancing in every direction. There was no breeze to wash away the heavy stench of stagnant pond scum that saturated the air and slowly permeated their clothing. It would follow them for hours.

Having never witnessed frog gigging, Mindy was only generally aware of the specifics. But this was something new she had not the slightest interest in learning about. So, she stayed in the car with arms folded as the boys and Julie got out. Envisioning boys in T-shirts and hip boots carrying a longed barbed pole and wading through a pond or creek, Mindy cringed at the thought of little croaking amphibians being skewered. So, it puzzled her as she watched the boys disappear down the curving dirt path in dress clothes, platform shoes, and carrying not a pole but a rifle with a telescopic sight.

A minute later, the repeated sound of gunfire startled Mindy. She sat frozen and wide-eyed as she tried to comprehend what was happening. Terrified, she looked around and was glad to spy Julie, who was nonchalantly ascending the dirt path toward the car without the slightest sign of concern. By the time Julie returned, Mindy was trembling uncontrollably and stuttered in distress, "*What are they doing?*"

Julie calmly replied, "Ed got a new rifle, and they're tryin' it out shootin' frogs." Mindy's stomach churned with disgust.

After squeezing off fifty or sixty rounds, the boys returned. Mindy sat quietly during the drive to Gallatin, having flashbacks of her distress on the day her family first arrived in Lafayette. She struggled to wash the image of mangled, disemboweled frogs lying motionless in blood covered mud from her mind and was happily relieved by the distraction when they arrived at the Pizza Inn. When the boys grabbed chairs at the exact same table she'd shared with Randy, Mindy looked to the sky and wondered, "How could the world possibly be so small?"

After waving goodbye to Ed and Julie, Mindy wasted no time before delivering Damien a verbal lashing, "I can't tell you how disgusted I am with you for shooting innocent frogs. That wasn't a date, that was a torture test. If you pull something like that again, I'll walk home if I have to. If you want to do such disgusting things, then do it on your own time, not mine."

Pseudo-submissively tucking his tail, Damien played dumb. "I don't know why you're upset. We do it all the time but usually bring 'em home for dinner."

On the following Tuesday, Mindy hitched a ride with Loretta to cheer practice, then to the ballpark. The home team was just taking the field as Mindy took a seat next to Julie. Damien came running from the dugout to approach Mindy in the stands and asked her to hold his wallet for him. Mindy received it without eye contact and thought, "He's trying to save face and convince people we're together."

As the girls chatted, Mindy thoughtlessly tumbled Damien's wallet between her fingers. Then she paused and wondered what boys kept in them that girls didn't keep in theirs. Curiosity won, and Mindy opened the inexpensive bifold for examination. She scanned the various compartments, then started her investigation. She found $18 worth of bills, which seemed like a lot. The clear vinyl pages held no photos but one horizontal slot was stuffed full. She pinched hard to pull out the stack of items to find an expired college ID, an insurance card, a yellowed Social Security card, several old receipts, a folded paper with phone numbers but no names, and a gold square aluminum packet adorned with a black helmet logo above which was printed "Trojan" in black gothic letters. Interrupted by a soft gasp, Mindy glanced up to find Julie staring wide-eyed and flushed with surprise. Mindy glanced back at the packet and let out a gasp of her own as she deduced what she held in her fingers. She clasped her hands between her knees to hide the evidence and immediately looked around for an escape route.

Without excusing herself, she stumbled over spectator feet and legs to the end of the stands and jumped. Taking a position behind the crowd, steam pressure rose in her head as she slid the little gold packet into her back pocket and returned the rest of the stack to the wallet. Her mind raced for a solution but found none. She felt sick and just wanted to go home. Studying the stands from below, she spied Ricky Hicks and considered asking him for a ride home, but worried what Julie might say if she left with another boy. Mindy hesitantly returned to the stands and sat with icy stiffness.   She considered whispering a denial of any wrongdoing in Julie's ear, but was convinced it would only make a bad situation worse.

As soon as the game ended, Mindy moved away from the small crowd and stood alone in the parking lot. It didn't take long for Damien to come bouncing around the dugout in her direction. His smile disappeared as Mindy coldly tossed him his wallet from eight feet away and walked silently to her car, but he missed her icy persona.

Revving the engine, Damien exclaimed, "Let's go for a drive."

Mindy cut him short, "No. Let's just go to Jones's. I need to eat something." She felt compelled to go somewhere public with as many ballpark people as possible. She desperately wanted them to know the little gold packet wasn't being opened somewhere in a tobacco field.

Frustration eroded Mindy's control, and she popped as soon as they pulled out of the parking lot. Retrieving the little gold packet from her back pocket, she waved it angrily six inches from Damien's nose. "And what is this?" she roared.

The scene turned Damien pale with horror. Stuttering wildly, he tried to explain, "It's — it's been in my wallet since college. I just had it — just in case. Oh, shit!"

He pulled over to a stop, shrunk in his seat and dropped his head between his arms. Convinced he was going to cry, Mindy leaned back and relaxed. With steam engine mechanics, she rolled down the passenger window and waited for Damien to look up. Slapping the little gold packet on his nose, she boomed, *"This is not for me!"* then whipped the small gold packet out the window like a miniature Frisbee.

Aloof and relaxed, the Valkyrie sat in her seat with arms gently crossed in observant command. She remained silent when Damien peeked in her direction. He let out a sigh of relief, wiped his brow, and continued toward Jones's. Damien suggested they eat in the car, but Mindy insisted they go inside where she ordered a burger, fries and chocolate malt. Public visibility was a must.

Back in the drive at Ellington, Damien thanked Mindy for not being too upset and tried to explain.

She threw up her hand to interrupt, "Stop. It doesn't matter. I don't care. I don't need or want to know. Just stop now while you think you're ahead."

Damien squirmed and wriggled with uncertainty. "Whaaa — what would you like to do this weekend?"

Mindy bluntly replied, "I have plans with the girls on Friday, but I'm open to suggestions for Saturday."

Damien chose his words carefully, "How about dinner at a nice place in Gallatin?"

"It would be nice to go someplace new. Thank you for the ride home. Goodbye," Mindy replied in a very business-like tone, then walked to the house unescorted.

After an afternoon of lounging on the patio with a book, Mindy migrated back inside and set the table as usual while her mother finished dinner preparations. She noted her mother seemed unusually quiet, but thought nothing of it at the time. After loading the dinner dishes into the dishwasher, Mindy's father surprised her when he said coldly, "Mindy, I'd like to talk to you in the living room."

Mindy obediently followed her father as she tried to anticipate the upcoming conversation. She took a seat and didn't have to wait long as her father got straight to the point. "Your mother tells me you've been spending a lot of time in the backyard. This is not a hotel, you know. You need to help out more around here."

Somewhat surprised her father was talking with her at all, Mindy couldn't remember him ever speaking to her in a condescending or critical tone. It was a blunt reminder of her mid-teen status in life. She nodded obediently and replied with a quiet, "Okay."

"Good," he said, then stood and walked out of the room.

Reeling, Mindy retreated her bedroom and thought, "If Mom wanted me to do more around here, why didn't she ask?"

Up early the next morning Mindy slipped into an old pair of jeans with worn holes in the knees, an old peasant top and a red scarf to hold back her unwashed hair. Feeling very much like a modern Cinderella, she marched directly to the kitchen where she planted herself directly across the counter from her mother. "What do you want me to do?" she asked coldly.

"What?" her mother replied with some confusion.

"Dad says I think this is a hotel and that I need to help out more. So, what do you want me to do?" Mindy flatly repeated. Her mother returned a blank stare, so Mindy continued, "I go to school most of the year, work at least two days a week at the bank — more in the summer — and have cheer practice at least twice a week. I set the dinner table and wash the dishes almost every day. I occasionally babysit your sons, drive them to ball practice, and run errands for you. I take care of my room and do most of my own laundry. I help you clean before and after Dad's work parties that I don't usually attend. I have three brothers who don't do a single thing around here but make a mess. But I understand I'm not doing enough. So, what can I do to help today?"

Mindy's shell-shocked mother was on her heels trying to think of some chores she needed done but came up empty. "I don't really need anything right now. Why don't you go outside and enjoy the day? I'll call you if I need you."

Mindy marched away to her room, wondering if there would be a pair of glass slippers waiting for her. She never heard another word about 'Hotel Murphy.'

The 4th of July weekend included a trip with Damien to "a new place for dinner" in Lebanon, Tennessee; Ponderosa. While waiting in line to order, Damien became skittish. Mindy assessed the scene and caught other males scanning her with hungry eyes. She realized this made Damien uneasy without Larry at his side. The remainder of the evening passed uneventfully.

A group of young adults met at Larry's mother's apartment the next evening to play cards. Mindy enjoyed socializing with the others, but Damien's ongoing habit of trumping her good tricks in

Spades frustrated her. No amount of explanation was successful in changing his approach.

Both evenings ended with the watchful silhouette of Mindy's mother peeking out the rec room window adjacent to the driveway. After Larry's, Damien was trying desperately to keep Mindy locked in conversation in the car, but the repetitive flashing of the light above the side door interrupted them. Embarrassed by her mother's monitoring, another wave of frustration pulsated through Mindy's veins. Suddenly she was angry with Damien, mad at her parents, and frustrated with her situation. She just wanted to scream.

With a huff, Mindy got out of the car and marched toward the door with Damien in pursuit. Approaching the side door, her mother's shadow disappeared and the night without fireworks in the local sky was more than matched by the lack of fireworks at the side door.

The highlight of the post-4th of July week was a trip to the RiverGate Movie Theater with Gina with plans to see the current front runner to win an Oscar for best picture, *Nashville*. But the summer weather left the girls thinking how nice it would be to be on the beach, so diverted to see the recently released *JAWS* instead.

With images of exploded chunks of bloody shark flesh dropping from the sky, the girls regained their wits, then had a grand time shopping after the movie. On the way home, Mindy silently hoped for an opportunity to spend more time with her friends over the summer.

Having hit puberty later than most girls her age, Mindy had always envisioned herself behind the physique curve; girlish, thin and angular. But the past few years had witnessed a dramatic evolution. She was fuller, well-proportioned, and stronger. So, Mindy wasn't disappointed when oppressive heat arrived in middle-Tennessee and presented the opportunity to wear a new bikini on a girls' trip to the Barren River. Modest as bikinis went, it would still easily be the least amount of fabric she had worn in public since she was a toddler in a diaper.

In her excitement to set her folding chair in the shallows of the river, Mindy probably sprayed more Sun-In into her hair than intended. By the time they began the return drive, Mindy's bright blonde hair was in sharp contrast to her already bronze skin. The other girls were beside themselves in disbelief and when she returned home, her two youngest brothers jumped to their feet to play an air guitar rendition of "Sister Golden Hair."

Those of the Barren River gang not too sunburned had agreed to meet again at the ballpark after dinner to watch the first round of softball playoffs. After a long shower sent sweat and tanning oil swirling down the drain, Mindy rooted through her drawers for an outfit that would be kind to her tan. Glancing into the dresser mirror, the underwear-only image captured her eye, and the visual transformation of her reflection astounded her. She gently pulled down the front edge of her underwear and was more amazed by the sharp linear contrast of her bronze, lightly six-packed abdomen and the soft baby white skin that disappeared under the dark curls of her pubic hair. "Oh, my goodness!" she thought.

She pulled out the yellow mid-drift top she had purchased at Gulf Shores the previous summer but hadn't worn since. She studied the short-capped sleeves and an embroidered blue flower over the left breast, then tried it on. It was immediately apparent her bust line was significantly larger than when the top was purchased, and it clearly revealed her sculpted bronze abdomen. A moment later she slipped into an old pair of hip hugger jeans and accented the look with white hoop earrings and clear lip-gloss.

She looked at the mirror a second time and had an out-of-body sensation as she studied the vision before her. The physical maturity of the reflection grew, and for the very first time produced a conscious recognition of her potential sex appeal. Her thoughts suddenly shifted, and a mischievous payback plan formed in her mind. "Now it's my turn," she thought.

She pulled on a loose blue blouse and buttoned it high enough to hide the tight mid-drift top. After a quick dinner, she stepped outside to wait for Phyllis. They arrived at the ballpark fashionably late, and Mindy slipped off the blue blouse, folded it neatly, and draped it across her forearm. Phyllis's eyes lit up, "Wow! You're gonna drop 'em in their tracks tonight." Mindy blushed with surprise but made no reply.

Many opposing players and observers of Damien's team referred to them as "Prock's Pricks," a nickname that accurately reflected what others thought. As Mindy took her seat in the stands, "The Prick's" were in the field. Their shoddy defense made for a long half-inning, but when it finally ended, Mindy felt flushed with embarrassment when a few of the 'boys' coming off the field stared at her through the fence. Undoubtedly promptly by teammates, Damien sprang out of the dugout to look into the stands and confirm their reports.

Catching sight of Damien in her peripheral vision, Mindy looked away and avoided even the slightest eye contact. Sensing his stare, Mindy sat straight and tall, then slowly arched her back and stretched her arms like spreading wings above her head to provide a full-frontal view. With ears tuned to hyperacuity, it was easy to hear Damien moan in pain, trapped on the other side of the fence. Untouchable, she thought, "*Suffer. You'll never get any of this!*" She slowly folded her wings across her chest and leaned forward with elbows on her knees and chin resting gracefully on her interlaced fingers.

As the game continued, Mindy felt the burn of a barrage of eyes coming from all directions. Her attire and appearance were attracting far more attention than she expected, and her growing embarrassment made her regret her clothing choice. She slipped on the blue blouse, buttoned it, and sat pensively for the rest of the game.

The innings passed slowly. Mindy became uncomfortable when some of the other girls teasingly discussed which boys they would consider dating as each stepped to the plate. Mindy had declined date offers from over half of Damien's team at one time or another, and she just shook her head. Then she laughed and thought, "They're called Prock's Pricks for a reason. There are no other date possibilities in that pack!"

Mindy wished she could disappear before the game was over, but Phyllis planned to stay to watch the next game. She considered asking one of the boys she knew in the stands to take her home, but stopped short. "They've all seen me dressed like this. They'll think I'm a slut if I leave here with another boy." She stepped out of the stands to watch the last innings from the parking lot. A short time later, the game was over. Damien went 0-4 at the plate, and his team was eliminated from the playoffs.

Mindy immediately sought the auditory protection of others as she mingled with friends in the parking lot. Damien arrived seconds later, panting with anticipation and forced out an air-starved, "Hi."

Mindy held up a cold index finger to indicate, "Don't interrupt," then calmly concluded her conversation with the girls before turning to acknowledge him. When she did, he anxiously motioned toward his car and Mindy followed slowly several feet behind. Despite his objections, Mindy insisted they go to Jones's for ice cream. She wanted to be visible and took every opportunity to talk with others.

Damien whispered, "My teammates are all jealous. They think you're the hottest thing in the county. Everyone wants to be with you — they all want to take you home." Mindy absorbed the jaded compliments coolly.

But self-confidence faded as she consumed an ice cream cone in near silence while Damien talked incessantly. By the time they pulled away from the neon lights, Mindy was a self-conscious young girl who needed time to think.

Damien pulled up hard into the Ellington driveway shadows. Mindy glanced past him to see her mother's shadow pass by the side window to take up station as a silent monitor. The maternal silhouette ignited a chain reaction of frustration. Mad at herself, she felt overwhelmed by a sudden need to strike out at the world. Without thinking, she leaned across the center console and delivered a kiss full of anger and devoid of affection, hoping her mother would witness it.

Before Damien had time to react, Mindy was already calmly reclined back in her seat staring blankly out the window piling on self-administered shame. She had let her inexperienced emotions strike out at both Damien and her parents when she didn't know who or how to hit.

Damien completely missed Mindy's anger. He stared. "Now what do you want me to do? You look — well, you look like — *that*. You look *incredible*. And then *this*. I want you more now than ever. *It's not fair*."

Mindy methodically fastened the buttons of her blouse all the way up to the collar. She turned slowly to look him coldly in his eyes. "You're right. It's not fair. It was wrong of me to do this. I will *never* do it again."

The door light flashed. Mindy marched toward the house with a single word flowing through her mind, "*Suffer*." She disappeared into the house without looking back, and the outside light immediately went dark.

Chapter 13
The Escape
July 10–September 6, 1975

Awakening the next morning mired in self-imposed shame, Mindy understood she must take personal responsibility for at least some of the 'bad' the previous eight months had accumulated. But it was hard to know where to draw the defining line. "Was I really so innocent? When and where did I transition from young and naïve to more mature, reflective, insightful, and occasionally even mean? How long ago *should* I have figured out he was bad for me? *Should* I have known as early as the virgin question or maybe the possessive phone call about going to RBS or maybe even as early as the first date and a Singapore Sling for a sixteen-year-old? Should I have known from the beginning? Looking back, it seems so obvious, but the bad things so easy to see now didn't seem so bad at the time." After another moment's reflection, she laughed at the vision of her younger self and concluded, "Yep, I was just a silly young girl. I was too trusting, too naïve to see what was really happening — to see what he was really like."

Her thoughts rolled on. "*He* is older. *He* should be more mature and more responsible for his actions. *He knew* I was a young girl. *He knew* from the very beginning what he was doing was wrong — that he was way too old for me. *He* was looking for an opportunity to take advantage of my innocence and my ignorance. *He* had no interest in being a friend."

Then it finally struck her, "Damien *never* even knew me. He *never* loved me. He doesn't know what love is any more than I do. I wonder if he even really liked *me* — who I am as a person. He just wanted to tell his friends he nailed a virgin. The balance of guilt has to lay heavily with *him*. But — I will never be able to completely absolve myself."

She accepted her faults and pitied his emptiness but remained convinced that conflict avoidance was the best approach for the short term. "I don't want to deal with silly soap opera controversy. I just want him to go away. Until I hear about a move, I'll be pleasant but won't let him break my rules."

Mindy cleared the breakfast table the next morning, feeling good and looking forward to the day. But her relative serenity was short-lived and the frustration of the previous twenty-four hours rebounded when her mother remarked, "Your father got a few phone calls from people who were at the ball game last night. He said you must have some big moths in your closet."

Mindy looked confused, so her mother clarified, "There must have been some pretty big holes in your clothes last night."

Mindy recalled her sexy reflection in the mirror, and her cheeks lit up bright red with embarrassment and hot with anger.

The omnipresent eyes of her small town had snared her again, and she could offer no plausible explanation or defense. The pressure grew until she popped, "I didn't do anything wrong!" She stomped into her room, stuffed the pretty yellow mid-drift top with a little blue flower over the left breast into a bag, marched outside, threw the bag hard into the trash can and slammed the lid closed.

With college behind him, Larry packed up his apartment and moved back to Lafayette into a two-bedroom trailer just outside of town. To complete his degree in physical education, he would return to his high school alma mater as a student teacher that fall. Mindy found it disheartening that an older guy, whom she considered an equal, who was routinely buying underage girls mixed drinks, and with whom she had danced, would be on the teaching staff. The saving grace was his appointment as a boys' PE student-instructor, so Mindy would have little or no interaction with him at school. Still, the thought seemed unacceptably weird and incestuous.

Billed as a "girls' weekend," Mindy and her mother were joining her Aunt Sue and Cousin Lori for a mother-daughter weekend in Gulf Shores, Alabama. In preparation, Mindy's mother went to the grocery store to stock up on food for the house. As Mindy helped unload and unpack, her mother reported, "I ran into Judy Green at the market. She looks like she's due soon and is almost as wide as she is tall. Her legs are terribly swollen, and she looked just miserable. I'll bet this heat is driving her crazy. I'm so glad that isn't you."

Mindy made no comment. She wasn't sure what to say or even what to think. The concept of being a seventeen-year-old mother was too overwhelming. Mindy asked unemotionally where her mother wanted the fresh vegetables, and the conversation promptly moved on to a new topic.

The girl's trip to the beach was fun and relaxing. Mindy had to laugh every time Aunt Sue said, "Let's go hang on the beach and enjoy the water, the company, and maybe a little wine." Her aunt and mother were two peas in a pod as they talked and laughed, floating on rafts in just inches of water for hours each day. Mindy listened to their girl talk from the beach and missed her friends all the more.

A broken water pump and an overheated engine interrupted the return trip to Lafayette. There was no choice but to sit at a small gas station in the middle of Alabama while they made repairs. Between waiting for repairs and the eight-hour drive, there was plenty of time to talk, but Mindy's mother seemed distracted, and Mindy noted the possibility of a move was suspiciously absent from the conversation. But she could hear a little voice whispering into her ear, "You know this mother-daughter trip means you'll be moving soon."

'The Pricks' post-season pizza party took place the following Friday. Mindy hurriedly slipped on her shoes when Damien arrived twenty minutes early and announced, "I forgot something at Larry's trailer and need to make a quick stop to pick it up." When they arrived, Damien suggested, "Come inside to wait. It might take me a few minutes."

Mindy cautiously followed along and scanned the rectangular pressboard palace with flashbacks of Sin City. She waited in the living room as Damien scurried into and out of back rooms, apparently searching. Mindy asked if she could help, but he flatly responded, "No."

With nothing to do but wait, Mindy's eyes wandered until she noticed a prescription pill bottle standing alone in the middle of the small kitchen counter just a few feet away. Out of bored curiosity, she picked it up and examined the label. The local McClard's Drug Store label was not surprising, but it seeing Damien's name printed on it filled her with uncertainty. Damien emerged from the back-bedroom empty handed and smiled when he saw the bottle in her hand. Mindy innocently inquired what he was taking medication for.

Damien explained, "I saw a doctor because I was having pains. He told me I was having prostrate problems caused by sexual frustration. He said that repeated excitement without release was causing damage to my prostrate. This medicine is supposed to help." He shrugged. "Don't blame me, you asked."

During the quiet drive to Gallatin, the pill bottle stuck in Mindy's mind. Although skeptical, her knowledge of the prostate gland and male genital physiology, in general, was limited to 5th and 6th-grade film strips during Sex Ed and had to wonder if there could be any truth to his story. "He does, after all, have a pill bottle, from a pharmacy, with his name on it," she thought. Then she shuddered to think, "If he's telling the truth, the town pharmacist and maybe everyone who works at the pharmacy knows about this. I don't want people thinking about such things. And what if this information leaks to the rumor mill?!" Mindy felt queasy and was ever so glad to arrive at the Pizza Inn in Gallatin; it was becoming like a second home.

The softball group took over a section of the seating area that allowed them to mingle and talk before the pizza arrived. Harry Whitmire, who was still dating Barb Gentry, took the opportunity during a relatively private moment to whisper, "Ya know, I'd still like to take you out sometime." Mindy just shook her head and walked away, wondering more than ever if there were any real men in the world, and kept her distance from "the boys" the rest of the evening. She so much wanted to tell Barb to run for cover, but admitted to herself she had been culturally trained to bite her tongue.

During the return drive, images of Damien's pill bottle grew larger, and Mindy's naiveté settled in for a return visit. The next morning, she cornered her mother in the kitchen and cleared her throat. "Mom, do you know anything about prostate problems?"

Her mother choked, sputtered and suppressed a laugh before she could respond. "Well, I don't know too much. But why do you ask?"

Mindy repeated much of Damien's speech and concluded, "He told me if a guy gets excited but no release that it damages his prostate. Do you know anything about that?"

Her mother just stared at her until Mindy told her the rest of the pill bottle story. It was, of course, immediately apparent to her mother that the bottle was a plant. "He just said that to make you feel uncomfortable. You tell him if he's having problems to come and see me. Tell him, I'll give him some money, and he can go see a prostitute in Nashville. You tell him he should leave our Mindy alone!"

Mindy didn't think much of the motherly advice but slapped herself on the forehead for being so gullible. She did, however, feel a tingle with the thought of tossing Damien a grenade.

The next day, Damien suggested they take a drive in the country, but Mindy sensed desperation in his voice and nixed the plan. To prevent any opportunity for an attack, Mindy embellished her need to be home early to pack for cheer camp but agreed to meet Damien at Clifton's while silently hoping to run into classmates while they ate.

At Clifton's, there wasn't much conversation before the food arrived. Damien had just taken a bite of fried chicken when Mindy nonchalantly pronounced, "My mom said she would give you money for a prostitute if you were still having prostate problems."

Damien nearly choked, and it took him a moment to recover. "WHAAAAT?!" he squeaked.

Mindy unemotionally repeated, "I told my mom you were having prostate problems because I won't have sex with you. She said she would give you money for a prostitute in Nashville. She also said you should stay away from me." Mindy shrugged, then coolly took a big bite of fried chicken.

Damien sucked hurriedly on the straw in his cold drink to clear his throat. He looked all around to make sure nobody was listening, then ducked his head to whisper in pitiful distress, "Oh, my God. Did you *really* tell your mother *that*? Do you tell your mother *everything*?"

Mindy shrugged again and replied, "Pretty much."

Damien buried his head in his greasy hands and lamented, "How can I ever come over to your house now? Your mother will laugh at me."

"That's your problem," replied Mindy before taking another bite of chicken.

The short drive back to Ellington was quiet. Mindy went inside to finish packing and crawled into bed, excited for the week of cheer camp ahead.

Up early, Mindy was ready long before the scheduled departure and was looking forward to a week of fun, exercise, and girl time. The school district was providing transportation this year, and the girls loaded onto a bus at the high school. During the drive, co-captain Kat campaigned hard to gain more authority over the team. It didn't matter that the power was more imaginary than real and Mindy was sad to see the squad unnecessarily divided.

Cheer camp otherwise proceeded much as previous ones had. The days were long, and the girls worked hard. To help stay cool, Mindy wore pigtails for most of the outdoor activities. A camp counselor approached Mindy during lunch on Friday and invited her to be a model in the cheer uniform fashion show that evening.

Mindy didn't hesitate to accept, and the counselor added, "We want you to wear your hair in pigtails just like this."

After the post-dinner competition, Mindy scurried off to the locker room to prepare for the show while the other camp attendees moved to the gym and sat tightly packed near mid-court. The overhead lights went off and roving spotlights beamed white light onto the gym floor to signal the start of the show. Each model would come skipping from off stage and do leaps and cartwheels to mid-court, then pause with hands on hips for a round of applause. As their name and high school was announced over the loudspeaker, their cheer mates would stand and offer a second burst of whooping and hollering. The model would then walk toward the stands, turn to show the back side, then stroll back to mid-court as the announcer described the style, fabric and various other fashion details of the uniform. After a jump or cartwheel, the model would bounce off the court to another warm round of applause.

On cue, Mindy bounced onto the court with a gleaming smile and her hair in high pigtails adorned with streaming purple and white ribbons. She wore a beautiful long sleeve royal purple sweater highlighted by sharp white trim. The sweater sported a squared-off white sailor's collar with purple trim across the upper back and a gold bow tie dangling across the chest. Under the bright lights, the pleated purple and white skirt seemed to flash with every movement of her hips.

Loretta approached Mindy after the show to say, "You were amazing! So beautiful in purple and so cute in the sailor top. But I have to tell you something. Before the show, Kat told the girls not to stand or clap for you. When you came out, they sat and laughed about your pretty pigtails. I just burned them with my eyes and Kat just about died. She whined, 'Just look at her. She *has* everything and *gits* everything. It's not fair. It's just not fair.' The other girls rolled their eyes, and Kat lost the respect she's been working so hard to earn."

The week was otherwise uneventful and passed quickly. Mindy was happy with the team's improvement but felt better when her freshman teammates quietly offered thanks for her guidance and support during the return bus ride.

The middle-Tennessee hills rolled by, and Mindy watched with melancholy sadness. She realized, "This was probably my last cheer camp ever. I'll miss the cheering, the competition, and I'll miss the girls." She tucked the memories into her soul, and by the time they pulled into Lafayette, her smile returned. "This time next year, I'll be getting ready to leave for college."

Back at MCHS, the girls shared a round of hugs, and Mindy didn't miss the fact that Kat's embrace was tighter and longer than the rest. They all waved and set off in different directions until the next cheer practice.

Mindy smiled and waved at her mother waiting in the Bonneville. She threw her bag into the back seat and jumped into the car. As they reached the Scottsville Road intersection, her mother slowed and pulled to the side of the road. Before Mindy could question, her mother announced, "It's official, we're moving. Dad has accepted a new job in St. Louis but hasn't told anyone at Carter yet. That means you still can't tell anyone."

After a silent pause, Mindy asked, "When?"

"We're not sure, but probably fairly soon," her mother replied.

Mindy's heart sank. She had seen the signs and knew it was coming. Saying goodbye to her friends and cheerleading was going to be hard, and she was already dreading the idea of being a new girl at school again. Aching with understanding that she was powerless to change the situation, Mindy crossed her hands tightly in her lap and remained quiet for the remainder of the short drive home.

After dinner, Mindy waited for her brothers to leave the table before confronting her father. He reiterated that no definite date had been set but alluded it could be anywhere from a few weeks to as late as Christmas. Recognizing the unfairness of his response, he offered a few options, "If we don't move until Christmas, you could graduate a semester early from high school and begin college in January, or we might consider the possibility of you staying with the Froedge's to finish the second semester here." Although both options sounded plausible on the surface, the little voice in Mindy's head told her neither was likely.

Mindy cleared the dinner table in silence. When she started for her bedroom, her mother tossed her a verbal reminder, "Nobody at Carter knows yet. You can't tell anyone, or there could be trouble for Dad." Mindy's heart fell into her stomach.

When Damien called a short time later, Mindy wanted to get out of the house and suggested they go get ice cream. Damien agreed but added, "Just come outside when you see my car. I don't want your mom to ask anything about my prostrate." Mindy just rolled her eyes.

Damien waited by his car with open arms, but Mindy barely acknowledged his presence as she crawled into the passenger seat. He completely missed her emotional distance during the short drive to Jones's where it didn't take much ice cream to unzip Mindy's lips. Ignoring her mother's instructions, she leaked the news of the upcoming move but likewise swore Damien to secrecy.

Initially dismayed, Damien quickly recovered when Mindy mentioned the possibilities of early graduation or staying with the Froedge's. As Damien spoke, his voiced faded and Mindy's thoughts drifted, "I should cut him loose. I should do it now and get it over with." She started to speak but held back. "It doesn't really matter when or what I tell him. Moving will negate the need for any drama. I'll just let it fade away."

Three days later, Mindy boarded a plane for Toronto. Planned months earlier, her family's move wouldn't change Mindy's itinerary or a family vacation in Canada. For Mindy, it was a timely opportunity to get away from Lafayette and gather her thoughts. She didn't want to be around Damien, and she didn't want to see her friends while tied to secrecy.

Similar to her previous visit, Vicki and Mindy rode bikes, shopped at the local mall, and enjoyed endless girl-talk while floating in the pool. Unlike past years, Vicki had a recently acquired boyfriend, and the girls spent lots of time with him and his friends on group outings. For the Canadian boys, Mindy was an immediate source of interest and hormonal fantasy. She absorbed their attention, which was a pleasant reminder of how silly boys her age could be.

The rest of the Murphy family arrived in Canada late in the week and picked up Mindy, who waved goodbye to Vicki, uncertain when, if ever, she would see her Canadian friend again.

As soon as they pulled away, Mindy's mother turned to face her in the back seat. "There has been a change of plans. Damien apparently told Charlie Donnelly about Dad's job change, and he notified Dad's boss at the Carter corporate office. Of course, they confronted Dad, and he had to tell them the truth. He's going to announce his resignation, and we'll be moving shortly after we get back. It will probably be better this way, anyway. You and the boys can get started at your new schools early in the year."

Mindy's stomach churned. She assumed the news would travel fast and felt terrible she wouldn't be the one to tell her friends. But it didn't take long for her thoughts to shift. She became angry with herself for not heeding her mother's warning, but even more upset with Damien. Betrayed by his breach of confidence, her irritation with him wouldn't fade for the remainder of her days in Lafayette. Instead, emotional distance would dominate.

The Murphy's spent the next several days in Algonquin National Park where Mindy enjoyed reading books along the lake shore and taking long solitary walks in the woods. She cultivated internal peace about her family's move and shifted her focus toward visions of her new home and school.

It was a long two-day drive back to Lafayette before Mindy took a few steps into her bedroom, then paused and gently lowered her suitcase to the floor. She scanned the room and thought, "This is a great bedroom, but I won't be sleeping here much longer." Images of listening to records with Anne, Gina, and Phyllis flooded her memory, but they rapidly faded. Her eyes fixed for a time on the cork bulletin board on the far wall, covered with pinned-up mementos of cheerleading. Sports schedules, school letters, awards, dried corsages, ribbons, and bows all represented moments of her past now frozen in time; an inanimate collection she would always remember fondly. After a soft sigh, she took a deep breath, ready to pack it all away and to step into not only the next chapter but a new book of her life.

Her eyes shifted again and caught sight of an envelope lying on her desk. Picking it up as if it might be fragile, she immediately recognized the handwriting but confirmed it with a quick glance at the return address; Connor Prewitt, Dahlonega, GA. With careful precision, she peeled it open, then curled up on her bed to read the pages. It began with the copied lyrics of Chicago's "Color My World" and expressed how much he missed her and hoped to see her again before leaving for college. Enclosed was a staged photo of him posed like "The Thinker" in front of a waterfall backdrop. The postscript asked, "Would you send me a recent photo of yourself so I can remember you better?" Those words tickled her, but the excitement didn't last.

Her thoughts shifted to her friends and what they may have heard about her family's move. She grabbed the phone, pulled it onto her lap and spun the dial. Over the next few hours, she happily learned that not one of her friends had heard the news but was still sad to inform them. Each of them, especially Kat, expressed regret for their loss and voiced their sympathy for Mindy having to make such a significant change to start her senior year of high school.

Migrating to the kitchen for a snack, Mindy was enjoying a Twinkie with a milk chaser when the phone rang. She was in no hurry to answer, and the sound of Damien's voice didn't surprise her. He sounded agitated. "I heard you were home. I've been trying to call all afternoon, but the line has been busy. I can't believe you haven't come to see me at the bank," he barked.

Mindy wasted no time setting him straight. "I wanted to talk to my friends first. Because you couldn't keep a promise, my dad had to resign early, and now we're moving in a few weeks." Damien tried to deny any wrongdoing, but Mindy quickly trapped him in his lie.

Damien arrived at Ellington minutes after the bank closed. Mindy's youngest brother let him in, led him into the kitchen, then had to remove a snarling Fi. Damien was forced to wait in the kitchen, nervously talking with Mindy's mother. Mindy heard his voice but remained in her room for a few minutes to give her mother time to inquire about his prostate gland.

After an acceptable delay, Mindy walked into the kitchen and, without comment, pointed to the patio.

Damien obediently followed. By the time he closed the patio door, Mindy was already seated. Before Damien slid into a chair, Mindy cut loose. She chastised him for breaking his promise, lectured him on his lack of class, and completed his quartering with a more-than-modest stretch of the truth. "My dad is furious. We were going to stay here until Christmas, but now we can't."

The sound of her own words made Mindy question herself. She silently wondered, "Why am I being so harsh?" but had no immediate explanation.

Damien shrunk in his seat and tried to defend himself, "Mr. Donnelly could tell something was wrong. He kept asking me, so I gave in and told him. But I told *him* it was a secret."

Reeling in her anger, Mindy softened her tone. "Oh well, it will probably work out better this way. It will probably be a good move for all of us, and I still have time to say goodbye to my friends."

Shifting to the front edge of his seat, Damien questioned in disbelief, "Wait. You don't have to go, do you?"

Mindy furrowed her brow, "Of course, I have to go. It's my family. Families move together."

"Well, you're still planning to come back here for college, aren't you?" he asked.

Mindy hadn't processed her thoughts that far into the future. "I don't know," is all she could say.

Later that evening, Mindy joined her parents at the kitchen table and tried to clarify the timing of the move. She asked, "Can we stay long enough so I can cheer for the first home football game?" She pulled the magnetic football schedule from the refrigerator door. "The first home game is September 5th."

Her father shocked her when he agreed, "Okay. We'll plan to move on September 6th."

A few days later, Mindy and her mother flew to St. Louis to begin house hunting. Mrs. Tilman, wife of Emerson Electric Vice President, Ralph Tilman, met them at the airport. Mrs. Tilman was a stereotypic corporate executive wife; expensive car, lots of jewelry, dyed and styled hair, perfect make-up, and fancy clothes. The first stop was for lunch at Bellerive Country Club, where Mindy's eyes popped at the prices on the menu. After lunch, Mrs. Tilman gave them a tour of residential pockets in St. Louis County that she thought Mindy's parents should consider for their new home. They drove past one custom mansion after another, leaving Mindy and her mother nearly speechless. From humble roots, the Murphy's had always lived cost conscious and conservatively. Opulence had never been their style.

They spent the next day with a real estate agent but returned to Tennessee exhausted at the end of the unsuccessful weekend of house hunting. The requirement of near-immediate occupancy so the kids could start school became a substantial obstacle that nullified many otherwise good options, and they arrived in Lafayette late Sunday evening with many thoughts but no contract.

Aware of Mindy's upcoming move, her teachers refused to issue her books on Book Day. With no books or homework, attending school seemed a waste, so Mindy left with her mother early Tuesday morning to resume house hunting in St. Louis. Again, they walked through many houses but made no offers and returned to Lafayette late Thursday. Mindy attended school on Friday, worked her last shift at the bank and cheered at the away football game that night.

Larry arranged a group outing Saturday evening to a Nashville nightclub as a farewell trip for Mindy. Damien called that afternoon to say he was on his way over from work and wanted to get on the road right away so they could get to Nashville early. He arrived minutes later, still wearing his work suit and tie. The bars Mindy was familiar with were very country-casual, and a business suit would certainly look out of place. When Mindy began to comment, Damien cut her off, explained he planned to change in Nashville and insisted they get started.

Ready to dance, Mindy was comfortable during the drive but wondered why nobody shared the ride with them. At the motel, it became clear when Damien grabbed his leisure suit from the car, then coyly smiled to announce, "I reserved a room for us."

Mindy stopped in her tracks. Damien ignored her obvious distress and said, "I'll get us checked in. We can relax in the room while waiting for the others." Mindy protested, but he cut her off again, "I thought we could spend more time together this way. Just call your parents and tell them you're going to spend the night at Julie's house. I'll get you back early tomorrow. They'll never know."

"I can't believe this. How stupid do you think I am?" Mindy screeched.

"Ah, come on. It'll be fun," Damien said as he passed through the doors toward the registration desk.

Mindy stepped into the lobby, dropped onto a bench seat near the entrance and tried to conger up an escape. Damien returned a few minutes later full of pride as if he'd done something special. Twirling the room key on his finger, he motioned toward the elevator.

Cheeks burning hot, Mindy growled, "I *am not* going up there."

Damien protested, "Why not? I'm just going to change. Look, this may be our last chance to be together for a long time."

"*We're not together, and I am NOT going up there,*" Mindy snarled.

Nervous perspiration rolled down Damien's face as he paced back and forth. Finally, he stopped and begged, "Ahhh, come on. This is just a way for us to spend more time together."

"*No!*" Mindy said loud enough to catch the registration clerk's attention. Flushed with embarrassment, Damien turned and dragged himself to the elevator.

Mindy was about to blow when Ed and Julie stepped into the lobby to find her seated alone. Ed looked around and asked, "Where's Damien?"

Mindy answered abruptly, "He's changing." She tried to sound calm but was too angry and embarrassed to hide her emotions. She studied Ed's expression, read unease in his eyes, and suspected he was aware of Damien's scheme.

Mindy thought seriously about asking them to drive her back to Lafayette right then. She wanted Damien to return to the lobby and not be able to find her. Mindy wanted him to feel panic, confusion, and loss. Instead, she sat quietly pondering her limited options but came to no conclusion before Damien emerged from the elevator looking like a leprechaun in his favorite green leisure suit and black platform shoes with large gold buckles.

Mindy glanced at Julie and read the unspoken questions in her mind, "Why is he on the motel elevator?" and "Where are his other clothes?" Mindy felt another wave of embarrassment and hoped the whole story wouldn't have to be told. She might have exploded, had Julie's thoughts had become words.

Ed gave Damien an awkward smile and tipped his head toward Mindy. Damien must have sensed the ticking bomb and suggested they all move to the bar. Mindy waited until the others walked away, then arose slowly to follow the pack off Julie's flank and as far away from Damien as possible. Sadness, disgust, and defeat crept through her veins were gradually displaced by anger. "It was so stupid of me to let this happen," she thought.

Larry and his date arrived a short time later and joined them in the bar. With no quick escape, Mindy settled herself and was pleasant to the others but said nothing to Damien. It was clear to Larry, who was obviously aware of the scheme, that something had gone awry. He and Ed shared uncertain glances but couldn't decipher the debacle before them. As a result, everyone but Julie squirmed with discomfort.

When Larry tried to order drinks for the girls, Mindy and Julie quickly declined. Julie was a Baptist abstainer, and Mindy didn't want to risk being expelled from the cheer team for drinking just before she moved. So, when Larry proposed a toast to Mindy, she raised her iced tea into the air without a smile or eye contact.

The tension became too awkward. Less than an hour after arriving, Mindy suggested they head back early and the others almost jumped out of their seats. Mindy hoped to ride with Julie and Ed until they announced they were going to stop in Hartsville and spend the rest of the evening visiting a cousin. She didn't consider riding with Larry a feasible option.

In the parking lot, Larry and Ed each sent Damien a "good luck" glance as they got in their cars and quickly pulled away.

Damien whispered in feeble defeat, "I need to get my clothes and check out." Mindy didn't want to stand in the parking lot alone so followed slowly trailing several steps behind. Before reaching the doors, Damien spun on his heels, "Won't you go up with me to get my clothes?"

His stupidity had gone beyond ridiculous. Mindy wanted to scream, but composed herself, then glared at him to reply calmly, "I'll wait in the lobby."

Minutes later, the motel clerk gave Damien a dumbfounded look when he checked out less than two hours after checking in. He dropped his eyes to the floor, drowning in his own miserable embarrassment.

Wretchedly pale, Damien tried to apologize in the car, but Mindy threw up her hand, "I don't want to hear anything you have to say." For her, this was his lowest maneuver ever. She remained silent the entire drive back and jumped out of the car as they pulled into the driveway. When Damien started to get out, Mindy raised her hand again, "Stop! Don't you dare get near me, or I'll scream."

The next afternoon, Mindy felt compelled to confess the motel room story to her mother. Her mother's only question was, "Well, did you go to the room?"

Mindy felt like she'd been hit by a torpedo. She wanted her mother to become unhinged with anger. She wanted her mother to yell and scream and cuss and maybe even throw things. She wanted her mother to say, *"You tell that son-of-a-bitch to never come around here again!"* But she didn't. She didn't seem to pass judgment at all.

Preparing for bed, memories of previous visits to the bar scene in Nashville floated through Mindy's mind. She got stuck with the realization that the last trip to Nashville for dancing was the night she got sick in April. She slapped herself for wasting so much of her summer hanging with Damien for trips to Nashville that never materialized.

With movers coming the following week, Mindy spent much of her last weekend in Lafayette going through her belongings to debride and organize. With no house to move into in St. Louis, all but a suitcase worth of her clothing and toiletries would go into storage, so careful planning was necessary to make sure she had what she'd need to get them through the house hunting process.

Pulling down mementos pinned to her cork bulletin board one by one, Mindy reviewed the fond memory in each. Carefully placing ribbons, medals, old sports schedules, souvenir balls, and cheerleading photographs into a box, she hoped to fix them into her heart and mind. She slowly folded the cardboard flaps closed, then sealed the box with far more tape than necessary.

Moving to her desk, she pulled out the bottom drawer which was stuffed with personal treasures that wouldn't mean anything to anyone else. Cradling each item gently in her hands, she paused to re-absorb their history. She couldn't part with a single memento until she came across a 5x7 inch cardboard picture frame. She knew what it held but didn't consider opening it. It hadn't crossed her mind since burying it after the Eagles concert. Without another thought, she flipped it Frisbee style to score a 3-pointer as it swooshed into the trash can seven feet away.

September 1st and Labor Day arrived. Mindy spent the afternoon visiting friends and snapping farewell photos. The goodbyes were solemn, and the weight of future uncertainty became heavy. She wondered, "What will my new home and new school be like? The school year will have already started; will it be too late to make friends or join any clubs or activities? It's likely I will end up in a much bigger pond. How will I fit in?" She considered this, then smiled with the reassuring thought, "I'll adapt. I have before, and I'll do it again."

That evening she pulled out her diary and wrote:

Dear Diary,
I'll miss my friends and Macon County High.
I hope to carry memories of them wherever I go,
especially my dear Anne. May my new home
have a good balance between "Somewhere over
the Rainbow" and "There's no place like home."

She closed the cover gently and packed her little book of memories into her suitcase.

Damien called that evening, but Mindy refused to come to the phone. "Tell him I'm busy," she instructed her mother.

Mindy daydreamed through every class the rest of the week but was happy when she put an X through September 5th on her calendar.

The first home football game of the season had arrived, and Mindy cheered at the top of her lungs. When the final horn blew, the Tigers had gone down, predictably, in another demoralizing defeat. It didn't matter. The Grim Reaper of reality had arrived and made his way onto the field. Mindy looked at her cheer mates with a sense of finality. They shared hugs, tears, and goodbyes.

An elderly woman paused on her way out to yell, "Don't be so upset, girls. The Tigers will get 'em next week!" The cheerleaders all burst out in laughter, then cried all the more. Kat cried the hardest and apologized but didn't say what for.

The girls slowly fragmented with each offering a final wave goodbye as they walked away.

Mindy stood alone and scanned the field and lights and the nearly empty stands to burn them into her memory. Sitting alone, high in the bleachers, was Damien. He looked shockingly small and worn and old.

Mindy moved toward the perimeter of the field to say goodbye to a few lingering friends and fans. When they walked away, Damien stepped to the same spot along the fence where Kat had introduced him at the end of the previous football season. "Can I talk to you?" he politely asked.

Standing at the end of her Tennessee story, Mindy softened. She nodded but stayed on her side of the fence.

"Do you think you'll be coming back for the second semester?" Damien asked.

Mindy didn't speak but shook her head no.

"So, is it really over?" Damien questioned.

Mindy considered her words before speaking, "If you've given it any thought, I suspect you've known it has been over for a long time. In fact, it never existed. My heart knew it wasn't right from the beginning. I just wasn't smart enough to understand it. We were never even good friends. But, it's as much my fault as yours. We only used each other. Me, for trips out of Lafayette and you for a false sense of heightened social status. That's all you ever really cared about — how you looked to other people. You didn't really care about *me*. I should have been more mature and insightful. I should have told you right away, but for no good reason, I didn't. Let me give you some advice, treat your next girl with honesty and respect. Treat her as a partner and a friend. Treat her like your *best friend*. Honor her. Don't just look to take advantage of her. I believe life will go better for you. I wish you the best of luck." She waited patiently to allow him to reply.

He stared blankly. His dull, empty eyes reflected no understanding. "He doesn't seem hurt or upset — that's good. He's showing no sadness or remorse — that's good too, but I wonder what, if anything, that means. I wonder if he'll ever really care about anyone. I don't think he has that kind of feeling in him," she thought.

"Well, you know I love you?" he emptily questioned without a single ounce of emotion.

"Goodbye," said Mindy, and she walked away.

——————— · ———————

The packing crew had emptied most of the contents of Ellington into a moving van during the day, so the Murphy's spent the night just two blocks from the high school with the Froedge's. When Mindy walked through the door, she became overwhelmed with fatigue. The psychological wear and tear of the past few weeks had taken its toll. But now it was over, and new challenges lay ahead. Despite curling up in a strange bed, Mindy closed her eyes, smiled, and slept ever so soundly.

Most of Macon County went to bed that night ignorant of the failed assassination attempt on President Gerald Ford earlier that day. Charles Manson follower, Lynette "Squeaky" Fromme, disguised herself in a nun's habit and carried a semi-automatic weapon under her skirt. Secret Service Agents had time to thwart her attempt because she had emptied the firing chamber of her gun before leaving home.

Awake before dawn, Mindy assumed control of the guest bathroom and was ready to go long before her younger brothers were awake. Eager to move on to the next chapter of her life, she purposely made enough noise to arouse her family and get them all stirring.

After a light breakfast, everyone migrated outside toward the cars. Mindy's mother had never been good at saying goodbye; she always had one more thing to say. This morning, the process that usually took thirty minutes took nearly an hour.

By the time they left the Froedge's, the morning shadows were being melted by the sun. The loaded Mustang and Bonneville made the short drive to Ellington to make a final pass through the house. A short time later, the moving van pulled away.

Mindy stood in the yard and looked back at the house. Once vibrant and so full of life, it was now only an empty shell occupied only by ghostly memories. Tears welled in her eyes as she waved and whispered, "Goodbye, old house."

As they reloaded the cars to begin the trek to St. Louis, Damien's car came to a rocking stop before them. He stumbled while getting out of his car with tears streaming down his face. Mindy felt responsible for dealing with him, so stepped forward and said firmly, "We're leaving now."

Damien spread his arms and jumped toward her, but Mindy's stiff-arm to his chest stopped him. The snot dangling from his skimpy mustache was repulsive and forced Mindy to turn her head and push him away. As she did, the tears waiting patiently in her eyes dropped onto her cheeks, although she was uncertain why. She whispered, "Goodbye."

Sliding into the driver's seat of the Bonneville with her mother riding shotgun, Mindy glanced into the back seat to see her two youngest brothers getting settled. Her father and oldest brother pulled away in the suitcase loaded Mustang just ahead of them. She dropped the transmission into drive, stepped on the gas and didn't bother to look back. Her brothers groaned. "Oh, my God! Did you see all that snot? Gross! I never thought a grown man could cry so much," they yelled, then broke into laughter.

Mindy stifled a chuckle as the scene hung in her thoughts for a moment. It was clear in her mind, "He's not crying for me or lost love. He's crying for himself. He's crying for lost social status. Maybe he's learned something, but I doubt it." She took a deep breath and pushed the accelerator a little harder.

The place to improve the world is first
in one's own heart and head and hands,
and then work outward from there.
Robert Pirsig, *Zen and the Art of Motorcycle Maintenance:*
An Inquiry into Values

Part III

The world is beautifully endowed with an array of climates, topography, vegetation, water, and life. Each place they visit is part of the same world but has been unique in its own way. They've walked countless miles together on paths that have varied from easy to rigorous. Most of those paths have sported spectacular vistas and have offered lessons in friendship, love, and humility. Hoping to learn something new about the world and each other, they take different paths on every trip.

"How are your knees holding up?"
"They're a bit sore, but this view is incredible and has been well worth the effort. You don't get to see these things without putting on shoes and walking out the door."
"I'm glad you walked into my life. It's been a fabulous journey growing up and getting old with you. I'm glad we've taken life's little trip together."
"Me too."

Chapter 14
Back to the Future
September 6–December 9, 1975

Passing beyond the last reminders of Macon County, Mindy shed one last tear for the familiarity she was leaving behind, and one tear for the uncertainty that lay ahead. Then it was over. She hoped her new world would open many new doors of opportunity. That hope gave her reason to look forward and step up to the challenges of a new school. With a quick wipe of her cheeks, her next life adventure was underway.

As they approached the Mississippi River, the colossal stainless-steel legs of the Gateway Arch came into view to announce they were very close. Even with no house, they were still happy to arrive at the airport hotel that would function as their temporary home. That evening Mindy crawled under the covers feeling washed out but anxious to learn what the next days and weeks would bring.

Mindy's parents spent Sunday with a real estate agent but returned without news. That evening they drove to West St. Louis County to have dinner with longtime friends and Mindy's Godparents, the Christmann's. They had a hearing and speech impaired daughter, Jane, who was also a senior in high school. As youngsters, Mindy and Jane had spent many afternoons together doing hundreds of cartwheels and backbends in the Christmann's front yard.

The Christmann's spoke glowingly of West St. Louis County and the local school district, which was considered one of the best public-school systems in the state. They admitted, however, that West County had its share of teen hooligan's just like anywhere else. They told the story of three teenage boys involved in a wreck literally right in front of their small subdivision home the previous fall, which demolished two cars. There were no severe injuries, but the further details of the story left Mindy wide-eyed.

On Monday, Mindy's father started his new job while her mother spent the next two days with the real estate agent. They left Mindy in charge of the boys, and the homeless kids filled their time splashing in the hotel pool and walking around a nearby mall while their peers were in school. With no house, there was no address. With no address, there was no registering for school.

Things changed when Mindy's mother returned Tuesday at dinner time to announce, "We've submitted a contract. We'll know within forty-eight hours if they accept it."

Mindy let out a yelp of joy. "So, we can start school this week?"

Her mother shook her head, "We'll have to wait to see if they accept our offer." Mindy's excitement quickly faded, but she was still ever so happy to see light at the end of the tunnel.

Happiness returned the next day when her mother hung up the phone to announce, "Our offer has been accepted, and the loan has been approved. We can move in next week." Their new home would be in west St. Louis County, part of the Parkway School District and just a few miles west of the Christmann's. Although Mindy's mother would have to drive the kids to and from school until moving in, they could register and start school the following Monday.

Everyone was up early for breakfast at the hotel restaurant, then piled into the car for the twenty-minute trek to West County. At the new high school, Mindy's mother completed the necessary forms within a few minutes and left in a flash. As she had been several times before, Mindy was now largely on her own to chart a new course.

The secretary escorted her to the counselor's office, where Mindy met with a senior counselor who was also the head football coach, Mr. Wells. He silently reviewed her transcript, penciled out a schedule, and handed it to her. "You've got just about all the required credits already. This should be a pretty easy schedule for you," he explained.

Mindy scanned the schedule and gasped. "These are almost all weak electives. I plan to go to college and probably have some catching up to do. I need to take Chemistry and a good English class along with Psychology and Sociology. It would probably be wise to take math as well."

Mr. Wells frowned, "Why don't you just have fun and enjoy your senior year? Look, you are from a small-town school, and you're already two weeks behind. You're going to have a tough time catching up as it is." But Mindy was insistent. So, Mr. Wells scribbled out a new course list which Mindy thought looked better but still omitted a math class. It was an omission she would come to regret.

During the subsequent locker assignment and tour, the size of the school was simultaneously impressive and overwhelming. There were three grades, 10 through 12, with over two thousand students. The school housed three separate gym floors, an Olympic swimming pool, a high-tech multipurpose auditorium, an expansive shop class, a state-of-the-art computer lab and a music conservatory for starters. Mindy thanked the volunteer for the tour, took a deep breath, and stepped into her second-hour class.

The 'girls only' version of The Art of Living was designed to discuss women's issues and practical everyday skills of adulthood. After brief introductions, Mindy took a seat and class resumed. Her eyes widened when the teacher announced, "We've spent the last few days discussing oral contraceptives. Today we'll begin our discussion of alternate forms of contraception."

Mindy's jaw dropped as the teacher sat on the front edge of her desk and held up before the class a diaphragm, a tube of spermicide and vaginal applicator. She described their use, then passed them around the room. "These things don't always work, so most experts recommend the concurrent use of . . ." She held up a small, square aluminum packet and continued, "a condom." Mindy's cheeks flushed with embarrassed recognition. The teacher opened the packet, unrolled the latex contents onto a banana, described its use, and passed it around the room. "Boys generally preferred not to wear them. My husband compares it to taking a shower with a raincoat on. But it ends up being *your* responsibility to insist that they do if you don't want to get pregnant."

Mindy trembled, and her mind drifted, "I'm pretty darn sure they don't have a class like this at Macon County High."

The bell rang, and Mindy made her way to gym class. Without a swimsuit, she had to sit poolside while the other students swam laps. Then she realized, "I don't own a one-piece swimsuit. Where does one buy a swimsuit in September?"

Beginning Acting followed and passed quickly. At lunchtime, Mindy followed the crowd out of the room but became confused when they dispersed in all directions. Steve Koontz, a skinny kid with long stringy brown hair and beaver-like incisors, followed her out of class and asked, "Hey, are you new here?" Mindy nodded. "Wanna go get high?" he matter-of-factly inquired, with no attempt to camouflage his words or voice. Filled with fear, Mindy stiffened and shook her head emphatically. Steve shrugged his shoulders and disappeared down the hall. Mindy never saw him again.

As the day progressed, Mindy felt a bit out of place as she made a note of the clothing styles at her new school. Her attire was relatively formal and quite feminine compared to the casual suburban style of her new peers. Tight shirts or sweaters that frequently revealed slivers of cleavage, and women's cut Levi or designer jeans appeared to be the norm.

Happy to be nearing the end of her first day, Mindy walked into her 6th-hour Interior Design class and took an open seat around a large design table. Allison Butler introduced herself and made Mindy feel welcome.

The class proceeded, and the students eventually stood to work on group projects. Another student at the table, Joan Hinkley, spoke at the earliest opportunity, "Alison, I've been meaning to ask you something. You lost a lot of weight over the summer. How did you do it?"

Alison smiled, "I lost forty pounds. It really wasn't hard."

"But how? You look great," Joan persisted.

Alison stated very matter-of-factly, "During the day I took caffeine capsules, and over-the-counter diet pills, then took a sleeping pill at night, so I wouldn't wake up hungry. I hardly ate anything all summer."

Joan and Mindy shared dumbfounded expressions. Mindy had trouble focusing for the rest of the class and wondered just what kind of crazy place her parents had moved her to.

After school, Mindy took a seat by herself on a bench outside to wait for her mother. She watched with amazement as an army of students climbed into seemingly endless lines of buses while additional platoons marched toward the student parking lot. Several boys did a double-take as they passed by, and a few said, "Hi," with blushing curiosity in their eyes. Their expressions put a positive spin on what had been a long day. But that didn't prevent Mindy from decompressing as soon as her seatbelt clicked in the car. She unleashed the invitation to get high and induced another rare speechless moment for her mother.

After dinner, Mindy grabbed her checkbook and made a quick trip to a nearby K Mart to update her wardrobe. But she had to go to a dedicated sporting goods store where the only one-piece swimsuit she could find was a $30 Speedo. Back in her hotel room that evening, Mindy did more homework in one night than she had done during her last three months at MCHS.

The next morning Mindy took an empty seat in her first-hour Chemistry class. Quickly identifying the new student, Jenna Manning's face lit up as she slid into a desk chair beside Mindy and introduced herself. Jenna was bouncy with big dark brown eyes that were in stark contrast to her pale powdered complexion and bright pink rouge. Her frilly girlish outfit and big pink hair bow deviated from the PWH norm and made Mindy wonder if she had just moved in from a small town as well. What was clear from the first moment was that Jenna liked to talk far more than listen. Always a good listener, that suited Mindy just fine.

Jenna happily volunteered her services to teach the PWH ropes and offer survival tips. She wasted no time in getting started as she passed Mindy several notes during class about various boys seated around them. By the time the first-period bell rang, Mindy already appreciated Jenna's levity and humility.

The next few days went smoothly. Jenna walked with Mindy between classes whenever possible to point out cute boys she should get to know and bitch girls to avoid while offering little personal caveats about each. Mindy heard about so many students so fast she couldn't keep Jenna's good-bad list straight or help but laugh at her lighthearted frankness.

The phrase "sexy and provocative" had never crossed Mindy's mind in reference to any teen girl before. That changed while talking with Jenna between classes. Mindy stared at a thin, buxom blonde surrounded by a drooling harem of boys who was gliding smoothly down the hallway in her direction. She was of medium height with long, flowing blonde hair, and wore a teasing touch of mascara and eyeshadow. Her tight, low-cut blouse worked like a tractor beam to attract male eyes by the score, and her skin-tight hip hugger jeans rode low enough to reveal a sliver of pink-white skin glimmering just above the beltline. The sex-goddess vision before her looked twenty-four and moved with womanly gait and confidence, oozing sensuality from her pores.

Jenna read the expression on Mindy's face and laughed, "Oh, that's Kim Cannon. Boys are just crazy about her. She's so far out of our league there's no need to bother even worrying about her. If she's in the room, I just leave. No boys will even give me the time of day." Kim and her consort continued past as Mindy watched in stunned disbelief.

While waiting for Mindy's mother to arrive after school, Jenna spoke at great length of her lost love and fellow senior, Doug Garrett. He had abruptly broken off their relationship eight months ago and had recently started dating her former best friend, Sharon Haskins.

A few weeks later, Jenna pleaded and convinced Mindy to talk with Doug on her behalf. Although reluctant to do so, Mindy stopped Doug in the hall at school and asked if there was any possibility he might consider dating Jenna again. Doug didn't hesitate to make it clear with an emphatic, "That will never happen." The intensity of the exchange left Mindy to wonder just what exactly had caused their break-up.

Janet "JT" Thomas injected herself into Mindy's life on her third day of classes. Like Mindy, JT was a senior year transplant from Evansville, Indiana but, unlike Mindy, she remained bitter about her move and struggled to fit in at PWH. A large boned-big busted girl, JT was never afraid to say what was on her mind and rarely hesitated to think before speaking. With difficult to control juvenile diabetes, JT had been in the hospital and missed Mindy's introduction to PWH but, like Jenna, immediately identified her as a new student, and latched on.

In desperate need of someone to share her frustrations with, it took JT no time to ventilate, "It really sucks, doesn't it?" Before Mindy could respond, JT described how much she liked her old school, old friends and how much she missed her boyfriend, Rod. JT was confident she had met her soul mate and planned to move back to Evansville after graduation, live with an older brother, get a job and get married as soon as they saved enough money.

Out of breath, JT paused to ask, "Did you leave a boyfriend behind in Tennessee?"

Mindy bristled at the word "boyfriend," and said, "No," but backtracked when teen social status reasoning kicked in. She added, "Well, I guess I had one. It was kind of on and off for a while. It's over for me, but he thinks I might move back over Christmas to finish school down there."

Mindy's response heightened JT's desire to hear more. "What have you decided about dating other people?" she inquired.

"Really, it's over. He was older and able to take me places boys our age couldn't. But he wasn't good for me, and I never really had any interest in him. I'll date here if anyone asks me out," Mindy explained.

Eager to tell her own story, JT launched into the details of her history with Rod; much of which Mindy didn't need to hear. JT's smile faded as she outlined their agreement, "Rod says he wants to be able to see other girls with me in St. Louis. So, we agreed it would be okay to date other people when we're apart, but we'll only see each other when I'm back in Evansville."

Mindy wondered when she'd heard a similar arrangement before, then cringed, "I just don't see how that can ever possibly work. It has to fail — probably sooner than later."

Following dinner that evening, Mindy was ecstatic about the arrival of moving day and her last airport hotel meal for a long time. Recalling her first bus ride to the trailer in Lafayette, she wrote her new address on a slip of paper and stopped by the office at school to learn her bus number and bus stop for her new home on Brass Lamp.

Too wired to sleep that night, Mindy turned on the television to find every major channel airing a "Special Report" on the capture and arrest of Patty Hearst. Soon the debate would begin: was she a willing accomplice all along, or was she really the victim of torture and brainwashing? Mindy, of course, would always believe the latter.

During Chemistry Lab the next morning, PWH socialite, Karen Cary approached, "Would you like to go out drinking with me and some friends this weekend?"

Knocked off balance by the unprefaced question, Mindy groped for a quick escape and awkwardly declined. "The moving van is unloading at our new house today. I'm pretty sure I'll be busy unpacking most of the weekend. But thanks anyway."

"Okay," Karen shrugged then walked away. She never spoke to Mindy again.

Jill Phillips, a soft-spoken classmate, had overheard the exchange and immediately stepped in to say, "I'm so proud of you for shunning temptations of the Devil. Would you like to join my youth group at church?"

Declining with political correctness, Mindy wondered where she would find balance in her new school.

Mindy had worn her new Speedo swimsuit exactly once when she went to gym class later that day and found her lock broken and the locker empty. She stood staring at the empty cubical, trying to understand what had happened. Realizing her brand new $30 swimsuit was gone forever, anger and frustration quickly grew. She stomped into the gym teacher's office and delivered a short tirade, "I can't believe it. They stole everything, even my deodorant. Who steals deodorant?! I'm not buying another swimsuit for thirty dollars. This place is awful! I just can't believe someone would do this!"

The teacher apologized and assured Mindy that such events were rare, but admitted there was nothing she could do to help. Mindy just fumed. Pacing in the gym foyer, she considered her options before concluding, "I already have enough gym credits to graduate. I'll drop gym class and take a study hall."

That afternoon, JT invited Mindy to join her and a neighbor, Cindy Hoefer, to watch a boys water polo game after school. Mindy readily accepted the invitation and thought, "I've never seen water polo — and sitting around a pool sounds much safer than a drinking binge, anyway."

After negotiating the bus ride to her new home for the first time, Mindy took a quick tour of the house and was pleased with its appearance and the spaciousness of her new bedroom.

The movers were still unloading, so her mother wasn't too upset to hear Mindy was returning to school for an hour or two. Waiting in the front yard for JT, Mindy looked around and thought, "I think this is going to work out just fine. I have new friends, I'm finally going to sleep in my own bed, classes are more interesting, and I'm going to watch water polo. Do they even play water polo in Tennessee?"

With Cindy driving, Mindy sat in the back seat and wasn't sure what to think as the other two talked with excitement about watching boys in bathing suits. The match was just beginning when they arrived, and red-cheeked embarrassment soon replaced Mindy's uncertainty as JT provided commentary about the various sizes of Speedo bulges around the pool.

After the game, the girls loitered in the gym foyer, but Mindy was unsure why. The reason became apparent when boys with wet hair began ascending the stairs from the locker room level, and the other girls' excitement re-emerged.

Several boys passed by offering looks of curiosity in Mindy's direction but didn't stop. This changed when Cindy waved and said, "Hi" to one of them. The boy waved back but didn't break stride until Mindy captured the sweep of his eye. Abruptly adjusting his course, Andy Sparks approached the trio, and Cindy stepped to the forefront. They chatted about the game for a moment until Andy took the first opportunity to look past Cindy and inquire, "Who's your friend?" After introductions, they all talked for several minutes before saying goodbye and heading home for dinner.

That evening Mindy considered her two new friends, JT and Jenna. They represented contrasting bookends and were very different as individuals, so Mindy was uncertain how their chemistry would mix if they did things together.

Mindy spent most of Saturday organizing and re-arranging her bedroom. That evening she sat down at her desk to follow through with a promise she'd made before moving and penned a brief letter to Connor. Fatigue soon took over, and Mindy crawled into bed. She scanned her new bedroom, then turned off the light and fell into a deep sleep with a smile.

Sunday passed slowly with several hours of catch-up homework after church. The relative quiet of the day left Mindy feeling a little lonely, but with three more hours of homework awaiting her, there was no time to dwell on it. Mentally exhausted by the time she finished, Mindy crawled into bed with side four of the Beatles' 1967-1970 greatest hits album on the turntable. As "The Long and Winding Road" played, she wondered what still lay ahead for her. After a few seconds of soft static, the needle lifted from the album, the turntable clicked off, and Mindy drifted off deep, satisfying sleep once again.

Just days later, Mindy received a reply from Connor, who wrote extensively about how much he was enjoying his college experience. The tone of the letter changed with a long paragraph outlining how much he missed her and hoped to see her again in the not-too-distant future. Poorly disguised as an afterthought near the end of the letter, he inquired, "How are things with your boyfriend in Tennessee?"

Mindy pulled out a sheet of paper and wrote a short reply to say, "Things are over with Damien. I broke up with him not long after your visit to Lafayette." Her eyes fixed on the blue ink image of "I broke up" and brought forth a sigh of relief.

Before their move to St. Louis, Mindy's mother had purchased plane tickets so Mindy and her eldest brother could return to Lafayette for Homecoming. Mindy had mixed feelings about the return but, with things going so well, she thought it would be a good time to see her old friends.

On the day of departure, Keith Little, a fellow senior in Mindy's Short Stories class, approached and nervously introduced himself. He was tall and thin, with small, low-set ears and wavy bangs that partially covered his eyes. When he threw his head back to clear his sight line, Mindy could read the look in his eye and knew what was coming. "Hey, would you be interested in going out to see a movie this weekend?" Keith politely inquired.

Having shared no previous conversation with Keith, Mindy replied with a well-rehearsed, "Sorry, I'm busy."

"Okay, maybe some other time," Keith replied, and he walked away unscathed. Mindy thought about the many cute boys she'd seen around the school; Keith wasn't among them. She sighed and moved on to her next class.

Since their brief introduction, Andy Sparks had been popping up outside of Mindy's classes frequently to engage her in conversation. So, it didn't surprise her when he approached after lunch. "Hey if you're not busy, would you like to go to dinner and a movie this weekend?"

Mindy felt like a recording. "Sorry, I'm busy," so she added, "I'm leaving town for the weekend in just a few hours." Also unscathed, Andy apologized for asking on such short notice and indicated he would talk with her again after her return.

On the plane later that afternoon, Mindy tried to explain her 'you can't go back' philosophy to her brother. "Don't expect Lafayette to be the same. Even though we've only been gone a few weeks, it will be different. It will feel different, and they will treat you differently. If you expect it to be the same, then you'll likely be disappointed." Her brother didn't seem to understand and just shrugged. Mindy wondered, "Where *are* all the real men in this world?"

The flight was short and smooth, but Mindy developed internal turbulence about the trip and was already regretting it well before the plane landed in Nashville. Mrs. Donnelly picked them up and dropped Mindy at the Froedge's and her brother at a friend's house just down the street.

Mindy quickly changed into a new outfit she'd purchased just that week. She experimented with a matching silk scarf until she settled on a necktie with a tight knot turned to the side and long trailing tails draped over the shoulder. She looked at herself in the small oval antique wall mirror and smiled at her sophisticated appearance.

Loretta arrived a short time later and seemed genuinely thrilled with Mindy's return. Mindy, on the other hand, was quite surprised to see Loretta wearing a new cheer uniform. Loretta explained, "Sonia Gann's mother cut one of her skirt patterns too short and can't find replacement material. So, we bought these right after you moved."

Mindy laughed to herself, thinking just how fast the world moves on in one's absence.

During the short drive to school, Mindy's anticipation grew with genuine excitement to see her old friends and watch them cheer. She had no desire to re-live old memories, but hoped the sights and sounds would help anchor the many good ones in her heart and mind.

"You'll be the next Homecoming Queen" was something Mindy had heard many times from classmates and was aware of a nagging desire to push herself past her own threshold of disappointment. She reminded herself, "It didn't happen, so get over it." She hoped seeing the 1975 crown being placed on someone else's head would release her from self-centered thoughts and sever any dangling psycho-emotional ties to her old school.

At the quiet pre-game field, Mindy shared greetings and hugs with her former cheer mates before fans filled the stands and homecoming festivities began. It thrilled her that the girls seemed happy to see her as they gave updates on town happenings since her move. Several of them noted, "You look different," but couldn't place their finger on it. Mindy knew it was her clothes. Somehow, she wasn't surprised that none of them asked a single question about her new school, house or friends. There was not even a question about boys in general.

With the home stands nearly full, the cheerleaders headed off to their cheer duties. Mindy waved and ascended into the stands where it didn't take for former friends and classmates to surround her to say 'hi' and recount their loss.

As Homecoming festivities unfolded, Mindy felt out of place. The coronation ceremony began as sports car convertibles made their way onto the track carrying the new queen and her court. Mindy envisioned herself riding in the car and waving to the crowd. The procession came to a stop, and the football captain and his court escorted the new queen and her attendants to the podium at mid-field. "Get over it. It didn't happen," she reminded herself again.

Kathy Smith interrupted Mindy's thoughts when she turned to say, "That would have been you. If you hadn't moved, you would have been queen."

Embarrassed by what felt like an unveiling of her thoughts, Mindy quipped, "No, the football team picks the Homecoming Queen, and Mack (the football co-captain) would have made sure the players voted for Teresa (his junior girlfriend)."

Kathy repeated, "Oh no, you would have been queen alright. This is the first time anyone can remember they didn't pick a senior. It would have been you for sure." The girls on either side of her nodded in agreement.

Leisa Gregory added, "Mindy, you were our only hope. It's just pretty sad they didn't think there was anyone else from our class good enough to be queen." Mindy sunk into her seat, ashamed at herself for her egocentric thoughts, and hoped Teresa would never hear such things.

Just before the opening kickoff, Mindy scanned the surrounding scene and shivered with a "you can never go back" sensation. She no longer felt part of the school or the town. Once the heart of her pride in this little town, MCHS unexpectedly looked small and old compared to her new school. Everyone she saw was pleasant, but most of their greetings didn't seem as genuine as they had in the past. Then she studied the new cheer uniforms and thought, "The skirts make everyone's butts look really wide. I would have vetoed them." With a sudden chill, Mindy felt uncomfortable and wished she were back in St. Louis moving forward, instead of treading water.

Glancing down at her new outfit, Mindy laughed at herself. "They're no different. *I* am different. I'm the one who has changed. I *have* moved on, and I've left my past behind."

The game ended and the stands quietly emptied with most spectators too disappointed to even complain about the score. As Mindy descended the stairs, she stopped for short random conversations with several girls she had missed earlier. They all said versions of the same thing, 'we miss you,' but she sensed they were just being polite.

Several girls met at Jones's for post-game ice cream, and a few wanted to know if she might return for the second semester. Mindy shook her head and tried to explain, "So much changes the day one steps out of one town and into another. If you've never moved, it's hard to understand. I'm in a new place. I have to adapt and look forward. That's what people do when they move." She wasn't sure what to think when they responded with only a mix of uncertain expressions.

Mindy rode with Loretta to visit as many friends as possible on Saturday. They greeted her with open arms expounded on local gossip updates from the night before, but not one of them expressed the slightest interest in Mindy's new home. Mindy wondered if they just didn't care or if the invisible walls of Macon County kept them so egocentrically focused on Lafayette and MCHS that it stifled their curiosity about what it would be like to live or grow up somewhere else.

As the conversation continued, Mindy stood on the outside looking in. She attempted to interject information about her new home but was quickly cut off, and the discussion shifted back to idle gossip that largely excluded comment by her. It saddened her to observe old connections falter before her eyes. By early afternoon she wished she could just pack up and leave for St. Louis. She dreamed of a world full of wonder, enlightenment, and imagination; a colorful vision of her life beyond high school and Macon County.

Quietly preparing for bed, Mindy retired to a bedroom the Froedge's had maintained as a museum in memory of their adult daughter who had left home many years previous. Before turning off the light, she looked around the room with the thought, "This would probably be my temporary bedroom should I push to come back for the second semester." She studied the high shelves around the bed filled with china dolls, all of whom seemed to stare with glassy dead eyes to where she lay. She trembled and turned off the light but could still sense the doll's icy stares and thought, "I could never stay here."

On the plane the next day, Mindy closed her eyes and let her thoughts drift. In her mind, she said a last goodbye to Lafayette, MCHS, old friends, cheerleading and, maybe most of all, to the popularity that came with being a big fish in a small pond. Her thoughts shifted to her new home, new school, and new opportunities. With college less than a year away, she was happy to think she would be the one mainly in charge of her next move. Before long, Andy Sparks made a random pass through her thoughts. "He seems like a nice enough guy. If he asks me out again, I'll say yes."

JT called that evening to ask about the weekend. Mindy explained, "I'm glad to be back in St. Louis. I enjoyed my time there, but Lafayette is in my past. I won't go back for anything other than short visits to see old friends now and then."

JT felt the opposite, "I love going back to Evansville. It always seems just the same. I could go back there any time and never have to start over." But Mindy could hear uncertainty in JT's voice and believed JT was looking through rose-colored glasses.

———————————

Relieved to be back in St. Louis, Mindy re-introduced herself to the importance of school and focused hard on her academic classes. As the days and weeks passed, her pool of new friends grew and represented a unique blend of personalities who were bright and intuitive. Often, their perspectives encouraged Mindy to open her eyes to a more panoramic view of the world. She appreciated and respected their opinions, but none of them would become a bosom friend.

The third week at PWH, Dr. Berger returned graded papers in Mindy's Short Stories class and asked her to stop by his desk after class. Scrawled across the top of her essay was, "A—good work." She was happy with her grade, but wondered if Dr. Burger was just being kind to the new student and wondered how her writing compared to other students in the class.

After class, Mindy waited patiently in front of Dr. Berger's desk as he cleared it. When he looked up, he spoke with great encouragement and expressed his pleasure with her writing skills. "Your writing reveals much potential. So, I took the liberty of checking your schedule and suggest you replace your study hall with a seat in my Honors English class. But I must warn, it's a lot of work, and you will have a lot of catching up to do."

Feeling the first pounding academic pulse of her heart in over two years, she relished the challenge and the opportunity.

That evening, Mindy made a conscious decision to focus even more on school. She planned to mail college applications in a few months and hoped to boost her GPA. "School must come first," she coached herself.

――――――――――― · ―――――――――――

The following weekend, Mindy mixed the girl chemistry and combined Jenna's and JT's personalities in the same outing as they attended a PWH football game together. The spectacle of the high school stadium impressed Mindy as they walked in. The home stands alone could comfortably seat several thousand spectators, everything looked brand new with fresh paint, modern concession stands, and the field seemed to glow with flawless green turf. The marching band moved like endless platoons of music playing warriors, and the crisp pounding drums sent rippling vibrations over her skin from one hundred yards away.

They took seats near mid-field, and Mindy studied the cheerleaders. It was immediately apparent that most were athletically talented, and she suspected many had significant dance and gymnastics experience. She watched in awe as they did backflips and a variety of gymnastic routines that she and her MCHS squad could only dream of. Letting out a soft sigh of disappointment, Mindy admitted to herself, "Making the cheerleading team here would have been a long shot."

By the end of the first half, the game had lost its luster for Jenna and JT, and they convinced Mindy to leave early. On the way out, Jenna drew Mindy's attention to the small army of eyes tracking her movement and lamented, "I wish they'd look at me like that. There's nothing like being pretty *and* new at school."

A quick glance confirmed Jenna's observation. Feeling flushed, Mindy quickened her pace until they approached the main gate. But she stopped abruptly when she noticed a boy with shoulder-length brown hair wearing a two-tone baseball undershirt, jeans, and well-worn three-stripe blue suede Adidas tennis shoes who never broke stride as he passed out the gate just ahead of her. Mindy had never seen him at school before, but he somehow seemed remarkably familiar. Before she could point him out to Jenna, he was gone.

――――――――――― · ―――――――――――

Schoolwork was substantial, time-consuming, and left little opportunity for play during the week. Jenna did, however, convince Mindy to go after school shopping with her one day and introduced her Monique's; a small discount clothing store in a local strip mall that sold mostly teen girl styles. The array of colorful clothing they offered thrilled Mindy, and she playfully searched through the seemingly endless racks. She would occasionally pull out a racy top for examination, then shake her head and laugh. "They definitely don't sell this stuff on the square in Lafayette."

After shopping, they retreated to Jenna's house to listen to records and talk before dinner. As a Beatles album spun on the turntable, Jenna curled up in a beanbag chair and lamented her lack of a date to the PWH Homecoming dance. It didn't take long for her to shift the focus to her lost love, Doug, and she weaved a detailed tale of woe. "We started dating in the middle of our sophomore year. I thought we were in love and believed beyond any doubt we would get married one day," she began.

With a self-deprecating laugh, Jenna continued, "I was stupid. Last January, on my seventeenth birthday, he told me he loved me. I really thought we were going to be married. So, I gave him everything. I sucked his you-know-what, then handed him my virginity. I thought we had consummated our relationship, but a week later he broke up with me. It devastated me and, now, eight months later, here I am — still hoping I can win him back someday."

After a pause, blunted anger replaced Jenna's remorse. "Then my best friend stole him. Sharon and I had been best friends for two years, and she knew how I felt about Doug. I just can't believe she did this to me." She chuckled again. "I'm so glad you moved in. Without you, I wouldn't have any friends here. Everyone at West thinks I'm crazy. Well, I *was* crazy. Lunatic became my middle name around here after being so unexpectedly dumped. My mother pushed me and I lost what little sensibility I had. I chased Doug obsessively at school and with phone calls. I baked him cookies and cakes and pleaded my case of devotion. One day, my mother drove me past the front of the school where Doug was waiting with others for the after-school activity bus. As we passed, I hung half-way out the window and screamed out my everlasting love for him. Rumors about what I did spread all over the school and I lost face. Many kids avoid me like I have syphilis, and Doug refuses to talk to me at all. They all think my mom and I are crazy. And they're right. We're as nuts as they come." Full of regret, Jenna concluded, "I wish I hadn't given myself away. I wish I could take it back. I wish I had saved it for someone who really loves me. But it's too late. Stupid, stupid me."

Mindy wanted to be supportive and searched her heart for a response, but couldn't find honest words. She drove home feeling Jenna's sense of loss. "She gave herself to someone who probably never loved her. Her virginity is lost — *forever*."

A flood of unhappy memories came out of nowhere, and Mindy wondered, "Why is it so easy for girls to be pressured into making bad decisions? Why do they fall for the 'You know I love you?' ploy." She trembled and felt so sorry for Jenna but arrived back at Brass Lamp so very relieved she hadn't made a similar mistake. She promised herself she never would.

A few days later, the trio of new friends attended the pre-Homecoming bonfire. The modest crowd seemed to have fun, but JT and Jenna spent most of their time crooning about lost boyfriends and the lost opportunity to attend their senior year Homecoming dance.

As the fire raged, JT spied Andy Sparks standing in the crowd. Nudging Mindy, she whispered, "I forgot to tell you. I heard Andy might give you a last-minute invitation to the Homecoming dance."

Mindy stiffened. She wasn't missing boys at all. In fact, Mindy was enjoying the freedom and the extra weekend time to do catch-up reading. So, she felt a wave of uncertainty when Andy approached for a fireside chat. Her thoughts settled as they talked and in the back of her mind decided, "If he asks, I'll say yes, just so I can go to the dance." But she didn't feel disappointed when Andy walked away without an invitation.

Seeking an alternative to Homecoming, Jenna had purchased tickets to see Head East in concert weeks earlier. After the friend she was taking accepted a late Homecoming invitation, Jenna gladly offered to take Mindy. Two nights later, the girls enjoyed the very entertaining concert, and Mindy never gave the Homecoming dance another thought.

The following week, Mindy sat in JT's bedroom, listening to records. As the dinner hour approached, JT grabbed a vial and syringe from her dresser. Mindy watched closely as JT drew up her insulin, then winced as the tip of the needle disappeared beneath the skin of her belly. After disposing of the syringe, JT reached into the top drawer of her dresser and pulled out a nearly flat round plastic container about the size of a compact. She deftly popped out a pill and swallowed it without water. When Mindy inquired whether it was also diabetes medication, JT just laughed. "No, that's my birth control pill, silly."

Mindy's eyes widened with surprise, and she whispered, "Does your mother know you are taking those?"

"Yeah, but she thinks I take them for bad cramps. But really, it's the only way to make sure you don't get pregnant. Lord knows I'd be pregnant if not for these little pills," she said nonchalantly. Mindy's expression prompted JT to ask, "Why such a look? Don't you take them? Didn't you have sex with your boyfriend in Tennessee?"

Mindy nearly choked. "Oh, my God! No! Of course not! I plan to wait until I get married."

JT flatly replied, "Most boys won't wait that long. I guess as long as it keeps Rod in my backyard, I'll keep giving it to him." JT's mother's call for dinner allowed Mindy to make her escape.

Struck by Jenna's remorse and the emptiness of JT's complacency, it was hard for Mindy to make sense of her mixed emotions. With a deep sigh of relief, she arrived home very happy with who she was and even happier to still own her virginity.

When the phone rang, Mindy waited until the fifth ring to answer. Andy Sparks wasted no time asking her out for dinner and a movie. He was pleasant and courteous, although his persona didn't live up to his last name. But that didn't matter. School was going well, and it seemed like a good time to do something new, so Mindy agreed.

Andy arrived right on time Saturday evening. After a quick introduction to Mindy's parents, they were off to dinner at Rich & Charlie's. Mindy scanned Andy's profile as he drove, but sensed no particular vibes or connection. By the time they arrived at the restaurant, she knew this would be a onetime date but was happy to be out. She planned to enjoy the evening and get a glimpse of "out there" in west St. Louis County.

Dinner conversation was pleasant, although Andy was too egocentric for Mindy's taste. The subsequent movie at the Manchester Dollar Theater, *Monty Python and the Holy Grail*, was entertaining. Mindy suspected she missed some of the satire, but Andy seemed confused by much of the movie. She thought it odd that he laughed hardest during the quartering of the Black Knight and remembered Don Holland laughing during *Walking Tall*. Afterward, Andy walked Mindy to the door and thanked her for going out with him. He made no move for a payback-goodnight kiss, and Mindy was ever so thankful.

JT inquired about the date the following Monday at school. After Mindy filled her in, JT informed her, "You know, my neighbor Cindy has had a crush on Andy for months."

With a flashback to the water polo game, Mindy realized how her new student status had blinded her to the obvious. Angry, Mindy wanted to know, "Why didn't you tell me this before? I never would have gone out with him," but JT had no reply. When Andy called the next day, Mindy didn't hesitate to decline his second date offer and suggested he consider calling Cindy. Unfazed, Andy thanked her for the recommendation. Mindy learned Andy took Cindy to the same restaurant and theater the following weekend. Mindy never saw or spoke with him again.

By the end of the first month at her new school, Mindy had dusted off her study skills and recaptured lost focus, organization, and efficiency. This combination allowed Friday evening and Saturday to become more typical play days, and she happily spent them doing little things like hanging with the girls, shopping and baking cookies.

The following week of school was very busy and filled with reading and study. But Mindy found her thoughts stopped in their tracks during Interior Design. When one of the larger busted girls in the class passed by their table, Alison pronounced without preface, "You can tell she gets felt up all the time." Mindy and Joan stared at Alison in disbelief. "What? Don't you believe me? Just look around the room. You can tell who gets felt up by how big they are. That's one of the things that makes 'em bigger — boy's playing with 'em," reported Alison without the slightest hesitation. "I can tell you guys don't believe me, but it's true," Alison concluded. Mindy had difficulty concentrating for the remainder of the class.

The next day, Alison handed Mindy a book and said, "Here, read this. You might learn a few things. I sure did. I've already read it a couple of times so, you can keep it." Mindy read the cover, *The Sensuous Woman*. She had no idea what was in it, but the title alone made her sweat, and she quickly slid the little book into a folder.

Mindy finished her homework early that evening, readied herself for bed and crawled under the covers with the gift paperback in hand. Thumbing through the pages, her heart raced as she read random paragraphs and her mind screamed, "Oh — my — GOD!"

Footsteps in the hallway forced the little book under the covers until convinced the coast was clear. Re-opening to chapter one, she consumed the first few pages, but curiosity drove her into later chapters. The first few paragraphs on oral sex made her hyperventilate as her heart raced faster. She snapped the little book closed and whispered, "Ohhhh — myyyy — Gooooddddd!"

The book made brief appearances from its hiding place each of the next few nights at bedtime. A voracious reader, Mindy could have finished it in a few hours but could only coax herself through a handful of pages at a time. It remained in its hiding place for about a week before she pulled it out and clandestinely returned it to Alison. "Here's your book. I don't think I can keep it at my house."

Alison grinned. "Did you read it?"

"Parts of it," Mindy replied with crimson cheeks. The briefest thought of that little book would make her sweat for months to come.

———————————

On each of the subsequent two weekends, Mindy attended open parties hosted by fellow seniors and advertised by word-of-mouth invitation. Without a complete understanding of West County party etiquette, Mindy and her friends were among the early arrivals on both occasions. The opening hour was relatively quiet and reserved, so Mindy and her friends stood together off to the side to chat and people watch as the crowd grew. In both cases, Mindy had never seen most of the party attendees, even in passing at school, which gave her a new appreciation for how large her new school really was. As the party crowd continued to grow and mix, she met a handful of new female classmates in passing, but boys, full of curiosity, arrived two to three at a time to introduce themselves. Jenna and JT watched in amazement as the power of Mindy's boy magnet effect became apparent. Mindy was unaffected by the boys, but she felt the alluring pull of teen craziness. Curiosity forced her to stay at the parties longer than her friends would have preferred.

Both parties became louder and evolved into scenes unlike anything Mindy had witnessed before. Parents were apparently willing to turn their upper-middle-class homes over to their teen children and remain out of sight for the night as high school kids arrived by the dozen seeking an uninhibited thrill. As a result, it was not uncommon to have a hundred or more partiers inside the house and another hundred outside, with others coming and going almost continuously. Many, mostly male, reveled in irresponsibility and general debauchery. There was open drinking and smoking. Spills were not uncommon, but no one seemed to care. It appalled Mindy to watch beautiful homes trashed by too many spoiled, unconcerned teens, and it re-enforced her resolve to never host another teen party.

Mindy caught the wandering eye of Bob Walton at the second party. He was tall with average looks and sported a beauty shop acquired afro, but seemed to be an unassuming young man. His introduction to Mindy was otherwise unmemorable but, like Andy Sparks, Bob started popping up frequently outside her classes at school and took every opportunity to share a few words with her. It didn't take long before Mindy recognized the look in his eye and knew he'd be calling for a date. "That would be okay. School is still going well, and it seems like a good time for some new adventures," she thought.

It had taken a few months but, for Mindy, the transition was complete. School, friends, and boys of the past had their chapter come to a close. She was moving forward into a new story and where it appeared to be headed pleased her.

———————————

Forward thoughts hit a speed bump just a few days later. Mindy's mother had been very active in women's groups and charity organizations in Lafayette and had enjoyed her own big fish in a small-town status as one of the town's menopausal queen bees. In West St. Louis County, she was just one of a million mothers trying to run a household and was having some minor withdrawal pangs. With schools closed the first Friday in November for a teacher's meeting and closing papers to be signed on the Ellington house, Mindy's mother considered it an ideal opportunity for a Lafayette fix. Mindy initially resisted, but her mother left her no option to remain in St. Louis, and she found herself unexpectedly on the way back to Macon County.

Loretta was warm and welcoming, and they were soon off to the football game. Mindy sat in the stands surrounded by many of her old friends, but noted they all sounded more southern than in her memory. She recalled the auditory struggles of the first weeks in Lafayette and had to laugh about her obviously de-acclimated ear.

She had always considered most of the MCHS girls seated near her as bright. But surrounded by many academically gifted students at PWH, her vision had changed, and she found herself measuring her old friends by a new standard. Then she thought about how hard she was working just to keep pace and wondered how her old friends would hold up under more intense academic pressure.

Awake early the next morning, Mindy lay in quiet contemplation until Loretta gradually aroused and they murmured about random topics. Before long, Mindy's stomach churned with both hunger and unease and reported, "It feels so weird to be back here. It feels like I've been gone for a really long time, and just don't belong here." Loretta had no response.

The trip back to St. Louis was long and quiet. JT called that evening to lament, "While you were in Tennessee, I went to Evansville. As soon as I arrived, people started telling me Rod was dating a sophomore. He didn't come to see me until 10:30 that night and admitted he'd been out on a date. He said it was too late to cancel when I called to tell him about my visit. He said he'd still like to see me whenever I came back, but I think he just wants to have sex when it's convenient."

Mindy felt so very sorry for JT.

———————————— • ————————————

School continued to be a bright spot in Mindy's new life. She was happy with her mid-term A's in Chemistry and Honors English, and the success encouraged her to work all the harder. She also started receiving phone calls from random boys whom she had met only in passing. Most seemed pleasant and harmless, but her heightened focus on school cut them short. "Sorry, I'm busy," became cliché.

There was one character in the boy crowd who was sadly comical in his approach. Even Dr. Berger made a pointed verbal observation at the start of Mindy's second day in Honors English when he noted how quickly Dick Parmley had moved his seat to be near her. Dick was heavy-set and loud, but generally meant well. He didn't hide his infatuation with Mindy and began making random uninvited visits to Brass Lamp. If Mindy wasn't home, he would maneuver his way into the house and talk to her mother until she returned. Her mother found his off-beat personality entertaining in short bursts but, for Mindy, his visits were intrusive, and she begged her mother not to let him in. Turning down his near weekly date requests for the remainder of the semester became passé.

A mid-week phone call caught Mindy off-guard. Damien had heard of her recent trip to Lafayette and called on the bank's WATS line to say, "I wish you would have let me know you were coming into town. I would have liked to see you."

There was no reason to be cruel or angry, but a cascade of unpleasant memories tumbled through her mind and she resisted the urge to punish him. Then she realized, "That's what I was doing all summer. That's why I didn't dump him for good him in

April like I should have." She cleared her thoughts and said, "You need to move on," and ended the conversation shortly thereafter.

A television news reporter caught Mindy's attention that evening when he announced the entry of Ronald Reagan into the race for the Republican Party Presidential nomination. She looked at her father in disbelief, "Ronald Reagan? Isn't he an actor? What's an actor doing running for president?" The report reminded her of a comedian running for president, and she bounced up the steps to her room singing, "Pat Paulsen for president! Pat Paulsen for president!"

———————

"Would you like to go to dinner and a movie with me this weekend?" Bob sang through the phone. With the answer already waiting patiently in her mind, Mindy readily accepted.

Bob arrived right on time, and Mindy introduced him to her parents. Her father didn't have much to say, but her mother was still talking as they left.

In what seemed to be an instant replay, Mindy could only shake her head when they went to Rich & Charlie's for dinner, sat at the same table she'd shared with Andy and ordered the same, and least expensive, item on the menu. Afterward, they went to the Manchester Dollar Theater for a movie re-run. Mindy laughed, "I thought things like this could only happen in Lafayette." On the upside, Mindy found Bob to be one notch higher than Andy on the interesting scale.

Mindy accepted Bob's second invitation to dinner the following Saturday. Service was slow, so they had time to chat about a variety of topics but stuck on popular music. Mindy was dubious about Bob's claim that "boys don't like the Beatles", and argued, "They couldn't have been the most popular band in the world with a female only following." She begrudgingly had to agree, however, when he extended that same generalization to Elton John. He then talked on and on about the current day boy bands and offered to lend her some of his albums. The music discussion turned into an ongoing debate. Mindy enjoyed this type of bantering, finding it softly educational, and wished it was more common during dates in general.

Still early, they returned to Brass Lamp after dinner and Bob walked Mindy to the door. Bob nervously leaned forward to deliver a quick kiss on the cheek, then said goodnight as he quickly walked away. Mindy went inside without giving Bob another thought.

The next week at school, Bob followed Mindy every possible minute and took an early opportunity to ask her if she'd like to go out again the following weekend. He was a nice guy, but Mindy wasn't interested in going out with him every weekend. To buy time to consider his offer, she informed him relatives were coming in for Thanksgiving, but was uncertain of their itinerary. "Let me check the schedule, and I'll let you know," she said.

Icy winds blew Wednesday morning, and a winter storm watch prompted school district officials to dismiss classes early to beat the arrival of snow and ice. Warm and safe at home, Mindy sat quietly at the kitchen table enjoying milk and cookies. With her mind full of thoughts about an Honors English paper due the following week, she paid little attention to the big, heavy snowflakes falling from the sky. Dr. Berger had continued to be very encouraging, and Mindy didn't want to disappoint him. So, she planned to spend much of the holiday weekend working on her paper.

After the last cookie, Mindy walked up the stairs to her bedroom with school books in hand. Two hours later, she put down William Faulkner's *Absalom, Absalom!,* and was just starting to mold the puzzle pieces of the story together when the phone rang. Answering on the fifth ring, it didn't surprise her to hear Bob's voice. "Hey, with the early dismissal I didn't get to ask, are you good to go out this weekend?" he anxiously inquired.

Mindy thought, "I'm going to need a break sometime this weekend," so replied, "Sure, how about lunch on Sunday after church," and Bob agreed. She walked downstairs to get a drink and was surprised to see four inches of snow had already accumulated while she had dissected Faulkner's tangled story.

The snow continued to fall, and Mindy continued to digest more Faulkner into the after-dinner hours until a repeated scrapping sound coming from the driveway broke her concentration. Too noisy and distracting, she walked downstairs to investigate and found her mother peeking out the window of the dark living room. Her mother whispered, "I think it's Dick Parmley. I'm pretty sure that's his truck."

"Oh, don't tell me that!" said Mindy as she moved to the window to peek out. Sure enough, there was Dick shoveling snow off their driveway in the dark.

When Mindy's mother suggested she go outside and thank Dick, Mindy replied with angst, "No way! I'm not giving him any encouragement."

Her mother pushed, "You really need to get out there. He's doing this for you."

Mindy shook her head emphatically, "He's not doing this for me. He's doing this for your three sons who should be out there. It's supposed to their job. Make *them* go out and say thank you," then ran up the stairs to her bedroom. An hour later the scraping stopped, and Mindy cringed when she heard the muffled voices of her mother and Dick in the entry foyer. "Please, don't call me down there!" she thought. Dick didn't stay long, and Mindy let out a sigh of relief as she sat down at her desk to decipher more Faulkner. The rest of the evening passed quietly until the interlaced perspectives of Faulkner's story of the old south had completely saturated Mindy's mind. She gently closed her book, readied herself for bed and crawled under her goose down comforter by 10 PM. Warm and snug, she drifted off to sleep, trying to piece together an outline in her thoughts.

Thanksgiving Day brought a new twist to the Murphy household as they bundled up and made the trek through nine inches of snow to Busch Stadium to watch the football Cardinals take on the Buffalo Bills and O. J. Simpson in his prime. The wind chill of 18 took much of the edge off the game, and everyone was happy to get back to the car to feel the warm air blowing from the car vents.

Back at Brass Lamp, Mindy quickly made her way up to her room to finish reading. A long yawn interrupted her thoughts just before 9 PM, and it was clear there was no room in her brain for any more Faulkner that evening. She drifted off to sleep with 'Absalom' resting on her chest.

Friday was a long day of helping her mother prepare for a dozen aunts, uncles and cousins that would arrive the next day for a belated Thanksgiving feast. As soon as she finished her chores, Mindy marched upstairs to take on more Faulkner. By that evening, she had meshed the various perspectives and symbolism of 'Absalom' into a single storyline and put together a rough outline for her paper.

Saturday was a busy but fun-filled day with food, relatives, and old stories. But as soon as the relatives said goodbye, Mindy escaped back to her room and started writing.

Bob arrived at noon on Sunday. Mindy was ready, and they left immediately for lunch. Eager to get back to her paper, Mindy kept the post-lunch conversation short. During the return trip to Brass Lamp, Bob nervously asked if Mindy would accompany him to his cousin's wedding the first week in January. Mindy hesitated to commit six weeks in advance, but the thought of getting dressed up and dancing at the reception captured her interest, and she agreed.

The conversation shifted to music, and they sat in the driveway at Brass Lamp for a short time. When Mindy indicated she needed to get inside, Bob leaned across to deliver a quick kiss. She thanked him for lunch and got out of the car.

Mindy found her mother waiting for her in the foyer. She was quick to say, "I don't think you should sit in the driveway with a boy."

Mindy scoffed, "I can handle this guy with my pinky." She wanted to add, "Where were you eight months ago when I could have used some help?" but didn't. She quietly marched up the stairs to her room.

After another date with her 'Absalom' paper, Mindy went to bed without another thought of Bob or his kisses. There was no passion, romance, or magic; only the business of dating. She closed her eyes and wondered, "Why don't I feel more excitement with Bob?" She already knew the answer and drifted off to sleep.

Writing and keeping up with other studies absorbed the next few evenings. After reviewing the first draft, Mindy worried it didn't reflect enough understanding or insight. So, she grabbed the car keys and drove to the nearest B. Dalton's bookstore, where she spent over an hour reviewing CliffsNotes on 'Absalom.' The next night she re-wrote her paper incorporating two concepts she had picked up at the bookstore.

Term papers due in Honors English and Short Stories plus tests in Chemistry and Art of Living classes made it a tough week. Damien called twice, but Mindy was at the library on both occasions and wasn't sorry to have missed his calls. Meanwhile, Bob was at her side every minute possible at school, and Mindy accepted his date offer for the following Saturday night.

Exhausted from studies by the time Friday arrived, the relief of surviving the week left Mindy ready to celebrate. JT and Jenna picked her up with plans to party hop that evening. Jenna reached under the front passenger seat to produce a nearly full bottle of her father's best gin and suggested they stop by a store to pick up some Shasta Tiki Punch as a mixer. They poured out about half the punch, then refilled the cans with gin.

Unable to find the first party and apparently lost, JT kept driving in a crisscross pattern through several subdivisions. During the search, Mindy consumed two cans of the punch flavored ticket to Buzzland and soon had slurred speech while the vain party mission continued. Turning into yet another subdivision, Led Zeppelin's "Stairway to Heaven" came on the radio and Jenna turned up the volume. Mindy dropped her head against the headrest. Fatigue mixed with alcohol to unlock a

Pandora's Box of memories and pent-up emotion. She sobbed; slowly at first, then the dam broke.

The song ended just as JT pulled up to a stop sign. JT and Jenna spun around to sing, "Oh my goodness. Mindy, what's the matter?"

Mindy cried even harder and sputtered, "Anne broke up with Matt, then Danny, and then she died. It was my fault, but it was a mistake . . ." She babbled on with unintelligible bursts of weeping sadness. Neither of the front seat passengers had any clue what she was raving about, but it was clear she could not make it to any party. They returned to Brass Lamp and had no choice but to help Mindy up the stairs, past her mother, and into bed. Jenna and JT were quite sober and played dumb about how or where Mindy had consumed enough alcohol to get drunk. They were, however, able to recite enough of her ramblings that her mother understood the tears and substantially softened her disciplinary approach.

The next morning Mindy enjoyed the gift of a hangover with a pounding headache but was lucid enough to apologize for being so stupid. Her mother asked what punishment Mindy thought would fit her crime. Mindy was in too much pain to consider options and simply suggested she cancel her date and stay in that night. Her mother agreed it would be a grand idea.

With White Pages in hand, Mindy retreated to her room and softly closed the door. Looking up Bob's number and slowly dialing the phone, she remembered the last time she had tried to call a boy to cancel a date. That call hadn't gone so well. So, she was happy when Bob answered the phone. Confessing her crime, she apologized for having to cancel on such short notice. He was disappointed but understanding, and they finished the call with plans to re-schedule for the following weekend.

Chapter 15
Changing Course
December 10–January 10, 1976

Mindy's heart pounded with anticipation as Dr. Berger handed back graded papers on Wednesday. Pausing a little longer at Mindy's side, Dr. Berger said, "Good job" as he laid her paper on the desk face down.

With sweaty palms, she quickly thumbed through the pages to read the short comments of praise or question. Reaching the last page, Mindy frowned upon seeing a circled "H" written in red felt-tip marker at the bottom of the page. Confused, she leaned to her left toward Julie Lindquist and asked, "What does this mean?"

Julie's eyes opened wide and whispered, "That's an H for Honors. It's higher than an A. That's the highest mark you can get."

Mindy blushed as she turned her eyes back to her paper. She blushed even brighter when she read Dr. Berger's final comments: "Excellent paper. Full of understanding, personal thoughts, and insight—except for the few CliffsNotes concepts. Trust yourself. You have good ideas of your own—use them." She never referred to CliffsNotes again.

———————————— · ————————————

With dreams of sharing life with Rod on the rocks, JT had fallen into a minor crush on one of Bob's friends, Tim Mermoud. Tim had returned no signs of interest, so Mindy decided to use her influence over Bob and strongly suggested he convince Tim to go out on an unofficial double-date. Bob was hesitant but couldn't refuse.

Thrilled to be out, JT became a one-woman comedy act with her off the wall comments and observations. The food disappeared quickly but, with no other plans, they remained in their seats until the waitress politely flushed them out. JT was happy and having a good time, so Mindy suggested they extend the evening and all return to Brass Lamp to play pool or pinball for the last hour before curfew. With no alternate suggestions, the boys readily agreed.

The foursome moved to the basement where, to Bob's dismay, Mindy dropped a Beatles album onto the turntable before they played a game of team pool. With none of them being pool sharks, the game took a long time and, with curfew approaching, Mindy suggested they switch to a quick game of pinball.

When Mindy took her turn at the pinball machine, Bob crept up behind her, slowly stretched his arms around her shoulders to grasp her wrists lightly and pronounced, "Let's make this a team game as well."

Feeling a wave of curiosity, Mindy didn't stiffen or resist. Bob misinterpreted her comfort level and squeezed her wrists tighter, but his interference allowed the silver pinball to disappear from the playing board with few points to show for her time. Disappointed with her score, Mindy glanced over her shoulder and caught Bob grinning at Tim. Suddenly the contact was uncomfortable, and Mindy shook her shoulders to escape.

By the time they were all walking back up the steps, Mindy's heart was heavy with disappointment. The three visitors passed through the front door onto the front walkway while Mindy stopped and stood firmly in the doorway to wave goodbye with no intention of following them to the car. Bob did a triple-take over his shoulder in disbelief. Mindy stepped back into the foyer and looked at the floor with no specific thought in mind. But dating Bob had clearly lost what little luster it had. She closed the door with an extra push that made the latch click louder than usual and left her feeling lighter inside.

Preparing for bed, Mindy felt a wave of exhilaration but was uncertain why until she realized she was free to choose whatever doors of opportunity that most suited her. She had been so busy with school the last several weeks she hadn't processed the evolution of her own heart or her visions of the future. Peace came with the understanding that any steady boy would restrict her freedom and flexibility. In what would be one of her last diary entries, she wrote:

Dear Diary,
I'm ready to be done with boys for a long time. I need
to focus on school, prepare for college, and start building
the future I want now.

Awakening with the first rays of the morning sun, images of the previous evening crept back into Mindy's consciousness. "Bob is a nice boy. He's pleasant and courteous — but he isn't *the* boy. It's time to cut him loose," she thought.

——————— · ———————

The end of the semester approached, and Mindy dove into her studies preparing for semester final exams and looked forward to

Christmas break. When grades came out, she felt disappointed and didn't understand the 'B' she received in Interior Design but was happy with an H in honors English and A's in the rest of her classes.

To celebrate, Mindy joined JT to see Barry Manilow in concert at the Kiel Opera House, where they sang along and laughed the evening away. Bob called the next morning sounding ill and dejected. While Mindy was out on the town singing with Barry Manilow, he had gone out drinking with friends and got in trouble when he came home drunk. His parents grounded him for a month, and he had to cancel their date that evening. Having had her own recent experience, Mindy was more than understanding. She also considered the grounding fortuitous as a freedom bell rang in her head. At the end of the conversation, Mindy breathed a long, soft sigh of relief. Returning the handset to the cradle, she felt better than she had in weeks.

Sitting quietly in her room, Mindy contemplated Bob and boys in general. To Mindy, Bob was just another boy; another ticket to "out there." She would never think of him or share bonds with him as her "boyfriend." His month-long punishment would provide time and space she was missing without having to push him away. She didn't want to go out with him again, but felt obligated to humor him until his cousin's wedding. She came to dislike doing anything purely out of obligation.

Christmas came and went uneventfully. Temperatures dropped, and the heart of winter finally arrived in the air. Mindy avoided visits by Dick Parmley, and the girls did the West County version of cruising a few times. Stopping late one evening for a snack at Steak 'n Shake, the girls were just coming out when a carload of boys unfamiliar to Mindy pulled into the parking space directly in front of them. As the boys got out of the car, she bristled when she overheard one of them whisper, "Hey, that's Bob Walton's girlfriend." More inaudible whispering followed, and before Mindy had time to react, the pack of boys descended upon her to lift off her feet and quickly deposited into the back seat of their car.

They were laughing playfully, and Mindy never felt she was in any danger, but she was angry none-the-less. "You let me out of here right now!" she yelled repeatedly. The boys giggled all the more and drove off. Shocked with the scene before her, JT jumped into her car and began a high-speed pursuit. The boys made a sharp turn down the dark two-lane Barrett Station Road to escape, but JT was already on their tail and flashing her lights wildly. Mindy heard "Bob's girlfriend" again and exploded, "*I am*

NOT his girlfriend! You stop and let me out right now! That girl back there is crazy, and she'll run you off the road if she has to!"

Glancing in the rearview mirror, the driver's eyes widened with the vision of JT's car bearing down on him. With sudden fear she might actually try to ram them, the driver yelled, "Hold on!"

The rowdy boys all became pensively quiet and nervous themselves. Gradually slowing in hopes of not being slammed from behind, the kidnapping car eventually pulled over and let Mindy out quickly. JT arrived at the driver's window. Banging her finger on the glass, she yelled, "If you ever do that again, I'll kick the shit out of you!"

JT was seriously concerned the boys may have assaulted Mindy in some way and wanted to notify the police. It took several minutes, but Mindy got her calmed down and convinced her she was unharmed. "It was only a stupid teenage boy prank."

One of the assailants apparently contacted Bob the next morning, and he called Mindy to apologize. She wanted to tell him, "I'm not your girlfriend," but didn't.

After hanging up, the upcoming wedding sat high in Mindy's forethought. She didn't want to go; even the opportunity to dance didn't seem worth it. Giving in to her thoughts, she asked her mother that afternoon if it would be poor etiquette to break her commitment at this relatively late date. Her mother was unsupportive, explaining they had probably already paid for her reception dinner plate and that it would be rude to cancel less than two weeks from the wedding. Mindy wondered if she could just send them $7.50 and call it even. She considered being "sick" and a variety of other excuses, but they all sounded lame. She resolved to go, but would gladly take a way out if the opportunity presented itself. In her heart and mind, she was done with Bob and wanted to be done with boys in general for a long while.

The Murphy's attended a New Year's Eve party at the home of longtime family friends. Just happy to be getting out of the house, a depressed and date deprived Jenna joined them. The party quickly wound down after a televised replay of the dropping of the Times Square ball announced the arrival of 1976. When Jenna left for home, she made Mindy promise to spend the evening with her on Valentine's Day, "I just don't want to be alone when everyone else is in love."

School resumed the following Monday. Mindy quickly learned it would be a challenging semester but happily dove into her classes focused and excited. "One more semester, then a summer of fun in the sun and finally off to college!" rolled joyfully through her mind. Being in control of her destiny remained a common theme of her dreams.

The other twist to the week was the arrival of Mindy's paternal grandparents. A bright and sassy pair in their youth, age had taken its toll on them. Her grandfather was dealing with rapidly progressive Parkinson's disease and, with his worsening dementia, living alone in their own home in Mt. Vernon, Illinois was no longer practical. They would spend the next five weeks at Brass Lamp awaiting the availability of a retirement apartment near Mindy's aunt in Austin, Texas.

Mindy spent long hours talking with her grandmother about things new and old. It was a humbling experience to hear tales of growing up in the depression, the ravaging effects of WWII, and stories of her father she had never heard before. She was sad to hear how her grandfather's Parkinson's disease had destroyed so many of their retirement dreams. They had worked hard and lived frugally to save for retirement so they could travel and explore the world. Her grandfather was diagnosed just as they were getting started with their adventures, and their grand retirement plans were changed forever. Visiting The Great Wall of China would have to wait for the next generation.

Homework filled the Saturday morning hours before the wedding. Mindy didn't want to go, but obligation forced her to her feet. As she stretched, the phone rang. She answered on the fifth ring and was dismayed to hear Damien's voice. She wanted to say, "I'm sorry, who is this again?" but didn't. After exchanging unemotional greetings, Mindy asked, "I don't have long, is there something I can do for you?"

Damien sounded pompously victorious as he announced, "I'm calling because I thought you should hear this from me. I'm dating Rita Green."

The tone of his voice made Mindy frown, and she could imagine the smirk on his face. Suddenly angry with his lame game-playing, she returned the barb. "Oh my, surely you can do better than that," she replied with a chuckle.

"She's — not what you think," Damien stuttered. Mindy wasn't sure what to make of this response but felt mad at herself, sad for Rita and disgusted with Damien. He repeated, "Really, she's not that bad."

Internal pressure rose and Mindy wanted to explode. She thought, "You manipulative prick, is that really the best you can say about her? You don't deserve her or any girl." But she bit her tongue and replied, "I have to go now."

Damien chirped, "Would you mail my college graduation picture back to me? I want to give it to Rita."

Mindy paused. "I don't have any idea where it is." Then she remembered tossing it across the room into the trash and quickly corrected herself, "I don't have it anymore."

"Oh. Well, I just wanted you to hear it from me," Damien squeaked.

Mindy dropped the handset hard onto the cradle, still feeling terrible for Rita.

——————————— · ———————————

Bob arrived on the day of the wedding spilling over with excitement, and his eyes popped when Mindy walked down the stairs in a gown. In an attempt to make up for lost time, Bob talked nearly non-stop all the way to the church. Mindy didn't have the heart to tell him it would be their last date.

Like most girls, Mindy enjoyed fanciful images of weddings. The decorations, flowers, gowns, tuxedos, music, and pageantry always captured her imagination, but she had never envisioned herself standing at the altar. So, she sat cool, calm, and collected while Bob sat next to her fidgeting and carefully avoiding even the slightest incidental contact.

As they walked down the stairs to the reception in the church basement, Bob proclaimed, "You are prettier than the bride." Mindy appreciated the compliment but noted that it elicited no emotional warmth. More than ever, it was clear Bob wanted something her heart could never give him. He offered to get Mindy a glass of wine but explained he wasn't allowed to even have champagne for the toast, "I'm still grounded ya know." Mindy declined the wine and enjoyed a glass of water.

Fun for a few and dull for most, the reception speeches seemed to drag on forever, and Mindy waited patiently for the music to start. She didn't know if Bob could dance, but that didn't matter. She had done her time and was ready to hear some good music and hit the dance floor. When the music finally started, Mindy felt a wave of relief. She had assumed all the young people at her table would head for the dance floor as soon as the wedding party dances were over. But, to her disappointment, none of them moved, and tombstone boredom settled in.

The bar had been open since the first guests arrived and, by the time Bob's mother made her way to their table, she was moving slowly and dropped heavily into the chair next to Mindy. "It's so nice to finally meet you. I've been hearing about you for weeks," she said with moderately slurred speech.

Embarrassed, Bob tried to escape. "Mom, we were just going to get something to drink."

"You go get us something. I want to talk to Mindy," she said as she waved her son off with a backhand flip of her wrist. She studied Mindy's eyes. "You're a beautiful girl. How did Bob ever get you?"

Bob turned bright red, "Mom!"

Without shifting her eyes from Mindy's, his mother coolly waved him off again with a double backhand flip and read deeper. Suddenly, she gasped and sat back her chair as if she'd been shot. "Ah! You're never going to go out with him again, are you?"

Caught very much off-guard by this bulls-eye insight, Mindy shrugged her shoulders. Bob just buried his head in his hands. "That's so sad. Still, I'm so happy I got to meet you," his mother lamented as she got up unsteadily from the table. She planted her palm in the middle of Bob's chest and shook her head, "Whatever made you think you could get a girl like that?"

Mindy just stared at the water glass on the table, wondering what his mother had seen in her eyes to unveil her secret.

"I'm so sorry about my mom. She's had a long day and too much to drink. Don't pay any attention to her," Bob pleaded.

Mindy nervously smiled and laughed. "Don't worry, I understand." They left the reception a short time later.

With JT's parents out of town again, Bob drove Mindy to JT's house where she would spend the night. He walked Mindy to the front porch where he immediately leaned in to deliver a kiss. Mindy stepped backward just as the front door flew open. JT stepped out into the chill of the night, "Hey guys, what-cha doin'?"

Startled, Bob jumped back. He waited on the front walkway, assuming JT would go back inside. When it became clear JT had no intention of leaving them alone, Bob thanked Mindy for accompanying him to the wedding, said goodbye, and walked away with drooping shoulders and looking at the ground.

JT stared as Bob got into his car and drove away. After a little huff, she summarily concluded, "You guys just don't look right together."

A short time later, Jenna joined them at JT's for a mini-slumber party, and the three of them talked and laughed almost continuously about nothing important. Eventually, they readied themselves for bed and, in a young girl slumber party style, decided to all share the king-sized bed in JT's parent's room. Mindy, the slimmest of the trio, ended up in the middle. Their chatter gradually slowed, moments of silence filled the gaps, and eyelids became heavy.

JT shattered the calm. "What's the farthest you've gone with a boy?" Mindy assumed JT was directing the question to Jenna and remained silent. It didn't take long for Jenna to recite her tale with Doug and JT to follow with tales of Rod.

Mindy laid rigidly still, hoping they would leave her out of the discussion. But she would have no such luck as JT rolled onto her side. "Well, Miss Virgin, have you ever been felt up?" Jenna's eyes popped open and rolled up on her side as well to sandwich Mindy between her interrogators.

Mindy pulled the covers close to her chin and coolly replied, "No, I can't say that I have. I'm going to save that *and* my virginity for the one I love, even if I have to wait a very long time." The interrogators rolled onto their backs and sighed.

Sensing the growing tension on her flanks, Mindy shifted the conversation to marriage. The other girls came back to life with happier thoughts of love and wondered which of them would get married first. They quickly concluded that Jenna would marry first, JT would be a close second, and Mindy would be a distant third.

Finally, the light went out. Before collapsing into a deep sleep, Mindy silently mused about the many boys she had dated and came to her own conclusion, "I don't know what true love is, but I certainly know what it's not."

Chapter 16
Blue Moon
January 11–January 16, 1976

Jenna called Sunday evening just to chat, and it didn't take long for her depression to seep into the discussion. Mindy tried to cheer her up and eventually shifted to the previous night's wedding; a topic she had avoided at JT's. When she recounted the story of Bob's mother and her visit to their table, it seemed to break the ice, and Jenna laughed and said, "I shouldn't laugh. My mom is even worse. Look at what she did to me."

"His mother was right. I don't know how she knew, but I decided weeks ago I wouldn't go out with him again after the wedding," Mindy revealed.

Jenna was beside herself. "Jesus! You can get any guy you want, any time you want, and then just dump them. I just want one!"

The conversation shifted again, and Jenna asked if Mindy was still planning to come to her birthday party on the 16th.

It was Mindy's turn to laugh. "Well, I don't think I'll be doing anything else. I certainly won't have a date anytime soon."

Jenna continued, "I'd like to have some girls over for cake, and ice cream, then head out for a wild night on the town. Wait, what does a new eighteen-year-old do for a wild night on the town?"

Mindy hedged, "Remember, eighteen is still a minor in Missouri, and some of us are still seventeen. I have no idea about a wild night on the town. You decide what you want to do, and the other girls will probably go along." Jenna agreed to give it some thought.

Two days later, Jenna grabbed Mindy at school. "I've got it! We'll go to a college party at St. Louis University!" Mindy was skeptical and had several questions about the logistics. Jenna led her to believe she had made several previous forays into the SLU nightlife world and knew the ropes. "They have great parties every weekend. All you have to do is bring something to drink, put it on a table, and they let you in. I know a freshman guy down there. I'll call him and get the details for this weekend."

Friday arrived, and Mindy scanned her closet, looking for something suitable to wear to a college party. She picked out a dark blue cashmere sweater with thin white horizontal stripes and light blue corduroy jeans. She reached for her brown moccasin style shoes but thought, "I haven't worn my blue and white saddle shoes for a long time, it's time to dust them off." She slipped them on, tied the laces, and thought, "They still feel good on my feet."

Jenna arrived a short time later and drove the circuit to pick up Mindy, Leslie Orrick, Linda Klutho and Julie Lindquist. They ate dinner at Coco's, then had cake and ice cream at Jenna's house. As they prepared to leave for the party, Jenna hurriedly slipped a bottle of her father's whiskey into Mindy's purse, "Shh, it won't fit in mine." A moment later, they were driving eastbound toward St. Louis University. During the drive, Jenna revealed she was unable to get in touch with her contact but reassured the others, "No worries, all we have to do is show up and ask around."

They parked behind Griesedieck Hall, then strolled past the front of the main campus dormitories. The atmosphere seemed ominously quiet, so they walked across the street to the student center, then doubled back toward the library. At every turn, the campus walkways were nearly deserted, and the girls were wondering if there was any life at this school.

Feeling embarrassed, Jenna ran into the nearest dorm and asked the desk workers to ring Keith Ebling's room, but there was no answer. She returned ready to give up when she remembered another former classmate who was also attending SLU. She quickly explained, "He was in our class but left high school early and started college last fall. I've seen him down here before and know he'll be able to help. Let's just go up to his room and ask." The others were reluctant but had no alternate suggestion.

Like five little ducklings, they marched through the main doors of Griesedieck Hall. Jenna checked at the main desk to get the right room number, and they all stepped into the elevators. Mindy scanned the buttons and noted they skipped from 12 to 14. "There's no 13th floor," Mindy announced, and they all laughed.

The door opened on the 11th floor, and the girls cautiously stepped into the elevator foyer. Nighttime lighting was already on and left the long hallway dotted with shadows. The pack quietly stepped into the main corridor. Jenna pointed to room 1105, "This is it." As she raised her arm to knock, the other four girls moved to the wall and held their breath.

The door opened, and there was a brief pause before Mindy overheard a faceless voice ask, "Can I help you?"

Mindy watched as Jenna seemed to look past the voice and smiled. "Hey, we're looking for a party but can't find one."

"Parties don't usually start until ten or eleven," the unseen voice replied.

Jenna glanced toward the girls then back to ask with some hesitation, "Well, can we wait here?"

A backlit figure took a half-step into the hall and glanced toward Jenna's trembling friends standing in the shadow and pressed against the wall. All Mindy could make out was his shoulder-length hair before he disappeared back into the room to pronounce, "Come on in."

Filled with uncertainty, Mindy watched as Jenna followed the voice into the room and wondered, "Should we be doing this?" The other girls must have felt the same way because their nervous jitters were palpable as they stepped toward the open door. They heard Jenna say louder than necessary, "Hi, I'm Jenna."

Linda was next in line and, hesitant to enter, she stopped. Mindy gave her a slight nudge from behind. And a second later heard, "And this is Linda."

Mindy took a deep breath and took one step inside the doorway as Jenna announced, "And this is Mindy."

Mindy's eyes met those of their dorm host, and time seemed to stop. There was no sound, and she was blind to everything but his all-absorbing eyes. She could sense him reading her soul through her eyes. Feeling a nudge from behind, she stepped forward.

"And this is Leslie — and this is Julie," Jenna continued as the last two girls crossed the threshold.

Mindy's vision blurred as her pupils widened when the dorm host's pointing finger immediately returned to her. Time stopped again as his eyes refocused on hers, and he confidently asked, "What's *your* name again?"

Mindy smiled and said her name with a sweet, bashful southern accent as if she'd never left Tennessee.

Time clicked forward by one second. In that very instant, Mindy felt her life change forever. Her heart opened with exhilarating recognition. With a silent gasp of ecstasy, she felt him gently touch her heart and kiss her soul with his. Mindy smiled bigger with the realization she could read his mind, could feel his heart pounding, and the warmth of his soul. She wanted him to take her in his arms and never let go.

Jenna cleared her throat loudly to break their trance and interrupt their melding.

With eyes still locked on Mindy, their host announced, "I'm Pete." then turned toward the interior of the room. Mindy turned as well and was quite surprised to see four other boys frozen in their seats. Pete continued, "And these guys are Tom, Mike, Steve, and Joe." The other boys sat in jaw-dropped amazement with the sudden and very unexpected appearance of five girls before them. Pete gestured with a swashbuckling wave of his arm, and they jumped like trained animals to their feet to offer their seats to the girls.

It was a typical dorm room; small and rectangular. Pete and his roommate had converted the beds into a bunk configuration, and two old upholstered chairs supplied additional seating, but the space still wasn't designed to accommodate ten people. The boys awkwardly rearranged themselves as the girls settled in. Mindy and two other girls took seats on the edge of the lower bunk. Pete's high-back chair directly across from Mindy remained unoccupied, so he plopped back into it and kicked his sock covered feet onto the ottoman.

Everyone in the room was all smiles, and the conversation was natural and fluid. As music poured from the stereo, the group fractionated. An invisible, nearly soundproof bubble formed around Pete and Mindy, and they talked to the exclusion of all others.

Full of curiosity, Mindy's eyes studied Pete, and somehow his two-tone baseball undershirt seemed familiar. Then her eyes focused on his three-stripe tube sock covered feet until he interjected, "Sorry, I'm just a white sock kind-a-guy. I wear this pretty much year-round. What you see is what you get."

Mindy smiled and felt her heart melt in her chest, "I like that."

"And I like your saddle shoes. You don't see those much these days," Pete replied. Mindy's heart melted more.

It was Mike Kush's turn to interrupt the Pete-Mindy dream state when he stood to suggest the group move across the street to the University Pub and the other freshman agreed. Pete grabbed a pair of jeans and held up a finger, "Give me just a second." He stepped into the hallway, and in a few seconds slipped out of his shorts, into his jeans and back into the room where he pulled on his well-worn three-stripe blue suede Adidas tennis shoes.

Mindy studied his shoes as he tied the laces and thought, "I know those shoes" but couldn't place where she had seen them before.

Pete held the door open with his foot as everyone filed out. Mindy suddenly remembered the bottle in her purse and was afraid it might get them into trouble at the bar. So, she lagged behind and paused just inside the door. She reached into her oversized purse and pulled out a 2/3rds empty bottle of Wild Turkey, "Is it okay if I leave this here?"

Wide-eyed, Pete took the bottle and set it on his desk.

At The Pub, the group took seats at a table for ten with Pete at the head, and Mindy seated to his immediate left. The bartenders ignored the fact that everyone was underage as Mike ordered two pitchers of beer.

Mindy watched closely as Pete filled the frosted mugs at his end of the table and served her first. They said "Cheers" and took sips without separating their eyes until Mindy focused on Pete's lips to watch the ice crystals melt.

Everyone else at the table chatted while Mindy and Pete re-enshrouded themselves in their own private bubble to shut out distractions. Their conversation was smooth and unbroken. Each little tidbit of personal information they shared was like finding buried treasure.

Pete was curious to hear how Mindy ended up at PWH, and she was happy to provide her family's complicated moving history. She felt warm inside as Pete's eyes lit up while she spoke. When her story finally delivered her to Brass Lamp, Pete said, "Wow, how do you do that?"

"What do you mean?" Mindy inquired.

"You started off with a normal Missouri accent, then shifted to a soft eastern Canadian accent, then back to Missouri. Then out of nowhere came a soft southern accent and now you're back to a normal Missouri accent! Your accent changed every time you moved."

Mindy blushed with embarrassment, "Sorry, I didn't notice."

"Don't be sorry. I'm amazed at how smoothly you transitioned," whispered Pete.

They talked uninterrupted for over an hour. Mindy shared her thoughts, dreams, and fantasies in a way she never had before. She followed Pete's eyes continuously. They were full of feeling, understanding, and warmth. With an upwelling of heartfelt emotion, she thought, "Nobody has ever looked at me this way. Nobody has ever made it past my smile or hair or shape. He's looking past all that. He's looking into my soul — and he's making it shine. I want to know more about him. I want to know everything there is to know about him."

The party came to an abrupt end when Jenna noted the time and screamed, "Oh my! It's late. We're going to be late!" The girls all jumped up, grabbed their coats, and headed for the door. Walking back across the street, the other freshmen made their way toward a party, and Pete waved them on.

Mindy slid into the front passenger seat and rolled down her window as they backed out. Pete's eyes fixed on Mindy's and he stepped toward the car, bringing it to an abrupt halt. Mindy held her breath as she grabbed the lower window frame with both hands. Pete leaned forward as well and gently placed his hands close just an inch from hers. There was a mesmerizing pause before Pete calmly said, "It was nice to meet you."

Mindy leaned through the window frame and could feel her lips being drawn to his. She wanted to kiss him goodbye but was disappointed when he suddenly withdrew.

Pete tapped the door frame, and his voice cracked ever so slightly as he whispered, "Drive safely."

With the softest of gasps, Mindy thought, "He's handing me his heart," and knew they would meet again.

The girls teased her for miles, "What's your name again? No, what's *your* name again? Sure, nobody cares what our names are." They all laughed.

When the teasing died down, Mindy trembled and pointed at Jenna, "He is so cute! We have to go down there again!" Jenna was quiet.

Back in West County, Jenna delivered Linda, Leslie and Julie to their respective homes. Each said goodnight and left Mindy with a parting tease, "What's *your* name again?" On the way to Brass Lamp, Jenna and Mindy discussed another trip to SLU the following weekend.

Mindy arrived home past curfew, but not late enough to get into trouble. She glided into the family room where her mother and grandmother were watching late night television. "Well, how was the college party?" her mother inquired.

Mindy replayed the evening in her mind, then looked at the well-worn saddle shoes on her feet. She had a new friend; a bosom friend and she knew she was bound to him in a most extraordinary way. She smiled and looked to the heavens to announce, "Well, I met the man I'm going to marry."

And the days of magic began.

Afterword

For those of you who have made it this far, here are my general thoughts on the fundamental life lessons of this tale.

For Parents:

Have high expectations and set lofty goals for your children congruent with their innate potential. Ask them to reach higher and go further than you. Ask them to be better than you were. With appropriate nurturing, encouragement, and the occasional push, the vast majority of kids will meet whatever expectations you set. Many will surprise you and far surpass your expectations or their natural potential. Push the next generation to be better. If you don't do these things, you shouldn't feel disappointed when your children struggle to succeed.

Be a good role model; lead by example. Enough said about that.

Be a guardian of your children's physical and emotional wellbeing. Obviously, the parent's role evolves significantly as kids grow up, but don't be premature in cutting them loose. Most kids remain at risk much longer than we care to admit. Every generation of kids is exposed to new fads, new technology, and new challenges. That does not change the fact that growing up and maturing still takes time. Despite the empty argument that kids grow up faster today because of cable TV and the internet, just being exposed to adult material doesn't make one mature. In reality, it still takes just as much time to "grow up" now as it ever has — probably longer. As parents, we need to be there for our children to guide and protect from infancy through at least the early twenties for most. Sometimes we even need to piss our kids off and interject our decision-making when they are at risk. They aren't always prepared or may not have the psychosocial tools necessary to make good decisions, especially through their late teens. This doesn't mean we should dominate them or never let them make their own decisions or learn from their mistakes.

There are some areas in which we need to be involved longer than they might like. Although these areas vary from child to child, there are clearly some common themes, one of which is in the arena of love and romance. There is no need and, in fact, there is probably danger in encouraging early dating and romance. Promoting anything other than group dates or school dances during high school is silly. Most adolescents do not have the maturity or insight to handle intimacy well. Subsequently, poor decisions outnumber good ones. If you must let your child date, have well-defined limits on who you allow your child to see, where they go and what they do. It's not just your kid you have to worry about, it's their date as well. Keep in mind that girls tend to be at higher risk than boys simply because they have a uterus. Sometimes one poor decision is all it takes to change their life (negatively) forever. So be guardians of their hearts.

Be on the same page; stand united when talking to your kids. Discuss personal perspectives and opinions in private, not in front of your kids. They will divide and conquer.

For Moms:

Ask lots of questions. Be nosy. Don't be afraid to say "NO!" when you see something wrong or merely questionable. Use your power over your husband to enlist help when necessary.

For Dads:

Let's keep this simple. Know your child, interact with your child, and protect your child. If a male who is obviously inappropriate for your daughter shows up at your door, point a finger pistol to the middle of his forehead and tell him if he ever messes with your daughter again, you'll blow his brains out. If you have a son who is chasing girls inappropriately, just do the world a favor, lock him in a cage and throw him a bone now and then. (My wife convinced me to lighten up on this one considerably.)

For Friends:

Be a good friend. If you see a friend doing or saying questionable things, speak up and tell them so. Question and challenge them. Tell them if you think they're being stupid. It may upset them in the short term, but they will learn to appreciate your friendship all the more. (This also applies to teachers, administrators, coaches, and other authority figures.)

For Girls:

Know your worth. Your touch and your kisses are priceless. They are yours alone to give. But be stingy, save them for someone worthy; for someone who loves you. They should never be reduced to a ticket to fun or required as payment for fun. Corollary: Believe that your heart is the most precious thing in the universe. Honor it, nurture it, and preserve it for one who will honor it and cherish it just as you do.

You don't owe a guy anything just because he takes you on a date.

If you find yourself wondering if a particular boy really loves you, then he probably doesn't. When a boy really loves you, it will be evident to you and the entire world.

Finally, don't be the wife or girlfriend that stays in or returns to an abusive relationship; no amount of rationalization will ever make it a good idea. Do yourself a favor. Pack your bags, cut your losses, and never return.

For Boys:

Never take your girlfriend for granted. If you do, you'll turn around one day, and she'll be gone. Treat her as if you're trying to win her heart every day. Corollary: Always treat your wife as if she's your girlfriend.

If you really love a girl, you must be more kind, more thoughtful, more honest, harder working, and forever more committed than anyone else if you hope to deserve her. If you can't do this, please walk away. If you can't walk away, do everyone a favor and lock yourself in a cage. (My wife got me to lighten up on this one too.)

For All:

Be a critical thinker. Become a good decision maker. Consider the consequences of your decisions. Take personal responsibility for everything you do. Your parents can and should help when you are young but, in the end, you are the most important person when it comes to making good decisions about you.

True Love is a rare and magic thing. You can't search for it, and you can't make it happen. Be patient. Wait for it to come to you. When it arrives, it sometimes grows fast and sometimes slow. But once present, you won't need to grab it or hold it. Its magic will bind you together.

———— • ————

I hope this tale will serve as a platform for teens, friends, parents, teachers and counselors to exchange their own thoughts about some of those difficult-to-discuss issues that are a part of our world while learning some worthwhile life lessons along the way. If that happens, I can believe I've contributed in a small but important way to help make the world a better place.

Acknowledgments

First and foremost, a loving thanks to my best friend and wife, Jane. None of you have any idea what I put her through for far longer than I should.

Next, a huge, heartfelt shout of thanks to all of you poor souls who helped make this little Chautauqua a reality. You all put up with more poking and prodding than I ever would have been able to tolerate myself. In no particular order: Jaynie West, Kathy Wilmore, Brian White, Danny McClard, Wynona Clayborne, Dewayne Cothron, the Macon County Times, Kim Kelce, Lori Rothschild, and Joe Williams. There are so many more. Trust me, I'll never forget you.

Of course, the list wouldn't be complete without a special thanks to my editor, Sue Christophersen for her guidance and insight.

About the Author

Working for over thirty years as an Emergency Physician, Mark Walsma, MD, has accumulated enough fodder for a dozen medicine-based novels. But he will tell you, "Medical stories about illness, dying and craziness may be entertaining, but they won't make the world a better place." So, his first writing venture addresses coming of age, love, friendship, parenting, and decision-making for starters. He hopes this story will make the reader reflect upon how they live their lives and raise their children. He believes that such reflection will help make the world a better place for all of us.

Raised in Manchester, Missouri, he is the product of mid-western values. As a youngster, he loved and played sports of all kinds but understood the importance of education as a pathway to the future. He married his high school prom date, completed medical school at the University of Missouri–Kansas City, and is the proud father of two successful children. His favorite authors include Ray Bradbury, Kurt Vonnegut, Ernest Hemingway, Carl Sagan, Robert Pirsig and many current day 'science for the masses' writers. Dr. Walsma and his wife are filling their empty nest years with travel, grandkids, and new ventures such as writing.

J.W.